8/23

CHRISTMAS
ON MAIN STREET

JoAnn Ross
Susan Donovan
LuAnn McLane
Alexis Morgan

A SIGNET BOOK

SIGNET
Published by the Penguin Group
Penguin Group (USA) LLC, 375 Hudson Street,
New York, New York 10014

USA | Canada | UK | Ireland | Australia | New Zealand | India | South Africa | China
penguin.com
A Penguin Random House Company

First published by Signet, an imprint of New American Library,
a division of Penguin Group (USA) LLC

First Printing, November 2013

 REGISTERED TRADEMARK — MARCA REGISTRADA

ISBN 978-0-451-41953-8

Printed in the United States of America
10 9 8 7 6 5 4 3 2 1

PUBLISHER'S NOTE
These are works of fiction. Names, characters, places, and incidents either are the
product of the authors' imagination or are used fictitiously, and any resemblance
to actual persons, living or dead, business establishments, events, or locales is
entirely coincidental.

CONTENTS

CHRISTMAS IN
SHELTER BAY

JoAnn Ross

To all the readers who've written over the years asking for Cole and Kelli's story: this one's for you

With appreciation to Sherrill S. Cannon and Kerry E. Gallagher for writing the holiday play Kelli's students perform.

1

It was beginning to look a lot like Christmas in Shelter Bay. Tinseled garlands and wreaths with huge red bows were strung across the streets, colorful holiday scenes had been painted by students on the windows of local businesses, and fairy lights sparkled in the branches of trees all over town.

Down at the pier, Cole Douchett was freezing his tail off stringing lights onto the cabin of his family's fishing boat.

"Why, exactly, are we doing this?" he asked.

"Because the mayor got the idea for the town to have a Christmas boat parade, like they do up in Portland," his grandfather Bernard said.

"She's hoping it'll bring in more tourists," Lucien, his father, added.

"Yeah, why go all the way to Hawaii for beaches when you can winter on the Oregon coast? In case you didn't notice, that's frigging sleet hitting your face," Cole complained.

"Boy's been in the desert too long," Bernard drawled

to his son. "All those years in Afghanistan and Iraq thinned his blood."

"I don't mind the cold," Cole countered. "I'm an effing Marine. We live for miserable conditions. . . .

"What I don't get is why we need to be out here turning into Popsicles in order to draw in more tourists. This is a *fishing* boat. It's not like we're going to be taking tourists for whale-watching rides around the bay."

And the boat wasn't even used all that often anymore, except for family sport fishing.

Whereas his grandfather had worked as a commercial fisherman until recently, his dad had left the sea years ago to open a restaurant with Cole's mother.

Unfortunately, the place had taken a hit by a vicious winter ice storm, only to be given a knockout blow two months after that when hurricane-force winds triggered by a Pacific typhoon came barreling through Shelter Bay. Which was when Maureen and Lucien Douchett had thrown in the towel, closed down Bon Temps, and retired.

Sort of.

They were currently running a bait shop on the harbor, but his father had kept the commercial fishing license, and whenever a recreational day on the water ended up with more crabs, rockfish, or salmon than the family could eat, the two men sold them to local vendors and restaurants.

"Didn't we mention both your grandmère and mother like the idea of a boat parade?" his father asked.

Slam.

Case closed.

There was nothing these two men wouldn't do for their wives. If Adèle and Maureen Douchett wanted the family to take part in this latest cockamamy marketing gimmick the mayor had come up with, that's exactly what their men would do.

"When you get married, if you're smart, you'll learn early on that when women get something set in their minds, it's easier to go along rather than get pecked to high heaven by ducks," Bernard said. "There's also the fact that your grandmère and maman *like* Christmas," he added pointedly. "Unlike some people in the family. Who'll remain nameless."

That unnamed family member being him.

It hadn't always been that way. Although his grandfather might have moved the family to the Pacific Northwest from Louisiana after Hurricane Audrey had wiped their bayou town of Petit Chenier off the map, the Douchetts had remained Cajun to the bone.

Which meant family celebrations were perched at the top of their priorities pyramid. Growing up, Cole hadn't fully appreciated the strength of his parents' and grandparents' long-term marriages. Until he'd learned the hard way that such commitment was a rare commodity.

"I didn't say I didn't like Christmas," he grumbled.

There'd been a time when he'd enjoyed the holidays. But that was then. And this was now, and what he mostly wanted was to just be left alone.

"You've been giving Scrooge a run for his money," Lucien said from atop the ladder as he arranged a long string of lights into the shape of a Dungeness crab.

"I was thinkin' more along the lines of the Grinch," his grandfather said.

"We understand you've got a lot on your mind, what with the decision you have to make." His dad's tone turned serious. "But your mother worries."

"Your grandmère, too," Bernard said. "You havin' nightmares?"

"Once in a while." On the rare occasion he could actually sleep through the night. "But that goes with the territory, right?"

The two older men nodded knowingly. They'd also both been Marines, and while they might never talk about the action they'd seen, Cole suspected he wasn't the only guy in the family with ghosts.

"I'm not pressuring you," his father said. "Whether or not you reenlist is a decision you can only make on your own. But the same way I've been keeping your brother's Camaro ready for when he returns home for good, we're holding on to this boat for you. Just in case you'd be wanting it."

"Not that you're obligated to take up fishing," his grandfather assured him. "Especially being that you got that fancy college degree. It's not like you'd have a hard time finding work. But you're the only one of the three boys who talked about someday taking the business over."

While his two brothers enjoyed sailing, neither of them had ever been all that enthusiastic about working on the family's fishing boat. Cole was the odd man out. He'd always thought a bad day out on the water was better than a good day on land. Which was why his brother Sax ragged him about becoming a Marine desert rat instead of joining the Navy so he could go to sea. Of course, the irony was that although Sax was a Navy SEAL, he'd ended up spending nearly as many years in the desert as Cole had.

Of the three of them, Sax had always been the one to buck tradition. Not to mention the rules. While Cole, as the eldest, had been the Eagle Scout in the family. The rock-solid dependable, "perfect" one.

The role model.

The first person in the Douchett family to graduate from college. Although he'd gone only because his parents had been adamant about the idea, he'd applied for a Navy ROTC scholarship with the Marine option. After graduating with an oceanography degree, he'd followed generations of previous Douchett men into the Corps.

Which made him the first officer in the family.

What neither of his younger brothers, who were always ragging him for being Mr. Perfect, realized was that it was damn exhausting always trying to live up to expectations. Just once, he thought, as he plugged in the lights and watched the oversized Dungeness crab begin to flash bright red, he'd like to be the Douchett Bad Boy.

Okay. Not really bad.

But reckless, like Sax.

Or impulsive, like his baby brother, J.T.

Of course, the last time he'd behaved impulsively, Cole reminded himself, it had turned his life into a train wreck he didn't want to ever repeat.

It wasn't that he didn't want to come home and spend the rest of his life fishing. One problem was that whenever he thought about returning to his coastal hometown, enjoying life on the water after all those years in the Iraqi sandbox and Afghan dustbowl, he felt guilty about the idea of leaving his men—guys who'd become as close as his own brothers—in harm's way. But time was running out; he needed to make a decision.

"You liked working the tourist fishing boats back when you were in high school," his father reminded him.

"Boy had a real knack for talking those rich city folks up," his grandfather agreed. "Ernie Martin always said his business brought in triple the amount of tips when you were showing folks how to bait their hooks and pull in their catch."

"That may have been more about the fact that Ernie didn't like people," Cole said. "I never could figure out why he switched from commercial fishing to charters, since I doubt if he said more than a dozen words to anyone all the hours we were out at sea."

"Fishing has always been an iffy way to earn a living." His father said nothing Cole already didn't know. "At least if Ernie didn't fill the boat's hold with fish by the end of the day, he'd still make a tidy profit from the charter fees. But he's finally closing down shop for good."

"Put his boat up for a fire-sale price the other day," Bernard said. "Seems he wants to escape the rain and retire in the Arizona desert."

Personally, Cole couldn't figure out why anyone would want to live in the desert by choice, but he figured if everyone felt the way about the Pacific Coast that he did, people would be flooding into Shelter Bay and ruining the town.

"It's a newer one than the boat you worked on that summer," his grandfather added. A bit slyly, Cole thought. "He had it rigged up especially for charters."

Cole felt a tug of interest. One of the things he'd been forced to think about was the high rate of veteran unemployment, even among officers with college degrees. In his case, due to his service years, his degree was eight years out of date. The idea that he'd actually not only have a job, but one he loved waiting for him, was tempting.

There was also the fact that he'd spent a lot of time, both while working his grandfather's boat and Ernie's, then during school, and over the past years, thinking about ways to expand the Douchett family fishing business. Maybe form a cooperative with other fishermen, one that could not only result in stronger marketing power and territory, but also fight for environmental issues that would ensure a bountiful sea.

"If I were staying, I'd already have a boat." This one, which was starting to remind him of Snoopy's doghouse in that old Charlie Brown Christmas TV special. Could they put any more damn lights on it?

"An old boat that's got decades of fish smell embedded into every board," his grandfather said. "Not that there aren't those who'd want it."

"We've had offers from fishermen wanting to expand," Lucien said. "If you wanted, you could sell it and put the money toward Ernie's newer shiny one."

Okay. That was an even more interesting idea. But . . . "I wouldn't take your money."

"We're doing just fine," his father said. "Especially since you and J.T. got together with Sax and pitched in to buy us our new place."

"We're family," his grandfather said. "What's ours is yours. You know," he said thoughtfully, "all this Christmas fuss and bother is probably making it tougher for you to focus and sort your choices through properly. Maybe you should spend some time alone at the cabin."

The two Douchett men had built the cabin themselves at Rainbow Lake during summer weekends back when Cole had been in elementary school. The adults in the family worked long and hard hours, so getting the time to escape for more than a day or two had been rare, but after Labor Day, once the tourists had mostly left town and the crabs were molting, putting a pause to the season, his parents would close Bon Temps, his grandfather would dock the boat, and they'd all spend the best two weeks of the year swimming, pole fishing, eagle watching, barbecuing, and just lying in a hammock, listening to the waterfall tumble over rocks into the lake while the breeze whispered in the tops of the towering Douglas fir trees.

There were times, more and more often lately, when memories of those carefree summer vacations had helped Cole survive deployments.

"I promised Mom I'd be home for Christmas," he said, even as the idea of being alone out in the woods while he tried to sort out what to do with the rest of his life sang its siren song.

"She'll understand," his dad assured him. "Though I'm not going to deny that she's been looking forward to getting her boys home again so she can spoil you all."

Which she'd definitely been doing. It was only his second day home and he'd already eaten more than he normally ate in a week. Of course, his mother's cooking, which people had paid to eat for years back when his parents had run the restaurant, was a helluva lot better than any MREs or military mess meals.

"Why don't you compromise?" his grandfather suggested. "Stay until after the boat parade and the annual school program. It's turned into a pretty big deal, since your grandmother's been working overtime helping Kelli with her kindergarten class's part in it. Then take off."

Kelli Carpenter was a blast from Cole's past. One that, unfortunately, in a town this size, he probably wasn't going to be able to avoid for long.

"If you're sure Mom wouldn't be upset."

"She's your mother," both men said together.

"She's always wanted the best for you and your brothers," his dad tacked on. "If you need time alone to get your head around what you're going to do next with your life, she'll be fine with the idea."

A memory of last year's Christmas tree lighting, when

Kelli Carpenter's blue eyes had flashed like lightning over a stormy sea the last time he had seen her, came crashing back. Although Recon Marines were no cowards, Cole was more than a little tempted to take his father and grandfather up on their offer to get the hell out of Dodge.

2

Kelli Carpenter had always loved Christmas. The carols, the shopping, the tinsel, and decorating the tree in bright lights and eclectic, mismatched but memorable ornaments collected over the years.

Although there were times when she might have wished that she lived somewhere she could experience a white Christmas, like in the song and seemingly every holiday movie ever made, she couldn't imagine living anywhere else but Shelter Bay.

The coastal Oregon town was where she'd been born. Where, in the sixth grade, she'd performed the role of the Sugar Plum Fairy in her Pelican Elementary School's production of *The Nutcracker*.

Shelter Bay was where she'd energetically waved her blue and white cheerleader pom-poms for the high school Dolphins, where she'd been president of the theater club and voted the most likely to star on Broadway. Where she'd fallen in love.

And, at one Christmas tree lighting she wished she could forget, had her heart shattered into a million pieces.

But she wasn't going to think about that now. This upcoming program wasn't about her. It was about making sure that the students in her kindergarten class would look back on tonight as a happy holiday memory. Also, hopefully, their parents and the rest of the audience members would enjoy the performance that she, Adèle Douchett, and Zelda Chmerkovskiy had been working on with the children since they'd returned from their Thanksgiving weekend.

"My nose doesn't light up," Cody Miller complained.

"Don't worry, cher," Adèle assured him. "This is just the dress rehearsal, so everyone can get used to wearing their costumes."

The seamstress of the team, Adèle had created the reindeer costume with a hood that left the little boy's face uncovered, partly so his parents could recognize him for their home video. But equally importantly, so he wouldn't go bumping into other singers, or worse yet, the scenery.

Last year, Kelli had made the costume from a pattern she'd found on the Internet. Unfortunately, with that hood having slots only for his eyes and mouth, the visually impaired Rudolph had walked straight into the tree, sending it tumbling down on two snowflakes and an angel, who'd ended up with a bloody nose.

It was not, Kelli thought, her finest moment. Unfortunately, it had also become a viral YouTube hit for the remainder of last year's holiday season. A bit of unwelcome fame she was determined to avoid this year.

"Mr. Douchett will add the battery before the performance," Kelli assured the five-year-old.

"Good," Allison Duggan said. "Because the song won't work if Rudolph's nose doesn't flash."

There were times when Kelli thought that she might

as well give Allison the role of codirector. The tiny blonde might look like the Christmas angel she was dressed up to portray, but the little girl was a demon when it came to getting the details right.

"It'll flash," Kelli said.

Yesterday, Allison's major concern had been whether or not there were enough rhinestones and sequins on her angel costume to sparkle properly beneath the spotlights.

ABC December was a simple and enjoyable play: Each of the children would do a little dance to the center of the stage, hold up a sign with a letter of the alphabet, sing two lines to fit their assigned letter, then dance off again.

It wasn't nearly as complex as the *Winter Snow Fairy* play the fourth graders planned to do. Or the annual sixth grade shortened version of *The Nutcracker*, which, years after Kelli had performed it, remained an audience pleaser.

Although she was trying to keep her mind focused, Kelli's concentration was that of a mosquito. Or at least a five-year-old.

"You seem distracted today," Adèle noted after the small performers had all gone home and the three women were packing up the costumes and alphabet posters.

"This time of year is always a bit stressful," she hedged, unwilling to admit to this woman she cared about so dearly that it was the older woman's grandson who was causing Kelli's mind to wander.

"You've always loved it so," the seventysomething woman said, studying Kelli with concern. "I still remember how you seemed to float above the stage when you danced *The Nutcracker*. You actually became a sugarplum fairy."

"I was eleven," Kelli pointed out. "Life was less complicated then."

"I suppose. Yet you've always embraced the holidays." Adèle's brow furrowed. "Actually, it's been only the past few days that you haven't seemed yourself."

Kelli shrugged. "I guess the weather's getting to me."

"It's winter," Zelda, who was replacing pink ribbons in a pair of tiny ballet slippers with white, pointed out. "It always rains on the coast in December."

Actually, it rained on the coast year-round, which had never bothered Kelli. In fact, she actually enjoyed the cool, misty days of "Oregon sunshine."

"Maybe I just need to get away for a few days. I wonder if it's too late to get plane tickets to Hawaii."

"With Bradford?" Zelda asked.

"No. Alone." She and Brad Archer had been dating for the past two months, but they were not anywhere near the stage in their relationship when she'd want to take a long flight and a beach trip with him.

"Alone?" Adèle looked at her as if she'd suggested taking a flight to Mars. "At Christmas? What about your parents?"

"It's not as if I'd be abandoning them." Merely escaping old memories she'd discovered she wasn't ready to relive.

"Cole's back home." Adèle pressed her case. "Have you seen him yet?"

"No. We haven't run into each other." And hadn't she done her best to make sure of that?

Over the past year, Kelli had tried to convince herself that she'd gotten over Cole Douchett. It wasn't as if they'd ever actually had a romantic relationship. He'd always treated her like a little sister, even when she knew, in her heart of hearts, that if he'd only wait for her to grow up, they could be so much more.

Kelli couldn't remember when she'd fallen in love with Cole. It seemed as if he'd always been hers. Living across the street, it was only natural that her older brothers would hang out with the three Douchett boys.

There were times when it was almost as if she had six big brothers.

But Cole had been different. He'd been the one who took her out for ice cream when Hershey, their chocolate Lab, had gotten run over and she couldn't stop crying. When she was seven years old, during a halcyon weekend when her family stayed with his at the Douchett cabin on Rainbow Lake, Cole had taught her to bait a hook.

Although she'd have rather eaten dirt than touch a wiggly worm, years later, Kelli could remember his large hands covering hers as he'd helped her pull in that gleaming rainbow trout. That night, while sparks flew upward into an uncharacteristically clear night sky, he'd taught her how to cook the fish—which he'd cleaned for her—over a campfire.

Although she'd tasted fancier preparations of trout in the intervening years, that simple fish remained the best she'd ever eaten.

"Bernard and I are just rattling around in our big old house," Adèle said. "I believe I'll throw a holiday *fais do do*." Which, although it translated to "make sleep," Kelli knew was Cajun for party. Nobody in Shelter Bay threw parties like the Douchetts. "It'll be fun to do for Boxing Day. You will come, won't you?"

"If I'm in town, of course." And if she didn't come

down with a case of the flu, which she could almost feel coming on.

Adèle started to open her mouth. Then closed it with a nearly audible snap. "Well, Cole's got another twelve days before he has to return to Camp Pendleton. There's plenty of time for us all to get together."

Too much time to keep coming up with excuses to avoid the man, Kelli thought with a sinking heart.

Hawaii was looking better and better.

3

The first thought that rocketed through Cole's mind when he saw Kelli arriving at the pier for the boat parade the next afternoon was that the little girl with the flyaway, dandelion hair, freckles, and braces had definitely grown up.

Her face, framed by the hood of her parka, reminded him of the ivory cameo his grandmother had inherited from her mother. Her eyes were wide and colored the gleaming blue of sunlight on summer water, her cheeks pink from the cold, and how could he have known her all her life and have not realized how kissable those full lips were?

She was with Matt, the eldest and most boisterous of her three brothers, plus his wife and kids, and some blond guy Cole didn't recognize.

"Hey, Cole!" Matt caught him in a one-armed guy hug. "Good to see you back, man. So, are you staying for good this time?"

"That's what I'm trying to decide," Cole said.

"Well, if you do decide to hang around, I'm selling cars at Gardner Ford and just happen to have a red Mustang GT on the lot that's got your name on it."

Since he already had a red dually diesel pickup he

used for hauling around the jet boat he kept docked at Del Mar's Camp Pendleton Marina, Cole needed a muscle car like he needed an extra head. But at least his old friend had gotten the color right.

He laughed. "It's good to know some things never change."

Despite what his father and grandfather had said about his ability to get along with people, Cole's people skills didn't come anywhere near this man's.

From their early days in Cub Scouts, when Matt Carpenter would win the top prize for Scoutarama ticket sales, he was always selling something: subscriptions to the *Shelter Bay Beacon*; crabs he'd buy at a discount from Cole's grandfather in the summer, then boil so fainthearted customers wouldn't be forced to commit crustacean homicide; hot cider and clam chowder every fall; Texas fruit cakes for the ski club trip fund-raiser; and Christmas trees from the Carpenter family's farm in the parking lot of Harbor Hardware.

The proceeds from all those years of salesmanship had paid for a degree in business from Oregon State University, and Cole had no doubts that someday his old friend could well end up owning the dealership.

He turned to Matt's wife, Meredith, who was holding a red-haired toddler by his mittened hand. A little girl he knew to be four years older had just caught the toddler's twin, who'd taken off running on the toes of his snow boots toward a trio of pugs an elderly couple were walking on leashes.

"Hey, beautiful," he greeted Meredith Carpenter. "How the hell can you be the mother of three when you look exactly the same as you did when you were sweet sixteen?" He tilted his head. Studied her. "I take that back. You look even better," he decided.

"You sweet-talking man," she said, fluttering her lashes as she scooped up the boy his sister had just managed to return to the group. "You should pay attention to the way Cole treats a woman," she told her husband. "Or I just might run away with him."

"Mama!" The little girl's eyes widened to blue saucers, and she tugged on the hem of her mother's jacket.

"Just kidding, darling," Meredith said. "You know I love your daddy to pieces." She secured the squirming boy more firmly to her hip and patted the top of her daughter's tasseled purple ski cap with her free hand. "You remember Mr. Douchett, don't you, Melanie?"

"You helped me build a sandcastle when I was little," the child—who was, as his grandfather would say, cute as a ladybug in a rug—said. "And you dug a moat."

"Gotta protect the home front from invaders," Cole said with a grin. "How you doing, sweetheart?"

"Fine, thank you," she said in a polite, ladylike voice far older than her years.

"I'm glad to hear that. You've grown up a lot since that beach day."

Another firstborn, he thought on an inward sigh. Already on the straight-and-narrow path of responsible behavior. Part of him admired her for being so conscientious at such a young age. A stronger part wanted to urge her to learn how to loosen up and play while she could.

Finally, because he couldn't ignore her any longer, Cole looked over at Kelli, who, in her pink hooded parka, matching ski pants, and white moon boots reminded him of a sugarplum. "Hey, Kels."

"Hello, Cole." Inwardly conflicted about his feelings toward this woman, he'd managed to keep his tone outwardly casual. Hers, while not exactly unfriendly, was as cool as a winter sea. Though an improvement over her inexplicable and uncharacteristic flare of temper last Christmas, it still wasn't all that encouraging. Maybe the guy she was with was the jealous type and she was just trying to avoid another scene. "You're looking well."

"I'm doin' okay," he said. Which was mostly true. "You're looking terrific." He wasn't sure she'd appreciate the sugarplum idea, so he kept it to himself.

"Thank you."

He hadn't exactly expected her to fling herself into his arms—they'd never had that type of relationship—but he also hadn't expected a deep freeze. After all, they'd known each other forever.

Younger and outnumbered by her three brothers and the three Douchett boys, for years she'd seemed like an adorable little puppy who was always following, wanting to go along. Possessing a determination far stronger than her size, she'd even, on more than one occasion, ignored the "Boys Only" sign and wheedled her way into the tree house Mr. Carpenter had built in their backyard. In fact, he remembered, looking back, it was where he'd found her crying her eyes out after her dog had died.

"Nice weather, for December," he tried again. When in trouble, always fall back on the weather. Although it was a few minutes to four, the sun was already lowering in the sky for the 4:22 p.m. sunset, and the temperature was dropping by the minute. Fortunately, the rain had stopped a little after noon.

"It's lucky it cleared up for the parade," she agreed.

"Yeah." A silence as thick as morning fog settled over them.

The guy she was with, seeming to sense the uneasy undercurrents, broke it. "I'm Bradford Archer."

Cole shook the gloved hand held out to him. "Cole Douchett."

When the guy put his arm around Kelli's shoulder, Cole could practically see the "Taken" sign flashing over her head. He glanced down at her hand, but the fuzzy white gloves she was wearing kept him from being able to see if she were wearing a ring.

"You're the Marine," Archer said.

"One of them," Cole said, wondering what Kelli had told him about their relationship. "One of my brothers is a Marine, too."

"Brad's principal of Pelican Elementary," Kelli said.

"Which would also make him your boss." Weren't there workplace rules against that? Apparently not. "Being an elementary school principal sounds like quite a challenge."

"Well, it's not on the level of fighting terrorism," Archer allowed. "But it's one I enjoy. Especially since I have the opportunity to work with such great and dedicated teachers." He smiled down at Kelli, who smiled back up at him.

Cole would personally rather be keelhauled than spend his day wrangling grade school kids, but he figured this Brad guy probably wouldn't fully appreciate parachuting into a remote location, then freezing your ass for hours on the cold, hard ground, scoping out a hole that led to a tunnel, which in turn led into a cave in the snowy Hindu Kush Mountains, waiting for a Taliban courier to show up.

It was funny to think of Kelli having hooked up with some guy. Not funny ha-ha, because she'd definitely grown up to be a desirable woman. Just funny odd. Being the baby sister of his best friend had kept him from thinking of her romantically or sexually, but in his mind, whenever he'd think about her, she'd stayed frozen in time.

Okay. That was a lie.

There *had* been that out-of-the-blue bolt of awareness of her as a very desirable woman last winter, which he'd managed to convince himself had been merely an aberration born from having been deployed too long.

Or so Cole had told himself. Over the past year in the mountains, he'd had plenty of time to second-guess a lot of decisions he'd made the last time he'd been home.

Another silence settled over them. Heavier, deeper, longer than the first.

"Heard the Douchett boat's going to be in the parade," Matt jumped in, turning the dial up on his natural enthusiasm, as if sensing something wasn't exactly copacetic.

"We spent yesterday putting lights all over it," Cole agreed, grateful for the conversational intervention. "And I hear this year's town tree came from your family's farm. Again." The red, white, and green lights draped onto the limbs of the towering Douglas fir tree in the park at the top of the hill were visible from all over Shelter Bay.

"Wouldn't be a Shelter Bay Christmas without a Carpenter Farms tree," Matt said. Just because he'd never enjoyed working on the farm didn't mean he wasn't proud of the family business. "Brian went into partnership with Dad after he got back from Iraq. I know he'd really like to get together while you're here, but this is his busy season. The farm's now one of the top five shippers in Oregon."

Which was saying something, given that the state just happened to be the top producer of Christmas trees in the nation.

"That's great."

"Yeah. Brian talked Dad into going after Costco,

which made a difference in profits. The big box stores may be really tight with their dollars, but they move a lot of merchandise. The old days of making a living selling from the local hardware store parking lot are long gone."

"Things change," Cole said. He might be talking to Matt, but he was looking at his old friend's sister, something that did not go unnoticed by Brad Archer.

"Well, we'd better get going if we want good seats in the viewing stand," Archer told Kelli.

For a fleeting moment, as her eyes met his and held, Cole thought he viewed a flash of the old Kelli, who hadn't even tried to hide her schoolgirl crush on him. But it came and went so quickly, he couldn't quite read it.

She'd not only grown up. She'd gotten a lot better at hiding her thoughts.

For some reason, one he'd think about later, despite having wanted to avoid her, Cole wasn't quite ready to let her go yet. "I hear you're working with grandmère on this year's play."

That earned a quick, uncensored smile that lit up her eyes. "She's been an amazing help. I swear she'd got as much energy as the kids." She arched a brow. "Are you attending?"

"Apparently it's a big deal for the family." Cole shrugged. "So, I figured I'd show up. She also mentioned a party the day after Christmas."

Which, until this minute, had been making him look forward to escaping to the cabin. One thing he wasn't up to was chatting with the crowd that would show up for a Douchett party, which always boasted the best food in town. Especially since he'd discovered that civilians all seemed to either talk about the war with him, or look at him as if they feared he was about to go all PTSD on them.

Now, though, he couldn't help wondering if Kelli was going to be there. And if she was, if she'd come with the territorial principal in tow.

"She invited me," Kelli answered. "But, unfortunately, I had to turn her down. Because I'm going to be in Hawaii."

When Archer opened his mouth, about to say something, she grabbed his arm and began leading him away. "Well, it's been nice to see you again, Cole," she said on a chirpy tone that even he could tell was as phony as the pollack some fish processors would flavor with a bunch of chemicals and pass off as crab. "Have a wonderful Christmas. And stay safe."

"Great seeing you again, too," he said. "Have a great Christmas."

As he watched her walk away arm in arm with Archer, their heads almost touching, Cole felt a sudden flare of heat. But having become intimately acquainted with dangers of all kinds, he banked that attraction just as quickly.

4

"Since when are you going to Hawaii?" Brad asked as Kelli practically dragged him toward the bleachers that had been set up as a viewing stand.

"I haven't booked any reservations," she said. "But after remembering how much the weeks of intense preparations for the holiday programs take out of me every year, I'm considering it."

Even more so now that she'd seen Cole Douchett. Damn, even with that too-short Marine haircut, he was better looking than ever. He was not really conventionally handsome. Not like Brad, who, especially when he wore his tweed jackets with their leather elbow patches, brought to mind a hot college literature professor.

Cole looked every bit the warrior he was. His face was all harsh, chiseled lines that cast deep shadows on his sexily stubbled cheeks and his full, firm mouth that for an unsettling moment she'd wanted to feel on hers. Back when she'd first been swamped by a tsunami of hormones in her teens, she'd fantasized about licking that delicious cleft in his chiseled chin.

How pitiful was it that her knee-jerk attraction to him

was every bit as strong as it had been when she was fifteen?

His heavily hooded, intense eyes were the color of the dark chocolate truffles she was regrettably too fond of, which partly explained the ten extra pounds she kept vowing to lose. They'd once been warm and, although more serious than his younger brothers', friendly. Not today.

It wasn't that he'd been particularly unfriendly. Or cold. In fact, if she were to be perfectly honest, she'd been the one to put the chilliness in their conversation. Nor could she describe those watchful brown eyes as remote.

At least not when they'd skimmed over her body. Although she'd fallen in love with the outfit when she'd first seen it in the window of the Dancing Deer Two boutique, Cole's appraising gaze had her thinking that she probably looked like a snowwoman some tagger had spray-painted pink.

She'd spent too many years wishing for Cole Douchett to look at her as if she were a female, and not a kid sister, not to recognize the fleeting flash of male interest. An attraction he'd immediately tamped down. She'd noticed the sexual conjecture was quickly replaced by another emotion that, as nervous as she'd been, she'd hadn't exactly been able to recognize.

"Lonely," she said suddenly as she climbed up the bleachers toward the top row. *That's* what had been in his heavily hooded eyes. Cole Douchett was lonely.

"What?" Brad, who was following behind, asked.

"Nothing." She waved off her inadvertent comment. "I was merely thinking out loud."

And even if she was right about what she'd seen in Cole's dark eyes, there wasn't any reason to feel sorry for him. Not only did he have his family to celebrate the holidays with, most of Shelter Bay's single women, and undoubtedly a few married ones, would jump at the chance to spend time with the hottie Marine.

"About going to Hawaii?" Brad frowned at the idea. "Because, as your friend, Kelli, I feel obliged to point out that spending the holidays all by yourself in a hotel room thousands of miles away would probably be very lonely."

"Probably." Though, now that she'd run into Cole, she was going to go online the minute she got home. "Then again, I feel as if I really need a break."

"Why don't we go together?"

"Together?"

Brad Archer was the least impulsive man she'd ever met in her life. Which was a good thing in his profession, she'd decided. But all his charts and diagrams and Power-Point slide shows, along with his tendency to plan everything down to the last detail, could get brain-numbingly tedious.

Which had her mind wandering toward Cole again. Of the three Douchett brothers, he'd always been the least impulsive. Not stodgy, certainly. But steady. Dependable. Steadfastness seemed an admirable trait for a Marine.

Then again, surely war wasn't at all predictable. So he couldn't be anything as rigid as Brad.

Not that she was comparing the two men.

Merely making an observation.

"I'm sorry." As she squeezed in sardine tight next to him to fit into one of the two open spaces left on the green steel bench, she realized Brad had been speaking to her. "My mind was wandering. To the play." Liar.

"I was suggesting that Hawaii at Christmas sounds like an enjoyable way to experience a different culture."

His initial undergraduate major, Kelli knew, had been archaeology. But while volunteering on a dig in the Mexican Yucatán between his freshman and sophomore years, he'd belatedly discovered that he disliked heat, insects, and mud, not to mention the deplorable lack of running water or room service. As soon as he returned to the States, he'd gone through drop/add and switched to education.

"I wonder if people decorate palm trees there," he mused.

"Some probably do." Spotting Cole's grandmother and mother waving to her from a few rows down, she waved back. "And Hawaii has Norfolk Island pines, which are really pretty, though they're not actually pines but conifers. Even so, they get a lot of trees shipped in from the mainland. The Carpenter farm has been sending them to the islands since before I was born."

"I'll bet that makes them expensive."

"Well, they're not inexpensive." Not that all that many profits ended up in her family's coffers by the time you factored in filing myriad government paperwork involved in ensuring the trees were disease free, along with the cost of shipping and distribution once they arrived in the Aloha State. "But a lot of people must figure it's worth it. And it's not exactly as if they could grow their own Noble firs."

"They could buy artificial."

"Don't suggest that to any member of my family," she warned as she watched Cole walk down the pier.

His shoulders, beneath the navy blue parka, were as wide as an ax handle, his back straight enough to get him on one of those posters in the Marine recruiting office on Main Street. He'd begun to shoot up in middle school, yet despite the muscle he'd put on over the intervening years, he somehow managed to move like a cat. A lion, she decided. King of the jungle.

His father and grandfather, who were no slouches themselves in the looks department, were already standing on the deck of the boat.

"It was merely an economic observation," Brad said.

"I'm not sure economics enter into the equation all that much when people are Christmas tree shopping. Plus, real trees just smell like Christmas. And fake ones end up being tossed out every five years or so, winding up in landfills while a real tree can be recycled into mulch.

"We've also been dropping trees into Rainbow Lake after the season. They become a good habitat for fish to lay their eggs in. And after Hurricane Katrina, we began shipping tree mulch to Louisiana to help rebuild coastlines."

"I didn't realize that."

"Well, now you know. It's not all tinsel and lights." Realizing that had come out uncharacteristically sharp, she forced a smile. "I'm sorry if I sounded snappish. I guess you can take the girl from the Christmas tree farm, but you can't entirely take the farm from the girl."

"Makes sense to me. You're right to be proud of your family business." He put his arm around her shoulders as the sun set into the water and the darkness gathered around them. "I could go online right now, from my phone, and see about booking tickets," he suggested.

She liked Brad. He was a nice guy and was wonderful with kids. Which would have made him a great catch in many women's eyes. But whatever relationship they had, it definitely wasn't to the point where she wanted to take a vacation with him. Especially since she had the feeling, from the way he'd behaved so oddly possessive when talking to Cole, that Brad was far more serious about her than she was about him.

He was a friend. A wonderful principal to work with. He'd undoubtedly make a terrific husband and father. Unfortunately, although she'd honestly tried, she just never felt any zing when she was with him.

While just seeing Cole again could set off sparks. All this time she had assured herself that no more sparks could fly up from embers that she'd firmly tamped down, especially after last year's debacle.

She'd been so wrong about that.

"Let's just watch the parade," she said. "We can talk about it afterward. Or tomorrow."

Although she had no intention of going to Hawaii with Brad, she truly liked him and didn't want to turn him down here, in front of so many people — many of whom were likely already eavesdropping on their conversation. One sure thing about Shelter Bay was that everyone knew everyone's business.

"Works for me," he said agreeably.

And somehow his affability only made her even more certain that the time had come to break things off. On the one hand, she didn't want a man who'd take away her independence by telling her what to do. But she also knew, having had to learn to be assertive growing up with three older brothers, that if she were to ever get serious and settle down with Brad, she'd undoubtedly walk all over him.

Which he'd come to hate her for.

Nearly as much as she'd hate herself.

The harbormaster blasted three sharp sounds on his air horn. A moment later, all the boats that had chugged out into the water turned on their lights, revealing a dazzling display of decorations as varied as the boats' owners. Among them were the more expected Christmas trees, Santa's sleigh, snowmen, reindeer, along with angels and a manger. Going with a more local angle, one featured a blue whale followed by its baby, another a huge goose, outlined in blue wearing a red scarf, looking as if it were flying off the stern of a sailboat outlined in white.

All were bright and wonderful in their own way, but the fishing boat that immediately drew Kelli's gaze was *Bon Temps*, with a giant red Dungeness crab opening and closing its claws.

Everyone around her was having a grand time. And why shouldn't they? It was Christmas, after all. Which had always been her favorite time of year. Or at least it had been at one time. But something had changed for her this year. Try as she might, once the decorations had started going up all over town, she hadn't been able to get last year's encounter with Cole out of her mind.

She'd always been easygoing—some would even say *perky*—Kelli. But despite realizing that Cole thought of her more along the lines of a cheerful puppy who was always trailing after him, she'd steadfastly believed that once she grew up, once he opened those Hershey brown eyes and realized that the freckle-faced girl with hair that always frizzed when it rained had matured into the woman he'd been waiting for all his life, everything would change.

Which had been why, for that one heart-stealing moment when he'd taken the jewelry box out of his parka pocket, although they'd never so much as kissed on the lips, she'd just *known* that he'd bought it for her.

She'd been so wrong.

And worse yet, the intended recipient of that pear-shaped diamond just happened to be her high school nemesis. The woman anyone with even a halfway working brain could see was totally wrong for him.

Unfortunately, although he might be a big bad Marine who could—according to the local press coverage regaling the act of heroism that had won him a medal for bravery—catch bullets in his teeth and spit them right back at the terrorists, that entire Christmas Cole had been home on leave, he'd acted as dumb as Dudley Do-Right, her family's ancient basset hound.

"He's a Marine on leave, honey." Matt had defended his lifelong best friend when she'd complained about the way Marcia Wayburn, whom Cole had dated off and on his senior year of high school, had him wrapped around her acrylic French-manicured finger. And that wasn't all that was fake. Kelli knew that for a fact, because Marcia had bragged all over school that her high school graduation present from her doting daddy had been a boob job. "Makes sense that he'd be thinking with his little head instead of his big one."

He'd flashed a grin that showed Cole wasn't alone. Which wasn't something Kelli had wanted to think about. At all.

"Guys who know they're going back to war are looking only for no-strings sex." He'd told her what she'd already figured out for herself. "And despite you always putting him up on a pedestal, Cole's still just a regular guy." He'd ruffled her hair the same way he had when she was six. "He's just reliving old high school days. He'll get over her."

Since her brothers had never lied to her, Kelli had believed him. Until the Christmas tree lighting when he'd flashed that diamond and informed her that he planned to give it to a girl named after that snobby, know-it-all Brady Bunch big sister, who, to Kelli's mind, was the most annoying character ever on television.

She'd never lost her temper. Ever. Until that night. Although much of what she'd shouted at him was a blank, she could remember throwing the pretty white jewelry box at his chest, where it bounced off and landed on the ground.

Which would've been bad enough. But before Cole could retrieve it, Ken Curtis's yellow Lab puppy snatched it up, slipped her collar, and had a dandy run around and around the tree, chased by seemingly every male in Shelter Bay before Cole finally caught her with a running dive that sent them both smashing into the tree. Fortunately, since her father and brothers had secured it well, the tree hadn't toppled over, where it could have crushed nearly the entire town who'd gathered for the annual holiday lighting.

But it had created a scandal that kept Shelter Bay talking well past the New Year. And if that debacle weren't bad enough, Cole and Marcia's breakup a mere four months later had only added grist to the gossip mill. Even now she cringed thinking about it.

Although Cole had been in Afghanistan at the time — thus avoiding all the talk — Kelli knew that he would've hated having all that attention on him. Especially since he'd always been the Boy Scout of the Douchett family.

Since her uncharacteristic behavior had created the scandal, Kelli was honestly surprised he'd spoken to her at all today.

Unfortunately, while their friendship might have gone up in flames on the pyre of his male cluelessness and her disappointment and jealousy, the one thing that hadn't changed was that Cole was still hot.

Make that *two* things.

Because, dammit, her raging crush on him was still alive and well.

And that was ridiculous. She was twenty-five years old. An adult. A professional, an honors graduate whom parents trusted five days a week with their precious children.

Crushes were for silly young girls who cut photos of Justin Bieber from *Popstar!* magazine and *Twilight* fans who wept copious tears in darkened theaters as Bella chose Edward over a brokenhearted Jacob, causing him to run off into the woods to live as a lone wolf.

How pathetic was it that just seeing him today, just hearing that deep, husky voice that she'd imagined too many times in her fantasies saying her name, had her remembering how knee-weakening the right kind of heat in the right places could be?

She'd already had her heart broken once by Cole Douchett.

She would not, Kelli vowed, make that same mistake twice.

5

Kelli couldn't believe it. With all the flights between Oregon and Hawaii, there wasn't a single seat on any plane flying out of Portland for her? Not even in first class—not that she could afford such luxury on her teacher's salary. Was no one staying on the mainland for Christmas?

If she were willing to go after the holidays, as long as she would settle for a middle seat in the very back of the plane, she could buy a ticket for an inflated last-minute price.

But by then she wouldn't need to escape because Cole would be gone from Shelter Bay.

Which was what she wanted.

So, why, she asked herself a few hours later, did the sight of him walking into the cafeteria, familiar pink bakery box in hand, cause her heart to hitch.

"Well, this is a surprise," she said.

"I ran into your mother this morning at the market," he told her. "She said that you couldn't get tickets to Hawaii."

"That was fast, even for this town. Since I struck out only last night."

He tilted his head. Frowned. "She wasn't gossiping, Kelli. I just asked her how things were going and it came up."

Had they been talking about her? Her mother had always liked Cole, who'd spent as much time at the Carpenter house as he had his own home.

"So, anyway," he said, "I brought you this." He held out the box, wrapped with white ribbon with *Take the Cake* written on the top in white raised script.

"You brought me a cupcake?" She could have easily been addicted to the shop's cupcakes if she weren't strict about how often she allowed herself to visit.

"I was walking by and the aroma wafting from the place drew me in. I was planning to get a box for the family when I saw this tropical one in the case. The bakery's owner bills it as tasting like a piña colada."

"It does." Which was what had gotten her thinking about Hawaii in the first place.

"After sampling one myself, solely in the interest of making certain she wasn't engaging in false advertising, I decided she had nailed it. So, I brought you Hawaii in a cupcake."

Kelli couldn't quite repress the giddy sense of pleasure that he'd been thinking of her. And had bought her something he knew she'd enjoy. Somehow it was better than a pirate's trove of jewels.

"Thank you. That's very thoughtful of you."

"Don't go giving me too much credit, Kels," he said. "There was more than a little selfishness involved."

"Oh?" She opened the box and breathed in the scent of rum, coconut, and pineapple. A bright yellow and white paper umbrella had been inserted in the middle of the toasted coconut frosting. Hawaii in a cupcake.

"I was hoping it'd get you to smile at me again. Like old times." He flashed a grin, the one that was such a surprising contrast to his rugged, almost harshly hewn looks. The one she'd never been able to resist.

Oh no. Kelli felt the moisture stinging at the back of her eyes and lowered her lids, fighting to control her tangled, complex emotions. Then finally she lifted her gaze to his steady, watchful one and gave him the smile he'd been waiting for.

"Thank you," she said.

"Friends?"

Because it seemed so important to him—and she reminded herself that he could, after all, be going to war, and she'd never forgive herself if he were injured, or worse, killed, thinking she was still angry at him—Kelli lied.

"Friends."

His shoulders visibly relaxed as he blew out a breath. "Great." His eyes warmed even further as his gaze skimmed over her face, and for one vivid, heart-stopping second, as they lingered on her mouth, she thought he was going to kiss her.

But, of course, he didn't. Instead he settled for the kind of quick, safe hug she might have received from one of her own brothers.

"Well." He flashed a quick, satisfied grin that told her he had, to his mind, fixed things and moved them back to the relationship they'd shared before her flash of temper had blown it up. "I'd better let you get back to work." He skimmed a finger down her nose. "Enjoy the cupcake."

Then he turned and began strolling back up the center aisle.

When he turned around halfway to the doors at the rear of the room, her foolishly romantic heart hitched. Her lips parted, ever so slightly.

Waiting.

Wanting.

"Break a leg," he called back to her.

"I think that's just for the actors," she said.

Since he'd already turned away again, her words were directed at his back.

"What's wrong?" Adèle asked ten minutes later. She might be in her seventies, but her eagle eyes never missed a thing.

"Nothing," Kelli lied, cursing as she touched up some painting on the backdrop for her class's play.

"You've seemed out of sorts since you arrived." Zelda looked up from where she'd been going through the music with two volunteer audio/visual students from Shelter Bay High School.

"I'm fine."

"Then explain the bags beneath your eyes." The former prima Bolshoi Ballet principal dancer might be somewhere between seventy and a hundred, but she was still as sharp as a stiletto.

"Okay, maybe not exactly fine," Kelli admitted. "But I *will* be dandy once tonight's over. I've just been stressed out from the pressure of needing everything to go perfectly."

Both women laughed at that idea.

"All your actors are five years old, dear," Adèle pointed out gently. "I doubt you can count on perfection."

"It'd definitely be a second Christmas miracle," Zelda agreed.

Which was unfortunately true. And if it had been any other year, Kelli would have admitted that she found the children's little screwups charming.

But this was not any other year.

"I just want to avoid us trending on Twitter or becoming a worst-ever Christmas play YouTube hit," she muttered as she dabbed some cadmium-orange paint onto a snowman's carrot nose.

"Things went very well in dress rehearsal," Adèle reminded her. "I wouldn't worry if I were you."

Easy for her to say.

"You have seemed unusually tense the past few days," Zelda said thoughtfully. "Maybe going to Hawaii isn't such a bad idea."

"That's off the table." Kelli moved on to covering up some dings on a red sled filled with presents.

"Oh?" Adèle turned from hanging up the costumes on a wheeled rack. "Are you and Bradford going somewhere else together?"

"I broke up with Brad after the boat parade," Kelli said.

"I'm sorry," both women said together.

Kelli shrugged. "It's been coming. It seemed best just to get it over with so he can take someone else to the New Year's Eve dance."

The conversation, which she'd broached on the drive to her house from the boat parade, had been surprisingly drama free. Which either meant that he truly was the nicest guy in the world, or that he might actually have been relieved. Surely she wasn't the only one who'd never felt sparks?

There had been one little obstacle to get over.

"What about the New Year's dance?" he'd asked as the wipers steadily swished the rain, which had begun to fall again, from the windshield. "I even rented a tux from Tux and Tails in Newport."

"I don't really feel like going this year," she'd said truthfully. "But I know, off the top of my head, of at least four women who'd jump at the chance to go with you."

He'd shot her a look. "Seriously?"

She'd nodded. "Absolutely."

"Who?"

"Laura, from Cut Loose, told me while she was trimming my hair that she finds you hot." Kelli had begun ticking them off on her fingers as he returned his attention to the road. "So does Jennie, who manages the catering for the Crab Shack, Audrey, from the bakery at the market, and last, but certainly not least, Patty, from school."

"Patty?" He had visibly perked up at that revelation; then he'd given her another, longer look. "My Patty? From the office?"

"Brad." Kelli huffed out a breath. "She's managed the principal's office for the past two years. Are you telling me you've never noticed she has a major thing for you?"

"Seriously?" he'd repeated. In an unconscious gesture, he rubbed his chin, which, while lacking any cleft, was still firm. In many ways, Brad had always reminded Kelli of Robert Redford, from his Sundance Kid days. Unfortunately, she'd always found Paul Newman hotter.

"Seriously," she'd assured him. "Why do you think she's always bringing you homemade baked goods?" November apple muffins and pumpkin bread had given way to December gingerbread and snickerdoodles.

"She says she enjoys baking."

"She enjoys baking for *you*." Since the bakefest had begun at the beginning of the school year, Kelli had found it highly unfair that Brad could eat all those carb- and sugar-laden treats without ever gaining a pound. "Trust me on this," she'd said.

And apparently he had, because she'd received a call from Patty shortly before coming here today to make sure Kelli didn't have any problem with her accepting the Pelican Elementary School principal's invitation to the dance. From the excitement in the other woman's voice, it seemed that she, at least, was going to be having a very merry holiday.

"Well, I'm glad no hearts were broken," Adèle said briskly. "I have to admit, now that you're no longer a couple, I'm not surprised. I'm also more than a little relieved."

"Why?" The older woman had never shown a single sign that she'd had any concerns about Kelli's love life. Or, more precisely, lack of it.

"Because we never saw any sexual sparks," Zelda answered first. Having heard stories of Zelda's many romantic adventures during her days as a prima ballerina for the famed Russian ballet, Kelli figured Zelda knew a lot about the topic.

"Passion is important to a relationship," Adèle agreed. "Bernard still tells me that he married me for the sex." Her smile hinted at a lot of truth behind her words.

Although she'd always found the couple incredibly sweet together, that only had Kelli feeling more depressed. How pitiful was it when a woman in her seventies was having a better sex life than you were?

Kelli thought again back to what her brother had said about Cole having hooked up with Marcia last year because he'd been in the desert too long. Well, she'd been living in a sexual Sahara for the past year. No. Longer. Doing some quick math, Kelli realized that she hadn't had an orgasm that didn't involve C cells for eighteen months.

"Maybe you do need to get away and recharge your batteries," Adèle said thoughtfully.

Given where Kelli's thoughts had just been, she laughed in spite of her mood. Her sour mood had actually worsened since Cole's attempt to make up. The owner of Take the Cake was incapable of making anything that wasn't excellent, but knowing that tonight the tropical cupcake would taste like dust, she'd handed it off to one of the high school kids.

"You know, no one in the family's using the cabin," Cole's grandmother mused. "The freezer and pantry are well stocked, and there's a generator and woodstove in case the power goes off. And mountain snow's in the forecast, so you might even have that white Christmas you've always talked about wanting."

"That sounds very appealing," she admitted.

As if sensing an opening, Adèle pressed a little more. "By the time the program's over tonight, it'd probably be too late to drive all the way up into the mountains."

"It'd definitely be dangerous, on those twisting roads in the dark, with all the black ice," Zelda agreed.

Not nearly as dangerous as spending the holiday here in Shelter Bay. Although she'd survived heartache and, to her mind, had come out a stronger, more independent woman, she had come to accept the fact that there was no way she and Cole could return to the easy, comfortable relationship they'd once shared.

Because the truth, as hard as it was to admit, was that she simply couldn't be around Cole and not want him. Unfortunately, he'd just demonstrated that her romantic feelings were, as they'd always been, one-sided.

"You could leave late morning or early afternoon and still be up there before supper," Adèle said, breaking into her thoughts. "I remember you enjoying the cabin."

What she'd mostly enjoyed was being there with Cole.

She pressed her fingers against her temple, where a headache was threatening. "I'd love that," she said. "Thank you so much." She hugged the woman she'd always loved as much as her own grandmother.

"Believe me," Cole's grandmother said as she hugged Kelli back. "It's my pleasure."

As she took her paint jars backstage to put them back into her prop supply kit, Kelli missed seeing Adèle and Zelda bumping fists.

6

After searching behind the stage and in the cafeteria's kitchen, Adèle found her husband on the floor in the auditorium setting up an extra row of metal folding chairs. Ticket sales had picked up after the boat parade, resulting in a sellout.

"Bernard, you have to run to the Sea Mist. Right now."

"Now?"

She nodded her gray head. "Now. We need wine."

He arched a wooly brow. "Don't tell me those kids have driven you to drink?"

"Ha-ha. *I'm* not going to drink it, but we need to get it before the restaurant shuts down for the night."

"Why not the market?"

"Because the Sea Mist serves a higher quality." It might not be up to the standards of what her son and daughter-in-law had carried at Bon Temps when they'd run the family restaurant, but it was definitely above what the small local market offered. "I'll call ahead and tell them you're coming. And get some champagne. The best they carry."

"Okay." Fifty-plus years of marriage had taught Bernard that going along with her was often the best way to get along. "Am I allowed to ask why?"

"I just offered Kelli the cabin for the holidays."

He tilted his head while rubbing the back of his neck. "You do know that Lucien and I already suggested Cole go there? And that he took us up on the idea after the boat parade?"

"Of course I do." She put her hands on the hips of her green and red plaid wool skirt. "Surely you don't think I'd send the girl out into the woods all alone? With a major snowstorm in the forecast?"

"Aha." He flashed a quick grin, catching on to her plan. "That's downright sneaky."

"I'm merely helping out two people who are very dear to me get through the holiday blues."

There was also the fact that she wasn't getting any younger and thought it high time one of her grandsons provided her with some great-grandbabies to spoil.

"Now, go." She made a shooing motion with her hand. "I need to call the Sea Mist and then I need to get hold of Doris and Dottie down at the Dancing Deer Two."

"Why them?"

"So they can gather together some decent clothes for the girl."

Bernard's gaze moved to the stage, where Kelli was on her knees, using black electrical tape to mark X's on the polished wooden floor. "I think she looks great."

"Well, of course she's always lovely. But she's wearing another of those silly Christmas sweaters."

Two days ago, a holiday toy train filled with presents had decorated a red sweater. Yesterday's was plaid, with a black Scottie dog wearing a red velvet ribbon around its neck. Today's was even worse.

"It's Christmas. And the kids seem to like the sweaters," Bernard said.

"Of course they do," she huffed with frustration. "They're five years old."

Honestly, men could be so clueless. Time was wasting; she couldn't stand here and explain every little thing to him.

"Since I don't remember her having such deplorable taste when she was younger, she no doubt bought them to brighten the holidays for her students. Which is a very sweet thing to do . . .

"But think back to when we'd started courting. Would you have ever even thought about tumbling me if I'd been wearing a red sweater with a Christmas tree that lit up?"

This time his grin was slow and, even after all these decades together, had the power to warm her the same way it had when she was an eighteen-year-old bride. "Like the song says, you can't hide beautiful," he said, the Louisiana delta drawl that he'd never entirely lost from his voice thickening like warm honey.

"I'd have wanted to tumble you even if you were wearing a burlap sack from Comeaux's Feed and Seed," he said. "But if you *had* been wearing a light-up sweater, I would've paid it no heed, because you sure as heck wouldn't have been wearing it long."

She felt the color rising in her face. "You shouldn't talk to me that way in public."

"Okay," he said, a bit too agreeably. He lowered his voice and leaned toward her, his lips against her ear. "I'll wait until we get home to continue this conversation. In private." He nipped at her lobe. "In bed."

"Oh, go on with you," she said, even as her toes curled in that old familiar way. "You have shopping to do, and I have calls to make. On your way home from the Sea

Mist, stop by the dress shop. Doris and Dottie will have the gift-wrapped boxes waiting. Then, because I don't want things to be too obvious, drop them by the Carpenters' house. It'll seem more natural for them to be gifts from Kelli's mother.

"The freezer at the cabin's already well stocked with meals. While you're out, pick up some things for a traditional Christmas dinner from the market. Then, right after Kelli's class finishes their part of the program, you and Lucien can run the things up there and make sure everything will be ready and in place when the two of them arrive tomorrow."

"If the president had put you in charge of planning military actions back when I was fighting in Korea, Del darlin', that war would've been over and I would've been back home in two days." He brushed her cheek with his lips, snapped a brisk salute, and headed up the aisle.

As Adèle allowed herself the luxury of watching him make his way toward the door at the back of the school cafeteria, she thought, not for the first time, how lucky she'd been to have met this man while home on summer vacation from convent school in New Orleans.

The moment he'd walked into the ice cream parlor— where she'd just bought a strawberry cone—romantically backlit by a late-June sun streaming in the window, the idea of becoming a nun had paled in comparison with marrying the handsome young fisherman and having his babies.

Decades later, Bernard was not only the love of her life, but her very best friend in the entire world.

Her grandson and Kelli were already friends. Or they had been until that boneheaded move he'd pulled last Christmas. Fortunately, he'd escaped a marriage that anyone with the sense God gave a duck could have seen would be declared dead on arrival at the altar.

Feelings had been hurt on both sides, but all the two young people needed was a little time away from the outside world for him to realize what everyone else in the family knew. That Kelli was not just a pretty, sweet girl.

But a keeper.

A best friend for life. The same way she and her Bernard were. And if Cole and Kelli needed a little push to make that happen, loving them both as she did, that's precisely what Adèle would do.

Now that she'd put her matchmaking plan into motion, she took her phone out of her skirt pocket and moved on to step number three.

7

How could a woman wearing a flashing Christmas tree sweater look so hot?

That's the question Cole was asking himself as he watched Kelli bustle around getting the children all lined up to go onstage. As the youngest of the classes, they'd go on first, but from the way they were bouncing off the walls, it looked as if they'd each ingested a pound of sugar.

He figured a drill instructor with a busload of green recruits would have had an easier job, though she seemed to be not only taking it all in stride, but actually enjoying herself.

Until, as if she felt him looking at her, she glanced over at him.

He flashed her a friendly two-thumbs-up. Only to have her turn away and begin straightening a tiny angel's halo.

So much for cupcake diplomacy.

Apparently, although she'd claimed otherwise, she was still holding a grudge from last Christmas. Which he couldn't exactly make amends for since he still wasn't sure what he'd done.

Okay, except get engaged. He'd rerun that scene over and over again in his head and still wasn't certain what had happened. He'd thought for sure Kelli would've been happy for him. The same way he would have been happy for her if the situation had been reversed.

That thought had him wondering just how far things had gone between her and the principal. Had Archer taken her to bed yet? Cole hadn't gotten the vibes that they'd actually gone there. But it was obvious during that little exchange on the pier that the guy had staked his claim. So, it was only a matter of time.

And what business is it of yours? a nagging little voice in the back of his mind piped up.

It wasn't. Not really. It wasn't like he had any reason to be jealous. Or pissed.

She wasn't his. She'd never been.

Whose fault is that?

"Shut up," he muttered.

"Did you say something, darling?" his grandmother, who was passing by with a pair of sparkly angel wings, asked.

"No. I was just talking to myself."

"Doesn't Kelli look festive?" she asked.

"She definitely lights up the room." Literally.

When a mental image of slowly peeling that flashing sweater up her body, kissing each bit of soft rosy flesh while revealing whatever lace she might be wearing beneath it caused his jeans to go painfully tight, Cole wondered where the hell her boyfriend had taken off to. If Kelli *were* his woman, he sure as hell wouldn't leave her alone where just any guy—like him, maybe—could hit on her with a toasted-coconut-topped piña colada cupcake.

The older woman laughed at that. "She does, indeed.

And the children adore her. Watching her these past weeks as we've worked on the play has made me realize what a wonderful mother she'll make."

Her hair had darkened from the pale blond of childhood to a deep, rich honey. She'd tamed it into a complicated braid that reached to the middle of her back. He was envisioning unweaving it and letting the waves tumble over her bare shoulders when his grandmother's words belatedly sank in.

His stomach dropped. Then clenched.

"She's not pregnant?"

"Oh no." A cool flood of relief swept over him as she waved away that question with a quick flick of the wrist. "Although"—she lowered her voice, as if any conversation could be kept private in this town—"there have been rumors that Bradford Archer was seen in Olson's jewelry store last week."

"I imagine Olson's gets a lot of business this time of year," Cole said through set teeth. Hadn't he shopped there last time he'd been home? "Was he looking for a ring?"

"I've no idea." She shrugged her shoulders. "There's always speculation when two young people start seeing each other. You know how Shelter Bay is. Rumors are always flying around. And Connie Olson is neither confirming nor denying."

"Well." Cole blew out a breath as he considered the possibilities.

Which weren't good. If she *did* end up getting engaged to the guy, she'd be making a terrible mistake. While Archer seemed nice enough, he was as bland as the tapioca pudding his mother used to make for him and his brothers whenever they'd get the flu.

Kelli was too full of life to spend the rest of her days married to man who couldn't fully appreciate her. Or satisfy her. Even though Cole had never so much as kissed her (not that he hadn't been sorely tempted earlier this evening), watching her now, with all her warmth and vibrant animation, he knew she'd wither away from boredom before her first anniversary.

Deciding that he wouldn't be a true friend if he didn't at least try to head her off at the pass before she made the same kind of impulsive, wrongheaded decision he'd made, Cole decided to invite her to breakfast at the Grateful Bread tomorrow morning.

Not a date, he'd assure her. Just a chance to catch up and clear the air. She'd always been levelheaded. Surely she'd understand that if he did return to town for good, they'd have to move on, not just for their own sakes, but also for their families, who'd be affected by any rift.

"Give the girl time," his grandmother said. "She has a level enough head not to make a mistake that important."

"I've no idea what you're talking about." Damn, he'd lied more in the last few days than he had his entire last tour of duty in Afghanistan.

"You're thinking about warning her against accepting Bradford Archer's proposal," Adèle said.

"I didn't think anyone knew if there was going to be a proposal."

"My point exactly. Kelli may look like spun cotton candy, but the girl's always had a mind of her own. Like someone else I know," she tacked on pointedly. "If you start trying to steer her in one direction, there's a good chance she'll take off entirely in the other."

"We're friends. *Were* anyway."

"And if you want to be more, don't go rushing things."

"Who said I want it to be more?"

"Your face," his grandmother said. "When she was opening that pink box, you were looking down at her as if she were an entire tray of cupcakes and you'd been starving for too long."

She knew him too well. He'd learned as a kid, like when he'd tried to take the blame for Sax breaking the Carpenters' front window with a curveball that had gone wildly out of control, that nothing got by Adèle Douchett.

When he and his brothers were young, she'd informed them that her own grandmère had been *a traiteur*, or healer, and seer. For years they'd been convinced that she truly did have eyes in the back of her head.

She didn't need that extra set of eyes as she glanced over at the object of their discussion, who was—damn—smiling up at the principal who'd finally shown up. "Give it time to play out."

If there was one thing being a Recon Marine had taught Cole, it was patience. And given how badly he'd screwed up last Christmas, he was willing to give his grandmother credit for knowing Kelli's female mind better than he did.

"I don't remember saying anything about wanting it to be more."

"Just because I'm old doesn't mean I can't see what's right in front of my eyes," she said mildly. "Think of it as another mission," she suggested. "Don't go rushing in without taking time to plan your strategy. Take a few days at the cabin. Give her time to realize she misses you." Her smile danced in her dark eyes. "And then you can come back and make your move."

Even as he felt an unexpected and decidedly unwelcome whip-sting of jealousy as he watched Kelli merrily chatting away with Archer, Cole managed a laugh. "You know, Grandmère, if the Pentagon had you planning battle strategy, all our troops would've been home years ago."

She went up on her toes and kissed his cheek. "Now, where have I heard that before?"

8

Just when she didn't need any more stress in her life, having Cole bring her that cupcake had sent Kelli's emotions on a roller coaster. She'd already made up her mind that as tempting as the man was, she was *not* going to allow him to break her heart again. Unfortunately, her heart didn't seem to be listening to her head, because every time she just happened to look at the back of the room, where he was leaning against the wall, arms folded across his broad chest, it began tumbling like a snowball rolling down a very steep hill.

She was a grown woman, respected by both her peers and her students' parents. And, as Brad was always telling her, loved by her students. She was smart, creative, and accomplished.

So how was it, she wondered, as Cole smiled and sent her rebellious heart tumbling yet again, that he could make her feel like an insecure, love-struck teenager?

As the stage lights came on and the music cued the beginning of her class's part of the program, she dragged her attention back to the stage.

As predicted, her young actors' performances weren't perfect.

Unsurprisingly, when it was Allison's turn to take the stage, she added a pirouette to her entrance that hadn't been in Zelda's choreography.

"C is for Christmas, the Christians' big morn," she sang out in a voice as clear as the bell in the tower of St. Andrew's church. The stage lights hitting all those rhinestones and sparkles made her appear to twinkle. "When they celebrate the December night baby Jesus was born." Adding a bit more choreography that hadn't been in the original plans, she mimed rocking an infant, her expression as beatific as a Madonna.

Oh yes, Kelli thought with a blend of humor and emotion. Whatever the girl decided to do with her life, she was going to prove unstoppable. That was one of the things she loved most about her job. The chance to see the natural, ingrained sparks in children before other life expectations would come along to dampen them.

Johnny Duggan struggled for a moment over the pronunciation of Hanukkah's dreidel for the letter *D,* and Denisha Lincoln's Kwanzaa costume headdress had teetered a bit dangerously as she'd spun like a colorful top onto the stage to announce the letter *K*, but neither slips were all that noticeable—and they didn't come anywhere near last year's reindeer collision.

They got through the rest of the alphabet with no serious hitches. When Jami Martin, looking darling in a blue snowsuit covered with white snowflakes, declared *Z* for "zero, a really cold day, the end of the alphabet and the end of our play," Kelli let out a long, heartfelt sigh of relief as the children bowed and curtsied the way Zelda had taught them to a standing ovation from the audience.

Unable to resist, as she wildly clapped her hands, Kelli glanced over her shoulder toward the back of the cafeteria, wanting to share this moment with the one person who still, despite all her resolve, mattered most. And discovered that sometime during the performance, Cole had left the building.

9

An icy rain was falling from a slate gray sky the next morning as Cole drove out of town, heading up into the mountains to the cabin. But on the way, he had a stop to make. He'd no sooner pulled his truck into the parking lot of Gardner Ford than Matt Carpenter came out the double glass door from the showroom floor.

"Hey, man," he said. "That was quick." He skimmed an appreciative look over the fire-engine red truck. "As much as I'd love to put you in some new wheels, that is one sweet ride."

"I like it," Cole said mildly. Which was a major understatement. He'd bought the truck last year, only to end up getting deployed shortly after driving it off the Oceanside Ford dealer's lot.

"I can see why." Matt ran an appreciative hand over the hood, which had been waxed and detailed to a mirror sheen. "And I guess this is where I've gotta tell you, man, you'd end up upside down in a trade because I can't give you what it's worth."

"I didn't come here to trade it in."

"You're going to go with them both? Wow, you must've gotten some beaucoup combat pay."

"I'm not trading it in, because I'm not in the market for new wheels. Even ones as cool as a Mustang GT." Which he'd admittedly lusted after back when Sax was tooling around Shelter Bay in his hot '97 white Cobra with the orange SS hood stripes.

"Then why *are* you here?"

"I need to talk with you about something." He glanced around at the lot. Despite the holidays, or—since many of the cars were sporting bright red plastic bows on the roof—*because* of the season, the dealership seemed to be doing a brisk business. "But I guess it can wait, because I don't want to cost you a potential sale."

"Hey, man." Matt shrugged. "Friendship trumps money any day. What would you say to taking a test drive?"

"The GT?"

A broad grin split Matt's face. "Now, that's what I'm talkin' about. Did I mention it's been tested at two hundred miles per hour on the test course? Let me just go get the keys."

They took the Mustang down the narrow high cliff coast highway, wide tires hugging the rain-slick asphalt. Befitting the coiled cobra emblem on the fenders, it cornered as slickly as a killer snake around a switchback, which made Cole feel just like Steve McQueen racing through San Francisco. Although he hadn't been born when *Bullitt* had appeared in theaters, he'd watched it more than once on DVD and had always considered it the gold standard of car chase scenes.

"This is damn tempting," he admitted with a long, wistful sigh. What it was, was pure adrenaline candy. And way more Sax's style than his. Which was almost enough to have him seriously trading in the pickup that had spent much of its life garaged while he'd been out fighting the war on terrorism.

Just thinking of the way heads would spin when he roared down Harbor Drive, all six hundred and fifty stallions straining for release—imagining all those busy tongues wagging about how steady-as-a-rock Cole Douchett must've gone crazy over there in the war—made him laugh.

"Something funny?" Matt asked.

"Just thinking what it'd feel like to drive this back to Camp Pendleton." Cole rolled down the windows, letting in the crisp scent of fir and sea. When he hit the gas, going full throttle, the menacing engine growl escalated into a lionlike roar even as the rear wheels fishtailed on the wet pavement.

"It's like the ultimate car." Sensing some weakening, Matt deftly shifted into sales mode. "Both a mega chick magnet *and* every car guy's wet dream," he said as Cole corrected the near spin.

Damn.

That was not the image Cole wanted in his head for this conversation. A frown replaced the grin that had felt frozen in place on his face since he'd pulled out of the dealership parking lot.

"It's about Kelli," he began cautiously, feeling as if he were crossing this conversational minefield while holding a grenade with its pin pulled.

"Kelli?" Matt glanced over at him. "What about her?"

"How serious is she about that guy Archer?"

"The principal?" Matt had to shout to be heard over the engine, which could've drowned out an entire carrier deck of fighter jets taking off. "Hell, I don't know. It's not like she and I talk about stuff like that."

"Well, you've got eyes, don't you?"

"Sure, but—" Those eyes in question widened as comprehension dawned. "Whoa. Man. Are you saying you're thinking of hitting on my sister?"

"No." Yes. Kind of. Cole closed the windows again, which lowered the engine noise to a level less likely to induce ear hemorrhaging. "I'm on my way to the cabin for a few days."

"Lucky guy. While you're spending Christmas Eve cross-country skiing and vegging, I'm going to be having dinner at my in-laws' and going home to put together a dollhouse and a pair of toddler balance bikes."

"And you love it," Cole said, feeling a little stir of envy.

Matt had what Cole had been picturing last Christmas when he'd proposed to Marcia. Okay, maybe three rug rats might be one more than had been framed in his imaginary Douchett family Christmas card, but if he had a wife like Matt's, he damn well wouldn't complain about dollhouses and toddler bikes.

"Abso-freaking-lutely," the other man said. "Plus, there's something to be said for sex on a regular basis." That idea had him frowning. "Shit."

"What?"

Matt scowled and raked a hand through his windblown hair. "Are you planning to have sex with my sister?"

"Now, see." Cole blew out a breath. "That's the problem. I don't have any sisters, but if I did, I probably wouldn't want to think about some guy doing them."

"Thank you for putting that image in my head," Matt said dryly, closing his eyes, as if that would help him unsee it. "I think, as soon as we get back to the dealership, I'm going drop by the parts department and find a sharp tool to jab into my brain to see if I can dislodge the picture of you and my baby sister. Naked. Together."

"I'm not talking sex." Another lie. Not that he was kidding anyone. They both knew damn well that he was. "I'm talking about maybe two people going to the New Year's Eve dance together."

"And getting up close and personal." Matt pressed his fingers against his eyes. "Christ Almighty, Cole, you're killing me here."

Cole allowed himself a moment to imagine Kelli's arms around his neck, her lush breasts pressed against his chest, her thighs moving against his. . . .

Oh yeah. Who was he trying to kid? They were definitely talking about sex.

"I just need to know two things."

"I'm afraid to ask." Matt blew out a long breath and shook his shoulders, like a boxer shaking off a punch. "And those would be?"

"How serious do you think she is about the teacher guy?"

"Principal," Matt repeated.

"Whatever." Cole shrugged.

"Like I said, I don't know. But Meredith says he's dull as dirt, so, if I have to venture a guess, I'd say he's just a temporary deal until some guy more to her liking comes along."

"Okay. The second question is whether you'd have a problem with that guy being me."

Matt rubbed his chin as he thought that over. "Depends. Are you going to hurt her like you did last year?"

"Hey, in case you've forgotten, she was the one pissed at me." He certainly hadn't thrown that stupid ring box against his own chest.

"Yeah. That's what I thought at the time, though I damn well couldn't figure out why. Then Meredith told me you broke her heart."

Hell. "Thanks for sharing."

"You're the one who brought my sister up in the first place," Matt reminded Cole. "Seems when you pulled that ring out of the box, she thought it was for her."

"Get out. You're jerking my chain."

"Nope. She told Meredith. Over a bottle of wine and a quart of Ben & Jerry's while I wisely took the kids to a Disney flick to avoid exposing them to female tears and estrogen poisoning."

Could things get any worse? No wonder she'd been so frosty at the parade and then had gone out of her way to ignore him at the program. That was why he'd bailed right after her students' performances. No point hanging around and watching her cozy up to a guy who wouldn't even know what to do with a woman that vibrant and filled with life.

"I swear I never did anything to give her that idea. I always treated her like a little sister. It would've been weird to think of her like, well, *that.*"

Which wasn't precisely true. Because there'd been that out-of-the-blue moment, which had freaked him out as much as it seemed to be doing to her brother.

"There's also the fact that when she turned sixteen and you noticed, I told you that if you so much as looked at her in *that way*, I'd break every bone in your body," Matt reminded him.

"There is that," Cole agreed, remembering the fraternal lecture all too well. Not that he'd needed the warning. The eight-year age difference had been major back then. Now that she was a very desirable twenty-five, not so much.

"She hasn't said anything to me, but you know how women talk to each other about everything. Meredith says the principal's probably on the way out," Matt divulged. "Though she may wait until after New Year's because hey, who wants to break up at Christmas?"

"You still haven't answered my question," Cole said. "About how you'd feel about her and me getting together."

"That's because I don't know. Let me think about it." He paused as Cole continued along the coast road. The rain was blowing in from the steely white-capped winter ocean. "Okay. I've thought about it."

"And?"

"Since I don't want her to end up an old maid—"

"I may not be married, but even I know you'd better not share that description with your wife," Cole said.

"Yeah. PC can be a bitch, but I hear enough of that at home that I don't need a lecture from you about it. My point is, I want Kelli to be happy. Which, for her, means marriage and kids. So, since that means her getting involved with some guy, I guess I'm okay with the idea of that guy being my best friend. With one caveat."

"I'd expect nothing less." Negotiating was, after all, woven into Matt Carpenter's DNA. "What would that caveat be?"

"You may be my best friend, and I love you like a third brother. But if you make my baby sister cry again, man, I'm going to have no choice but to rip out your lung and stomp all over it."

Mission accomplished, Cole spun the leather-covered steering wheel, making a wheel-squealing illegal U-turn to head back to the dealership. "Makes sense to me," he agreed.

10

Kelli's mother bustled around the homey kitchen, brewing tea and cutting a coffee cake that smelled so good Kelli could picture the calories attaching to her hips before she'd even taken a bite.

"I'm so glad you were able to stop by before you left town, darling," Laura Carpenter said as she placed a red and green plaid linen napkin next to the Spode Christmas tree plate.

Kelli knew that people thought she wore all those flashy holiday sweaters for her students, but the truth was, when you grew up in this woman's home, you viewed the calendar as twelve months of holiday-themed opportunities. With Christmas like a living Advent calendar, each day brought a new surprise for the Carpenters all the way into the next year's Epiphany.

"I'd never leave without saying good-bye," she assured her mother. "And it's not as if I'm heading off to Timbuktu."

"I know." Her mother offered a bright but slightly wobbly smile. "It's just that however grown-up you'll become, in my heart you'll always be my baby, and this will be the first Christmas since you were born that you haven't been at the table for dinner."

"I'm sorry. I just need a break. To recharge my batteries," she quoted Adèle.

"You've been working very hard," her mother allowed. "But then again, you do every year." She got up from the table when the kettle whistled and poured the water over loose leaves in a pot shaped and painted like a gingerbread house. "Does Cole Douchett have anything to do with this sudden urge to leave town?"

Kelli was glad her mother's back was turned as she steeped the tea, because she feared her expression would give her away.

"Not really."

"But he's one of the reasons?" Laura brought the pot to the table on a reindeer trivet and poured the fragrant tea into a cup that matched the tree plate.

Kelli knew better than to lie to her mother. "I've loved him forever, Mama," she said, scooping some sugar from a bowl and stirring it into the tea. "I thought that after last Christmas I'd gotten over him. I mean, I certainly tried hard enough this past year—"

"Including dating a man who, while very nice, was so wrong for you."

"True. But that's over."

"So Adèle told me. She also said you'd fixed him up with a new girlfriend."

Kelli shrugged. "Like you said, Brad's a nice guy."

She could've done worse. But he wasn't the man she wanted. Sometimes she wondered if any man could ever live up to the masculine perfection of Cole Douchett shimmering in her mind. What if she was destined to spend her life alone, playing doting auntie to her brothers' children?

Wasn't that a depressing idea?

She added another, larger scoop of sugar to her tea.

"Anyway, it was obvious that Patty, from the school, is in love with him. And from the way he seemed to be floating on cloud nine last night when he told me about the two of them going out for a late supper at the Sea Mist after the program, I'd say it's reciprocal."

"That's lovely. But it doesn't address your relationship with Cole."

"I know. And it's honestly another reason I want to get away for just a few days. I need to decide what to do about him."

"Do you want him?"

"Like I want to breathe. But it's complicated." She might be in love. But she did, after all, still have her pride. Not to mention it had taken a very long time to put all those shattered pieces of her heart back together again.

After polishing off the piece of coffee cake and allowing herself to be talked into taking the rest of the cake to the cabin, she exchanged gifts with her mother, promising to open one on Christmas Eve. A cherished family tradition, going back to when she and her brothers were young, was that each of them could open a single gift before going to bed after midnight Mass.

"It'll be as if we're all together in spirit," her mother said as she handed her that special Christmas Eve gift in a box wrapped in the familiar Dancing Deer Two silver Christmas foil.

The snow on the road up into the mountains to Rainbow Lake was fresh, wet, and slick, and it appeared Kelli was ahead of whatever plows the county might be sending out.

"Are we having fun yet?" she muttered as she cautiously maneuvered around a particularly nasty curve, trying to stay in tire ruts that were getting filled by the moment as the snow fell faster and thicker. Although she'd turned on her headlights, the beam merely bounced against the wall of snow.

Deep purplish black shadows, cast by the towering, shaggy fir trees lining the road, had her feeling as if she were driving through a narrow white tunnel. She could have been the only person in this wooded world, which wasn't the least bit encouraging.

The only sound was the crunch of the snow beneath the tires and the voices on the radio, which kept announcing road closures all over the western part of the state.

"Well, you've always wanted a white Christmas." Heavy white flakes had started to pile up on her windshield, and her wipers were losing a valiant struggle to keep up as outside temperatures plummeted, turning the snow to ice. "Maybe this will teach you to be careful what you wish for."

By the time the GPS showed her half a mile from the cabin, her jaw was aching from having clenched her teeth for the past ten miles and her fingers had been gripping the steering wheel so tightly she feared it would take a crowbar to release them.

"Almost there," she assured herself as the GPS counted down to three-tenths of a mile.

One of the best things about the cabin was the bubbling hot spring on the property, which Bernard and Lucien had tapped into when they built the cabin. Providing them with a seemingly endless supply of heat and hot water.

Since Adèle had assured her the place was stocked

with everything she could need, the very first thing Kelli planned to do when she reached the cabin was pour a huge glass of red wine. Then she was going to drink it while soaking away the stress in that deep, lion-footed tub she remembered so fondly.

She was enjoying that warm mental image when her left front wheel slid off the road's shoulder.

A moment later there was an ominous crunching sound as the car came to an abrupt, bone-jolting stop.

11

"Damn, damn, damn!"

Kelli slammed her gloved hands onto the steering wheel. Wasn't this the last thing she needed? Taking a deep breath, which was meant to calm but didn't help at all, she put the car in reverse and tried backing up. But the tires only spun, and after two more tries, it was readily apparent that all she was going to do was get herself even more stuck.

Heaving a sigh, she pocketed the key, took her overnight bag from the backseat, and left the car. She wasn't going to worry about the gifts in the trunk right now. If anyone did manage to make it all the way out here, they were free to try to steal them.

As she trudged through the snow, bent against the wind, Kelli couldn't help wishing she were lying on a warm, sun-drenched beach sipping a mai tai while a deeply tanned cabana boy catered to her every need.

With the forest draped in snow, nothing looked familiar, making her uncertain exactly how much farther she had to go and remembering everything she'd learned about always staying with the car in situations like this.

Then, just was she began to fear she was lost, she turned a corner and there, surrounded by towering fir trees, was the Douchett cabin.

That was the good news.

The bad news was the fire-engine red pickup parked in front.

"Well, there's no turning back now," she muttered. Rather than use the key Adèle had given her, she knocked on the heavy wooden door.

A moment later it was opened by Cole, who was dressed in sweatpants, a soft, well-washed black sweatshirt with a Tun Tavern emblem, and thick black socks. Kelli knew, because Cole had told her when he'd signed up for ROTC, that the Philadelphia tavern had been where the Marines had held their first recruitment meeting in 1775, even before the Declaration of Independence.

"What are you doing here?"

"Merry Christmas to you, too," she shot back, her nerves and temper frayed.

"Hell, I'm sorry." He ran a hand over that too-short hair she was actually starting to get used to. It definitely defined those razor-edged cheekbones. Which was so not what she should be concentrating on right now! "It's just that I wasn't expecting you." He glanced past her. "Where's your car?"

"It's down the road about a quarter of a mile. I slid off the shoulder and got stuck. Hopefully nothing's broken."

"You walked all that way? In this storm? Didn't your dad teach you to stay with the car?"

"Yes. But it wasn't that far, and weighing the options, I decided to risk being eaten by bears or getting lost rather than spending the night all alone out there."

He shook his head, but didn't argue her point. Instead

he took the overnight case out of her hand and moved out of her way. "Come in and warm up."

After stomping as much snow off her boots as she could, she walked into the cabin, nearly weeping with relief at the warmth of the fire, which cast a glow over the walls of logs she knew had been milled by the Douchett men from trees grown on the property.

He skimmed a look over her. Her jeans, which she'd worn instead of waterproof ski pants because she hadn't planned to be wading through snow, were soaked nearly to her knees. "You'll want to get out of those wet clothes. Maybe take a hot bath."

"I've been imaging that tub for the last hour," she admitted, unzipping her parka.

He helped her out of it, hanging it on a hook by the door. "Lucky for you, we've unlimited hot water."

She smiled at that idea. "I was thinking about that, too."

He smiled back, and for a suspended moment, it was almost like old times. Just two friends enjoying the same thought. "Did you leave anything else in the car?"

"A larger suitcase and gifts from my family in the trunk."

"Give me the keys." After she'd handed them over, he walked into the kitchen area and retrieved a heavy black garbage bag, which she assumed he intended to use as waterproofing against the snow, from beneath the sink. "I'll go get them.

"Would you like some coffee, brandy, or wine before I go? My grandmother wasn't kidding when she said the place was well stocked. We've got enough booze to open our own bar."

Her nerves were already so jangled from the drive, Kelli knew if she drank any more coffee, she'd never get to sleep. And brandy might be more than she could handle right now. "As it happens, wine was involved in that fantasy," she said.

"Red or white?"

"Red."

"You've got it."

He pulled a bottle from the cupboard and deftly opened it with an attachment on a black folding knife.

"That's very MacGyverish of you," she said.

"We Marines pride ourselves on making the most with the least. And, hey, this Leatherman is Oregon made." He smiled at her as he poured the ruby wine into a glass. "Here you go."

His fingers brushed hers as he handed her the fat, stemless glass. At first she'd thought he might have done it on purpose, but his friendly, harmless expression gave nothing away as he sat down on a bench by the door and began pulling on his boots.

"So, I'll retrieve your stuff while you run your bath," he said. "Unless you'd rather I hang around and warm you up myself."

Surely he was kidding. Wasn't he?

"The wine and bath will be fine," she said mildly. "But thank you for the offer. It was very generous of you."

"Always happy to help out," he said cheerfully. But there was a devilish gleam in his brown eyes she'd never seen from him before. "Let me know if you change your mind."

With that, he was out the door, leaving her wondering if she might have actually been safer staying in the car.

12

"Think of it as another mission." Cole mimicked his grandmother's voice as he carried the bag of presents and the bright polka-dot suitcase that matched the smaller one she'd shown up with back to the cabin. Although the car was definitely stuck, from what he could tell, she hadn't broken the wheel, so he should be able to pull it out in the morning.

"Don't go rushing in without taking time to plan your strategy," he continued. "Give her time to realize she misses you. . . .

"Thanks a bunch, Grandmère."

It was an obvious setup. Thinking about it, both families had to be in on it. At least some of them. Matt had seemed oblivious—though, since they were tight, it was possible the others had been afraid he'd spill the beans.

Cole was not alone in his thinking.

"We were set up," Kelli announced the moment he entered the cabin. She was standing in front of the fire, the wineglass cradled in her hands.

"That'd be my guess." She hadn't changed, but he

could hear the water running in the oversized tub. "Which room do you want?"

She shrugged. "It's your family's cabin. I don't care."

"I'll move my stuff out of the master and you can have it."

"There's no need."

"It looks out onto the waterfall. Which, by the way, is starting to freeze."

"Really?" She followed him into the bedroom, which had always been his parents', then stopped in front of the French doors to stare in wonder at the view. He had to admit it was pretty freaking incredible.

"Oh, wow. How cool is that?" Her blue eyes widened with pleasure, reminding him of a child who'd just been informed it was a snow day.

"It's got to get pretty cold to freeze that much water," he said.

He went into the adjoining bathroom and got a large beach towel from the linen closet, which he put on the floor so the snow from the suitcase and trash bag wouldn't dampen the rag rug his grandmother had hand hooked decades ago.

"It's so magical out here," she said on a long, happy sigh. "Enough that I'm not going to get mad at our families for tricking us."

"What about Archer? How are you going to explain spending Christmas out here alone with me?"

"I don't have to explain anything to anyone. And, although it really isn't any of your business, Brad and I are no longer seeing each other."

"Are we sorry about that?"

She folded her arms and shot him a look over her shoulder. "No more sorry than we are about Marcia Wayburn being out of the picture. And, for the record, I wasn't jealous about you proposing to her. Just disappointed you displayed such poor judgment."

"Yeah. Sure. The same way I was going to warn you about Archer."

She'd gone back to looking out at the swirling flakes that were coming down faster and harder by the minute. But that drew her attention again.

"Why on earth would you have wanted to warn me about Brad? He's totally harmless."

"That was my point. It never would've worked because that guy never could have satisfied you."

"Oh, really?" The frost in her voice was chillier than the temperature outside the paned glass doors. "And what would you know about what satisfies me?"

He nodded at that. "Your point."

One he was planning to rectify. But deciding that his grandmother was right about not pushing, Cole decided to take things slowly. Let the situation play out.

He still wasn't exactly sure what he was feeling toward her. The one thing he did know was that their families could manipulate things until doomsday, but he was damn well going to make his own choices.

And for now, for this stolen time away from war and family and the over-the-top holiday celebrations that his hometown loved to indulge in, he chose Kelli Carpenter.

"The tub's probably filled," he said. "Why don't you take your bath while I start dinner?"

"You don't have to cook for me."

"I'm not. Along with all the liquor, the freezer's stocked with meals."

"I didn't realize your family had elves," she said dryly.

"Neither did I. But someone's definitely been busy. We could probably survive until spring before we'd have to stoop to squirrel stew.

"There's also a small roasting turkey and all the fix-ings in the fridge. But I guess we're expected to cook it ourselves. I suppose that's to encourage us to put aside our differences and work together."

She shook her head, but her lips quirked. "It might be humiliating to be set up by our parents at our age, if they weren't so obvious. And I'll have to give them an A for effort. But I'm not some puppet they can make dance to their matchmaking scheme."

"That makes two of us."

"So. We'll eat their food and drink their wine and catch up on each other's lives. Enjoy ourselves like the old friends we used to be."

"And if there are strings to be pulled, we'll be the ones pulling them."

She rewarded him with a dazzling smile that sent something beneath his heart tumbling. "Exactly. Now, I'd better get to that tub before we flood the place."

13

Cole sipped thoughtfully on a dark ale as he heated up a pot of gumbo. Having grown up in a culture where the men did much of the cooking, he had no problem cooking the rice himself. He knew his mother would've thrown herself off the Shelter Bay Bridge before ever stooping to instant.

He'd put on a CD, and in the background Billie Holiday was singing the blues.

Kelli had changed in the past year. She'd toughened up. And while his grandmother was right about her having always had a mind of her own, she'd acquired more of what his grandfather Bernard would've called good old-fashioned spunk.

And it looked damn good on her.

And speaking of good . . .

"Did you mean that?" she asked as she walked into the kitchen, engulfed in a plush, pastel pink robe that had him thinking of sugarplums again. Beneath the robe he could see a bit of blue pajamas printed with polar bears. Apparently, her winter-theme wardrobe extended beyond the sweaters.

The outfit shouldn't have been sexy. And it might not have been, had it not been for the way she'd piled her hair into a messy topknot that just begged to have the pins pulled out of it so it'd tumble down. Even more distracting were the beads of water gleaming on the rosy skin revealed by the robe's neckline. She was wearing striped pink, blue, and white socks.

"Mean what? About having to resort to squirrel stew? Because if you're worried about starving, I can assure you that Marines are taught all sorts of cool survival techniques." He turned the heat on the water, getting ready for the rice. "I even know how to build a snow cave." He shot her a look. "And how to share body warmth to stay alive."

More color flooded into her cheeks. "I was referring to what you said about staying warm together."

Then he noticed that the glass she was holding was nearly empty. He took the wine bottle and topped it off. "I'm a guy. We're always serious about sex." He put the bottle back on the counter. "For now, why don't we just try this?"

He framed her face in his hands and, taking advantage of the fact that her hands were occupied holding that wineglass, he lowered his head, pausing just a breath away from actual contact.

Her eyes darkened, and he heard the little intake of breath. He waited, giving her time to say something. Or move away.

But she didn't. She just stood there, fingers tightening around the glass, deep blue eyes offering him a silent invitation no man with blood still stirring in his veins would have been able to turn down.

As he touched his mouth to hers and she slid easily,

naturally into the kiss, Cole wondered why the hell he'd waited all these years. She tasted warm and feminine. Of wine and temptation. And in that moment, his entire world shifted and he knew that he would never be the same.

All the time, she'd been right there. Hiding in plain sight.

Because he wanted to make sure she understood that this thing between them wasn't some convenient sex in a snowed-in-cabin scenario, although it took every ounce of his self-control, Cole kept his hands on her face.

"That," he murmured, as he leaned back, enjoying the delicious mingling of desire and confusion in her eyes, "was worth waiting for."

"I don't understand." She pressed her fingertips to her lips as he poured the rice into the water, which had begun to boil during the kiss. The water wasn't the only thing that had heated up. "What happened to being friends?"

"Wasn't that friendly enough for you?" he asked easily as she gulped down her wine. Drawn to the silk of her skin, he returned to skim the back of his hand down her cheek. "We can try it again, if you want."

"No." She backed up. "I need to think."

"Fine. You can sit here and think while I finish heating up dinner. Then we can watch a movie, if you'd like." He knew her weakness for Christmas movies. And suddenly, although it was the last thing he'd been expecting when he'd taken his grandfather and father up on their suggestion to come out here to the cabin, he was in the mood to celebrate the holiday with Kelli. "I found a DVD of *It's a Wonderful Life*."

"Oh." She sighed happily. "I love that movie."

"I know." She'd always been a romantic. Which had him determined to do this right. "Then, afterward, I'll walk you to your door, like a true officer and a gentleman. And maybe you'll let me kiss you good night."

"I suppose that sounds all right."

What it sounded like was a start, Cole decided.

14

Dinner was delicious, as Kelli would have expected. There'd been a reason that Bon Temps had been one of the most popular restaurants on Oregon's mid coast. Maureen Douchett was a genius when it came to elevating humble Cajun comfort food to something close to sublime.

And speaking of sublime . . .

The movie, which she'd seen more times than she could count, was as romantic as ever. Oodles more so with Cole sitting next to her. She sighed when Jimmy Stewart promised to rope the moon for Donna Reed.

"A bit impractical," Cole, who was sitting next to her on the couch, his arm around her shoulder, said.

"It's a metaphor."

"I get that." He pressed his lips against her hair—it had, with some help from Cole, come tumbling down sometime between when George's brother, Harry, had fallen through that ice and when George and Mary started dancing, after George finally saw Mary for the amazing woman she was. "But I guess, with women, it's the thought that counts."

"Exactly." She smiled up at him. "And maybe not as impossible as giving a woman Hawaii in a cupcake."

He didn't answer. At least not in words. But the slow, savoring way he pressed his lips to hers for their second kiss spoke volumes.

"Of course, it goes downhill from here," he said, as he left her trembling and returned to eating popcorn.

"For a time," she allowed, wondering if Cole would feel cheated, like George Bailey initially had, if he returned to Shelter Bay for good. "But it all works out in the end."

"And good old Clarence gets his wings." He held out a piece of buttered popcorn.

She thought about pointing out that she was perfectly capable of feeding herself. But although it was merely corn from a package, popped in a microwave with a bit of melted butter poured over it, she found the gesture, and the rich taste, which her own air-popped unbuttered corn could never equal, unreasonably seductive.

"You like happy endings," he said while holding out another piece for her.

"Of course." She closed her teeth around the fat white kernel. "Doesn't everyone?"

He continued to feed her bites as George and Mary sang "Buffalo Gals."

"I always knew you were a romantic."

"Perhaps the world needs more romantics."

"Roger that," he agreed. He sniffed at her tumbled hair. "God, you smell fantastic."

Then, before she could respond, he kissed her again, and as his tongue swirled up to taste the drops of melted butter on her lips, Kelli decided that she'd never be able to eat popcorn again without thinking of this night.

The rest of the movie went by in a blur as they shared

popcorn and kisses and he drew her so close, nestling her under his arm, she could have sworn, by the time Zuzu announced that the bell on the tree ringing meant an angel had just gotten his wings, Kelli was on the verge of melting herself.

"Well," he said, clicking the TV off. "All's well that ends well." As she put her hand in the one he held out to her, her heart did a slow, dizzying spin of anticipation.

After all these years of waiting, the night she'd dreamed of had finally arrived. Refusing to worry about whether the closeness they were experiencing would last beyond this stolen time together and what things would be like when they returned to town, as they walked to the master bedroom, hand in hand, Kelli decided she was going to stop worrying about the future and live in the moment.

She'd reached out to open the door when he tugged her back and turned her around.

"Put your arms around my neck."

More than a little dazed by the roughness of his deep voice and the storm swirling in his dark eyes, Kelli could more easily fly to the moon on gossamer wings than refuse him.

"Better," he said with a satisfied quirk of the lips.

He put his hands on her hips and moved closer, pressing her against the heavy wooden door. As their bodies touched, center to center, he brushed his mouth against hers. Touching, then retreating, touching again and ratcheting up the desire until she was practically clinging to him for support.

Kelli was not naive. Nor innocent. She'd been kissed before. She'd made love before. But never had every atom in her body been so focused on the havoc being done to her mouth. His tongue traced a line across the seam of her lips, encouraging them to open for him.

Which, seeming to have taken on a mind of their own, they did.

He nipped at her bottom lip, pulling it into his mouth, drawing a ragged moan from deep in her throat.

"Nice." He murmured the words against her lips before slipping his tongue inside, in an impossibly slow possession that blurred her vision.

Heat was building in her core, spiraling outward, fingers of flame reaching through her blood, touching her all the way outward to the tips of her fingers and toes. And all the time his gaze stayed locked on hers, watching, measuring, discovering all her secrets. Learning her every weakness.

She couldn't speak. Couldn't think. Her mind had gone blank and she'd lost control of her senses.

And then, impossibly—although, with his body against hers, there was no hiding his arousal—he . . . *backed away*?

"Cole . . ." The words wouldn't, couldn't come.

Terrific. Now she'd gone mute as well as blind.

But not so blind she couldn't see his slow smile.

"Say good night, Kels."

Surely he wasn't going to leave her? Not like this?

She was dazed, confused, but although he'd left her in a puddle of need, he'd not claimed her pride. She tried to regain some self-control.

She would not whimper. Nor beg.

Summoning up her inner warrior goddess, she lifted her chin even as her legs felt like water. "Good night, Cole."

"Good night." His eyes softened and gentled as he skimmed a fingertip over those lips he'd so expertly ravaged. "Sleep tight." He opened the heavy door. "I'll see you in the morning."

"Morning," she repeated. Then somehow, on unsteady legs, she made her way into the room and shut the door behind her. Leaning against it, she sank bonelessly to the floor, where she bent her legs, wrapped her arms around them, and lowered her head to her knees as she listened to Cole whistling "Buffalo Gals" as he strolled the few feet to his own bedroom.

It was much, much later, after finally falling asleep following hours of frustrated tossing and turning, that Kelli woke to an odd, unrecognizable sound coming from outside the cabin. Without turning on the light, she climbed out of bed, padded to the French doors, and pulled aside an edge of the curtain.

There, bathed in the spreading glow of a full moon, stood Cole. Despite what had to be freezing temperatures, he'd stripped down to a brown thermal underwear shirt and was wielding a huge red-handled ax, lifting it over his head, then bringing it down again and again as he split log after log, sending pieces of wood scattering in the snow all around him.

The shirt fit tightly enough that it took no imagination at all to envision tan flesh stretching over sinew and muscle, rippling as he attacked the wood.

Which was, hands down, the sexiest thing Kelli had ever seen.

She could have stood there forever. But, not wanting to get caught watching him, she forced herself away from the window and back to the too-lonely bed.

15

After pulling Kelli's car out of the ditch and towing it back to the cabin, Cole was on his second pot of coffee and was frying bacon when Kelli came out of the bedroom the next morning looking deliciously warm and tousled.

"I'm sorry I overslept."

"It's a vacation," he said. "You're supposed to sleep." Which didn't explain the lavender circles appearing like bruises beneath her eyes.

She glanced out the window. "You've already rescued my car?"

He shrugged. "I was up, so I figured I might as well. Want some coffee?"

"I'd love some."

"Great. I was just making breakfast."

"I don't usually eat breakfast."

"You should. It's the most important meal of the day."

"So I've heard, but—"

"Besides, you'll need your energy."

"Oh? For what?"

"We're going snowshoeing."

"You're kidding."

"Well, we could just wade through thigh-deep snow. But I figured it'd be easier to bring the tree back if we're on snowshoes."

"We're cutting down a tree?"

"I suppose I could call Brian to deliver one from your family farm. But it is, after all, their busy season, so it only makes sense that we should forage for ourselves."

"It's snowing."

"Which makes it more romantic," he countered. "Trust me, Kels. You'll love it."

If he'd been alone, as planned, there was no way he would've gone traipsing out into the woods to cut down a Christmas tree. But the idea of decorating it together, while carols played on the CD player and flames crackled merrily in the fireplace—and God knows he had enough firewood piled up to last into next year—was proving vastly appealing.

He put the bacon in the oven to keep warm and moved on to the hash browns.

"I suppose I might as well get some exercise," she muttered as she crossed the room into the kitchen area. "If I don't want to weigh as much as a moose by New Year's."

"I think you look terrific," he said as he handed her a mug of steaming-hot coffee. He couldn't wait to get her out of those clothes and taste every bit of lush, fragrant flesh.

Patience, he reminded himself. *Keep your eye on the mission.*

Easier said than done when she smelled like a spring meadow and looked good enough to eat.

"Flatterer," she complained without heat.

"It's not flattery if it's true." Because he couldn't be

this close to her without touching her, because raging sexual need had forced its way even into his nightly insomnia and tangled in his mind, he fisted his hand in her hair, holding her as he swooped down and took her mouth in a hot, hard, hungry kiss that instead of easing the ache, resulted only in a more powerful slap of lust.

Cole's heart hammered against his rib cage, and his pulse surged. Despite his vow to take things slowly, he was on the verge of lifting her onto the counter or dragging her to the floor—either one would do—and taking her now. Before he went totally insane from the temptation she offered.

"Cole." The coffee sloshed over the mug as Kelli pushed against his shoulder.

"Just a minute more." His hand slid between them to untie the robe, giving him access to her breast.

"No. Really." She pushed harder. "You have to stop now."

"Soon," he promised as he cupped that rounded flesh and struggled to resist ripping the flannel polar bear top off. Which, on the plus side, would mean she wouldn't be able to wear it anymore.

He dragged his mouth back to hers, swallowing her protests, until he belatedly realized that the clouds of smoke surrounding them weren't from the flames scorching through his body.

But from the forgotten hash browns burning in the frying pan.

"Shit." He released her, grabbed a lid, and covered the pan to cut off the oxygen, then opened the windows, letting in a blast of frosty air as he began trying to wave the smoke out with a dish towel.

"I tried to tell you," she said, retying the robe.

"So you did." He sighed and shook his head as he

took her in. Shadows like bruises darkened the skin beneath her eyes, her dark honey hair was a wild tangle around her shoulders, and there was a coffee stain down the front of that pink robe. None of which stopped her from looking hot as hell. "I guess you're off the hook for the hash browns."

"But not the snowshoeing."

"Not on a bet. I promised you a Christmas tree hunt and that's exactly what you're getting.

"Or," he suggested, with a wag of his brows, "we could stay here and spend the day in bed."

"You want me." She was obviously pleased by that idea.

"Nah. I'm just horny as a goat and you're the only female I happen to be snowbound with."

She laughed at that, as he'd meant her to. Then held her mug out to him. "Get me some more hot coffee, and you should know that I take my eggs scrambled with my bacon. I'll be back as soon as I change into something more suitable for trudging through the snow."

"You're going to wear that pink parka, right?"

"Since it's the only one I brought, yes." Her eyes narrowed. "Why?"

"Because I like it." He decided, since they were getting along so well, to go for broke. "When I saw you wearing it at the pier the afternoon of the boat parade, I thought you looked like a sugarplum." His smile was quick and wolfish. "Good enough to eat."

As pleasure flooded into her unguarded eyes, Cole decided that when he got back to town, he was going to send his grandparents on that Greek cruise they'd always talked about. Because he figured he owed them. Big-time.

16

Although she'd been admittedly less than enthusiastic about the snowshoe outing, Kelli couldn't deny that being out in the forest, walking through the heavily snow-frosted trees, was exhilarating.

She was also grateful for the yoga and Zumba classes that kept her able to keep up with Cole, as he seemed determined to drag her all around the lake, searching for the perfect tree.

At least she'd probably burned off a gazillion calories. Or this morning's bacon.

"I love snow." The sun was streaming through the trees, making it sparkle like a white carpet of diamonds. "It's like a fairy tale."

"Says the woman whose car was stuck in a ditch."

She smiled sweetly. "Fortunately, I had you to pull it out for me."

She stopped a moment later when a particular tree caught her eye.

"Something wrong?" he asked, turning around when he realized she was no longer behind him.

"Nothing. I think I found it."

"You're kidding." He stared at the tree in question. "It looks like Charlie Brown's tree."

"That's what I like about it," she said. "It has character."

"And very few limbs. And the ones it does have are crooked."

She shook her head and folded her arms across the front of her parka. "I never would've taken you for a tree snob. If you want a perfect tree, you should've bought one from my family's farm."

"It doesn't have to be perfect," he countered. "But looking like an actual tree would be a plus."

"I like it."

He angled his head. "You really mean that."

"Of course I do. All it needs is a few decorations and it'll be perfect."

He shrugged. "If you want it, you've got it."

She grinned, feeling foolishly happy. It was a homely tree. Which was exactly what she liked about it. Anyone, even people in Hawaii, could have a perfectly shaped Christmas tree. This one was unique.

"Thank you." She lifted her smiling lips to his, getting in one lovely nip before he broke away to get the hatchet and saw from the sled he'd brought along to cart the tree back to the cabin.

She wasn't surprised that he managed to topple the tree and tie it to the sled in less than ten minutes.

"I think I have a new fantasy," she said.

"Other than George Bailey?"

"Oh, he's not a fantasy." She waved away that idea. "Fantasies are for cowboys and pirates and sailors."

He stopped in the process of securing the hatchet on top of the tree. "Sailors? You fantasize about sailors?"

Ha! She knew that would get under his skin. "How could a girl not? Those snazzy dress whites, a girl in ev-

ery port, those big, big ships." She heaped a double helping of innuendo on the word "big." "If you get my drift.

"And SEALs." She fanned herself as if just the idea of
a Navy SEAL was enough to make her swoon. "They're
like the ultimate sailors."

"You fantasize about freaking frogmen." He shook
his head in disbelief.

"You're jealous." And didn't she just love it?

"Of a SEAL frogman? No way."

"Well, it doesn't matter. Because, as I said, I've discovered a new fantasy. Thanks to you." Her lips curved in a
siren's smile that had Donna Reed only pulled out in
Bedford Falls, George Bailey never would've considered
jumping off that bridge. She pulled off a glove and
chewed thoughtfully on a fingernail as she treated him
to a slow, judicial, up-and-down study. "I never realized
a lumberjack could be so sexy hot."

She walked over to him, belatedly realizing it was really hard to glide seductively while wearing a pair of
snowshoes. "And speaking of hot." She ran that fingernail around his lips. "As soon as we get back to the cabin,
I'm going thaw out in the hot tub." His jaw tightened as
she trailed her fingers around it. "While I fantasize about
getting manhandled by some sexy mountain man."

She could tell from the way Cole's eyes went all dark
and hooded that he was right there with her. Wanting to
drive him as crazy as he'd left her last night, she licked
her lips, which she feared would be unappealing and
chapped if they didn't get back to the cabin soon.

It worked!

The hatchet fell to the snow, forgotten, as he pulled
her to him. "Do you have any idea what you're doing?"
His voice was rough and ragged, growled from deep in
his throat.

"I'm trying to seduce you." She smiled up at him. "Is it working?"

Pulling her in for a passionate embrace, he pressed her tight against him.

Oh my. She was not going to faint, Kelli assured herself. The only reason her head had suddenly gone light and all the air had whooshed out of her lungs was because they were at such a high altitude.

"If you don't do something soon, I'm going to have no choice but to murder you," she warned him. "With your own ax."

He laughed at that even as he rotated his hips. Even through all the layers of under- and outerwear, she had no trouble feeling exactly how much mountain manliness he was promising her.

"Then we'd better get going," he said. "Before I'm forced to take you right here. In a snowdrift."

"We'd get frostbite," she said as they followed their tracks back to the cabin.

"Good point. Change in plans. I'll ravish you on a bearskin rug in front of a blazing fire."

"You don't have a bearskin rug."

"Hey, you women aren't the only ones allowed to fantasize."

Although Kelli donated to the Sierra Club, she couldn't deny that the fur rug, as a fantasy, had its appeal.

"Then I guess we're back to the manly lumberjack. Who's worked all day chopping down forests with his manly ax. Which is why he has to work out the kinks in the bubbling hot tub."

Pulling the sled with one hand, he reached out with his free one, lacing their gloved fingers together. "Sweetheart, you had me at kink."

17

They didn't make it to the hot tub. At least not right away.

They'd no sooner entered the cabin when their lips crashed together, tongues tangling and desperate hands ripping at clothes.

Even as parkas, sweatshirts, and thermal underwear went flying, their hands were never still. Cole's mouth plundered, streaking over every bit of newly bared flesh as she strained against him, wrapped around him, her own hands as greedy as his.

"If you want me to stop, Kelli, tell me now," he said as he yanked off her snowy boots so he could rid her of those pink ski pants that had pooled around her ankles.

"Don't you dare," she said breathlessly, lifting her hips as he hooked his thumbs in the lace waistband of her reindeer panties and ripped them away. "I've been waiting my entire life for this moment."

Despite his brain feeling as if it were going to explode, Cole managed to remember the condoms. Which were, unfortunately, in his shaving kit on the bathroom counter.

"Where are you going?" she asked, grabbing his wrist as he started to stand up.

"Condoms," he managed, thinking that if he had planned a military mission as badly as he had this one, he never would have made it home to be naked with this woman.

"It's okay. *I'm* okay. Seriously," she promised. "And I'm on the pill."

With any other woman, he might doubt her claims. But not this one.

"Me too," he said. Which was totally true. He hadn't had sex with any woman since his last physical, and the Marine doctor had tested him.

"Well, then." She went to work, pulling the sweatshirt over his head. Just when Cole was certain he'd go insane with hunger for her, they were finally naked, stretched out in front of the fire, not on the fantasized soft bear rug, but on another of his grandmother's braided rag ones.

Her body was lush and curvy and perfectly made for a man's hands. And mouth. He lifted her breasts, and as her fingers splayed on the back of his head, he feasted, his teeth and tongue creating a trail down her torso, over her stomach, which quivered as his tongue glided over it, then lower still.

Her short nails dug into his back and she arched her back like a bow as he brought her to the edge. Again and again until finally, with one quick, slick stroke of his tongue, he felt her shatter.

But still it wasn't enough. Not for him. And not for her.

"I want you inside me," she said. "I need you."

Not as much as he needed her. The staggering truth, which hit Cole's brain like an ax blow, was that he wanted Kelli Carpenter more than he wanted to live.

He pushed her knees up, encouraging her to wrap her legs around his waist.

Although he'd been picturing this in his mind since the boat parade, even as he'd struggled to safely wall off the mental images of sex in a million ways with her, Cole wanted to watch Kelli come.

But he didn't have to tell her to look at him, because once again, they were on the same wavelength.

Her eyes were locked on to his as he filled her slowly, giving her time to adjust to his size—which her long, happy sigh assured him lived up to her fantasy mountain man—before he began to move.

Faster. Deeper. Until he was taking her, claiming her, watching her incredible eyes glaze over.

When she came, the deep climax ripping a choked sob from her throat, Cole was right behind her, his mind emptying right before he collapsed onto her.

"That was . . . wow," she murmured.

"Yeah. But . . ." He glanced around at the clothes strewn all over the room. "We didn't make it to the hot tub."

"Next time," she said on another blissful sigh as she cuddled up against him like a warm kitten.

"Which would be now," he said, pushing himself to his feet, then pulling her up as well.

"Oh. My." Her eyes widened as they took in the hard-on that, having been deprived for so many months, was ready for round two.

"Forget the lumberjack." He tried to shield her from the cold blast of frigid air that hit them as they walked out the door onto the deck and he flipped open the cover on the hot tub. "Along with the damn SEAL frogmen and sailors. If you want real stamina, sweetheart, call a Marine."

"Ooh-rah," she said as she slid into the hot water.

"Exactly." He sat down on a bench and pulled her onto his lap facing him as he lowered her onto his erection. "The Marines have landed and the situation is well in hand."

18

Kelli woke the next morning to an empty bed. The bed where Cole had spent much of the night making such slow, sweet love to her, he'd actually made her weep. The sheets on his side were cold, revealing he'd been up for a while.

When she heard the steady *thunk*, *thunk*, *thunk*, she understood why.

And this time her tears were not from joy, but for whatever demons he'd brought home with him that seemed to be keeping him from sleep.

Part of her wanted to ask. Another, stronger part decided that he'd tell her when he felt safe with her. And in order for that to happen, she was going to have to practice patience.

After all, she'd waited for Cole her entire life. She already had so much more of him than she'd had only two days ago. What would a little more time hurt?

The next three days passed in a gilt-edged blur. They'd slipped back into their old friendship, something she'd feared they'd lost forever, as they decorated her foolish little tree, played in the snow like children, made love in that oversized, lion-footed bathtub, watched the sappy movies that would always make her weep and sigh with pleasure, and when they weren't doing those things, they were making love in every way possible. And a few Kelli hadn't, even in a million years, imagined.

"I just realized," she said, as they sat in front of the fire, watching the dancing flames as Bing Crosby crooned about missing a white Christmas. "It's Christmas Eve."

"So it is." He drew her mouth to his and kissed her with an easy familiarity gained from a great deal of practice over the past few days.

"I promised my mother I'd open one of my presents tonight. So it'd feel like our family was all together."

The gifts were under the lighted tree. "Which one?" he asked as he crouched down.

"The silver one. From the dress shop."

When he handed it to her, Kelli found herself wishing that she'd thought to buy him something. But they hadn't exactly been on the best of terms when they'd parted after the holiday program.

She carefully took off the silver wrapping, then folded back the tissue paper. "Oh," she breathed as she held up the white silk nightgown. "It's obvious my mother was in on the subterfuge."

"Apparently." His took in the silk pooling over her hands. "Are you going to try it on for me?"

"Absolutely." Feeling a strange modesty at odds with the nudity she'd grown comfortable with around Cole, she took it into the bedroom, stripped off her robe—she'd quit wearing the flannel pajamas because he'd certainly provided her with enough heat—and felt it skim over her body like a silken waterfall.

"Oh wow." She looked at herself in the mirror. It was almost as if a stranger were looking back at her. The perky kindergarten teacher had vanished, leaving in her place the type of siren portrayed in all those movies that were her second-favorite genre behind holiday ones. Rita Hayworth, Susan Hayward, Ingrid Bergman, Bette Davis, all wrapped up into one sexy silk package. The kind of woman who could treat a man wrong and make him beg for more.

Enjoying that idea, she fluffed her hair with her hands. Dug through her cosmetic bag and located a scarlet-as-sin lipstick she'd bought on a whim for the Christmas program, only to chicken out at the last minute. Wishing she had a pair of the marabou mule slippers sexy seductresses in those films always seemed to wear with their filmy negligees, she decided she had no choice but to go with bare feet.

Taking a deep breath, she channeled an inner temptress she'd begun to discover lurking inside her, and opened the door.

Cole was rearranging the fire while sipping from a glass of brandy when she walked toward him on her closest approximation of a siren's glide.

"Merry Christmas, Santa baby," she purred, as Bing gave way to Eartha Kitt.

"It is, indeed, that," he managed after choking slightly on the brandy. "You look amazing."

"Do you think so?" She skimmed her hands down her body, from her breasts to her thighs, drawing his attention to curves only days earlier she would have wanted to try to hide.

"Actually, amazing is a serious understatement." He sat down in a brown leather chair and made a twirling motion with his finger. She turned slowly, revealing the way the nightgown bared her back to below the waist, accentuating the flare of her butt.

"So, Kelli . . ." His voice had slid into the rough, sexy timbre that she could feel vibrating inside her. "Have you been good?" he asked as she turned around. "Or bad?"

She tilted her head coyly and looked up at him through her lashes. "Aren't I supposed to be sitting on your lap to answer that question?"

"Absolutely." As he took her hand and settled her onto his lap, Kelli could feel his arousal and finally understood what had allegedly kept Adèle and Bernard Douchett together for half a century. She knew that she'd certainly never tire of making love to this man.

"Well?" he asked.

"Aren't you going to give me my candy cane?"

"You know how it works."

"Well then." She sighed. "I guess, since I can't lie to Santa—"

"It would be ill advised," he agreed.

"I'd have to say I've been bad." She wiggled a bit, knowing exactly what she was doing to him. "So bad, you might even say I'm good."

His answering grin was a wicked slash, like no department store Santa she'd ever seen. "That definitely calls for a special treat."

"Oh, Santa baby." She felt herself melting into a little puddle of need as his hand slipped beneath the flow of white silk and his wickedly clever fingers began trailing up her thigh. "I really do believe in you." She thought about tossing out the line from the song about wanting a ring, but decided that would be pushing it. "Do you believe in me?"

"Why don't you let me show you how much?"

And as he took her mouth, he proceeded to do exactly that.

19

He'd slept through the night. That was the first thought Cole had when he woke up to find Kelli's head on his chest and her leg flung across his. He ran a hand down her back, skimming over the silk negligee she was still wearing.

Although he loved her body, even in those silly sweaters, flannel pajamas, and most of all, naked, when he could look and touch and taste at will, there'd been something about that nightgown that had enticed him to explore each little region of the delicious female territory that was Kelli Carpenter bit by bit. Piece by piece.

The feel of the silk—like a cool waterfall in the empty desert that his life had become—had proven an aphrodisiac, not that he needed one when he was with her.

For someone who moved so fast while awake, she roused slowly, stretching, sighing, her eyes the last thing to finally join the world. When she realized he was still lying with her, playing with her hair, which was splayed over his chest, those sea blue eyes widened.

"Merry Christmas. . . . You're still here."

"Yeah." And he would have happily stayed there for

the rest of his life. But having changed the dynamics of their relationship, he knew it was only fair that he be open. And honest. Which he hadn't entirely been to himself. "And we need to talk."

"Today?"

Her reticence suggested she expected the worst. And why shouldn't she?

"Today," he repeated. "Let me start the coffee."

"That sounds ominous."

Her hands were clutching the sheet like a lifeline. He uncurled her fingers and lifted each one to his lips. "There are things you need to know."

"Like why you chop wood in the middle of the night."

"That's one of them." Then he gave her a kiss that, while light and short, was one of the most heartfelt they'd shared over this stolen time apart.

He couldn't be going to tell her it was over, Kelli assured herself. That being here together was only a stolen time that had no relation to their real lives. Because, all right, maybe this hadn't exactly been a normal everyday existence. But it was real. And no way was she going to let him claim otherwise.

He was standing at the kitchen window, looking out at the snow, which had begun to fall again. Her long-dreamed-for white Christmas.

"If you're planning to try to tell me that 'what happens at Rainbow Lake stays at Rainbow Lake,' I'm not buying it," she said. "Because, whether you want to hear it or not, I love you."

"Which is handy." He handed her a mug of steaming black coffee that was, dammit, sweetened exactly the way she liked it. "Since I love you, too."

That was so not what his grim face had her expecting.

"Oh. . . . Well. Why do you sound as if your dog just got run over?"

That question clearly had them both thinking back to that day when he'd been the only person who could unbreak her heart.

"Remember when I broke my shoulder?" he asked.

Another surprise. "Of course."

The only reason all those college scouts had come to Shelter Bay was to see the six-foot-three-inch quarterback who could throw bombs from the pocket and run like a sprinter. When his shoulder was shattered, any chance of a football scholarship had flown out the window. Even at nine years old, Kelli had realized what that had meant to him. And how devastated he must have been.

Refusing to indulge in any pity parties, before he could even rotate that arm again, he'd signed up for ROTC so Uncle Sam would pay his way in exchange for him risking his life in several deployments in two different wars.

"You baked me brownies."

As sad as that time had been, she smiled at the memory. "Here's where I confess that they were from a box."

"It doesn't matter. The important thing was you were the only person I could talk to about it. Even though you were still just a kid. It wasn't really until this past year that I realized how unusual that was."

"Not if I loved you. And you were destined to love me," she suggested.

"Yeah. I thought about that a lot, too. About how much fate plays a part in our lives. Why one guy on a convoy gets blown up and another one, standing a few feet away, doesn't even get a scratch. The randomness of life sucks."

She wasn't going to argue that.

"Are you trying to tell me you're reenlisting?" She could live with the man she loved being deployed, Kelli decided. She wouldn't like it. At all. She'd worry the entire time he was gone. But she'd understand that it was his choice. And living with fear every day for months on end trumped living without Cole Douchett.

"I was probably going to. Because I felt guilty about getting on with my life while leaving my brothers behind."

She knew he wasn't talking about Sax and J. T. Douchett. But his band of brothers. "Aren't there always new Marines cycling into units?"

"Yeah."

"Then when would you leave, Cole? Or do you intend to be the last Marine to leave Afghanistan in a flag-draped casket?"

His lips curved, but his smile held no humor. "You've never held back with me."

"I did once. When I didn't tell you that Marcia was all wrong for you. And I nearly ruined everything. For both of us."

"I wanted to get married," he surprised her by saying. "I came home and there was this one moment, when I had a flash of you and me together, and suddenly I knew I wanted the life our parents have. The life your brother has. A house and kids and a damn picket fence I'd have to paint and a big, stupid dog. And I wanted you."

"What?" She'd been pacing the floor, but that stopped her in her tracks. "You wanted *me*?"

"Yeah. You've no idea how much."

"You're right about that. Since you proposed to Marcia Wayburn."

He dragged a hand over his head. "I knew her in high school."

"So, I hear, did half the guys in town." She lifted a hand. "Sorry. That's merely gossip." After all, she had no proof that the woman was a slut. Though, actually, the way she had dumped Cole and, it appeared, even kept the ring didn't do the woman's reputation any favors, in Kelli's opinion.

"She was someone familiar for me. She wanted to get married. So did I."

"Uh, maybe you should've asked me."

"Yeah. Matt told me you thought the ring was for you." Another swipe over that Marine haircut. "I'm really sorry about that. I honestly had no idea."

"You talked with my brother? About me? Last Christmas?"

"Hell no. He told me about it the other day. Before I came out here, when I asked if he'd have a problem with me being with you."

"You actually asked permission from my brother to go to bed with me?"

"No. Not exactly. Damn. . . . The thing is, he'd warned me, back when you turned sixteen, exactly what he'd do if I ever even looked at you."

"Matt threatened you?" Color rose in her cheeks, waving like furious flags. "He had no right."

"He had every right. You were sixteen years old, Kels. I was a twenty-four-year-old Marine. Hell, if I had a sister, or someday a daughter, you can bet I'd do the same thing."

"I loved you!"

"Puppy love."

"No." About this she was very sure. "It was real. It was real when I baked those brownies, it was real when I was sixteen, and it was real last year. When, by the way, I was twenty-four years old. Which, last time I checked, is legal in all fifty states and probably every damn country in the damn world!"

"It felt weird, okay?" he shouted back at her. "I've known you almost my whole life."

She shook her head, trying to wrap her mind around their situation. "What makes this year so different?"

"I've had the past year to think about it, to figure out I was an idiot. That I was worrying about all the wrong things. Like wanting you to have a chance to fall in love with someone besides me."

"Like that was ever going to happen," she muttered. "You broke my heart last year, Cole." She felt the tears filling her eyes and this time didn't even try to hold them back. "Do you have any idea how long it took me to put all the pieces back together again?" But she hadn't really succeeded. Because this man still held her entire heart in his hands.

"Yeah. Because mine was pretty much torn up, too. Like it had been hit with shrapnel. . . . It just took me a while to realize what I was feeling. And when I finally did, my grandmother advised me to take things slowly."

"You talked to *her*, too? About me?"

"When she offered the cabin. She said that if I tried to push you into doing something, you'd only run the other way. That I should take my time to achieve my mission."

That would be true. In any other case.

She put down the mug of cooling coffee and folded her arms. "So now I'm a mission?"

"That's not what I meant. Not exactly. There's this thing Recon Marines have. A creed."

"A creed."

"Yeah. I'm not going to recite the entire thing now, but the part that fits our situation goes: 'Conquering all obstacles, both large and small, I shall never quit. To quit, to surrender, to give up is to fail. To be a Recon Marine is to surpass failure. To overcome, to adapt, and to do whatever it takes to complete the mission.'

"And then there's some more military-type stuff. Until it ends, 'A Recon Marine can speak without saying a word. And achieve what others can only imagine.'"

"So, how long were you going to give me to be overcome so you could complete your mission?"

"I hadn't thought that out. That's what coming out here was supposed to be all about. To come up with a plan."

"I see. A plan that would convince me to marry you and have your children and put up with a big stupid dog burying bones in my garden without you having to say a word."

He saw the trap. Too late.

"You want the words."

She arched a brow, proving that Recon Marines weren't the only ones who could speak without words.

"Okay." He blew out a breath. "I love you, Kels. I think I always have, which is why, the past year, not having you in my life has been hell."

His fault, she thought, but there was no point in rubbing salt into the wound. Not when she was so close to getting the Christmas present she'd wanted her entire life.

"I love you and I need you, and although I have to go through the separation process, I promise I'll come back to Shelter Bay as soon as the military releases me. And I'll build a fence to keep the dog out of your garden, and if you don't want children—"

"I've always wanted children." *His* children.

"Great. Okay. Well."

Since her big, bad, sexy Marine was actually looking more than a little out of his comfort zone, Kelli took pity on him and decided to help him out.

"However, I'm old-fashioned," she said. "Plus, I like

things in order. I realize that marriage isn't imperative for having a family. But." She shrugged. "As I said, I'm old-fashioned."

"You want me to propose."

"Unless you intend to wait until I do."

"No. I mean I'm tired of waiting, and I'm old-fashioned enough to think it's the guy's thing. So . . ."

He squared his shoulders in a way that had him looking as if he were facing a firing squad. Her heart went out to him, but Kelli refrained from asking if he wanted a blindfold and a cigarette.

"Will you marry me, Kelli Carpenter? And live with me and be my wife. Forever and ever? Amen?"

She'd imagined this day so many times, Kelli had believed she'd known exactly what it would feel like.

She hadn't come close.

"It certainly took you long enough." With joy bubbling in her veins and her heart floating up to the cabin rafters, the future Mrs. Cole Douchett laughed and flew into his outstretched arms.

"Yes." She kissed him. Then quoted the Randy Travis lyrics back to him. "Forever and ever. Amen."

While they cooked the holiday dinner together, the way they both knew the crafty Adèle had planned for them to do, Cole admitted that he'd been diagnosed with PTSD. Another reason he'd been leaning toward returning to civilian life.

"But it's not bad enough that I'm dangerous or anything," he assured her. "Hell, I doubt anyone comes back from any war totally free of problems. In my case, it's mostly just insomnia."

Which explained that mountain of wood outside the window.

"Well then," she said as she broke apart pieces of corn bread for the Douchett family's traditional andouille sausage and corn bread stuffing. "I'll just have to make sure you're all worn out every night."

"Works for me," he agreed easily, feeling more relaxed than he had in months. Maybe years. "I also was going to ask, before you got me off track, what you'd think of being married to a fisherman."

"As long as that fisherman is you, I love the idea."

When he told her about his chance to buy Ernie's newer, shinier boat, she agreed that was a great idea. Then she said, "As much as I'm enjoying this time together, I'm wondering if we should go back tomorrow."

"For Grandmère's Boxing Day party," he said as he fried the sausage in the pan.

"Everyone went to a lot of thought and trouble to set this Christmas up," she said. "We probably shouldn't keep them wondering how things turned out."

"Good point. Though, since they were so sneaky about it, there's no point in giving them their satisfaction right off the bat."

She turned from chopping the celery, onion, and bell pepper, which Cole had told her was the holy trinity of Cajun cooking. "We'd just go in for the day," she suggested. "We could leave my car here and drive back to town together in your truck. Then you could drop me off at your grandparents' house and go buy Ernie's boat before someone else snatches it up."

"While, meanwhile, you keep them guessing why I'm not with you."

"Exactly. It's going to be so much fun when we tell them they've been punked." Kelli grinned happily at that idea. And they'd never suspect such behavior from responsible, serious Cole.

She loved the fact that although they were very different people, years of being friends had them so often thinking in the same way.

Like now, just when she was wondering why she'd never realized how sexy a man in the kitchen could be, he pulled the pan of browned sausage off the burner, turned off the gas, took the knife out of her hand, and drew her into his arms.

"What would you say about having your dinner a little later than planned?"

She twined her arms around his neck. "Late dinners are fashionable." Last summer she'd attended a teacher's conference in Seattle and thought she'd starve to death before their banquet dinner was served.

"Terrific." He scooped her off her feet and headed toward the bedroom. "Let's be fashionable together."

20

The Boxing Day party was in full swing when Cole arrived at his grandparents' cliffside home. From the number of cars parked in front, it appeared his grandmother had invited half the town.

He smiled as he thought about how frustrated she must be at Kelli's refusal to spill the beans about what had happened up at the lake. Fortunately, she was a good enough sport he knew she'd laugh at being caught at her subterfuge.

And speaking of surprises . . .

His nerves tangled a bit when he took the pink box from the passenger seat.

The buzz of conversation immediately stopped when he walked into the room.

"It's about time you got here," his grandmother complained as she caught sight of him. "We've all been waiting to hear about your Christmas."

"It was okay."

He had to bite back a laugh when his grandmother shot a frustrated look at his grandfather, who just shrugged.

With far more important things on his mind than their game, which he'd already lost interest in, Cole crossed the room to Kelli, who looked drop-dead delicious in a fluffy pink sweater that exposed her shoulders, a short gray pleated wool skirt, and black suede boots that went nearly to her knees. All gifts from her mother.

She'd told him, when she'd opened the boxes from the Shelter Bay boutique, that she suspected the women in their families had been trying to sexy her up, to which he'd answered that personally, he considered her just as hot in that flashing Christmas tree sweater or polar bear pajamas. Especially once he got her out of them.

Which had caused that cute pink color to bloom in her cheeks.

And speaking of pink . . .

"Since it's Boxing Day, I figured a box was in order," he said, pulling the familiar pink one from behind his back.

She drew in a sharp breath as she opened it and saw the piña colada cupcake, like the one he'd given her before the play. With one important difference.

"We've already done Hawaii in a cupcake," he said, surprised at how nervous he was, since she had, after all, already accepted his proposal. "So, I was thinking this time, maybe I'd try for a Hawaiian honeymoon in a cake."

"It's absolutely perfect." She cupped the box in her hands as he untied the slender white ribbon Sedona Sullivan had used to attach the ring to the umbrella topping the coconut frosting.

"It's a pink sapphire." The oval-cut stone was set off by tiny chips of diamonds on either side that extended onto the band.

Before meeting Ernie at the harbor where he docked

his boat, he'd talked Henry Olson into opening his store, which had been closed for the day. Although he'd readily agreed when Cole explained his mission, the jeweler did warn that this was going to be the last engagement ring he ever sold him. Which wasn't going to be a problem.

He took the ring and slipped it on her finger. It fit perfectly. Just like them, Cole thought.

"It reminded me of you." He leaned forward, sensing everyone in the room straining to hear the murmured words meant only for her ear. "And sugarplums."

From the way her eyes darkened and her cheeks flushed again, he knew she was remembering how he'd told her he loved tasting her. All over.

"Well, it certainly took you long enough," Adèle said briskly, as everyone in the room began to applaud and Mrs. Carpenter began dabbing at her misty eyes with a tissue. "But you two finally got your happily-ever-after ending."

"It's not an ending," Cole corrected, feeling the grin splitting his face, as Kelli lifted her beautiful, smiling pink lips to his. "It's just the beginning."

ABOUT THE AUTHOR

JoAnn Ross is the *New York Times* and *USA Today* best-selling author of the Shelter Bay series. She lives with her husband and three rescued dogs in the Pacific Northwest. Visit her Web site for a video tour of Shelter Bay.

CONNECT ONLINE

www.joannross.com
facebook.com/joannrossbooks
twitter.com/joannross

A SEASIDE
CHRISTMAS

Susan Donovan

1

"Gather 'round, ye maids. A storm brews."

Mona Flynn gestured for members of the Bayberry Island Mermaid Society to hurry into position around the fountain and its statue. Under the glow of flashlights, fifteen feet of bronzed female grandeur gleamed in the darkness. Mona knew it was a sight that never failed to delight and inspire their kind, a reminder that anyone who sought the mermaid's guidance in matters of the heart would find their way to true love.

The wind suddenly kicked up, whipping the members' long tresses and misting their upturned faces with icy spray from the Atlantic.

"O, Great Mermaid!" Mona cried out, her voice nearly carried away in the wind. "Hear this plea of pure heart!" She waited patiently for the impassioned echo of her words that was supposed to begin every Society ceremony. Instead, what she got was a lackluster grumble.

"Ladies?"

"O-Great-Mermaid-hear-this-plea-of-pure-heart."

"Not great, but better." Mona knew she couldn't fault the group for being less than enthusiastic. Standing in the icy rain on a black December night in nothing but a set of seashells and a spandex mermaid tail wasn't exactly invigorating, even for a group of women prone to hot flashes. Just as Mona opened her mouth to intone the ritual of emergency love intervention, her eyes noticed a tiny reddish glow on the opposite side of the sacred circle.

"Polly!" Mona waved her flashlight around in the darkness. "Are you *nuts*? You almost set your wig on fire the last time you tried to smoke in the wind!"

"Keep your shells on, Mona." Polly Estherhausen hiked up her mermaid tail and begrudgingly ground out her cigarette with the heel of her L.L.Bean snow boot. "Do you think we can zip this along? My bum knee is freakin' killing me."

Mona sighed. Honestly, serving as president of this group wasn't for a woman with a weak constitution. Nevertheless, it was her sacred duty to keep them on point. "Did we not agree that Annabeth Parker needs our help?" she asked. "Do our bylaws not state that an equinox—either the summer or winter solstice—is the best time to seek the Great Mermaid's intervention? Is the winter solstice not ideal because it's a time of rebirth and new opportunities?"

"Excuse me," Izzy McCracken said. "I think I got lost with all the double negatives."

"Every party needs an English teacher," someone mumbled.

Mona threw up her hands. "Is tonight not the winter solstice, people?"

The women nodded.

"Fine. Let's start over, shall we?" Mona took a cleansing breath and gazed at the vision of aquatic grace and mystery towering above them. Even in winter, with her majestic fountain plumes of water silenced, she was a joy to behold. "O, Great Mermaid! Hear this plea of pure heart!"

This time, the group's response was loud and clear, which made her smile. Mona continued. "On this night, a daughter of the island is in need. She awaits her heart-mate, yet stubbornly refuses to ask for your help. Great Mermaid, look down upon our sister Annabeth Parker. Hear our plea on her behalf. Soften her resistance. Allow the water of love to flow through her. Light her way to shore."

The group responded on cue. "Help us."

"Soften her resistance," Mona intoned.

"Assist us."

"Allow the water of love to flow."

"Guide us."

"Light her way to—"

"I need a hot toddy like a son of a bitch."

Mona's head snapped around. She glared at Abigail Foster in annoyance.

"Well, excuse me, Mona, but this ice is frizzing my new wig, and it's so cold out here that my nipples are like drill bits."

Guffaws erupted all around. At this point, Mona couldn't help but join in. "Oh, the hell with this, then. I guess Annie's on her own."

A collective sigh of relief went through the circle. Everyone clicked off their flashlights, grabbed coats from the park benches, and cautiously made their way down the icy boardwalk to Polly's house, where hot toddies and a roaring fire waited.

"Annie will be fine," Abigail yelled, zipping her parka and keeping her head down against the wind. "That girl gets a new toy boy every tourist season. Sooner or later the tide's bound to wash up someone decent."

"It's boy toy, not toy boy," Izzy said, none too charitably. "And the Mermaid Society is about true love, not just boinking."

"Hey, I'd be happy with some good, old-fashioned boinking, thank you very much," Polly shouted.

Mona rolled her eyes. Certainly, this hadn't been one of the Society's most dignified gatherings. But she was certain Annie needed their help and she needed it *now*. The girl was her daughter Rowan's lifelong best friend, and Annie could prance around like an independent, modern woman all she wanted, but Mona could see through the facade.

Annabeth Parker needed a loyal, passionate, and courageous man, a man whose devotion knew no bounds, the kind of man who would not run from the awesome power of true love.

Well, hell. They all did.

His callused, sea-roughened hands clutched at her glistening flesh. Their mouths met in a fierce tidal wave of a passion, the force of which threatened to wash him away, drown him. Yes, it was taboo. Forbidden. But Captain Forrest Burroughs didn't care. He simply didn't care!

As Annie's fingers flew over the laptop keyboard, a shudder of pleasure went through her. No doubt about it. *Desire at High Tide* was going to be her most popular installment yet. Fans of the Sea of Lust mermaid erotica franchise were going to love this shit!

"Take me! Take me!" Neptunia cried, her glistening tail whipping around the captain's torso, capturing him, pulling his masculine form to her heaving, shell-covered bosom.

Annie's fingers stopped. She scrolled back to the previous paragraph and shook her head in exasperation. She'd already used the word "glistening" and certainly couldn't use it again so soon. She'd have to wait at least two pages for the mermaid to glisten again. Annie deleted the word and replaced it with "slippery." Good enough for the first draft.

Absently, she reached toward the end table for her mug of hot cocoa, but got a handful of cat whiskers instead.

"Mmmmrrrow."

"Oh, all right, Ezra. Hop on."

The big black kitty with white paws jumped from the table to her shoulders, where he draped his heft around the back of her neck like an overfed fur stole. Sure, this arrangement gave her a wicked backache after a while, but it made Ezra happy. And besides, his purring acted as a poor woman's vibrating massager.

"Now, where were we, E?" Annie sipped the cocoa, settled deeper into the club chair, and stretched her sock-covered feet toward the fire. She returned her attention to her laptop. If all went according to schedule, she'd have this one finished by March and could squeeze in at least half of another novel while preparing the store for the season. Added to the six she'd already written, that would bring her to seven and a half self-published books in six years—not bad for the off-season hobby of a tourist-town shopkeeper.

Before her fingers could connect with the keys, her cell phone rang. With a groan, Annie snatched it from the side table to see that Rowan was calling.

"How's the interspecies porn coming along?" Her best friend, Rowan Flynn, wasn't known for subtlety.

"It was going along fine until my phone rang."

"Well, sorry for the *mermaidus interruptus*, but I wanted to make sure you were all right."

"I'm fine. Why?" Annie had to nudge Ezra off her

neck. His purring was so loud, she could barely hear Rowan's snarky comments.

"The storm. We're supposed to get a couple of inches of ice tonight. Maybe even some power outages. I swear to God, this island has more annual power outages than residents."

"Huh." Annie peered out the front windows of her narrow little clapboard cottage to view the island's boardwalk. "All I see is rain."

"Nope—it's ice. It's supposed to worsen as the night goes on. If I didn't have a customer coming in on the ferry, I'd be over there to keep you company."

Annie laughed. "Captain Forrest Burroughs is keeping me company just fine, but I appreciate you checking on me. Everything okay over at the B and B?"

"More or less. It's six leaks and counting up in the attic, and another shutter just flew off. This place is falling apart faster than my love life."

Annie sighed. It had been about a year since Rowan left Manhattan and washed up on the familiar shores of Bayberry Island, her pride and spirit in tatters. Not only had Rowan's fiancé crushed her heart, he also had talked her into investing what was left of the Flynn family fortune in what turned out to be an investment scam, leaving him indicted for securities fraud, Rowan without a home or a man—and the family flat broke. As a way to make amends to her family, Rowan offered to run the Flynn's Safe Haven Bed and Breakfast. So far, it had been like a jail sentence for Rowan, and her wounded heart had been slow to heal.

"I'll come over tomorrow and help you look for the shutter," Annie said.

"I already called Clancy." Rowan's middle sibling, Clancy Flynn, was the island's police chief and everyone's go-to guy for off-season home repairs. "He said he'd patch the roof, too, while he was over here."

"But I really don't mind—"

"Oh, stop. I didn't call to rope you into doing odd jobs. I just wanted to make sure you're good."

Annie smiled. "I am, thank you."

"Then give Captain Burroughs a big ol' wet one for me."

"Sure will."

"Has he discovered the '*Piscem* Problem' yet?"

Annie laughed again. Rowan had helped her brainstorm many a mermaid tale, either in person or on the phone from New York. Her friend knew the challenges of writing a hot-and-heavy love scene featuring an anatomically correct human male and a half-fish, half-woman mythological creature. Rowan dubbed it the "*Piscem* Problem" after an ancient poem by Horace, a Roman dude who hadn't been much of a mermaid fan, apparently. He wrote that what began as a beautiful woman ended in the ugly, blackened tail of a fish. "*Desinit in piscem mulier formosa superne.*"

Annie long ago decided that Horace—and all the other haters and doubters out there—could just stick it. These were her books. It was her world. Her stories. If she wanted to make it simple for her dashing sea captains and fetching seamaids to mate, then that's what she'd do. It wasn't as if she were reinventing real biology, for heaven's sake. So she decided from the get-go that all her captains would have standard—albeit above-average—equipment, and all the mermaids would be like seaplanes—able to manage in water and on land with some minor adjustments. So far, she'd received only a few nasty online reviews, including one from a reader who claimed to be an actual mermaid. This made Annie think she must be doing something right.

She said good-bye to Rowan, took another sip of cocoa, and got back to work.

The captain lifted her effortlessly from the foaming surf, his mouth claiming hers roughly. In awe, he noticed that her mermaid tail had begun to split in two, a woman's lovely, long legs taking shape in the summer air, a woman's perfect nethermouth appearing at their ~~glistening~~ moist vortex.

"Pffshew," Annie said, fanning herself. She knew she'd be wise to switch from cocoa to cabernet if ol' Forrest was about to hoist the mainsail.

"How ya holdin' up there, sir?"

Nathaniel Ravelle raised his watering eyes to the ferry conductor but kept the seasickness bag pressed to his mouth. He nodded that he was all right, which was a lie. One more pounding wave like that last one and he'd be face-first on the concrete floor of the passenger cabin. Maybe it was a good thing he hadn't eaten anything but a bag of airline peanuts thirty thousand feet over Iowa City, a good seven hours before landing in Boston, getting a taxi to the Cape, and catching the ferry to Bayberry Island.

"Takes some gettin' used to, eh? Wintertime seas can get rough around here. Looks like we're getting a nor'easter. My name is John. Let me know if there's anything you need."

Nat nodded.

"I bet you wished you'd stayed in Los Angeles."

You have no idea.

"All right, well, only about fifteen minutes till Bayberry. You're the only passenger getting off there. Have to say they don't get many tourists this time of year. Mostly just during summer. They have a Mermaid Festival every August, you know."

I know. Trust me.

"You should be glad you're not going all the way to Nantucket tonight, because that would be another half hour. Not much fun in your condition, to be sure."

Nat nodded.

"I hope you've made arrangements for someone to pick you up at the dock. This is no night to be wandering around in the—"

Mercifully, the conductor noticed a woozy passenger darting out into the rain for relief, and he ran off in pursuit. Nat rested his forehead against the cold glass of the ferry window and talked himself out of getting sick. The conductor would never know this, but the fact that one little choppy ferryboat ride could flatten him like this was nothing short of an embarrassment.

Nat had grown up in Green Bay, Wisconsin, where he'd made the acquaintance of moody Lake Michigan before he'd learned to walk. He spent every available moment boating and fishing as a kid, and later taught sailing lessons in high school to earn money for college. Maybe his mother had been right when she'd admonished him a few months back, claiming that a dozen years in LA had changed him.

The ferry lurched, rising up with a wave and slamming down again. Nat stared out into the blackness, knowing that he'd feel less nauseated if he could spot the horizon line. Suddenly, he saw a blurry strip of lights break through the sleet, and he smiled at the promise of solid ground. The smile didn't last.

Why, exactly, was he out here on the stormy Atlantic in a 150-decible, diesel-spewing tin can of death? What, in his executive producer's bizarre little mind, was so critical that Nat was booked on a plane stuffed with holiday travelers and shipped off to the East Coast on a moment's notice?

Fucking mermaids.

Seriously, as soon as Nat got back to LA, he was getting a new job. He didn't care that he was the only one of his film school friends with a career in entertainment that didn't involve squirting butter on popcorn. Four years as a segment producer for the cable paranormal reality show *Truly Weird* was about three and a half years too many. In the name of advance-location scouting, he'd been sent to chat it up with Sasquatch witnesses in southeastern Ohio, alien abductees in Alabama, and enough alleged victims of demonic possession and ghostly hauntings to fill every seat in the Staples Center.

Nat wasn't entirely clear why this particular assignment was shaping up to be the proverbial last straw. Maybe the disgust was cumulative. But, really, an island full of insane people who thought a mermaid statue had been setting up happily-ever-afters since the nineteenth century? An entire population brainwashed into thinking a bronze fountain could grant requests like a disc jockey at a wedding reception? People who actually believed there was such a thing as true, abiding love between a man and a woman in today's world?

Sure. And Bigfoot shopped at the Trader Joe's on La Brea and Third.

There was only one good thing about this trip. His whole family happened to be in Boston for the holidays, because his big sister lived there with her kids and husband. Nat had already told his mom that he'd be joining them as soon as he could get the hell off Bayberry Island, news that made her cry with happiness. It had been years since they'd all been together for Christmas.

The boat engine began to slow. It wasn't long before Nat's feet were on the slippery dock and the ferry pulled away, belching fumes in his direction as a final insult. He looked around, making several observations. First, he couldn't help but notice the largest live Christmas tree he'd ever seen towering over the public dock, decorated in festive lights and topped with, of course, a large mermaid, now swinging precariously in the wind. Next, he saw that the promised taxi was not waiting for him and there wasn't another human being in sight. And last but not least, he realized the stuff coming out of the sky was ice.

This wouldn't be good. His leather jacket and smooth-soled Jack Purcells might work for brunch in Malibu but not for a December nor'easter off the coast of Massachusetts. He grabbed his cell phone to call the B and B. Dead battery. Of course.

Figuring the place couldn't be too far away, Nat decided to walk. He strapped his laptop case across the front of his body, grabbed the handle of his rolling suitcase, and took a step. He almost landed on his ass. Seasickness? The inability to walk on ice? Ridiculous. He was a child of the blizzard belt. There was no way he would let a little winter weather stop him from getting where he needed to go.

Twenty minutes later, Nat had progressed about two blocks down the boardwalk. His hair was a helmet of ice. His hands were numb. The Christmas decorations along Main Street were charming, but he decided to keep his eyes on the placement of his feet, just to be safe. He did so until he passed a quaint tourist shop with a name that made him laugh out loud—A Little Tail. He wondered if the naughty double entendre was intentional and decided it couldn't be. The kitschy store was probably run by a little old lady with a white bun and a cat who slept near the cash register. Nat smiled at the idea just as he noticed the list of products for sale within: "Mermaid-themed souvenirs, mermaid/sea captain erotic novels, adults-only cakes and chocolates, X-rated sea shanties."

"What the—?" Distracted by the sign, he took a step without noticing the slight downward slope to the boardwalk, and his feet flew straight out in front of him. His body planked parallel to the walkway and ice pelted his face,

Just before his body slammed to the boardwalk, Nat realized this was going to be even worse than he thought.

2

When Annie heard the loud *thump!* she jolted with surprise. What an odd sound. And it seemed to have come from outside the front door of her house. She cocked her head and listened carefully, but all she heard was the clicking sound of ice hitting the front windows and the faint whistle of wind.

Her cat looked at her and meowed loudly.

"Thanks for the heads-up, Ezra. I heard it too." Annie placed the laptop on the floor near her chair and walked to the front door, stretching her arms over her head as she moved. Maybe she'd lost a shutter, too. Or maybe the shop sign blew down. Only one way to find out.

She opened the door and gasped. Her hands flew to her chest. She staggered back in shock and almost tripped over her own stocking feet.

That was no shutter. That was a man. And he'd obviously just wiped out and landed on his back at her doorstep, his body already coated in a shiny fondant of ice.

"Oh boy. Oh hell. Oh God." Annie peered down at him. "Uh, sir? Are you all right? Can you hear me?" She squatted next to him and patted his cheek, which was freezing. She got no response, though she could see he was breathing. The man was young, handsome, and wearing an expensive, albeit useless, leather jacket. She noticed that a rolling suitcase had skidded to a stop on the cobblestones of Main Street. This had to be Rowan's B and B reservation.

Annie remembered from her lifeguard days that anyone with a possible neck injury shouldn't be moved unless there was another immediate danger. So she left the man outside, ran into her living room, and grabbed her cell phone. Her 911 call got her transferred to the emergency room on Nantucket. A helpful doctor gave her some good news and some bad news—yes, she could go ahead and move the man indoors because of the risk of hypothermia, but no, no one could make it to Bayberry until the next morning because of the storm. The doctor gave Annie suggestions for getting the man warm and dry and making him comfortable, then told her to call back as soon as he'd regained consciousness.

Annie took a deep breath and told herself she could do this. She slipped on her snow boots, jammed a heel against the doorjamb for support, and then grabbed the man by his feet, shaking her head in disbelief as she did. No wonder he fell! What kind of idiot wears hipster Converse sneakers in an ice storm? With the first yank, she spun him around so that his feet were across the threshold. With the second yank, she had him half inside. The third yank was followed by a steady pull, which was enough to get him toward the center of the hardwood floor. Next, Annie called Rowan.

"You're not going to believe this, but there's a man in my house."

Rowan snorted. "You got a man over there? But tourist season is five months away!"

"He's passed out on my floor."

"Like I said—"

"Just get over here and help me, would you? I think he's your ferry passenger."

Annie pulled the man's briefcase strap over his head, then ran out into the storm to fetch his suitcase. Once back in the warmth of her cozy front room, she stared down at her lifeless guest, feeling something akin to panic.

"Okay, Annie. Keep it together." She knelt down, un-zipped and removed his jacket, then tossed it aside. She snagged a toss pillow from her writing chair and put it under his head. The sheen of ice was melting, and Annie saw that he was soaked. Slowly, with trembling fingers, she removed his stupid shoes and soggy socks, and was in the process of figuring out how she could remove his stylish V-neck cashmere sweater and his undershirt when Rowan blew in the front door.

"No time for foreplay?"

Annie rolled her eyes. "He's wet." When her friend had no snappy comeback, she looked up to find Rowan's eyes wide. "What?"

"I'm not even going there." Rowan tossed her parka to the boot bench by the door. "What can I do to help?"

Annie sat back on her heels and rested her palms on her knees. "I guess we should get him stripped and in my bed—and keep your clever retorts to yourself."

"Jeesh. Fine." Rowan knelt down on the other side of the man. "He's pretty cute, really." She leaned close and felt his forearm. "Ooh, strike that—he's *reeally* cute. He's got hottie muscles! Smells nice, too. Did you check his ID to be sure he's my guest?"

"I'm not sure he'd appreciate you poking and sniffing him like he was a melon, and no, I didn't look for an ID."

Rowan raised a brow. "Allow me, then." She reached into both his front pants pockets and found nothing but a giggle, then reached for his wet jacket. She pulled a wallet from an inside pocket. "Aha! Yup. Nathaniel Ravelle, age thirty-four, six-one, one ninety-five, brown hair, green eyes, from Los Angeles." Rowan looked up. "He's booked for two nights in the blue suite. He's on island to do research for a TV show. Did I tell you that?"

Annie snatched the wallet from her friend, examining the driver's license and credit cards. She opened a slim business card holder and read aloud, "Senior producer, *Truly Weird*." Annie felt her mouth hang open. "Oh *God,* Rowan! Have you ever seen that show? I have, and it's complete trash. I take it they're doing something on the Mermaid legend?"

"What else?" Rowan took it upon herself to undo Mr. Ravelle's belt and unzip his trousers. "He said the crew plans to film during next year's festival week. They've already booked three rooms and two suites for ten days. Here, help me pull these off."

"Wait a minute." Annie grabbed the lap rug from her writing chair and draped it over the guy's hips. "He deserves some privacy. What if he doesn't wear underwear or something?"

Rowan smiled. "Then he automatically qualifies for a discounted room rate."

The two women pulled off his sweater and T-shirt, and Mr. Nathaniel Ravelle of Los Angeles, California, lay almost totally nude on Annie's floor.

"Holy Moses," Rowan whispered.

Annie would have said something similar if she'd been able to form actual words. Instead all she could do was breathe too fast and stare. Truthfully, this was the finest naked man to grace her home since Todd "the

Bod" Townsend from the 2009 season. Todd had been the only lover for whom she'd been tempted to reevaluate her no-man-past-Columbus-Day rule. But in the end she decided it would be best if he packed up and returned to the mainland, like all the others.

This Nathaniel Ravelle guy was even better looking than Todd. His body was gracefully athletic but not bulky. His skin was a rich peach color, and his chest was touched by fine dark brown hair, which continued down the center of his abdomen all the way to his . . . lap rug. Eventually, Annie got her voice to work. "We need to lift him, Rowan."

"Say what?" Her friend blinked at her. "Can you dead-lift a hundred pounds off the floor?"

Annie pursed her lips. "I would have no way of knowing the answer to that."

"Well, I know *my* answer to that. I'll call Ma. She'll bring reinforcements."

Not five minutes later, eight senior members of the Mermaid Society arrived, most in formal wig-and-scale regalia and three sheets to the wind, a sure sign that Rowan's call had interrupted a Mermaid Society "meeting." The women spilled into Annie's small front room and stared in disbelief.

"I'll be damned," Polly Estherhausen said, her mouth unhinged.

"That's got to be some kinda record," Izzy McCracken slurred.

"There's a naked man on your floor, Annabeth." Mona stared at her in shock.

"He's harmless, Mona. Don't worry. He's a Safe Haven guest who arrived by ferry. I found him outside my door on the boardwalk after he fell on the ice."

"Damn! No way! You're messing with us, right? What time was this, because that is just completely impossi—"

Abigail Foster slapped a hand over her mouth, as if she'd said something she shouldn't have.

"What's going on?" Annie looked from one woman to the next, aware that the group's behavior was more odd than usual, if that were even possible.

"Nothing," Mona snapped. "So, how can we help you?"

Rowan answered her mother. "We need help lifting him and carrying him to Annie's bed."

"That shouldn't be a problem." Everyone removed their coats. Mona immediately went to Nathaniel's shoulders and propped him up. She assigned the legs and arms, then instructed others to put their hands under his back. Annie ran ahead to open her bedroom door and pull back the covers. She turned around in time to see the middle-aged mermaids stagger around with Nathaniel Ravelle's limp body, nearly banging his head on the wall in the process.

"He's slipping!" Abigail screeched.

"Hold on, ladies." Mona backed through the bedroom doorway and coordinated delivery. "This side of the bed, everyone. Hurry. On the count of three, let's swing him."

"No swinging, Mother!" Rowan yelled. "Just set him down gently."

Izzy grunted with effort. "We can't just set him down because we're all standing on the same side of the bed. He'd end up on the floor, and I'm sure as hell not going to pick him up again!"

"Yeah," Polly said.

"I'm gonna drop him!" Abigail screeched once again.

"Ready?" Mona nodded toward the bed. "Let's aim for as close to the middle as possible. One. Two. Three!"

"Oh Jesus. The lap rug!" Annie tried frantically to cover him but wasn't quick enough.

A silence fell over the room.

Izzy was the first to speak. "That boy's drawers are so wet, they're see-through," she said, looking slightly shell-shocked.

"I need another hot toddy," Polly said.

"Ladies, come with me to the kitchen, please." Mona began ushering her charges into the other room while speaking to Annie. "We'll make a pot of tea for when he wakes up. Anything else we can do for you?"

"Uh, I don't think—"

"We'll be back in just a jiff." Mona closed the bedroom door.

Annie shook her head. "They're up to no good."

Rowan snorted. "Of course they're up to no good. It's what they live for."

Annie put her hands on her hips and sighed. "Well, our guy can't get warm with wet boxers plastered to his body, so help me get them off. You hold up the comforter and I'll try to yank them off without looking."

"You always get the good jobs."

"Let's just get this over with, okay?" Annie shook her head. "Honestly, I feel uncomfortable touching a naked man I don't even know."

"Really?" Rowan held the comforter up and away, trying to suppress a laugh. "So who are you, exactly, and what have you done with my friend Annabeth Parker?"

"Shhh! Keep it down! I'm serious!" Mona herded the ladies through the kitchen, out the back door, and onto the covered porch. "Gather 'round, ye 'maids."

The women formed their sacred circle.

"I don't think this has ever happened before," Mona whispered. "Polly, you're chapter historian. Are you aware of another occasion when the Great Mermaid has acted almost instantly?"

"No." Polly screwed up her face in concentration. "Not unless we count the time Liz Tantillo's groom missed the ferry from Hyannis and the wedding was called off and she fell in love with the party rental guy from Martha's Vineyard only two hours after he petitioned the Great Mermaid to find him the girl of his dreams."

Izzy shook her head, clearly annoyed. "We've never formally ruled on that case and you know it."

"I know!" Polly looked hurt. "That's why I prefaced my analysis with the words 'not unless we count. . . .'"

"Never mind," Mona snapped. "All we can do is look at the facts, and the facts are: We petitioned the Great Mermaid to intervene on Annie's behalf, and less than an hour later there's a naked man in her bed. It cannot be a coincidence."

Everyone nodded in agreement.

"So this is unprecedented," Mona mumbled. "I'm at a loss here, ladies."

"If I may say something." Abigail glanced around hesitantly. "I think we're overlooking the most shocking part of the night's events."

Mona crossed her arms over her chest. "Go on. We're listening."

"Well, um . . ." Abigail's eyes widened. "Am I the only one who's noticed how . . . well . . . how *similar* this is to the origin of the Mermaid Legend?"

A collective gasp rose from the circle, and one by one, the ladies contributed to the discussion.

"A nor'easter!"

"An injured man!"

"Unconscious, even! Soaked to the skin!"

"And a lovely young woman brings him in and nurses him back to health!"

"Maids!" Mona lowered her voice to a raspy whisper. "This is huge. Mind-boggling, really. We must take the sacred pledge to never speak of tonight's intervention, not until Annie and ..." She stopped. "Does anyone know her heart-mate's name?"

All members shook their heads to the contrary.

"Well, anyway, not until Annie and Mr. Whozits are in a committed love relationship. No matter how long that takes. No matter if it's years. You know how vital this is. If even one of us breaks our pledge, their love will be lost and will never return, and I know none of us wants *that* on our heads."

Each woman placed her right hand above her left shell and recited the pledge of secrecy, their lips moving in silent unison, their expressions solemn.

"Mr. Ravelle? Nathaniel? Can you hear me?"

She was indescribably lovely, this vision, with very long dark blond hair and pale blue eyes. Her touch was gentle on his cheek and her voice sounded like soft music playing very far away. But where was he? Odd.... He was in a bed, but what bed? Whose bed? Was it hers? How did he get here? The smell of wood smoke floated into his nostrils. He felt light-headed and just a little unsteady. Was he ill? Drugged? *Dead?*

More female beings began to hover nearby. It was difficult to figure out what was happening, but they seemed to be bickering, nudging at one another, and peering at him curiously. There was something strange about these creatures. Their long hair seemed dull and thin. Why were they wearing shells? And what was that iridescent, shiny stuff below their waists? Were those *scales*?

"Fucking mermaids!"

Nat tried to sit up but couldn't. His plan was to force

himself awake and end what was obviously another work-related nightmare. He'd had them before—a Loch Ness Monster in his condo swimming pool, cute little werewolf pups free to a good home outside the Ace Hardware in Koreatown, zombie hairstylists at his neighborhood barbershop. This time, however, his eyes were wide open, but the paranormal populace of his dreams hadn't vanished. In fact, the creatures stared down at him like he was the only freak of nature in that room. One mermaid, who reminded him a little of his mother, looked as if she might cry.

"That was entirely uncalled for," she said.

Just then, Nat realized the reason he couldn't sit up was the wave of pain that rolled from his hips to his head via his spine. That's when he had a vague recollection of erotic chocolates and losing his footing on a slick sidewalk.

The lovely blond-haired vision shooed everyone away from the bed. She pulled up a small wooden chair and sat down near Nat's shoulder, touching him through the fluffy down comforter pulled up to his neck. "My name is Annie Parker, and you're in my house on Main Street. You fell on the boardwalk right outside my door. You've been unconscious for about fifteen minutes, but you're going to be fine."

He blinked. Nat raised his right arm and was relieved to see it move. This Annie woman smiled down at him and it had to have been one of the most divine smiles he'd ever seen. "So you're not an angel?"

A young woman standing near the fireplace snorted with laughter. "Got that right." She smiled at him, and Nat noticed she had normal, shoulder-length hair, a very cute face, and was most definitely not a mermaid. She walked to him and patted his arm. "Welcome to Bayberry Island. I'm Rowan Flynn and I run the Safe Haven B and B. We spoke on the phone. I think you were heading to my place when you wiped out on the ice."

Things were beginning to make sense. "Yeah. About that. The taxi didn't show, so I had no choice but to walk."

Rowan cringed. "I sincerely apologize. It's embarrassing to admit, but we have only one driver in the off-season, and he's pretty iffy, even when the weather is perfect."

"He smokes the wacky weed," someone volunteered.

Nat was almost afraid to look in the direction of the voice. Very slowly, his attention moved to the group of mermaids clustered near the doorway. His eyes traveled over way too much exposed, wrinkly skin, something not often seen in LA. He noticed how each of their stretchy, scaly skirts ended in a big fish tail opened at their ankles, revealing a collection of snow boots. One of the women clomped forward.

"Hello. I'm Mona Flynn, president of the Bayberry Island Mermaid Society. We were having an important meeting when my daughter, Rowan, called to ask us to help carry you to the bed. That's why we're in our costumes."

"We all chipped in," said another woman.

"That was very kind of you." Nat produced a quick smile before he had to look away. He would never be disrespectful to any woman of a certain age, but damn— there should be some sort of law forbidding the tying of shells to your boobs past the age of fifty. "Thank you, ladies," Nat said, seeking the safety of the pretty face of his guardian angel. "Uh, my things? My laptop? I had a video camera in my suitcase."

Her beatific smile appeared again. "Everything's right

next to the bed." She inclined her head and gazed at him with concern. "Unfortunately, we have only one full-time doctor between Martha's Vineyard, Nantucket, and Bayberry during the off-season, and she's not going to be able to get here until tomorrow because of the storm. But she's given me instructions on how to make you comfortable until she arrives. To rule out concussion, the doctor wants me to wake you every couple hours to check on your mental state."

"You might want to check the rest of the island while you're at it," Rowan said.

Right then, Nat became aware that soft flannel sheets touched his warm, bare skin—*everywhere*. That meant that he was naked. "Excuse me." He didn't know to whom he should address the question, so he looked to Annie Parker. "Do you know what happened to my clothes?"

"Time to go!" The head mermaid ushered her group out the doorway while they all waved and told him to feel better soon. Annie's friend Rowan said her good nights, too, and asked Annie to call her in the morning.

Suddenly, the house was still. Annie remained in the chair at his side, smiling sweetly. She was incredibly beautiful. He was completely nude. At any other time, this wouldn't have disturbed him.

"We had to remove your clothes, Mr. Ravelle. I apologize for taking those liberties, but you were soaked to the skin, and the doctor said getting you warm and dry was our first priority." Annie appeared the slightest bit sheepish. "We tried our best not to look."

Nat laughed. "We?"

"Rowan and I."

"So not the entire mermaid population of the island?"

Annie laughed, too. It was a lyrical sound, and it

seemed to fill the room with light and happiness. It wasn't a girl's giggle — it was full, womanly laughter, and he loved it. He couldn't help but stare at her. He simply couldn't take his eyes off her.

"I have a couple questions, if you don't mind," she said.

"Yes."

"So you *do* mind?"

"I don't mind. But I figured we'd save time and let you know that my answer to anything you might ask is yes."

She chuckled. "Moving right along, are you allergic to cats? Do you have any food or medicine allergies I should know about?"

"Yes. I'm very single."

Annie's face froze. For a moment, he feared he'd gone too far, too fast. He didn't know what had gotten into him. Nat was usually so cool around women that he'd been informed on more than one occasion that he came off as disinterested even when the opposite was true. So this type of flirtatious, pushy come-on was, well, it was truly weird.

He watched Annie's cheeks redden as she averted her eyes, but she couldn't stop the smile from forming on her full lips. "Good to know," she said, looking at him again. "And what about the actual questions I asked?"

"Oh. Cats are fine. Not allergic to anything that I know of."

"Good." Annie glanced toward the floor and patted her knee, and the biggest black cat Nat had ever seen thudded onto her lap. "This is Ezra. He might jump in bed with you tonight, so be forewarned."

Nat felt his eyes widen. "Just so long as he promises not to smother me in my sleep."

Annie laughed again. "Yeah. He gets a little chunky

in the winter months." She put the cat on the floor once more, but he immediately hopped up on the bed and found a spot against Nat's right thigh. "I'll go get you some water and Tylenol, which is what the doctor suggested, and I need to call her. She asked me to let her know when you woke up." She patted his shoulder as she stood. "I should be back in just a minute. Yell if you need anything."

It was so wrong. Nat was flat on his back and in pain and had no idea where his clothes were, but the only thing he cared about was how this woman moved, how graceful her arms swayed as she walked, how firm and luscious her thighs were in those jeans, and how he could almost feel her perfect bottom cupped in his hands.

Nat became vaguely uncomfortable and turned to see Ezra glaring at him, his yellow kitty eyes narrowed into slits. "My bad," he whispered to the cat.

3

Nathaniel seemed more comfortable since he'd spoken with the doctor, took his pain reliever, and was propped up on a stack of pillows. Annie had already apologized to him about her bed—the mattress and box springs were brand-new, but the scrolled wrought iron of the antique headboard wasn't exactly designed for lounging. She'd helped him into one of Todd the Bod's left-behind sweatshirts. Nat had been embarrassed that it hurt to lift his arms over his head, but Annie hadn't minded one bit because it gave her an excuse to touch him. The feel of his solid, warm flesh had sent a shiver of sensual awareness through her.

Annie was pretty comfortable herself. She'd moved her writing chair into the bedroom near Nat and lit a hot cedar and oak fire in the bedroom fireplace. She sat with her feet curled up under her and a cup of tea cradled in her hands. She studied the subtle details of his face and enjoyed the rich, deep tone of his voice as he talked.

Nat had a husky, happy laugh. She'd become fascinated by the way his thick brown hair had curled at the nape of his neck as it dried. She noticed his eyes were a dusky sea green, heavy lidded, and accented by dark lashes and brows. She decided the shape of his face wasn't exactly square, but it wasn't round—it was a perfect, masculine combination of curves and planes, washed in gold by the firelight and the small bedside lamp.

It was strange. Annie wasn't the type to be transfixed by a man. Sure, she'd been ferociously attracted to men before—about one man a year, to be exact—but she'd never understood when her friends would claim they could barely breathe in the presence of a certain man. That kind of talk had always struck her as ridiculous. At thirty-one, Annie certainly had known her share of hot and fun-loving men, but no one had ever caused her respiratory system to go on the fritz.

Tonight, though, something unusual was going on inside her. Whatever it was had affected her pulse rate, the temperature of her skin, and okay—her breathing, too. In fact, she felt a little shaky, like her nerve endings were too sensitive. If she were alone, she'd assume she was coming down with the flu.

Annie continued to gaze at Nat Ravelle, unaware of how much time had passed. They'd certainly touched on a lot of background information during their chat— childhood highlights, family, college, hobbies, work—but none of it in any real depth. She kept waiting to hear some tidbit about Nathaniel that would bring her back to the practical skepticism for which she was known, the ability to cross a man off her "maybe" list with absolute certainty and never look back.

But so far, nothing. In fact, the opposite seemed to be happening. Everything she'd heard made her want to know more. Nat had earned his bachelor's in film and TV. He was smart and funny and was still close to his family. He'd ended a long-term relationship about a year before and had decided to be happy on his own for a while. If the right woman came his way, he said he'd try his best to be open to the possibilities, but he wasn't looking.

In other words, he just kept getting better and better. This had to stop.

"So do you enjoy your job with *Truly Weird*?" Annie figured that question would put an end to her infatuation with the handsome stranger. She long ago decided that the island had reached its maximum crazy-person load, and she would not sleep with an imported supernatural-loving lunatic of a man, no matter how stunningly attractive he might be. So she braced herself for his answer. This is where he'd tell her he'd seen the yeti with his own eyes and had since devoted his life to the pursuit of the unexplained. He would say he was honored to come to Bayberry to witness the awesome power of the mermaid.

Instead, he howled with laughter.

"Here's the thing," he said, once his outburst had died down. "I hate my job. I hate everything about it, and I've already decided that as soon as I get back to LA, I'm going to find something else. I took the gig only after I lost my previous job, which I happened to have loved."

"Oh?" Annie took a sip of her tea. "And what was that?"

"I made music videos. I'd been working for a production company but had a major falling out with the owner and got my ass fired." He shrugged his shoulder and immediately winced with discomfort. "LA is notorious for stuff like that. You just have to catch the waves when they're good. I never intended to keep the *Weird* job as long as I have, and I've definitely hit the wall."

"Actually, you hit the boardwalk."

Nat chuckled. "Don't I know it."

"So making music videos was your dream job? Is that what you've always wanted to do?"

Nat shook his head. "Not really. It was fun and it was a wonderful experience, but I went to film school because I want to produce and direct documentaries. That's my real passion, I guess you could say."

For a moment, the two of them said nothing. They simply looked at each other. Annie waited for the inevitable awkwardness that comes when strangers lock eyes for too long and the rawness of it become unbearable. That moment never arrived. Instead, the experience mellowed, and as the seconds ticked by, it seemed as if they'd reached some kind of understanding.

"Can I ask you something?" Nat tipped his head and grinned at her.

Honest to God, that smile was magical. Annie felt like she was under some kind of spell every time it was pointed in her direction. She swallowed hard and responded with a croak. "Sure."

"Please be assured that I mean no offense, but there are a couple questions I need to ask. I want to make sure I understand something."

Annie put her mug of tea on the bedside table and wrapped her arms around her knees, thinking this couldn't be headed anywhere good. "Go right ahead. If I can answer you, I will."

Nat glanced up at the ceiling, then took a breath. "Look, I know Bayberry Island is synonymous with the Mermaid legend, and I respect that." He leveled his gaze with hers once more. "I realize it's tied to the history of this place, but, well, do you ever wonder if maybe it's just a bunch of bullshit?"

It was Annie's turn to guffaw. Nat looked a little surprised by her reaction, so she held up her hand to assure him she was almost done with her outburst. She finished with a sigh. "You're asking me if I've been drinking the local Kool-Aid."

"I wouldn't put it that—"

"No, Nat. I don't *wonder* if it's a bunch of bullshit—I *know* it is. Just because I was born on the island and have lived here most of my life doesn't mean I'm a head case."

A faint smile broke out on his face. "I guess I'm happy to hear that."

"Rest assured we're not all certifiable around here. Mona and her groupies? Yeah, they're pretty out there, but it's harmless, you know? They just run around in their spandex and blather on about true love and mystical forces and all that crap. But they don't hurt anybody."

Nat was visibly relieved.

"I wish I could say that the Mermaid Society is the weirdest thing on this island, but that would be a lie. There's also another group of older ladies who call themselves the Fairie Brigade. They wear Tinker Bell outfits with big-ass wings."

Nat's eyes bugged out. "Are you kidding?"

"No. And the Fairies are usually up in arms with the Mermaids about something or other. Lately, it's been the resort plans for the island, and it's getting really nasty."

"What resort?"

"Well, there's a Boston real estate developer who wants to turn much of the north beach into a vacation resort—a championship golf course, a hotel and casino, and a big, swanky marina. The Mermaids are against it and the Fairies are for it. At a recent zoning hearing, one of the Fairies got into it with one of the Mermaids, and there was some hair-pulling and face-scratching going on. The police were called."

Nat howled with laughter. "This is great! Please tell me they were in costume at the time."

Annie laughed, too. "They were. It provided some much-needed comic relief, let me tell you. So if you add all this development drama to our baseline Mermaid Festival madness—the parades and the plays and the costume contests and the drunken, naked beach parties—you've got yourself an interesting little island."

Nat went very still. "This would make an incredible documentary," he said, mostly to himself. "Do you know if anyone's ever done one?"

Annie thought for a minute. "I don't think so."

"Obviously, I was too quick to judge." Nat shook his head. "I barely read any of the advance material our researcher put together for this trip because I just couldn't face the crazy. But it sounds like this time the crazy is crazy good."

"I can't say I blame you for not wanting to read about us." Annie stretched her arms over her head, just then realizing how long she'd been seated and how stiff she'd become. "Unfortunately, when you live here, the crazy is sort of inescapable. Plus, it's the way I make my living."

"Yeah. About that." Nat situated himself so he was sitting up taller, a sure sign that his pain was subsiding. "The truth is, I might not have fallen if I hadn't walked by your shop."

"How do you figure that?"

"Your sign for adult desserts and erotic novels distracted me and I lost my footing."

"Ah." Annie felt her face flush and took the opportunity to get up from the armchair and add more logs to the fire. She remained with her back to Nat for as long as possible. She was embarrassed! How bizarre! It surely wasn't the first time she'd heard a man's flirtatious commentary about her particular brand of tourist tchotchkes. In fact, she had a whole list of standard responses designed for every variety of male customer, from the sweet and shy to the complete ass. But she'd never been truly *embarrassed*. Maybe that was because she'd never cared what a man thought of her wares—if the guy wanted to buy something, great, but if not, fine—until this very second.

Annie straightened, seeing her reflection in the antique mirror over the mantel. It wasn't the only reflection she saw. Nathaniel Ravelle was staring at her booty like a starving man eyeing a center-cut pork chop. She whipped around. "Are you hungry, Nat?"

He looked up, not in the least bit ashamed that he'd just had his eyes glued to her ass. "You have no idea."

Sure, his answer could be interpreted more than one way, but the flirting didn't worry her. What worried her was how she'd just offered her guest something to eat when she had almost nothing in the house. Her weekly off-season grocery delivery was due in from the mainland in the morning. Talk about embarrassed.

Annie returned to her chair and leaned her elbows on her knees. "How hungry are you, exactly?"

"Starving." He wigged his eyebrows. "I haven't eaten since I left LA, maybe ten hours ago or more."

"Oh great." Annie caught herself. "Sorry. Don't mean to be snippy. It's just that I wasn't expecting company, and my groceries are being flown in from the Cape in the morning—and that's only if the weather breaks. In the meantime, the pickings are slim."

Nat served up one of his magical smiles, stretching his hand toward her. Without thinking, Annie took it. His fingers were long and smooth. His flesh was warm. And that simple touch was enough to make her yearn for more—more smooth and warm flesh, to be exact. His naked flesh. His naked flesh pressing against her naked flesh, everywhere there was naked flesh to be found on their two bodies.

Annie gasped, yanking her hand away like she'd just been electrocuted. She stood again and headed for the kitchen. "I'll go see what I've got."

"Annie."

She stopped, her fingers gripping the thick, painted trim of her bedroom doorway. She needed to get ahold of herself. On any other night she would be her usual, reasonable self. Her behavior would be casual and friendly. Her voice would be relaxed and her hands steady. But there was nothing usual about the way Nat made her feel, which was nuts. It occurred to Annie that there was a very good reason why she'd never allowed a man to have this kind of effect on her—she hated not being in control of her emotions.

So she didn't dare turn around when she finally answered Nat. "Yes?"

"Are you all right?"

"I'm fine. I'll be right back." She took one step before Nat spoke again.

"If I interrupted your plans for tonight, I apologize."

"No plans. Would you like to listen to some music while I'm in the kitchen?"

"Sure."

In a seamless series of motions, Annie grabbed her iPod and earbuds from the sitting room, tossed them to the bed—nearly hitting a half-awake Ezra in the skull—and scurried out of the room. She closed the kitchen door and called Rowan.

The raspy sound of her friend's greeting revealed that she'd been asleep.

"I'm sorry I woke you," Annie said, rubbing her forehead as she paced the small kitchen. "I don't even know what time it is."

"It's . . . hold on . . . it's twelve forty-five. Are you all right? Is Nathaniel all right?"

"Fine. We're fine. No, wait—he's fine. Really, really fine. I'm a wreck."

"Uh-oh." Annie heard Rowan sit up in bed and feel around for the lamp switch. "What's going on, sweetie?"

"I've never acted so stupid in my life!"

"Stupid?"

"Yeah! Goofy. Peculiar. I'm so nervous around Nat that I can't think straight. It's like I've lost my damn mind!"

"I'm sure you're exaggerating."

"I'm not! Seriously, when have you ever known me to get all shaky and unsure of myself around a guy?"

Rowan chuckled. "I've got two words for you— Fletcher Vickers."

Annie closed her eyes and sighed. "That was sixth grade. I hadn't hit my stride yet."

"All right, well, Nathaniel is pretty damn cute. Maybe that's all it is."

"Every man I've ever had in my bed has been pretty damn cute!"

Rowan paused a moment before she spoke again. "You have a point. All right. Let me get dressed. I'll be over there in a few minutes."

"No!"

"But . . ." Rowan chuckled. "Let me get this straight, Annie. You called because you're all jacked up over some dude in your bed, but you don't want me to come

over and help you out? Why? Do you need privacy because you're planning on having sex with him?"

Annie stopped pacing. "Of course not," she hissed.

"Then relax. Maybe it's PMS."

Annie opened the refrigerator and took stock of what
she had on hand. One egg. Some butter. About two ta-
blespoons of milk. Wilted salad greens. She went over to
the pantry and began moving cans and plastic storage
containers around, getting more frustrated by the second. "It's not PMS, but I'm telling you, something's
wrong with me."

"Maybe you're in love. You know, some of that good,
old-fashioned mermaid voodoo kind of *luuuuv*." Rowan
started to snicker. "Hey, I bet that's it! The Bayberry Island Mermaid has finally slapped some major mojo on
you! You took one look at the adorable Nathaniel Ravelle
and your heart leaped for joy! You suddenly lost all—"

"Good night, Rowan."

"Good night, Annabeth. You'll be fine. Call me if you
need to talk more. Love you."

"Love you, too." Annie set baking ingredients on the
counter, frowning at the limited possibilities. "Hey wait.
I really am sorry I woke you up, Row."

"Oh, please, woman. How many times have I woken
you up in the last year crying my guts out? Compared to
me, you're so sane you're boring."

"Ha! Good night." Annie stuck her phone in her
pocket and headed back into the bedroom to inform Nat
of his menu options. The instant she reached the doorway and saw him, she felt dizzy with delight. Nathaniel's
head was tipped back and resting on the pillows. His
eyes were closed. He was listening to music on her iPod
and his fingers stroked Ezra, now curled up on his stom-

ach and purring so loudly the house vibrated. A heat slowly spread from her belly into her chest.

The man was *beautiful*.

She must have sighed out loud because Nat partially opened his eyes and gave her a sleepy grin. He pulled the headphones from his ears. "You have very eclectic music tastes, Miss Parker."

"Oh yeah? What did you settle on?"

"Well, your Snoop Dogg catalog definitely called out to me, but in honor of Bayberry Island and its claim to fame, I picked Debussy's *La Mer.*"

Annie leaned against the doorframe and crossed her arms under her breasts. "You're funny. It's an LA sort of funny."

He laughed. "Thank you."

"Would you like to hear the evening's à la carte choices?"

"Please."

"Tonight's appetizer special is peanut butter on saltines. Entrées are either the canned baked beans, an omelet made with freezer-burned spinach and the only egg in the place, or, if you can hold out a little longer, I've got all the ingredients to bake you a small mermaid cake, which would be our catch of the day."

One of Nat's eyebrows arched high on his forehead. "I'll have the peanut butter appetizer and the mermaid entrée, please."

"Of course."

"And I'd like to help you." Nat smiled shyly. "I'm not in anywhere near as much pain as I was and could probably move around a little."

"Oh no, you don't." Annie walked to the side of the bed and tucked the comforter around him. "The doctor said you shouldn't move more than what is absolutely necessary."

"I feel uncomfortable having you wait on me."

Annie giggled. "I'm just baking a cake for an injured man. It's no big deal."

As she returned to the kitchen, she reminded herself that it wouldn't be a big deal except for one small detail—she'd never baked anyone a single-serving mermaid cake unless they were willing to shell out $7.95 in the form of cash, debit, or credit.

Ev-*er*.

4

Nat swam up from the depths of sleep, opening his eyes to a familiar vision peering at him—long blond hair, blue eyes, angelic smile. It hadn't been a dream.

"Are you still hungry?"

Suddenly, he became aware of a crushing weight on his chest. He tried to breathe but found it difficult. "What the—?" Nat looked down into the narrow, golden eyes of the corpulent cat named Ezra, and everything started to come back to him. "Oh man. Sorry, Annie. I must have dozed off."

"You did," she said, her voice gentle. "I let you sleep while the cake cooled enough to frost, but I was about to wake you for your mental status check."

He laughed a little, pushing himself up. He noted the twinge of discomfort at the base of his spine, but the rest of him was much looser. The sleep and the pain reliever had probably helped relax his muscles. "And yes, I'm still hungry. I can't wait to find out what goes into making an adults-only mermaid cake."

Annie placed a laptop computer on the floor next to her chair. She'd obviously been writing while he slept,

161

which reminded him that he needed to make sure his secret was still safe. Very slowly, he stretched his arm along his side and under his left thigh, verifying that the paperback remained hidden from sight. It had been a close call earlier when Annie had fiddled with the comforter. She'd nearly caught him reading *Ship of Surrender.*

"You good, Nat?"

"Great, thanks."

She stood, looking down at him with the faintest frown between her brows. "If you say so. More tea with your cake?"

"Please."

Nat kept his head still while shifting his eyes to watch her leave. Ever so slowly, he grasped the book with his fingers and began to slide it up along the flannel sheet. Just as the paperback was about to clear the edge of the comforter, Annie poked her head back in the room.

"Any preference?"

Nat froze. "Yes. I mean, no. Whatever kind of tea you've got is fine."

"You sure you're okay? Maybe I should call the doctor."

All this chatter had disturbed Ezra, who suddenly rose up, stretched, and decided it was a great time to begin kneading the comforter. Before Nat could do anything to prevent it, the big cat had pulled the covers down just enough to expose the corner of a hot-pink book cover.

Busted.

Annie placed a hand over her mouth to hide her smile, but it didn't work. By now Nat knew that his benefactor's smiles engaged her whole face, from her cheeks to her nose to her eyes to her forehead. And clearly, she found the situation hilarious. "That was the very first book I ever wrote. How far have you gotten?"

"Uh . . ." Nat let his head fall back on the pillows. "Well, the captain and mermaid are just about to get busy."

Annie laughed. She marched over to the side of the bed and grabbed the paperback, letting it drop to his lap. "That doesn't narrow things down much, since that plot twist occurs every twenty pages or so. If you're good, maybe I'll read some to you while you eat your cake."

With that, she leaned down, planted a chaste kiss on his cheek, and left the room, leaving a sweet-smelling breeze in her wake.

"Damn." Nat raised a hand to his face and touched the spot she'd just kissed. It tingled. It felt hot. His chest felt tight. He figured he was either having a stroke or was falling for Annie. He slapped himself for good measure.

Something wasn't right. He felt almost as if he were drunk, which of course he wasn't. Even a concussion couldn't account for the variety of odd sensations coursing through him at that moment. This was about Annie Parker. He was sure of it. She was somehow doing this to him. Yesterday, he was fine. Today, he was off balance, like a sailor having to walk on solid ground after months at sea. And what was the difference between yesterday and today? Annie Parker and her mermaid erotica and her charming old seaside cottage and fragrant flannel sheets and her pornographic cakes. Not since high school had Nat lost himself in a woman, and since that was also the only time he'd been blindsided by heartache, once had been enough.

Nat stared toward the empty doorway, listening carefully for the return of the Bayberry Island temptress. Enough of this helpless invalid shit, he decided. He needed to regain his mental composure and physical strength. Because without those things, a man was vulnerable to being seduced by the first woman he encountered who happened to be extremely pretty, kind, smelled good, and lived in a quaint but funky house by the sea with a real Christmas tree in the main room and natural evergreen boughs hung along the fireplace mantels.

Nat decided to test his body to gauge his physical condition. He gently raised and lowered his shoulders and rotated at the waist. He gingerly bent forward and reached for his toes. And then, when he was sure he was able, Nat pressed his hands down into the mattress and raised his body off the bed. Sure, it hurt a little, but a typical longboard wipeout at Venice Beach hurt a lot worse. He was fine.

"Here you are," she said, returning with a plate piled high with cake, a fork, and a mug of steaming tea.

Nat lowered himself back to the mattress.

"Are you sure you're comfortable enough to sit up to eat? You can have some more Tylenol if you need it."

"I'm good for the moment. Thanks, Annie."

She placed the tea on the table and handed Nat the plate. He almost dropped it. There, staring up at him, was a serving of sex and chocolate—a voluptuous mermaid with her tail flipping and her breasts pouting and her only covering a set of strategically placed jujubes poking up from fudge frosting. He stared a long time. "Annie?"

"Yes?"

He looked up at her. "I don't know whether to eat her or ask her out."

Annie laughed, and as hungry as Nat was and as tasty as the cake appeared, he could do nothing but gaze at his angel of mercy. As he blinked in wonder, a few things occurred to him. Her beauty was 100 percent natural. She didn't need haute couture—she looked hot as hell in that old wool sweater and jeans. There wasn't a streak of makeup on her. Her hair was flowing and shiny and thick, and though it was quite long, it was her own actual hair growing from her own actual scalp. No Botox had paralyzed her forehead. No collagen had been shoved into her lips. Her nose hadn't been whittled down to toddler proportions. And her breasts—those full, round, bouncy breasts—those babies had come from the man upstairs and not a plastic surgeon with second-floor offices overlooking Rodeo Drive. It was almost a shock to Nat's system.

Annie grabbed the pink paperback from the bed. "Should I start reading just any-old-where?"

"I was on page fourteen, to be real honest with you." Nat slid his fork into a fluffy matrix of chocolate mermaid scales. "The first mate had just yelled to the captain that all was lost." He was noticing that his confession seemed to please Annie just as he raised the fork to his mouth and the cake landed on his tongue.

Oh God. It was *really good.* The flavor was rich and deep, the consistency was as fluffy as cotton candy, and it melted in his mouth almost as fast. Nat's brain began to buzz with sensual delight as Annie's sweet voice filled the room.

"Could no one else see her? Oh, but how could that be? She was immediately there, portside, surrounded in a storm-tossed halo of light. The exotic creature's long hair fanned out around her in the waves, and her eyes bored into the captain's soul. Somehow, he knew she'd come to save him. Somehow, he knew his crew would not perish on that dark and treacherous night, and perhaps even his heart and soul would be saved from eternal emptiness."

"Oh, that's damn good stuff," Nat mumbled, his mouth full.

"The cake or the story?"

"Both. Keep going. But you can skip to a juicy part if you want."

Annie chuckled and thumbed through the pages. Nat figured she knew every word by heart and must get a lot of satisfaction from reading one of her own books. Just then, she groaned in frustration.

"What's wrong?"

"There's one particular scene that I think you'll like, but I can't find it. I don't remember where it is."

Nat thought that was odd. "Don't you have the whole thing memorized?"

She laughed loudly and looked up from the book. "I can't even remember writing this, to tell you the truth. It was six years ago, and once I've published something in electronic format or send it off to be printed, I don't read it again. I keep books handy in case I have a continuity question, but that's it."

His fork stopped in midair. He smiled. "I understand."

"You do?" She looked surprised.

"Yes. When I finish final edits on a film, I have to let it go. I can't keep watching it over and over because it will just make me insane—I'll always find a hundred things I wish I'd done just a little differently, just a little bit better."

"Exactly," Annie said, tilting her head as if she were fascinated by what he said. "When you're done, it doesn't belong to you anymore. It belongs to the reader—or the viewer, in your case—and you have no business hanging around looking over their shoulder as they experience it."

Nat felt himself blink. He knew he was staring again. But this was so strange that he couldn't help himself. His beliefs about his work had always been his own, and he'd rarely met others who felt the same way. But now Annie was echoing his philosophy exactly. The whole night's events had been odd. It was almost as if a force had brought Annie and him together, the sound of the cosmic *click* so loud that everyone on earth had to have heard it.

"Do you want me to keep reading?"

Nat just smiled.

"Hey! I found it!"

"That's excellent news."

As Annie's sweet voice rang out once more, Nat raised his fork and placed another delicate morsel into his mouth, wondering if there was such a thing as too much pleasure, too much joy, and wondering if he might be ready to find out.

"Captain Smythe ran his palms up the exquisite creature's smooth and rounded hips, fascinated by how her scales had dissolved in the heat of the hearth. He was a man of science. He understood the sea, the stars, and the magnetic pull of God's earth. But the idea that her mermaid features had simply disappeared was fantastical, almost too bizarre to be believed. Yet how could he deny the truth? She had saved him and all his men from certain death. It was by her hand and her light that their boat arrived safely on shore.

"At that moment, however, Captain Smythe was aware he couldn't be bothered with science. His eyes beheld a thing of impossible mystery and beauty, her female nature exposed and open to him, beautiful and glistening in the firelight."

When Nat dropped his fork to the plate, it made a terrible crashing sound. Annie stopped reading. Nat was breathing hard. "Sorry." He swallowed, not sure if it marked the end of the cake or his life as he knew it. "Please go on."

"I can't." Her cheeks reddened.

Nat put the empty plate on the side table. "Don't be shy. It's a beautiful story."

"No. It's really not." Annie shook her head and closed the book. "I use that word way too much."

Nat was puzzled. "What word?"

"'Glistening.' Over and over in all my novels, the mermaids *glisten* their asses off. They glisten in the sand. Glisten in the bed. Glisten on the deck of the sailing vessel. I can't believe I've been so careless about that! It's just lazy writing."

"You're too hard on yourself." Nat smiled and touched the top of Annie's hand. The brush of his fingers on her warm skin produced an electric flash that traveled to his core. He wanted her. He wanted her like he'd never wanted any woman, and it was a strange and crazy and completely illogical desire. It was almost as if he wasn't in charge of his own life! "Maybe we can brainstorm," he managed to say.

Annie's eyes widened. "You want to brainstorm with me?"

"Why not?" He began to stroke the top of her hand with his fingers. "I bet there are a hundred ways a mermaid can glisten."

"You think?"

"Sure. For starters, she can shimmer or shine."

Annie started to breathe hard. "I guess they can."

"Anything is possible."

Very slowly, Annie rotated her hand so that her soft palm was laid open to his fingertips. That was a gesture any man could decipher. It was about as subtle as a hard slam on an icy boardwalk. Annie had just offered herself to him. Simple as that. Nat felt the comforter rise, and he didn't give a damn whether she saw it. She needed to see it. His own breathing became shallow.

"Or she could be moist," Annie whispered.

Nat insinuated his finger up inside fuzzy cuff of her

sweater. The inside of her wrist felt tender and hot to the touch.

Annie gasped.

"She could glow," Nat said, deciding to take her up on her overtly sexual offer. He brought her wrist toward him with one hand while pushing the sweater up to her elbow with the other. Slowly, so slowly, he lifted her arm to his mouth and lowered his lips to the delicate tendons and bones of her inner wrist.

Annie whimpered. "Or, maybe she's just wet."

Fuck. Nat's focus began to narrow as the comforter expanded. He removed his lips momentarily. "Drenched."

"Dripping."

He introduced the tip of his tongue to her skin, then left openmouthed kisses from her wrist to the crook of her elbow. He looked up at her. "Maybe she's soaked."

"You're very creative, Nat."

"Take your clothes off and get in this bed with me."

"Why?"

"So I can show you just how creative I am."

With that, his kind and sweet caretaker reclaimed her arm from his mouth, stood by the edge of the bed, crossed her hands at her lower belly, and yanked the sweater up over her head. The move displayed a tight white T-shirt, which revealed every aroused and puckered detail of her body that the sweater had hidden.

"Wow."

She smiled down at him, her thick blond hair falling over one all-natural breast. "Do you think you have the strength to help me get out of these clothes?"

"I'll die trying." Nat sat up and splayed his fingers across her tight belly. Then he fingered the button of her jeans, releasing their stretch across her hips. Just for fun, he slapped his hands on her ass and pulled her closer, using his teeth to open the zipper. And even as they both laughed, an outlandish but dead-serious thought wafted through his mind: *This is how perfection feels—the sun on his face, the wind in the spinnaker, the water rushing by, all the forces of nature in concert as he's delivered to his one true destination.*

Nat pulled at Annie's pants, his eyes flashing as a bare strip of tummy was revealed, then pale blue-green panties, then the tops of her thighs. He pressed his lips to all those places, one by one, tasting the sun and the wind, smelling the salty air, hearing the crash of waves inside his head. Annie suddenly pulled away. He felt privileged to watch her get rid of the jeans and socks, then the T-shirt, leaving her in only the sheer panties and the even sheerer bra. When she began to climb up on the bed and straddle his legs, Nat's mouth went dry.

Something large poked into his ribs, and Nat saw that Ezra was still there, annoyed that the bed had become crowded. This presented a dilemma. He needed to lose the cat without alienating the nearly naked cat owner now perched on his upper thighs looking sexy as hell.

"Beat it, dude," Annie said, lifting the animal. Ezra immediately jumped from her hands to the comfortable chair, where he shot a nasty look Nat's way before getting settled.

"I'm impressed," he said, stroking Annie's silky thighs.

"Oh yeah?" She pushed her hands up under the sweatshirt, caressing his stomach. With care not to jar him, she lifted each arm from each sleeve, then pulled the sweatshirt over his head. The pleasure of her gentle touch was so intense that Nat moaned out loud.

"What impresses you most?" she asked, tossing the shirt to the floor.

Nat chuckled. "I hardly know where to begin, but it

was really impressive how you tossed your cat to the chair. Not all women would do that."

"Really?" Annie placed her hands on the mattress near Nat's head, then leaned close. Her eyes sparkled and her mouth twitched. The instant her soft lips made contact with the side of his neck, Nat moaned even louder. He closed his eyes and continued his shameless moaning as her kisses traveled to his collarbone, up his throat, to his jawline and the side of his face. The kissing stopped abruptly, and Nat opened his eyes to see her smiling down at him. "I don't know what kind of girls you've been hanging out with, Nat, but I have a strict rule—only one pussy is allowed in this bed when I have company."

Nat laughed hard. She laughed with him.

He reached for her hair. It was the first time he'd touched it, and it felt like water flowing between his fingertips. Eventually, their laughter slowed, then stopped. When Nat looked into Annie's eyes, a rush of emotion hit him so hard that his chest felt like it would burst into flames. It took him a moment to pull himself together.

"Any other rules I should know about, Miss Parker?" Nat dropped her hair and smoothed it against her shoulder, then ran his hands along her sides, her ribs, her back muscles, her soft belly.

Annie arched into his touch and made a humming sound. "I usually have a lot of rules."

As he noted her use of the word "usually," Nat moved his hands to her thighs again, but this time he dared look between them. It was obvious that mermaids weren't the only females glistening around here. "Like what?"

"You really want to know?"

"I do." His fingers strayed to the silky flesh of her inner thighs, and he stroked her there.

"I have a one-man-per-year rule," she said, her voice suddenly matter-of-fact instead of teasing and seductive. "I pick one at the beginning of the tourist season and ask him to stay with me for the summer. Then I kick him out in the fall."

Nat's mouth fell open. He had to concentrate in order to snap it shut again. "Seriously?"

"Yes. Rowan teases me about it all the time, but I've decided that's the way I want it to be."

"Why?"

She shrugged. Something about the movement revealed a vulnerability he hadn't yet seen in her. He knew to proceed with caution. "You can tell me, Annie."

She looked away, giving Nat a chance to study her profile. She was stunning. She was also a little sad. "It's just safer that way," she said, still not making eye contact. "We both know ahead of time that there's a beginning and an end and there's no room for unrealistic expectations. Nobody gets hurt."

Something about this didn't make sense to Nat. "But isn't summer the time of year that you have the least amount of time to spend with someone?"

She turned, looking his way again. Nat could see tears forming in her eyes. "That's the point."

Breath whooshed out of him. "That's harsh."

"It is."

"But you're breaking that rule with me?"

"In a big way." It was obvious that Annie was struggling with her emotions, too. "I let you in my house four days before Christmas. I let you in my bed. I actually want to spend time with you. And you're . . ." She stopped.

"I'm what?"

"Different." A tear fell onto her cheek. "I want you. I

want you here. I want us both to have expectations, which is completely insane because I live here and you live in LA, and anyway, I don't even know you."

"Come here, Annie." Nat opened his arms and felt her body lay against his. He caressed her back as he spoke, aware of her diaphragm moving as she breathed, the heat of her skin, how truly wonderful and unexpected all of it was. "If it makes you feel any better, I broke a rule with you, too."

"Really?" She squeezed him tight with her thighs but kept her face hidden against his neck, where she cried softly. "Tell me, Nat."

"It's my only rule, really, but it's hard and fast."

Annie wrapped her arms under his back, so that she was clutching him. "It must be an important one."

"It is." Nat pulled her closer. They were locked as tight as pieces at the center of a puzzle. "I never let myself get lost in a woman. What I mean is, I never allow myself to get in so deep that I lose control of the situation. It happened to me only once, when I was very young, and I promised myself it would never happen again."

Annie stiffened in his arms. A long moment later, he felt her exhale, relax, and push herself up and away from him. She looked bewildered.

"What's going on here, Nat?"

"I have no freaking idea."

"We haven't even kissed yet."

He smiled, deciding now was the perfect time to try out his strength. Without giving her any warning, Nat grabbed Annie, rolled with her, and flipped her onto her back. If it weren't for the fact that the covers were now twisted around them, it would have been a flawless execution of a fairly complicated maneuver.

"What the—?"

Nat covered her mouth with his, letting his lips and his tongue tell her that everything would be all right, that no matter what was happening to them, it was all right because it was completely, magically, insanely, 100 percent mutual.

He shoved his hands in her hair. He tried to use his legs to open hers, but the covers were a tangled mess. Nat removed his mouth long enough to rip the bedclothes from both their bodies and then start in on Annie's underwear. He couldn't help but laugh at her stunned, but happy, expression as he removed her bra and panties like a man who didn't have a second to spare.

Because right then, Nat knew that he'd wasted too many seconds in his life. He would make up for every one of them. Starting now.

5

"What if you hurt yourself?"

"I'm fine."

"But the doctor said to stay in bed."

"I am in bed. With you. And we're both naked."

"But—"

"Shh."

Nat ended Annie's objections by lowering his lips to hers. The slick, sweet heat of his kiss left her so weak that all she could do was moan. The kiss felt decadent. Reckless. Which brought her right back to reality.

"I'm worried this might make things worse and—" Her words were muffled by his continuing kiss, and she felt something hard and long poke into her belly. Nat sure didn't appear to be physically impaired. In fact, he seemed robustly healthy. Gifted, even.

"I want you, Annie." He pressed her wrists against the mattress and continued to leave soft and leisurely kisses along her neck, shoulders, and chest. "I want to make love to you. I want you to call out my name and beg for more. I want you to *glisten,* baby."

Annie chuckled, knowing she'd long ago passed the

glistening stage, sure he knew it, too. Her laughter turned into a gasp of pleasure the instant his soft lips brushed the top of her left breast, then her right. Involuntarily, she began to wiggle and arch up beneath him. When Nat gently bit down on a nipple and sucked, she nearly shot off the bed.

"You like that, huh?" Nat moved on to the other nipple. His hands left her wrists and traveled up into her hair again, then down her arms to her sides, eventually settling on her hips. Annie felt his fingers claim her flesh as he pressed his weight—and his way-above-average erection—into her stomach. Nat's touch had an unusual intensity. His skin felt so hot. The sensation of his tongue and lips was extraordinarily electric. Her body hummed with awareness from her scalp to her pinkie toes. And in what she suspected would be her last moment of clear-headedness, Annie fumbled around inside the drawer of her bedside table until she found a condom.

"Are you always this prepared?" Nat asked, raising his head from her breast and taking the foil packet from her fingers.

"Yes." She wrapped her legs around the backs of his thighs and squeezed.

"Are you always such a greedy little sex vixen?"

"No."

When Nat smiled, his eyes flashed. Annie couldn't decide whether it was a spark of delight or a warning to her that things were about to get interesting. She hoped it was a little of both.

"Annie Parker, I'm going to ravish you. I'm going to make you mine." Nat began to slowly push himself further down her body, his lips and tongue trailing down between her breasts toward her belly button, which he greeted with a quick flick of his tongue. At that moment, she felt him pull away and push her legs apart, a move that made her whimper in anticipation. Oh God, she wanted this. She wanted him.

Nat looked up, his gaze locking on to hers, as he used his hands to press her wide open. Annie couldn't remember the last time she felt so helpless, so exposed. Maybe she never had. Maybe she'd never allowed herself to.

Nat gave her a wicked little grin, then resumed using his lips and tongue to drive her insane. First she felt his kisses on the inside of her thighs. Next came a series of nibbles and licks, his mouth making its way toward her sex. The instant she felt Nat's tongue slide along her opening, Annie tipped her head back and gasped at the acute pleasure.

And that was it. She knew there would be no turning back, no second-guessing. Whatever was happening between them was too powerful and too perfect to question. She knew that all she could do was hold on and enjoy her good fortune.

Nat took his sweet time teasing her with a trick bag of sexual moves that left her defenseless. There were long, deep licks and quick touches of the tip of his tongue. There were intervals of sucking—soft, then harder—that segued into one, two, then three fingers entering her, only to leave and start again. When he focused all his skills on her hard clitoris, she couldn't help but scream. Before she could regain her composure, he'd slipped on the condom, realigned himself, and positioned himself against the entrance to her body.

"Annie," he whispered.

She opened her eyes and realized she could barely see him through her tears. She couldn't speak, so she nodded.

Nat smiled as he stroked the side of her cheek and

brushed away her hair. "I need to be inside you now," he whispered.

"Yes." Annie felt how she'd instinctively opened wider for him, her body welcoming him. "Please, Nat."

His mouth covered hers. She tasted herself—salty like the sea, rich and female—the juices of a greedy, love-starved woman. And as Nat pushed inside her in a single long, slow thrust, she swore she heard the waves crashing through her heart, through her soul.

Annie opened her eyes, took a breath, and knew that everything had changed.

One of her legs was thrown across Nat's thighs and her head rested on his chest. His body felt hot and firm against hers, and their feet were entwined. Her hand lay on his hard belly, and his hand covered hers protectively.

Nat was asleep, his breathing deep and slow. Annie peeked up at him and saw how relaxed and peaceful his face was, how handsome. Suddenly, she felt a twinge of guilt for being such a terrible nursemaid. In fact, she sucked so bad at nursing that she had no idea what time it was or how long Nat had been asleep, which was a real no-no. Plus, she'd just had wild, bed-rocking sex for hours on end with a patient who was supposed to be resting and might even have a concussion, an offense that surely would be frowned upon by everyone—except maybe Rowan.

Though Nat stirred, she continued to observe him. He had a strong neck and a firm jawline. She noticed that his face had become scruffier as the hours passed and de-cided a bit of beard looked unbearably sexy on him. His hair was just long enough to give him some bad-boy pos-sibilities. But those lips! They were the most erotic lips of any man she'd ever known, smooth and straight, soft, the foundation for that magical smile. And, boy, did he know how to use them. Annie thought it amusing that Nat had grown up in what sounded like one of the most ordinary places in the world, yet he was the most extraordinary man she'd ever known.

At first she'd found him slightly intimidating, with all that cocky male energy and his hipster clothing. But he'd grown on her. Fast. And it was difficult to believe that she'd just met Nat and he'd already accomplished the impossible—he'd gotten her to let down her guard.

She closed her eyes and nestled in to him again, a sudden sadness enveloping her. It wasn't fair. The idea that Nathaniel Ravelle would be leaving as soon as he'd finished whatever he'd come to Bayberry Island to do made her want to cry. All night she'd been trying to push away the knowledge of the inevitable, but it kept returning, even in moments of extreme pleasure. But how could she pretend to be surprised by this? She'd let him in. She'd taken the most deadly of all fatal missteps. She'd allowed herself to want him, *to have expectations* about their relationship, though she had no idea if Nat had any of his own.

Annie sighed, promising herself two things: She would keep her anxiety to herself, and she would enjoy what time she and Nat had together, no matter how brief it might be.

Though she didn't want this moment to end, it was time to wake Nat to check that he was alert and oriented. Plus, she needed to know how much time they had before the doctor showed up, because finding them naked together in bed, clothes and cats thrown every which way, probably wouldn't go over well with a health care professional.

"I know you're awake," Nat whispered, gently stroking her hair.

When Annie smiled, her cheek pushed against his chest. "How could you tell?"

"I hear your brain working."

She giggled. "It works when I'm asleep, too."

"Not like it is now." He pulled her tighter. "Right now, your brain sounds like a 767 taking off from LAX. Care to share what's going on in there?"

She shrugged. "Just that if I were a good nursemaid, I would rouse you, make sure you were still thinking straight."

Nat began to move her hand, the one resting on his belly, pushing it under the blankets. Her fingertips encountered a part of Nat that she'd already become quite familiar with. It was silky, hard, and thick. It was perfection. It had turned her into a helpless and oversexed wreck of a woman who now had all kinds of *expectations*. She couldn't help but smile. "I said 'roused,' not '*a*roused.'"

"My bad."

Annie stroked him, feeling how rapidly he grew in her hand. She loved the effect her touch had on him. "Don't get me wrong. I can work with aroused."

"Yes, you certainly can." Nat turned on his side, facing her. He cradled her head in the crook of his left elbow and slid his right hand along her ribs, into the valley of her waist and up along the rise of her hip and back again. All the while he gazed into her eyes and smiled softly.

"You are so beautiful, Annie."

She'd heard this dozens of times that night, but she didn't mind him repeating himself. "Thank you."

"Do you know what I find to be the most beautiful thing about you?"

Nat's voice had become rough with emotion. The sudden change put her on alert. "You have a favorite thing in particular?"

"I do." He continued to look at her, a gentleness in his expression that she hadn't seen before.

Her hands stilled. Somehow, Annie knew the conversation was about to veer away from playful sex talk and move into a deeper place. It surprised her a little. It scared her even more. As it was, she was barely containing her anxiety.

Don't go. Don't leave. Stay with me, Nat. Stay with me always.

"Do you want to know what it is?"

She nodded.

Nat brought his finger to her throat and slid it down the front of her chest. "The most beautiful thing about you is"—he brushed across the top of both her breasts, then pressed his index finger into the center of her sternum—"right here. It's your heart, Annie Parker. You are impossibly beautiful in your heart, the most beautiful woman I've ever known."

For a second, she forgot how to breathe. The tears built and there was nothing she could do to stop them.

"But there's something that comes a close second." Nat dragged his fingertip up from her chest, over her chin and lips, and along the bridge of her nose. He tapped her forehead. "Your mind."

Annie smiled through her tears. She wished she could come up with a clever response, but her emotions were so strong she couldn't speak. All she could do was nod softly.

"It's okay, sweetheart," he said. "I feel what you feel. All I've been thinking about is how I could make it work here."

"*What*?" Annie's pulse just spiked. What was he saying?

"I've been trying to figure out how I could spend a lot of my time here on Bayberry Island, with you."

Nat kissed her then. It was sweet and earnest and it seemed to reach deeper inside her being than any kiss that had come before it. It knocked the breath from her.

He eventually removed his lips and leaned his forehead against hers. "There's something I need to ask you to do for me, Annie."

She pulled back and looked at him. The last time a man started a request that way, he was gunning for two thousand dollars to bail his brother out of jail on the mainland, plus thirty bucks for the round-trip ferry ride. Instead, he'd gotten a one-way trip out of her life. But, as if Annie needed further proof that she'd completely lost all grasp of reality, she simply said, "Anything, Nat."

He smiled. "I need you to tell me a story."

Annie narrowed one eye at him and tipped her chin down. "Say what?"

"A story."

"Are we talking a mermaid-and-sea-captain kind of story?"

He was embarrassed! His cheeks had just flushed and he looked away. "Yes," Nat said.

Annie had no idea where he was going with this, but she trusted him. For some reason, she trusted Nathaniel Ravelle completely. "Should I get one of my books?"

"Actually, I'd like hear the *original* story. The legend. The whole thing." He glanced up at her again. "Like I said, I didn't read up on it, and I think it would be much better coming from you."

Annie brushed away any remaining tears. She touched his chin and studied him. "Is this to prepare for your show?"

Nat shook his head. "I want to hear the story for *me*."

She blinked in surprise. "Is there any particular reason why you—"

"I think it might be an important tale for me to hear. I have a lot to learn about love. This could be a good place to start. Besides, I happen to be naked and in bed with the island's storyteller-in-residence at the moment."

"I see." Annie felt her mouth twitch. So the California-cool customer wanted to hear the over-the-top romantic tale of her little island? "I'd be happy to tell you, Nat. Unlike one of my own novels, I really do have this story memorized. I've been hearing it since first grade."

She cleared her throat before she began. "Once upon a time ... well, on March 14, 1881, to be exact, an Irish immigrant named Rutherford Flynn was out on his fishing boat when an epic nor'easter hit."

"Is that your friend's relative?"

"Oh yes. He was Rowan's great-great-great grandfather, to be exact. In a way, the Flynns are like the island's first family. Rutherford started Flynn Fisheries when he settled here, and it became the island's largest employer, the basis of the entire economy for more than a hundred years."

"Interesting."

Annie kissed Nat softly, which distracted her. "So, where was I?"

"The nor'easter."

"Right. So Rutherford was at the helm of the *Safe Haven*, the lead fishing boat in his company's fleet, when the storm hit. As the story goes, he fought valiantly to guide the boats to shore, but all seemed lost as the gale-force winds and sea swells tossed them off course."

"Sounds dramatic."

"Well, all good stories are. Then, suddenly—as Rutherford would later explain in great detail to anyone who would sit still long enough to listen—he spotted a mermaid at the boat's side, strangely illuminated in the dark, swirling water. Her raven hair fanned out around her. Her beautiful, dark eyes locked on his as she smiled reassuringly."

Nat frowned.

"Is something wrong?"

"No, please go on. This is great. I clearly picked the right person to tell me this story."

She smiled. "Anyway, Rutherford watched in awe as the mermaid pulled his boat to the cove, and the other boats followed, saving most of the male population of the island and its future generations in the process. Now, this is where things get good."

"I can't wait."

"According to the legend, poor Rutherford was so overcome with emotion that the instant his ship was secured, he dove into the frigid Atlantic in search of the divine creature who had saved them, attempting to pledge his undying love and devotion to her. The fool nearly drowned, of course, but his men managed to pull him from the crashing ice-cold sea. They dragged him to the inn, where he slipped into a fevered illness for days."

"I'll be damned."

"When he awoke, his eyes landed on the beautiful innkeeper's daughter, who had been nursing him back to health. And what did he see? The same shiny raven black hair and dark, beautiful eyes that he'd seen in the mermaid! Despite the girl's protests, Rutherford swore the women were one and the same, and he rolled off his sickbed to one knee and pledged to cherish her and love her until the end of time."

Nat's eyes went wide.

"According to the legend, they ended up insanely happy together, and Rutherford's business boomed and his family grew. He built a luxurious mansion for his wife, which is now the Safe Haven B and B."

"Ah, okay. Makes perfect sense."

"Now, ol' Rutherford, who some believed had lost his entire pack of marbles by that time, commissioned a bronze mermaid statue and fountain for the center of town to be made in his wife's likeness. You have to remember that this was during the Victorian era and this was New England, right? So when the huge, nearly naked mermaid was unveiled, the locals freaked. But what could they do? By that time, Rutherford was not just the biggest employer on the island, he was the mayor."

"Sounds like Chicago."

Annie laughed. "So, soon after the statue was unveiled, stories began to circulate about her special powers. Overemotional girls swore the mermaid could reveal to them their true loves. But only if they asked with a pure heart."

"You mean they had to be virgins?"

"No. I mean they had to have good intentions. I'll get to more of the rules in a minute."

"This story sure has a lot of damn rules."

Annie grinned. "Baby, we're just getting started."

Ezra chose that moment to thud onto the bed again. He tried to shove his fat cat body between them, but Annie and Nat guided him toward their feet, smiling at each other the whole time.

"I lost my train of thought."

"The mermaid rules."

"Oh, right. So young women swore the mermaid could deliver their true loves. The men who kissed the mermaid's hand claimed to fall under a magical spell. They said they suddenly were consumed with a passion beyond reason for one particular girl they envisioned in their mind's eye—often one they'd never met and had no name for! As the years went by, this basic legend evolved into its expanded, modern-day form."

Nat looked slightly upset.

Annie thought maybe the story was too long. "I can stop here if you want me to."

"Hell no. Don't you dare!"

She laughed. "Okay, so here's the legend as it stands today: True love is like the sea—beautiful, deep, and life-giving but unpredictable, powerful, and even dangerous. To succeed at love, you must set out on your journey with a true heart and be prepared to be tossed by waves of passion, be willing to drown in love's undertow. The legend claims that anyone who comes to the mermaid, kisses her hand, and pledges to go wherever love leads will find happiness. But beware." Annie wiggled her eyebrows for effect. "Anyone who comes to the Great Mermaid with preconceived notions about the 'who-what-wheres' of true love will find heartache instead."

Nat's face blanched white. He looked almost seasick.

"Are you all right?"

He blinked at Annie. "Yeah. But I need some clarification on something you just said."

"Sure."

"All this stuff that's supposed to happen—you know, the passion beyond reason thing and the magical spell and undertow shit—that can happen only if you go to the mermaid personally, right? I mean, someone else can't go to the mermaid and plead your case without your knowledge, right? The mermaid just can't throw something like that on an unsuspecting passerby, right?"

"No. You have to go to her yourself and make your request—if you believe in any of this crap, that is."

Nat nodded and thanked her for telling the story, but she could tell something still troubled him.

And then she remembered . . .

"Hold up," she said. "I take back that last part. There's supposed to be another way the mermaid juju can get you, but it's just as goofy as everything else about the legend."

Nat's eyes got big again. "What's the other way?"

"Well, back when we were teenagers, Rowan told me that Mona and her minions have a bunch of secret rituals that no one's supposed to know about—pledges and chanting and handshakes and stupid stuff like that. But one night, Rowan eavesdropped on them.

"She overheard them talking about performing a ritual—I think they even called it an 'intervention.' It was for a woman who refused to believe in the power of the Great Mermaid. Apparently, they were waiting for a solstice or special moon phase or some ridiculous thing, and when it came, they planned to put on their wigs and scales—"

Annie stopped. They jolted up at the same time, startling Ezra so much that he hissed before he thumped off the bed. Annie and Nat stared at each other in silence for a very long moment.

Then Nat said, "I think yesterday was the winter solstice."

6

"What a charming house you have, Miss Parker." The doctor stomped her boots on the rug by the front door. "Sorry I'm a little late."

"Oh, it's no problem. I'm very glad you got here safe. Please, come in." Annie took her coat and gestured toward the bedroom. "Is the weather letting up at all?"

The doctor shook her head. "It's still a mess out there, but the temperature's rising. How's the patient?" She walked alongside Annie toward the bedroom.

"He's wonderful. Very alert. His appetite has been good. He says his pain is much better, too."

The doctor gave her a sideways glance, then smiled a little. "This is all great news. Were you able to wake him every couple hours, as I suggested?"

"Yes. As a matter of fact, we were up most of the night."

"You don't say?"

Annie realized her choice of words might be giving the doctor the wrong impression. Or the right impression. Which would be the wrong thing to give her. "Talking," she said. "We were up talking. Nat is an interesting man. After you." She gestured for the doctor to enter the bedroom.

"Thank you."

"I'll be in the kitchen if you need anything," Annie said, walking away. The instant the kitchen door shut behind her, Annie was on the phone with Rowan. It was the sixth time that morning.

"Well? What did you find out?"

The doctor was an older woman with a kind face and a quiet touch. She'd checked his pulse, his blood pressure, the dilation of his pupils, and his reflexes. Then she began to gently nudge and tug on his limbs, asking if anything hurt.

"My concern is that you lost consciousness for a rather long period of time," she said, patting his arm. "You seem fine, and I'm not overly worried, but concussions can be tricky to diagnose without a CT scan, so you should have one after the holidays. I will write you a prescription." She returned her stethoscope to her doctor bag and sat down in Annie's writing chair.

"Any headaches, Mr. Ravelle?"

"Just at first. Nothing now."

"Nausea or vomiting?"

"No."

"Are you seeing flashing lights?"

"Aside from the ones on Annie's Christmas tree?"

The doctor grinned. "Those don't count."

"Then no."

"Persistent confusion?"

"No."

"A noticeable change in your usual thought process, emotions, or behavior?"

Nat scrunched up his mouth.

"Mr. Ravelle?"

"Uh . . ."

"Absolutely nothing," was Rowan's answer. "My mom denies they did any kind of ritual."

"Of course she does."

"I was on the phone with her for a half hour, trying to get her to crack, and then I went over there to see her in person. But she just keeps telling me the same thing—she has no idea what I'm talking about, and there is no such thing as a love intervention anyway."

"Whatever."

"She thinks maybe you've been spending too much time alone, writing about captains and mermaids gettin' it on in the sea of love."

Annie nodded. "Right."

"So after I was done with my mom, I marched over to Abby's, Izzy's, and even Polly's, and they all said the same thing—they have no idea what I'm talking about. I will say this, though—Abby seemed real nervous and even shut the door in my face."

Annie sighed. "Well, I really appreciate you going out and doing the Sherlock Holmes thing for me. You're the best friend I could ever hope for."

Rowan laughed. "Oh, come on now, Annie. You and I both know there's nothing to the mermaid crap."

"Of course." Annie leaned against the counter, hearing the doctor's soft murmur from the bedroom and the sound of Nat's laughter. They seemed to be getting along great.

"Look, I did tell my mom that they needed to mind their own damn business. But even if they did have one of their pagan parties in your honor, they did it because they love you and just want you to be happy."

Annie smiled. "I know."

"Annie?"

"Yeah?"

"Is there something you're not telling me?"

"What do you mean?" Annie began rinsing out cups in the sink, thinking that keeping her hands busy would somehow magically stop this conversation.

"Well, you called me last night completely freaked out because you were a nervous wreck around this guy. Then this morning you call me completely freaked out because you're suddenly convinced the mermaids are messing with your love life. And, since I'm Sherlock Holmes and all, what it looks like to me is you suddenly *have* a love life."

Annie froze. "You know, I should probably go. The doctor's here and—"

"Oh my God! You're in love with him!"

"Oh please, Rowan." Annie stepped out onto the small back porch to finish the conversation. "I don't even know him. How could I be in love with him? Don't go getting all crazy on me, all right?"

"You're lying to me, Annabeth Parker. Liar, liar, liar."

"I really need to go."

"You love him and you've never let yourself love someone before, so you're worried that the Great Mermaid had something to do with this, that she used her tractor beam of love to deliver him to your door. Am I right?"

"The mermaid story is ridiculous. I don't believe in the mermaid."

Rowan giggled. "That's great, sweetie. But what if she believes in you?"

The doctor waited patiently for Nat to answer. This was a dilemma. He knew it was important to share everything with a doctor. Your life could depend on it. He also knew that if he told her the truth—that his thinking process and consciousness had been radically altered, that his emotions were on kamikaze autopilot, and that he'd even entertained the possibility that a bronze mermaid fountain might have directed him to his one true love—she'd order a psychiatrist to go with that CT scan.

Nat stared at her. All he could manage was a laugh.

"You know, Mr. Ravelle," she said, "I live in the world of science, but science isn't the be-all and end-all. Working as a physician, I've seen things I have no explanation for, and I've reached the conclusion that there's more to life than we can prove with empirical data."

Nat really liked this woman. "I'm listening," he said.

"I grew up on Nantucket," she said. "I've been coming to Bayberry Island all my life. I've always known there's something extraordinary about this place." She raised her eyebrows. "I met my husband here."

"No kidding?"

The doctor's expression seemed to glaze over for a moment. "Yes. At a totally kick-ass beach party during the 1980 Mermaid Festival."

"So I need a CT scan, huh?"

She chuckled and reached for a prescription pad. "I understand that your reason for being here is job related, but if I may ask, what were your holiday plans, Mr. Ravelle?"

He noticed she'd just used the past tense. "My whole family is in Boston for Christmas. My plan was to spend a couple days on this godforsaken piece of rock and take the first thing smokin' back to Boston."

The doctor smiled as she wrote out something on her pad. "Well, those plans have changed. I've just written you a note excusing you from your job for two weeks.

Have them call me if they have any questions. And here's a referral for a CT scan."

"But . . ." Nat was bewildered.

"I want you to stay put for a while. For the next few days, don't leave this bed unless it's for meals, showers, and maybe some slow dancing in front of the fireplace, but only if you feel up to it. And I think you should consider inviting your family to Bayberry for Christmas, since it's better that you don't travel. You can get your CT scan on the Cape." She tore off both slips of paper and handed them to him.

Nat knew his mouth was hanging open. He looked from the piece of paper to the doctor and back again. "What's my diagnosis? Is it serious? What do you think is wrong with me?"

She grabbed her bag and stood by the side of the bed. "Nothing that a couple weeks on this island with Miss Parker won't cure. Merry Christmas."

Now it was official. There had never been so many people crammed into her tiny house at one time. And the walls had never tried to contain so much chatter, laughter, music, and the sound of kids playing. Annie loved it. She couldn't stop smiling at the idea that all these people—the ones she'd just met yesterday and the ones she'd known all her life—had come together to celebrate Christmas Eve. And they were here in her house, which she had expected to be cold and empty over the holidays.

The only one who wasn't enjoying himself was Ezra, now with a bow on his head and being carried around by Nat's six-year-old niece.

"What an adorable place you have, Annie." Nat's mother had followed her into the kitchen. "Has this property been in your family a long time?"

"Only for about the last one hundred fifty years, give or take." Annie smiled at her. She was a lovely woman who seemed enamored with the island and deliriously happy that her family could be together over the holidays. She also seemed just the teeniest bit curious about Annie and her life—and probably her shop's dessert menu. It was obvious that Mrs. Ravelle hadn't followed her into the kitchen only to help carry out more bacon-wrapped scallops.

"May I ask you something?"

"Of course."

Mrs. Ravelle had donned a pair of mitts to remove another tray of appetizers from the oven. "Well, Nat has told us a bit about you, and I have to say I'm a little surprised by the situation."

Annie turned to face her, puzzled. "You're surprised he would be interested in me?"

"That's not what I meant at all!" Mrs. Ravelle laughed. "There's no surprise there. Any red-blooded man would be interested in you. You're beautiful, smart, funny, and I'm just glad you seem as smitten with Nat as he is with you."

"Scared me there for a minute," Annie said.

"I'm sorry. What I meant was . . . well, dammit, I'm just going to come right out and say it." She took a breath and rested the oven mitts on her hips. "Nat has never brought a girl home for us to meet, not once since he moved to California for college. He had a girlfriend in high school, and I really thought he was in love with her, but that was it. We were starting to think, well, you know. He's in his thirties now. He lives in LA."

Annie laughed out loud. "Nat is definitely not gay."

"Oh, thank God! Not that there's anything wrong

with being gay. We just weren't sure, and it's such a relief to know one way or the other." With that, Mrs. Ravelle grabbed Annie and squeezed her tight. "Thank you, my dear girl."

"That was your question?"

"Oh no. I just had to get that out of the way before I asked what I really wanted to ask."

Annie crossed her arms over her chest and leaned against the counter. "Fire away."

"Would you consider—and you don't have to if you are sick of doing it at this point—but would you consider telling us the story of the mermaid legend after dinner? I think the girls would love to hear it. They're in that phase, you know."

"Which phase is that?"

"The true love stuff. Fairy tales and princesses. Magical powers. Knights in shining armor."

"Ah, that phase," Annie said, grinning. "I think I remember it."

Many hours later, Annie's friends and neighbors had returned to their homes and the Ravelles had settled in at the Safe Haven B and B. She and Nat were in the kitchen washing dishes and listening to Christmas music.

"Let's take a break," Nat said.

"Is your back bothering you?"

"Nope, but this is my favorite carol." He grabbed Annie by the hand and led her into the sitting room. He flipped off all the lights, leaving only the Christmas tree and the fire to cast a warm glow.

"What are you—?"

"Shh. This requires ambience."

She giggled as he pulled her to the front of his body and began to sway to a slow and jazzy version of "Have

Yourself a Merry Little Christmas." Since the room had already been rearranged for maximum party space, there was plenty of room for dancing.

Nat gazed down at her, his eyes sparkling with the lights. "Annie Parker, before this night ends, I wanted to be sure to thank you."

"For?"

"Saving me. Bringing me to shore."

7

Six months later ...

"Fifteen minutes to Bayberry Island, Mr. Ravelle."

Nat looked up from his shooting budget and smiled. "Thank you very much, John."

"Beautiful June day out here. Water is as smooth as glass."

"Yes, it is." Nat began to gather his things, tapping his shirt pocket to make sure he had his sunglasses.

"Staying on for good? I think you told me last time that you hoped to be. Will you be here for the whole summer? Will you be here for the Mermaid Festival?"

"I will, John."

"Will your family be coming?"

"Yes. They'll all be here in August for festival week."

"That's lovely. Very nice people, your family."

"Thank you."

"How's Annie doing? I got to chat with her the last time she was on her way to Boston to catch a plane to see you. She tells me that Los Angeles is more than six

197

hours away by jet! I've never been much of a flyer myself. I prefer to travel by sea, you know."

Nat smiled again. Yes, he did know. In fact, by now the only thing about John that remained a mystery was his preferred brand of underwear, and the ferry conductor seemed dangerously close to revealing even that before they reached the public dock.

Just then, a little boy and his mother ran for exit, the kid clearly suffering from seasickness.

John puffed out his chest and pulled on his belt. "Tourists," he whispered to Nat, rolling his eyes. "Anyway, welcome home, Mr. Ravelle. Nice chatting with you, as always. Give Annie my regards."

"I certainly will. Take care of yourself, John."

Nat grabbed his carry-on and tugged the strap of his laptop case across his chest. He'd shipped the last of the remaining boxes from LA before he caught his flight. His *Truly Weird* coworkers, neighbors, and friends had thrown him a going-away party two nights before. He wouldn't lie to himself. He would miss some things about LA, and he'd definitely miss his friends. But he'd already hired a few of them to work with him on the mermaid documentary, and they'd be joining him later in the summer. The rest of them were so charmed by Annie, and by tales from Bayberry Island, that they were all planning to visit.

Nat stepped out onto the passenger deck, the sea spray hitting his face as the sun beat down on his skin. He breathed deeply, filling his lungs with salt and wind. He heard the cry of seagulls and the beat of the ferry against the ocean. As the engine slowed, he opened his eyes. He saw her right away, and his heart somersaulted in his chest. Each time he returned, he was happier to see her. Each time, he loved her more. And very soon now, everything would change.

As he waved to Annie, his cell phone rang. He ran back inside so he could hear.

"Everything's ready," Rowan said. "We've got the champagne. We'll be hiding in the bushes on the other side of the fountain. Is the ferry on time?"

"Yep. Just pulling in now."

"Great. See you in about ten minutes. Hey, Nat?"

"Yes?"

"I—" She sniffed. "Never mind."

"Ah, man, Row. You're not crying, are you? Nothing's even happened yet!"

"I know. I know. I'll pull it together. It's just that I'm so happy for Annie! For you! It's just such a happy day! She's going to be so surprised!"

"I sure hope so. Thank you, Rowan. See you in a few."

Nat put the phone away and checked his pants pocket for the velvet box. It was there. And this was it.

Moments later, Nat stepped onto the dock, and Annie threw herself into his arms. He lifted her up and held her against him for a long time, so tightly that he was afraid he would hurt her.

"I've missed you so much, Annie." Nat buried his nose in her fragrant hair, kissing her neck again and again. He let her slide to her feet so he could kiss her properly. Her lips were sweet and soft against his. When she moaned into his mouth, he felt himself being pulled into a vortex of love and happiness powerful enough to drown a weaker man.

"Let's take a walk to the square," Nat said. "I hear the mermaid is pretty spectacular when the fountain is up and running."

Annie smiled at him. "She positively glistens."

About the Author

Susan Donovan's novels have won accolades for being witty, sexy, and entertaining—"brain candy for smart women," as she puts it. She's a *New York Times* and *USA Today* bestselling author whose novels have been translated into a dozen languages. Susan is a two-time RITA Award finalist and her novel *Take a Chance on Me* was named "Best Contemporary Romance of 2003" by *RT Book Reviews*. She earned bachelor's and master's degrees from Northwestern University's Medill School of Journalism and worked as a newspaper reporter in Chicago, Albuquerque, and Indianapolis. These days, she lives in Maryland with her family and dogs.

CONNECT ONLINE

www.susandonovan.com

MISTLETOE ON MAIN STREET

LuAnn McLane

1

Santa Claus Is Coming to Town

"Oh no!" Ava Whimsy gripped the handle of her big wicker basket tightly as she dodged past dancing elves and then cut through a Girl Scout troop decked out in cookie costumes. The line for the Cricket Creek Christmas parade was organized chaos at best, and this was no time to be running late.

"Santa, where are you . . . ?" Ava stopped and twirled around so fast that the red velvet skirt of her Mrs. Claus dress billowed out like an umbrella before settling down around her calves. The basket tilted, sending a few candy canes sliding to the concrete, but she didn't have time to pick them up. Ava knew the Santa's sleigh float brought up the rear, but seriously, the end of the line was nowhere in sight.

"Where in the world is Santa's sleigh?" Ava shouted to Noah Falcon, owner of the Cricket Creek professional baseball team and grand marshal of the parade. Even though the weather had a threat of snow flurries, the top of the flashy red convertible was down, allowing Noah and his wife, Olivia, to wave and toss Cougar baseball caps to the eager crowd.

"Back . . ." Noah began, but the high school marching band started playing "Jingle Bells," which drowned out his answer. Ava looked in the direction of Noah's thumb jammed over his head. *Finally* she spotted the flying reindeer jutting up in the air all the way over at the other end of the parking lot.

The jolly old man might have to ride in the sleigh solo this year. But after taking a deep breath to ready herself, Ava lifted her red velvet skirt with one hand, put one dainty laced-up boot in front of the other, and then hurried as fast as she could past floats and other Christmas-themed participants. It didn't help that this was one of the only times of the year that she wore a dress. Ava preferred her jeans and favorite cowboy boots. Her basket, laden with tiny toys and candy canes, swung back and forth, making her gait resemble that of a penguin.

A last-minute customer at Ava's toy store, just a few blocks away on Main Street, had her running behind, and then to make matters worse, her dog had decided to shred her white wig to pieces. Apparently, Rosie, her usually sweet little rescue mutt, didn't take kindly to Ava's recent long hours stocking A Touch of Whimsy in preparation for the holiday rush. In a panic, Ava had pulled her chestnut brown hair into a bun and sprayed it with the fake snow she'd been using for the front window display. Judging by the white crusty flakes falling from her head, it wasn't her best idea. Although she considered herself a creative person, she kept her makeup to a minimum and wasn't really equipped for situations like this.

The label at least *said* the contents were nontoxic, so she hoped that meant her hair wouldn't fall out.

For the past ten years, she and Pete Sully had played Santa and Mrs. Claus during the three-day celebration filled with food and festivities along Main Street in Cricket Creek. Pete also made Santa appearances at her store throughout the holiday season. With his real beard, round belly, and booming voice, Pete played the part well. Although perhaps more suited to play a cute elf, Ava dressed up and portrayed Mrs. Claus at Sully's Tavern when he hosted Toys for Tots and Teens, a charity event to benefit local children in need. Ava just couldn't fathom any child not having a toy on Christmas morning.

"Finally!" Ava muttered when she reached the row of plastic reindeer. Sure, they had seen better days, but the worn, rosy cheeks and chipped paint somehow added a nostalgic appeal that Ava found endearing. Rudolph's red nose blinked as if in welcome, and Ava sighed in relief. She'd made it.

"Hey there!" Ava waved to Braden Greenfield sitting on the big green tractor that was going to pull the float. A huge red bow adorned the front grille. When Braden tipped his cowboy hat at Ava, she grinned and tossed him a candy cane, which he deftly caught.

"You took your sweet time getting here, Ava," Braden called over to her.

"Long story," she shouted back. The Greenfield farm butted up to her family's farm, and Braden was like a little brother to her. "Catch ya later!" Ava turned and accepted Santa's white-gloved hand as she took the big step up and slid onto the black leather seat.

"Sorry I'm late," Ava apologized a little breathlessly and set her basket down on the floor. She leaned over to pick up a few candy canes that had tumbled around her feet. "I had a customer who couldn't decide whether to purchase trains or airplanes." Sitting back up, she arranged her velvet skirt just so and brushed away a mist of white flakes that continued to flutter from her head when she moved. "And then a wardrobe situation complicated matters." She pointed to her head. "So, how's it going, Pete?"

"Pretty good, but um . . . I'm not Pete."

Ava chuckled as she tugged at her tight gloves. "Right. Sorry. . . . You're Santa. I forgot that you like to stay in character." After flicking another powdery flake from her skirt, she reached down for a handful of candy canes and finally glanced his way. "Would you like one?"

"Thanks," Santa said, reaching for the treat. But when their fingers brushed, for some odd reason, Ava felt a little tingle.

"You're welcome." Ava smiled. *Whoa, wait a minute.*

She peered at Santa over the top of her granny glasses, and her heart started to thud. "W-why do you have a fake beard?"

"Shhh. I'm not the real Santa," he replied in a stage whisper. "Only a helper. I'm a very big elf."

Ava looked into light blue eyes accentuated by tan cheeks visible above the beard and felt another tingle of awareness. She swallowed hard.

No, it couldn't be.

The candy canes slid from her hand and into her lap. *Clint?* The name slammed into her brain but got caught in her throat and stayed there.

"Dad couldn't make it, so I'm filling in," he explained, confirming her suspicions.

"Clint?" The single word that was a tangle of so many emotions tumbled out of her mouth. Of course it was Clint. Pete had only one son.

And she hadn't spoken to him since he'd broken her teenage heart fifteen years ago.

"Yeah, it's Clint." His full lips curved slightly between the white mustache and beard. "Good to see you, Ava. Or should I say, Mrs. Claus?"

Ava blinked at him, not knowing how to respond. She finally managed a rather choked, "Yeah . . . um, you too." In the years since Clint left Cricket Creek, Ava often wondered if she'd run into him when he came home from California to visit his father. Early on after their breakup, she'd fantasized about having Clint coming home and throwing pebbles up to her bedroom window and then serenading her like a scene from a movie. Perhaps they'd kiss in a rainstorm like in *Sweet Home Alabama* or see each other from across the street and end up in each other's arms. Sometimes, though, she imagined she'd remain aloof and distant and give Clint a mere lift of an eyebrow only to have him run after her, spin her around, and kiss her senseless.

Never for a moment did she think that she'd be dressed as Mrs. Claus with crusty fake snow falling from her head. But then again, how would Clint react to her *without* the disguise? The last time he'd seen her, she had blond hair instead of her natural brown, had been ten—okay more like *fifteen*—pounds lighter . . . and oh dear Lord, fifteen years younger.

Fifteen years! Perhaps she was better off disguised as Mrs. Claus after all.

"When did you get into town?" Ava asked lightly, hoping that her breathless voice didn't give away her sudden fit of nerves. She was actually surprised she hadn't known. Gossip spread like wildfire in their small Southern town—and the return of a favorite son always had tongues wagging—but then again, she'd been busy working extended holiday hours in her shop.

"A few days ago. I've been keeping to myself, hanging out with Dad."

"Oh, that's . . . um, nice." When she nodded a bit too hard, a few flakes fell from her head and fluttered in the breeze. Embarrassed, she quickly brushed them away and then patted at her hair. She busied herself scooping her candy into a neat little pile in her lap. Awkward silence followed.

"The baseball stadium is something else. No wonder Noah Falcon is the grand marshal of the parade. I think it's pretty cool that he moved back here."

Ava nodded, but then, unable to help herself, she looked up into his intense blue eyes. "Noah and Olivia will light the tree in town square too. The honor is well deserved." She smiled, but then her lips had to go all rogue on her and quiver. Mortified, she quickly glanced away, wishing that the bench seat had more room between them. Dear Lord. When she'd woken up this morning, everything had seemed so normal.

"Do you go to any of the baseball games?"

"Whenever I get the chance. Summer at my shop isn't as busy as this time of year." Ava looked away, suddenly overcome with emotion. Clint was one of the reasons she'd always loved baseball. They'd bonded first over their love of the game—something a high school jock from town and a feisty little farm girl could share. The memory brought a lump into her throat.

"Still ride the umpires, Ava?" Clint's grin was partially hidden by the beard, but there was a sudden twinkle in his eyes.

"When they don't know the strike zone," Ava swiftly replied, drawing a chuckle from Clint. She gave him a small smile. Her emotions were tipping back and forth between the pure joy of seeing him and the pain of his departure, making her feel a bit off balance. Looking away again, she played with a plastic candy cane wrapper and really wished the parade would get under way so she could wave and throw treats instead of having to make small talk with the boy who broke her young heart.

"It really is great to be back in Cricket Creek." His voice sounded like the Clint she knew but with a deeper timbre ... a husky quality that stirred her blood. The boy she knew was now a man.

"You could have warned me." Ava didn't really mean to say those words out loud but was suddenly glad that they'd tumbled out of her mouth. It was unfair to be put in this awkward position.

"Would you have backed out?"

"Of course not," Ava sputtered. Clint looked at her as if he wasn't buying what she was selling, and in truth, Ava wasn't sure what she would have done. "But a heads-up would have been, well, fair warning." A candy cane crunched in her clenched fist, and she looked down at it in surprise.

"I'm really sorry," Clint offered quietly.

Ava looked at him, and his eyes suddenly appeared serious, making her wonder if he meant much more than showing up unannounced. Something fluttered in her stomach.

"Look, Ava—"

"Don't," Ava interrupted softly but firmly. She wasn't quite sure where Clint was going with this, but she knew sitting on a Christmas float dressed as Santa and Mrs. Claus wasn't the time or place to discuss their past. In fact, annoyance that Clint would dare to show up out of nowhere and apologize tipped the scales against her enjoyment of the parade. She decided she'd rather just leave and let Santa and his reindeer fly solo. But as soon as she stood up, the float lurched forward. To Ava's horror, she tilted sideways and landed with a *plop* on Santa's lap.

"Whoa there." Clint's hands grabbed her around the waist, and she heard him chuckle. Ava wanted to remain aloof, but a delicious warmth spread through her at his touch. "Well, now, what would you like for Christmas, Mrs. Claus?"

"Let me up," Ava's brain demanded sternly, but her voice refused to cooperate. As if on cue, the band started playing "Santa Claus Is Coming to Town."

Clint chuckled again, and the deep, rich sound of his laughter rumbled in her ear, sending a hot shiver of awareness sliding down her spine. For a split second, Ava was brought back to a place and time when they shared playful moments like this. "Have you been a good girl?"

"Clint!"

"Santa," he corrected. "Or Kriss Kringle, if you prefer. Father Christmas is too formal."

Ava nearly giggled, but his big hands spanning her waist and the warmth of his peppermint-scented breath on her cheek made thoughts go through her head that would certainly put her at the top of the naughty list, and it brought her back to reality. "Really, people are *looking*," she pleaded, even though they were bringing up the rear so it wasn't really true.

"Sorry," Clint said, although the remaining laughter in his voice indicated otherwise. Thankfully, he released her, and she scrambled back to her side of the sleigh, putting a much-needed couple of feet between them.

Ava stole a look in his direction and then leaned down to scoop up the scattered candy canes. After they pulled out of the parking lot, she started tossing the treats to people lined along the road watching the parade. The route took them past the banks of the Ohio River. Even though the trees were bare, Ava appreciated the stark beauty that winter brought to the countryside. The addition of park benches and streetlamps along a paved sidewalk lured people outdoors for morning jogs and evening strolls even during the colder weather, an activity Ava enjoyed but hadn't had time for lately.

"Wow. I haven't been back since most of the new development. Dad was telling the truth. Things have changed," Clint commented as they passed a relatively new row of shops built to resemble the quaint buildings on Main Street in Cricket Creek. Bright red bows and pine wreaths added a festive touch.

"For the better," Ava answered with a touch of pride. "Cricket Creek has been through some tough times, but when Noah Falcon built the baseball complex, we all banded together and brought this town back to life. It took some doing, but hard work goes a long way. I wasn't about to lose my store without putting up a fight. I'm happy to say that I made it through the recession. Next summer, I'll celebrate my tenth year of being in business."

Clint shot her a grin. "Ah, so you're still a little spitfire, huh?"

"When it comes to things I care about." She gave him a slight shrug but then grinned back at him. "You know me. I'm pretty quiet until you get me riled up about something I believe in."

"I'm glad to know you haven't changed." Clint's grin remained, and Ava had the urge to yank the beard down so she could get a good look at his face.

"I guess being the youngest with three older brothers

played a factor," Ava answered lightly. In fact, she'd never been self-conscious of her tomboy ways. Ava enjoyed the outdoors and never really wanted to be a girly-girl. The closest she came was lightening her hair for a while, and to this day her brothers would call her Blondie just to get her goat. When Clint, who was big man on campus in high school, had asked Ava out, she'd had to look over her shoulder, thinking that surely there had been some cheerleader standing behind her in the hallway. "I had to learn to hold my own." She shrugged. "I guess some things really haven't changed."

"Yeah, some things sure don't," he agreed, giving her a look she wished she could read. How could Clint be so unaffected and playful? Didn't he remember the painful way they'd parted? It had hurt her to the bone that even after Clint had failed to make it to the major leagues, he'd never seemed to look back at his past in Cricket Creek, at her. Why hadn't he returned to Cricket Creek, his friends and family?

And come home to me, slid unwanted into Ava's brain.

Rattled, Ava turned back to tossing candy, but she remained acutely aware of Clint sitting next to her. Although Ava would never have admitted it out loud, for a long time she'd secretly hoped Clint would come back home to rekindle their relationship. But after a while she'd given up on that fantasy and concentrated on her toy store. As her pain faded, she often smiled at fond memories, sometimes prompted by a song on the radio, a favorite movie they'd laughed at, or simply watching a baseball game. As the years passed, she would think about Clint now and then with a twinge of sadness, sometimes wondering what might have been but mostly because the beauty of their young love had ended with such bitterness.

MISTLETOE ON MAIN STREET   213

Ava swallowed a sigh. Evidently, even dressed up in that Santa suit, the man could still get to her. And for some reason that she couldn't quite explain, it darn well ticked her off! She had given Clint the power to hurt her once, and she wasn't about to give it to him again. With a quick intake of breath, she tossed a handful of candy canes so hard that a group of onlookers actually ducked.

"Underhanded, Mrs. Claus." Clint reached down and grabbed a handful of candy from the basket and demonstrated. "Ho, ho ho!" he called, drawing a cheer from the crowd. Ava narrowed her eyes at him over the top of her granny glasses and then made a grand gesture of throwing the candy ever so gently. Clint laughed, and the twinkle in his eyes nearly had her smiling back at him. But she pressed her lips together instead.

Normally an even-keeled kind of person, Ava was mortified that she was behaving peevishly and yet she just couldn't help herself. "Merry Christmas!" Ava waved at the crowd and started humming along with the band's lively rendition of "Rudolph the Red-Nosed Reindeer." But her smile faded when they turned down Maple Street and Cricket Creek High School loomed in the background like a giant memory. A new addition had been added since Ava and Clint attended classes, but the original redbrick building remained in front, along with the row of oak trees that had been there as long as she could remember.

She found her gaze drifting to the baseball field where she had watched Clint play countless games. They'd shared their first kiss beneath the stands one night after Clint had knocked in the winning run to clinch the district tournament. Tender, sweet, and full of promise, the kiss haunted her still.

When emotion filled her throat, Ava bent down to get

some candy canes. Out of the corner of her eye, Ava caught Clint staring at the stands and she wondered if he was remembering that first kiss too. Flustered, she tried to act as if the memories didn't bother her. After waving to the crowd, she removed the plastic wrapper from a candy cane, cracked off a bite, and rolled the piece of peppermint around with her tongue. When the silence became uncomfortable, she asked, "How's your mom doing?"

Clint hesitated slightly and then answered, "She's enjoying living in Nashville."

"Is she singing?"

"A little bit at the Bluebird Café, but mostly songwriting."

"That's good. I remember that she enjoyed her music." Ava nodded, but when he didn't elaborate, she didn't probe. Clint had taken his parents' divorce really hard. "So, um, how long are you in town for?"

Clint hesitated for a second and then said, "Haven't you heard?"

"No." Ava shook her head. She casually raised her eyebrows, but her heart pounded like she had just had a double shot from Starbucks. "Heard what?"

"I'm moving back to Cricket Creek."

2

Sleigh Ride

Clint watched Ava's mouth open, shut, open, and then shut again. He couldn't blame her. First he showed up without warning, and now he dropped this little bombshell in her lap.

"That's . . . good. I mean, I'm sure your dad is happy," Ava finally responded, but her tight smile and stormy eyes told another story. "And your mom lives only a couple of hours away."

"Yeah, all of that warm weather and sunshine was just too much to handle any longer," Clint joked, but if Ava got it, she didn't laugh.

"I bet." She popped the rest of the mini candy cane into her mouth and then looked away. Clint had an odd urge to reach over, take her hand, and squeeze it, but he refrained. In truth, he'd come back to Cricket Creek to check up on his father, who'd started having heart issues but had stubbornly refused to go to a specialist. Afraid that his dad might suffer a heart attack if he didn't change his lifestyle, Clint had decided to come back to help out at the tavern for an extended period.

He'd also contacted Noah Falcon, offering to help coach the Cricket Creek Cougars, but it wasn't until the float turned up Maple Street that Clint started feeling as if he should consider moving back for reasons other than his father's health. Plus, after several years of trying to make the major leagues, including a few seasons playing in the Dutch League in Europe, he'd returned to USC to coach instead. As it turned out, he enjoyed working with players. He'd hoped to someday land the head coaching job at USC, but it didn't appear as if Jake Barnet had any intention of stepping down anytime soon. Everything seemed to be pointing in the direction of Clint coming home. The clincher, though, came when the bleachers came into view and he heard Ava's soft intake of breath. Clint understood. He remembered that kiss as if it were yesterday.

But it wasn't yesterday, he reminded himself. That first kiss had occurred nearly seventeen years ago, and for two years Ava Whimsy had been his girl. But soon after graduation day, everything changed.

Of course, at the tender age of eighteen, Clint had thought that everything would work out. Surely his parents would come to their senses and reunite. He would get drafted into the minor leagues and return home after becoming a baseball superstar like everyone had predicted. But Clint soon found out that life wasn't that easy. He'd been a big fish in a small pond in Cricket Creek, and he wasn't quite prepared for the intense competition in a Division I school and major-league baseball. Until then, Clint had sailed through life effortlessly, unprepared for the frustration of failure. As Clint continued to try making the majors, one year blended into the next, and now here he was wondering why he'd stayed away so damned long.

Clint sighed. Of course, Ava couldn't have heard that he was moving home because he hadn't really fully decided. So why in the world had he just blurted out that he was moving back to Cricket Creek instead of just here for an extended visit? Clint snuck a glance in Ava's direction. He guessed his unexpected announcement was to see her reaction, and he felt his chest tighten. Over the years, thoughts of Ava would hit him unexpectedly, and he'd sometimes wondered what might have been. He would never ask his father about her, fearing that the answer would be that Ava had married and had three kids or something. But she hadn't. And now here he was sitting next to her, wondering if he might have a second chance.

"Ho, ho, ho!" Clint shouted before sneaking another look in Ava's direction. She remained turned toward her side of the street, waving and shouting holiday greetings. They'd both known that he had to take the scholarship, but what Ava didn't know was that to this day, leaving her remained the hardest thing he'd ever had to do. But on their last night together, emotions had been running high. Looking back, he realized that the anger, the arguing, had been the defense mechanism they both used for masking the pain of separation. Living across the country from each other simply wasn't going to work and the truth hurt. They'd had to break up. But that didn't mean he liked leaving her.

"Happy holidays!" Ava shouted before tossing a handful of candy in the air.

Clint closed his eyes. He had missed the sound of her voice, the touch of her skin. He'd lie awake at night in his dorm envisioning her pretty face, her sweet smile. Ava could make him laugh even after a lost game, and she had been his soft place to land while his parents struggled to keep their marriage together beneath the stress of a failing business. And Ava wasn't prissy like so many of the other girls in his class. They'd gone fishing and four-wheeling, but the best part was that she didn't just watch his baseball games. . . . She *knew* baseball—and basketball and football, for that matter. He'd never found anyone else like Ava Whimsy and had never really stopped missing her. He just didn't know how much until now. Clint had dated over the years. He'd even had a couple of serious relationships, but they'd never lasted. Were they both still unattached because even after all these years they were meant to be together?

Ava suddenly turned toward him. "Why move back now?" she asked so softly that Clint barely heard her over the music and revelry. Were her thoughts going in the same direction as his?

"Dad's having some health issues," Clint replied. He watched her dark brown eyes widen.

"Oh, I didn't know! Why didn't he tell me? Is it something serious?" She put a hand to her chest and waited for his explanation.

"No." Clint shook his head. "At least not at this point. But Dad needs to get a handle on his heart health, slow down, and lose weight. All of that bar food and beer has taken its toll."

"I can imagine."

Clint chuckled and then tugged on the beard that was starting to itch his face. "I'm even trying to convince him to switch up the menu and offer some healthier choices other than wings, fries, and burgers. He balked at the idea, but I'm going to cook for him and show him that healthy food can be tasty too."

"You can cook?" Ava finally seemed to forget to be guarded and grinned.

"Yes, and very well I might add." He'd spent a long time on his own and had needed to learn healthy cooking to stay in shape for the game and then later preached the importance of nutrition to.the kids he coached. Ava pushed her granny glasses up from where they kept slipping to the tip of her nose. "Wow, I'm surprised."

"I guess there's a lot we don't know about each other," Clint said. *And a lot I'd like to explain*, he thought with a touch of sadness.

"Yes, it's been a long time," Ava agreed. Her guarded expression returned. She remained quiet as the parade headed down Second Street, past a neat row of houses decorated with an abundance of Christmas cheer. The sun was dipping low in the sky and a breeze was kicking up, but colder temperatures didn't seem to dissuade the citizens of Cricket Creek from watching the parade.

Clint reached into the basket for more candy but instead encountered carved wooden toys. "What are these for?" He held up a cute little rocking horse.

"Oh, those are for Santa to hand out when we reach the big celebration on Main Street." She pointed to a gold sticker on the bottom. "A bit of self-promotion, I'm afraid. All of the toys in A Touch of Whimsy are handmade. And many of the crafters are local," she added with a lift of her chin.

Clint examined the toy, leaned closer to her, and whispered, "By local elves, you mean."

Ava tilted her head back and laughed.

God, Clint loved the sound . . . feminine and throaty. She might be dressed in a silly costume with white stuff sprayed on her hair, but underneath it all was still pure Ava.

Suddenly the parade came to a halt and everyone including the band became silent.

"What's going on?" Clint asked with a bit of alarm, but Ava put her index finger to her lips. Clint waited a minute but wasn't satisfied, so he scooted closer and whispered, "Seriously, Ava, what's happening?" It was then that Clint got a whiff of her perfume . . . the same light floral scent that she wore back in high school.

Ava turned her head slightly toward him and whispered back, "The parade is much better than when we were kids. Just watch. You'll see. . . . It's magical."

"Okay . . ." Clint nodded, but he was reluctant to return to his side of the sleigh. Temperatures were dropping, and when a gust of wind hit them, she shivered. It was all Clint could do not to put his arm around her shoulders and keep her warm. When he stayed close, she didn't protest, and so he didn't move.

It finally dawned on Clint that they were waiting for the sun to completely set. A few moments later, the big ball of fire dipped beneath the horizon. Lights . . . hundreds—no, thousands—of them sprang to life all at once, turning Main Street into a shining beacon of Christmas joy. Each shop, all of the trees, and every streetlamp lined along Main Street glittered against the backdrop of the darkening sky. The band started playing "It's Beginning to Look a Lot Like Christmas," and the crowd, including Ava, started cheering. The next song, "Silent Night," felt like a sweet breath of peace, played softly so that the town could sing along with their voices sounding as one.

Joy felt like a collective emotion, and for the first time in a very long while, Clint felt the spirit of the holidays grab him. When he started singing, Ava turned to him and smiled. He longed to take her hand and hold it, but he refrained.

"Start handing out toys, Santa! The children know what's coming and will be clamoring close to the sleigh with outstretched hands."

"There won't be enough for every kid," he said.

Ava patted his leg. "Don't worry. They know that if they miss out, all they have to do is come by my store to get a toy. It's the honor system."

"Generous of you, Mrs. Claus."

"It's not much, but all in the spirit of Christmas," she said brightly. When she noticed that her hand was still resting on his leg, her eyes widened over the glasses, and to his disappointment, she quickly pulled away. It was odd because Clint knew exactly what she was experiencing. In so many ways, it felt like old times, as if the fifteen years apart had never really happened. But on the other hand, he could feel the raw edges of the hurt that he had caused by disappearing so completely from her life when they had meant so much to each other.

When the parade started moving forward, Clint began tossing toys into eager hands. Each little toy was cuter than the next. "I'm looking forward to seeing your toy shop, Ava."

"It's located in the old hardware store. Ed moved to a bigger location just outside of town."

The heart and soul of Main Street remained the same, but the buildings looked fresh and vibrant. Myra's Diner, the hot spot after high school games, was now called Wine and Diner. While the original building remained, there was an addition and a brick-paved courtyard off to the side. "So Myra sold her diner?" The thought made him a little bit sad.

Ava shook her head. "No. When the diner was struggling to keep up with the chains, Myra's niece Jessica came back to town."

Clint thought for a minute and then nodded slowly. "Oh yeah. I remember that Myra took her in when she was a pregnant teenager. Didn't she become a big-time chef?"

"Yes, at a fancy restaurant in Chicago."

"Right, Dad told me some of this."

"Well, she came back with her daughter, Madison, who now teaches at the local college and is a playwright. Jessica married baseball star Ty McKenna, who, I'm sure you know, coaches the Cricket Creek Cougars."

"Wow . . . This little town has attracted some movers and shakers." He grinned when he pointed to Grammar's Bakery. "Still the best butter cookies on the planet?"

Ava groaned. "Yes, and such a temptation since it's located right across the street from my shop. The smell of baking bread is nearly impossible to resist."

Clint smiled when he spotted A Touch of Whimsy on the other side of the street. The structure was an original Cricket Creek redbrick building, but she had added some gingerbread trim painted white. The big picture window had a Christmas village display, and a huge wreath adorned the front door. He wanted to hear all about her business and her life, but he decided to go slowly.

"It must be fun owning a toy store."

Ava turned to face him. "Oh, it is! Everything in the store is pretty simple, requiring imagination rather than batteries. You won't find a video game in there." Ava shook her head but then grinned. "Growing up, I wanted all of the latest stuff, not realizing that the homemade toys beneath the Christmas tree were true treasures."

Clint swung his hand in an arc. "And obviously this is your busiest time of the year."

Ava nodded. "You're right. This is the most important season for most shops, but of course, especially for a toy store. There have been some lean years, for sure, but I've added arts and crafts, tea parties, and birthday parties. Dad teaches a wood workshop for children interested in making their own toys." She shrugged. "I'll never be rich, but I love what I do, and that's more than some people can say. I feel blessed."

"True," Clint said, thinking that he wished he felt the same peace within himself that Ava seemed to have. He wanted to ask her more, but she turned away once again, as if she was opening up and didn't want to give up more of herself. But he'd made her smile, heard her laughter. It was a beginning.

Here and there were other new shops that Clint didn't recognize, and although he remembered Cricket Creek as being a quaint river town, there was a fresh vibrancy, an air of excitement that he could see on the faces of the crowd.

And suddenly, to Clint's delight, it started snowing! Big, fat fluffy flakes swirled in the crisp night air. He couldn't have asked for a more perfect night to be reunited with Ava, and he didn't want to waste the opportunity to have her back in his life.

"Oh my!" Ava laughed with pure joy. "It's beautiful!"

Clint raised his gloved hands skyward. "Ho, ho, ho, cue the snow!"

"I wish it were that easy! We've hoped for snow for years, but it's never happened, at least while I've been part of the parade." She tilted her face upward and laughed again when the cold flakes hit her cheeks. She turned and smiled at him. "I guess you've missed snow."

"I've missed a lot of things."

Ava blinked at him for a moment, as if she wanted to

ask him more but was hesitant. "Main Street looks like a lovely scene inside a snow globe!" Her smile remained bright, but there was a nervous edge to her voice.

"Yes." Clint nodded. "You were right, Ava." With the fat flakes swirling in the wind and colorful Christmas decorations everywhere, Cricket Creek glittered with Christmas cheer. "It's truly magical."

Ava's smile widened, and she seemed to relax if just a little bit. Her cheeks were rosy from the cold, and she looked so adorable in the silly outfit that he wanted to lean over and kiss her. Something in his expression must have given him away because her smile faltered..

From that moment on, she kept her attention focused on the crowd. Disappointment settled in his gut, but he understood. He'd hurt her a long time ago, and they needed time to get to know each other again. But he knew he wanted to regain her trust. Fifteen years was a long time to be away, but there was still a strong bond between them. He could feel it.

A few minutes later, the parade and music halted once again. Noah and Olivia Falcon got out of the Corvette and headed over to the tall pine tree in the middle of the town square.

"It's time for the lighting of the tree," Ava explained.

A moment later, the tree exploded with color and the crowd roared with approval. The band started playing "O Christmas Tree," and once again Cricket Creek became a collective choir. Ava, though, remained quiet this time. Halfway through the song, a single tear slid down her face. She quickly brushed it away, leaving Clint to wonder if the show of emotion was for the lighting of the tree or if it had something to do with him. Once again, he wanted to reach over and take her hand, but he held back.

Clint didn't know if he could rekindle what they once had, but he was up for the challenge. He wanted to explain some things to Ava, and whether it closed the door between them or opened it for another chance, she deserved an apology.

Clint smiled softly. She might try to avoid him, but he was Santa Claus in Cricket Creek. He had that power, at least, and he wasn't above using a bit of holiday magic of his own.

3

Winter Wonderland

"Rosie, get over here!" Ava called from her back door. Rosie paused from playing in the snow to look up at Ava. "Come on, girl!" Ava coaxed, but Rosie's tongue lolled out of her mouth and she gave Ava that pleading look that said she wanted Ava to join her. "No, it's too cold!" Ava shouted as if Rosie understood English.

"Don't you want your treat?" Ava asked, but Rosie gave her an are-you-kidding-this-is-way-too-much-fun bark and then proceeded to frolic in the winter wonderland.

"You silly thing." Ava shook her head and pulled the edges of her pink terry-cloth robe closer together. She couldn't help but laugh when Rosie buried her nose in the snow and then flung some up into the air. The playful pup had shown up on Ava's back deck one cold and rainy night three months ago and had been living with Ava ever since.

After closing the door against the chill, Ava shivered

and then walked over to the kitchen counter to pour a cup of coffee. The fragrant steam cleared the remaining cobwebs from her head as she added cream and sugar. Rosie wouldn't venture very far, and after she had her fill of the snow, she would come scratching at the back door begging for a treat.

Ava lived in the apartment above A Touch of Whimsy, making her morning commute to work a mere walk down the stairs. The open floor plan made the space feel bigger than it actually was and she liked the rustic beamed ceiling, hardwood flooring and exposed brick walls. Her furnishings were mostly purchases from antique and thrift stores in Cricket Creek, except for the sturdy kitchen table built by her father. Beautiful rugs woven by her mother added a shot of color that brightened the otherwise neutral decor. While Ava still enjoyed trips out to her family's farm, she liked the convenience of being able to walk to many of her favorite stores and restaurants in town. Knowing how tough it was to stay in business, Ava preferred to spend her money locally. Now that the economy had picked up she shopped more often and it was such a blessing to see store owners thriving instead of the constant struggle.

After the snow flurries had turned into snow showers, last night's festivities had been cut short in an effort to get everyone home safely. Thankfully, the squall had only amounted to an inch or so and the streets were already safe to drive. With no more accumulation in the forecast, the rest of the Main Street events for the weekend should go on without a hitch. Well, unless you included the return of Clint Sully, but Ava refused to think about him before finishing her first cup of coffee.

Cradling the warm mug in her hands, Ava walked over to the front window and looked down over Main

Street. Bright sunshine had melted the snow on the pavement but it remained on the grass and rooftops, making the bright red Christmas bows and greenery look even prettier.

After yawning, Ava took a sip of the coffee she'd brewed extra strong since sleep had pretty much eluded her last night. All she could think about was Clint. She wondered what he looked like beneath the Santa beard and padded costume. He'd been tall and lanky up until senior year when he'd filled out, making him even more of a threat on the baseball field. Doubles and singles turned into home runs but he had remained fast on the base pads, rare for a catcher. She'd loved watching him play and almost never missed a game even if she had to stay up late doing her homework. Ava smiled at the memories that came flooding back. What would have happened if Clint hadn't moved to California? Would they be married with a house full of children?

"Don't go there," Ava grumbled. "That ship has sailed." She took another sip of coffee and tried to push thoughts of Clint from her brain. With an effort she started considering what to eat for breakfast when she spotted a black BMW Z4 convertible rolling down Main Street. Except for people like Ty McKenna and Noah Falcon, Chevys and Fords were the norm in Cricket Creek, and when the black beauty slid into a space across the street in front of Grammar's Bakery, she watched to see who would emerge from the driver's side. The door opened and long, jean-clad legs unfolded followed by wide shoulders in a black leather bomber jacket. A dark head of hair long enough for a girl to run her fingers through became ruffled in a sudden breeze. Silver aviator sunglasses glinted in the sunlight, shading his eyes, but Ava would have known that strong jawline and prominent nose anywhere. Her heart started beating faster.

Clint.

When he looked over at her shop Ava moved away from the window and flattened against the brick wall so fast that coffee sloshed over the top of her mug and splattered on her slippers. She wasn't sure if he knew she lived in the loft apartment but she wasn't taking any chances at being caught gawking at him. Still, she tiptoed — why she felt the need to tiptoe she didn't know but she did — back over to the corner of the window. Pressing her lips together, she peeked past the chocolate-colored panel curtain that was almost always kept open to let in sunshine. Ava watched Clint pause in front of his convertible and dig into his pocket. A moment later he answered his cell phone. "Oh boy . . ." she breathed when got a nice shot of denim-clad butt beneath the black leather jacket.

Wow . . . Clint Sully was all grown up and looking mighty fine! The Santa belly had been all padding. She watched until he opened the door and entered the bakery and then decided that a bowl of Special K would be an excellent choice for her own breakfast.

Still, Ava stood there for a moment, gathering her wits and sipping her coffee. After inhaling a deep breath she blew it out and said, "Just act natural around him." Taking her last swallow of coffee she added, "You know . . . casual." *And whatever you do, don't bring attention to yourself*, which was unfortunately something she had a knack for doing without ever trying.

Knowing she had to get downstairs Ava poured her cereal, wishing she had a banana to liven it up, and then got the treat out for Rosie. She waved the rawhide chew out the back door and finally managed to coax the happy puppy inside. "Hold still, you squirmy thing," Ava pleaded with a laugh. After wiping Rosie's wet paws with an old towel kept there for that purpose, she rewarded her dog with the chew. With her tail wagging furiously, true to form, Rosie scampered away to hide her beef-flavored treasure in back of the sofa.

"You should really mix it up with a different hiding place," Ava suggested when Rosie came back to get her ears scratched. "But I understand. I do the same thing with my stash of Reese's Cups." While Rosie crunched her puppy chow, Ava ate her cereal even though a warm and gooey cinnamon roll from Grammar's Bakery was calling her name. She suddenly remembered that powdered-sugar doughnuts and butter cookies had been Clint's treat of choice and she wondered if that's what he'd just bought.

"Who cares? Stop thinking about him!" Ava said so loud that Rosie paused in her crunching and gave her a you-humans-are-wacky look. *Perhaps you can't stop thinking about him because you do still care*, argued the voice inside her head that she longed to silence. After an exasperated groan, Ava grabbed a pen and paper, another cup of coffee, and starting making a list of things to do in order to prepare for the crowd of people attending the rest of the weekend celebration. A Touch of Whimsy was a part of the Christmas walk open house later that afternoon but the entire day would be a busy one. Pete usually played Santa for a couple of hours in the afternoon. With a little of flash of excitement Ava wondered if Clint would show up instead of his dad.

"I hope not," she mused out loud but then sighed. "Oh who am I kidding? But I'm just curious . . . nothing more," she told herself. Maybe instead of trying to act casual she should just give him the cold shoulder? Pretend indifference? She closed her eyes and sighed, acknowledging that it was pretty doggone difficult to give a cold shoulder to a man who made you feel warm all over. The thought snuck into her brain that maybe this was their second chance but she quickly squashed it. Getting over Clint Sully had been heart-wrenching and she didn't want to go through that pain ever again.

Even as she told herself that she wasn't going to do anything special because Clint was in town, Ava took extra pains with her makeup as she got ready for her day. And although she usually pulled her hair into a ponytail, today she curled it into what her cute little clerk Ronnie would call beachy waves and then fluffed it around her shoulders. Since Ava often got hands-on with the toy displays she normally dressed in jeans and a casual button-down oxfords with her logo stitched above the pocket but today she opted for a festive red sweater with pearls, sewn into the neckline. She added a green silk scarf and knotted it halfway down her chest. After taking a step back to look at her reflection she told herself she was simply celebrating the season but she knew darned well why she was dressing up. But when the image of sexy Clint in his leather jacket and jeans filtered into her head she was hit with a flash of insecurity. Sadly ironic, since Clint had been responsible for making her, an outdoorsy farm girl, feel beautiful. It didn't help knowing that he'd been living in LA on a college campus where all the women must be gorgeous. But then Ava fisted her hands on her hips and glared at herself in the mirror. Wasn't she the one who stocked uplifting books on self-esteem and acceptance in the book nook corner of the toy store? Didn't she always make sure that each and every girl felt like a princess at her Saturday tea parties? She was about to give herself an extended and much needed pep talk when her cell phone started ringing. Of course she never had the doggone thing next to her when it rang and had to hustle back into the kitchen and locate it.

When she saw that the screen said Grammar's Bakery, Ava answered. "Hello."

"Hey there, Ava, it's Mabel at the bakery."

"Oh, hi, Mabel. Are my cookies ready?"

"Yes, they sure are, sugar. I'll have them delivered."

"Oh, Mabel, I know you're swamped. I'll have Ronnie come over later and pick them up. I'm not going to put the cookies out until the Christmas walk open house or they will be long gone."

"Are you always such a sweetie?" Mabel said. "But listen." She lowered her voice to an excited whisper that had Ava's heart beating a little faster. Ava actually held her breath so she could listen more closely. "That's not the only reason I called."

"What's up?" Ava asked, even though she already had an inkling of where this was going.

"Guess who just stopped in here," Mabel continued in a low voice, but she didn't wait for Ava to answer. "Clint." She paused and then said in a lower tone, "Sully! Clint Sully," she then said together so that there would be no confusion.

"You don't say," Ava commented calmly.

"I'm not playin'! He said in all of LA there wasn't a bakery as good as mine," Mabel boasted and then lowered her voice again. "He's single, Ava. I know 'cause I asked."

"You asked?"

Mabel chuckled. "Hey, eligible bachelors in this little town are hard to find."

Ava grinned. "Are you going to make a play for Clint?"

"Oh, I wish! Sugar, when he walked in, my brain went

straight to you. Although I did admire how he filled out those jeans."

"Miss Mabel . . ."

"He's looking pretty doggone fly, I might add."

"Fly?"

"Hey, my employees are mostly teenagers. They rub off on me. Mercy me, but I remember how cute of a couple you two made back in high school."

"That was a long time ago," Ava reminded her.

"Child, seems like yesterday to me," Mabel said with a sigh.

A hot lump of emotion gathered in Ava's throat.

"Anyway, there's no need to send Ronnie over."

"But—"

"When Clint saw your name written on the box of cookies sitting on the counter, he offered to deliver them to you."

Ava's eyes rounded and she stood up straighter. "Is he on his way?"

"Just finishing up his coffee and a second powdered-sugar doughnut. I'm so glad that I added that café section in the bakery. He'll be over shortly, though, I imagine. Thought I'd give you fair warning. Hope I didn't do the wrong thing," Mabel added, but she didn't seem at all concerned.

"No, of course not," Ava assured her even though her heart continued to race. Matchmaking was a common practice in Cricket Creek. Ava supposed it was because in a small town everybody knew everybody. And Mabel was right. Eligible bachelors were a hot commodity in town, especially those over thirty.

"Well, I've got to get back to work. I love the Christmas season, but I'm already plumb tuckered out and it's just started. Oh, would you just listen to me whine? It wasn't too long ago that I wondered how I was going to keep the doors open and now I've expanded. I should count my blessings. Bye now, sugar."

"Bye, Miss Mabel," Ava said absently. After ending the call, she stood there for a second and then was suddenly galvanized into action. When she ran back into the bathroom to check her hair, Rosie seemed to know something was up and scampered after her as if she could somehow help. "Dear Lord but I'm *hot* and I don't mean in a sexy way. I'm sweating! Why did I put this sweater on?" She looked at Rosie, who gave her another humans-are-wacky look. "And I think this hair is . . . eighties big." She plucked at the sweater and then did an armpit check. "Oh, I *am* sweating!"

In a true panic, she yanked the sweater over her head but forgot about the scarf and somehow, someway, the entire thing became tangled around her shoulders with her arms stretched upward. "What the . . . ?" Ava tugged, nearly turning the slipknot on the scarf into a noose. The small tag on the scarf must have gotten snagged in the pearls.

"Grrr . . ." Ava tugged harder and suddenly found herself in a Houdini-type situation. This had happened to her once in a dressing room. She had found herself in a similar situation when she tried a dress on that had been two sizes too small and had to enlist the help of a clerk after she managed to zip it up but not down. But there wasn't a clerk here, only Rosie, who wasn't going to be any assistance. Ava wiggled wildly and at least managed to get the edge of the sweater down far enough to see. She looked into the mirror and decided that she looked like a red version of SpongeBob SquarePants.

Ava gave the sweater one last big tug. What was snagged popped loose, and it sailed over her head so fast

that she stumbled backward while the sweater went flying. Rosie thought it was a chase the sweater game, and
she went running to where it landed on the floor in her
bedroom. "No, Rosie!" Ava went chasing after her. The
sweater was a gift from her mother, and she didn't want
Rosie to ruin it.

"Stay!" Ava commanded as she chased after her little
dog, almost catching up to her just as she reached the
entrance into the kitchen. But then the doorbell rang.

To Rosie the doorbell meant visitors, and she went
bounding toward the door with the sweater hanging
from her jaw just as Ava went skittering after her into
the kitchen. Knowing she was going to be in full view of
the window, Ava tried to stop her forward progress, but
in her sock feet, she went sliding across the ceramic tile
floor as if on ice skates.

With mounting mortification, Ava realized that the
dark hair and leather jacket belonged to Clint. He stood
with his back to her, but when he turned and reached for
the doorbell, his eyes widened. She wasn't sure it was
from the fact she was clad only in her bra and jeans or if
he thought she was going to slam into the door. Luckily,
she came to a stop just before the collision. She dipped
down and retrieved her sweater from Rosie, who was at
this point more interested in the visitor than her prize.
Ava tugged it over her head, did a quick little smoothing
action, and then stood up. With a flip of her beachy
waves that now probably resembled a hurricane, she
opened the back door. "Clint? Come in," she said and
stepped back for him to enter. "What brings you here?"
She was going for casual, but the chase left her
breathless . . . or maybe it was seeing him that made her
breathless.

"You'll have to give me a minute while I get the image

of you in that pink lacy bra out of my head," Clint said as he set the box he carried onto the table.

Ava felt a blush steal into her cheeks that were probably as pink as the bra. "Ready now?" she asked while Rosie begged for his attention.

"Nope. I do believe the image is in my brain to stay. Sorry. I'm a guy and you're a beautiful woman. What can I say?" He gave her a slight shrug, and then before she could think of a reply, he knelt down to give Rosie some much-needed attention. But two words stuck in Ava's brain: "beautiful" and "woman." They weren't kids anymore. This was a whole new ball game.

"Whoof!"

"You have a face only a mother could love," Clint said with a chuckle. "You're a Heinz 57, for sure."

"He insulted you. Bite him," Ava said, and Clint chuckled. They might be adults, but the connection that started when they were kids remained.

Rosie responded by rolling over to her back. "Oh, you want a belly rub? Well, here . . ."

Rosie made little mewling noises of ecstasy, causing Ava to shake her head. "You've got a friend for life now."

Clint glanced up and gave Ava a smile that made her heart beat fast. "A good thing to have. I'll take it."

4

I'll Be Home for Christmas

Much to Rosie's sorrow, Clint stood up. "Your hair is pretty, Ava." He didn't really intend to voice his observation out loud. "I like that you've gone back to your natural color."

"Much better without the fake spray snow."

"That's what that stuff was?" His eyes widened.

"I read the label, Clint. It clearly said it was nontoxic," she replied in a defensive tone.

"So was the Kool-Aid that you used to dye your hair red for that Halloween party. You had pink hair for about a month."

"Hey, pink hair is in style now. I was just ahead of my time."

Clint laughed. "Your mom was so mad."

"I had extra chores until the pink Kool-Aid came all the way out. I took three showers a day and got into even more trouble when I used up too much water from the cistern." When she tipped her head to the side and laughed, Clint felt her guard slipping. Something in the air shifted, changed, taking them backward and yet forward at the same time.

"I brought the cookies from the bakery."

"You didn't have to do that."

Clint took a step closer to her. "I know. It was an excuse to see you."

"Clint, I—" she began, but when he saw protest in her eyes, he pulled her closer and kissed her. He felt her stiffen slightly, but when he cradled her head and deepened the kiss, he felt her relax and melt against his chest.

Clint ran the tip of his tongue over her full bottom lip, tasting, savoring, and teasing until he heard her soft moan asking for more. He threaded his fingers through her hair and kissed her again slowly, lingering until he finally pulled away to look into her eyes. He wanted to say something flirty, clever, but he was too blown away by his reaction, and emotion clogged his throat.

She swallowed, licked her bottom lip. "You kissed me," she said softly. Clint got the impression she wanted to sound accusatory but she failed, sounding more like she felt a sense of wonder.

He tilted his head and tucked a lock of hair behind her ear. "You kissed me back, Ava."

"You took me by surprise." She frowned slightly. "I . . . I . . . got caught up in the moment. Why did you do it?"

Clint rubbed the pad of his thumb over her chin. "Because I wanted to kiss you from the moment I saw you . . . even in that Mrs. Claus outfit."

She glanced down, swallowed hard but then tilted her head up and looked him square in the eye. "No, Clint. I meant why did you leave Cricket Creek instead of coming back here to live?"

Oh, that was such a loaded question. Clint had answers and she deserved to know them, but they stuck in his throat.

Ava took a step back and came up against the sink. "Was it that easy for you? A clean break?"

"Ava . . ." he began, and she looked at him expectantly but he couldn't go on.

"I guess it was." She lifted her chin and shoved past him.

"Ava!" He gently grabbed her arm.

She shook him off, but when he failed to leave, she slowly turned around. "I waited, you know. Hoped . . ." she began but trailed off and shook her head.

"I'm so sorry."

Ava looked at him for a long measuring moment and then shrugged. "We were young. And you had an offer you couldn't refuse. I get that." Ava's voice shook, but when Rosie trotted over and sat down by her side, she seemed to somehow draw strength from the little dog and get her emotions under control. After a deep breath, she said, "But when you didn't return, I went on with my life, Clint. And I'm doing well. It's not fair for you to come back here and wreck it."

"That's not my intention."

She blinked as if fighting back tears, and it clawed at his gut. "Then stay away, Clint. You had your chance with me." Her tone wasn't harsh or unkind but firm. "Please."

"What if I want another chance with you, Ava?" He took a step closer.

Ava stood her ground but lifted her chin and looked him square in the eye. "You waited too long."

Clint nodded solemnly and then shoved his fingers through his hair. "Okay. I understand how you must feel. But you don't know everything. There's more to this than meets the eye. Look, I know you have to get downstairs, but we need to get together. I want to explain some things." He felt the door that had opened earlier about to slam in his face. He shouldn't have given in to the moment and kissed her.

"You had fifteen years to do that, Clint. You could have looked me up when you came into town to visit your father. But you didn't."

"I know." He nodded again. "I *understand* how you must feel, but I'd welcome the chance to get together and talk about it."

At Ava's stony silence, Clint turned and walked away. When he reached the doorway, he paused and turned around. "There's still a spark between us, Ava. Don't deny it."

She swallowed but remained silent.

Clint shoved his fingers through his hair. It was all he could do not to drag her into his arms and kiss some sense into her, and judging by the rise and fall of her chest, she was feeling the same reaction. "I take that back. Not just a spark, Ava, but a damned flame."

5

Christmastime

Ava watched Clint leave, fighting the urge to go chasing after him. "What is it about Clint that turns me to mush?" she grumbled. No one in their right mind would run after a man who left her without looking back. What reasons could he possibly have to never even make an attempt to contact her over the years? "Seriously?" When Ava fisted her hands and groaned up at the ceiling, Rosie whined. With a crooked smile, Ava knelt down and scratched her dog behind the ears. "It's okay, girl. And thanks for having my back, well, until you rolled over and let him scratch your belly. But your heart was in the right place. I'm going to get you one of those gross pig ears that you love so much."

After thinking about it, Ava opted to leave the sweater on in an effort to remind herself that getting involved with Clint would only cause her to get all tangled up inside. Inhaling a deep breath, she retied the scarf and straightened the sleeves. As long as she didn't think about Clint, she wouldn't overheat.

But while Ava tamed her messy hair, she had a tough time not recalling how bone-melting it felt to have Clint's hands cradling the back of her head while he kissed her deeply, thoroughly, like she had dreamed about for years. She touched her fingertips to her bottom lip. Oh, Clint had been a good kisser when they were teenagers, but *that kiss* blew those memories right out of the water.

If the kiss was any indication, Clint would be an amazing lover. Not that she was going to find out. "Wow . . ." Fanning her cheeks, Ava hurried back to the kitchen. After pausing to fill Rosie's water bowl, she stopped to pat the little dog on the head. She gave Ava an I-know-you're-leaving me sad puppy face and then trotted over to her bed, flopped down, and rested her face on her paws. "I'll be back later to let you out, Rosie," Ava crooned. Rosie's eyes were already looking heavy. The morning romp in the snow was taking its toll.

With a smile, Ava picked up the cookies and then headed down the stairs leading to the toy store. "Hi, Ronnie," Ava called as she set the box behind the counter. "Sorry I'm a little bit late." She smiled at the cute little college junior who helped her out on weekends and during the holiday rush.

"No problem. I used my key to get in. And we're pretty much ready to open." Ronnie stepped back from the display of wooden blocks she was arranging into a castle. "Do you think it needs a moat?"

"Of course."

"That's what I was thinking." Ronnie was dressed in a fun little elf outfit and wore black knee-high boots. "Well, would you look at those rosy cheeks of yours?" She flipped her long strawberry blond braid over her shoulder and arched one eyebrow.

Ava put her cool palms to her warm cheeks. "I've been, you know, rushing around." She pointed to the sweater and plucked at the fabric. "And this thing is hot."

"And seriously boring."

"I prefer the term 'festive.'"

Ronnie sighed. "You're so gorgeous, and for some reason you don't play it up. I'm dying to take you shopping. Oh ..." She wiggled her eyebrows. "Speaking of gorgeous, tell me all about your hot boyfriend who just walked across the street and climbed into that sexy BMW."

"Clint?"

"Is that his name?"

"Yes—but wait. He's not my boyfriend."

Ronnie fisted her hands on her hips. "Okay, *was* your boyfriend."

"Some fifteen years ago." When Ronnie's eyes widened, Ava said, "Yeah, you were a little kid at the time." She waved a hand upward. "Ancient history. Wait. How did you know that anyway?"

"Are you kidding? Are you forgetting where you live? This is a small town, Ava." Ronnie shook her head, making her cute elf hat slide sideways to a jaunty angle. "And Facebook sure does accelerate small-town gossip." She laughed. "Even my grandma has an account. This news just might be trending on Twitter."

Ava put her hand to her pearl neckline. "Since when did little old me become great big news? I mean ... are you joking?"

Ronnie laughed. "A tiny bit, but the town is talking. Seriously, Ava, you need to do more in the way of social media."

"The store has a Facebook page and a Twitter account. I update it almost daily. The Christmas village is now our cover photo. And I tweeted about the twenty percent discount with a canned goods donation."

"I mean you personally."

"What would I tweet about? What I ate for breakfast?" She wrinkled her nose, thinking about the Special K that ended up having some sort of strange dried strawberries that got mushy with milk.

"So tell me all about what's going on between you and hot stuff."

"Nothing! Clint is Pete Sully's son. He came home to keep an eye on his dad's health. Coming back here has nothing to do with me." She twisted the scarf around her index finger for a second. "So do you think he's hot?"

Ronnie grinned.

"Okay, forget I asked that last part."

"Yes, he is seriously hot, you know, for an older dude."

Ava rolled her eyes.

"What?" Ronnie flipped her palms upward. "Why do you always act like my compliments are insults?"

"Someday you'll understand."

Ronnie went back to building the castle but said, "So, I also heard that Clint was playing Santa in the parade instead of Pete. How was that?"

"Awkward."

"Will he be stopping by the store later during the Christmas walk?"

Ava busied herself lighting a pine-scented candle. "I sure do hope not."

"You are such a terrible liar."

"See now, I take *that* as a compliment."

"Weirdo," Ronnie said but laughed.

"Hey, normal is way overrated," Ava commented as she walked around the store making sure that everything was ready for the busy day. When Ava had first opened the shop, her mother had often pitched in to help out. But once her brothers had started having children, her mother's free time was taken up with babysitting. Hard-working and free-spirited Ronnie was a good fit for working in the toy store, and Ava had grown quite fond of her over the past few years. Ronnie had the perfect personality for putting on puppet shows and hosting birthday parties. Ava was going to miss her when she graduated from college and moved on with her life.

"Are we ready to open, Ava?"

"I think so. We'll put the cookies and punch out at one o'clock. Just plug in the train on the Christmas village. Oh, and don't forget the two canned goods thing."

"Gotcha." Ronnie saluted as she walked over to the front door. But when she glanced out of the front window, Ava saw her stop and stare.

Ava felt her heart skip a beat, thinking Ronnie had spotted Clint once again, but when she followed Ronnie's gaze, it was Braden Greenfield who was commanding her little elf's attention. "Well, now," Ava said in a teasing tone.

"What?" Ronnie asked lightly, but there were two pink spots of color in her cheeks.

"You can't fool me. You're blushing."

Ronnie lifted her braid. "Ginger problems. We're always blushing."

Ava nodded toward Braden, who was coming out of Grammar's holding a large cup of coffee. "Braden's pretty hot, you know, for a *young* guy."

"Ha-ha," Ronnie said and then lifted one shoulder. "I guess so, if you're into the whole cowboy look. Personally, I go for frat boys. Spiky hair. Abercrombie and Fitch."

Ava shook her head. "You're kidding me."

"Of course I'm kidding you. Those Wranglers, boots, and that hat? Mmmm-mmm." She gestured palm up toward the window. "Would you just look at him?"

Ava laughed. "You had me worried for a minute. I babysat Braden. He's like a little brother to me, but yeah, he's a hottie, for sure."

Ronnie let out a long sigh. "I know."

"Make a play for him, Ronnie."

Ronnie turned away from the window and wrinkled her nose. "He's dating stuck-up skinny-as-a-stick Stacy Meadows."

"Are they exclusive?"

Ronnie shrugged. "I don't know. But, Ava, she has mile-long legs and great big boobs." She cupped her hands beneath her chest to demonstrate.

"Ronnie Carlton, you're gorgeous!"

"Ava, I'm five foot two and wear a push-up bra to make the most of my itty-bittys," she said in a deadpan tone. "At best, I'm perky and"—she shrugged—"cute." She lifted her braid. "And I'm a ginger."

"Are you kidding? Just look at you in that elf outfit. And your hair color is natural and very pretty."

She rolled her eyes and pointed to her nose. "Freckles that makeup hides for, like, a minute. Like I said, *cute*. Not a blond bombshell."

"You're also smart and funny."

"Yeah, well, long legs and big boobs get the guys."

"I think you're selling yourself short."

"No pun intended, right?"

Ava laughed but then sobered when a thought occurred to her.

"What?"

"Nothing."

"Ava, you have that look on your face. You know I

won't let up until you tell me. Just get it over with and save us both a lot of trouble."

Ava leaned against the counter for support. "It's just that I used to think the same thing about Clint. He was big man on campus, and I was just this little ol' farm girl. I wondered what he saw in me. I even lightened my hair thinking I needed to be blond . . . even though I'd never be a bombshell."

"Ava! You're beautiful and funny and . . . Hey, did you trick me into this?" She fisted her hands on her hips but then smiled slowly. "Well played, Whimsy. Well played."

Ava laughed and then wiggled her fingers. "You're like putty in my hands."

Ronnie rolled her eyes again and seemed about to reply, but a knock at the front door reminded them that it was time to open up. Customers immediately started pouring in, and the steady stream of business continued all morning long. The only time Ava took a break was when she hurried upstairs to let Rosie out to tinkle before the Christmas walk started.

"So, do you think Clint will show up?" Ronnie asked while Ava replenished the tray of cookies. Clearly she wasn't going to give up on their earlier conversation. Unfortunately, there was a break in the action while the high school band played a Christmas concert over on the town square.

"I asked him to stay away, Ronnie."

"Ava! Have you lost your mind?"

"It's better that way."

"You don't know that. I mean, what if— "

Ava raised a hand in protest. "No more 'what ifs' or 'maybes'. I've been down that road."

Ronnie picked up a tree-shaped cookie. "You're forgetting one important thing."

"And that is?"

"Clint is back, Ava. And that changes everything."

"It changes nothing."

Ronnie shook her head. "It's Christmastime. Anything can happen. You just wait and see."

6

Have Yourself a Merry Little Christmas

"Would you just put the Santa suit on and head over to Ava's shop, Clint? You damned well know you want to."

"That beard makes me itch."

"I meant you know you want to see Ava. The Santa thing is just an excuse to head over there."

"Dad." Clint finished drying a wineglass and then whipped the towel over his shoulder. "You need me here at the tavern. As soon as the Christmas walk is over, you're going to get slammed with thirsty customers."

"Son, I'll handle it."

Clint turned and rested a hip against the sink. "Are you forgetting that I came back to help you so you'll slow down?"

Pete sat down on a barstool. "I've got plenty of hired help and they'll be here soon enough. I just wanted everybody to have the chance to join in the festivities up on Main Street before their shifts."

"I mean help for you personally! Stop being so stubborn and let me help run things around here."

"No need to get so testy."

"Sorry, Dad." Clint started pouring peanuts into small bowls lined along the bar. "I didn't mean to sound like an ass. I'm just worried about you."

"There's more to your mood than this. Tell me."

Clint sighed. His father had always been perceptive. It made him a great bartender. "Ava told me to stay away from her."

"Well, so what? Don't do it," he said.

Clint had to smile. It was just like his father to get straight to the point. They had been so close during Clint's childhood but had drifted apart after the divorce. The health scare made Clint realize that had to change.

"Um, I don't plan on becoming a stalker," Clint stated with a shake of his head. He suddenly needed a beer but didn't want to drink one in front of his father, who was doing a pretty good job of cutting back.

"Don't stalk her, Clint. Woo her. Win her over." There was a bit of a haunted look in his father's eyes that made Clint wonder if he was thinking of the mistakes he made with Maria, Clint's mother. "Don't blow having a second chance," he said, but instead of his usual booming voice that Pete Sully was known for, his words came out low and gruff. "You might never get another one."

Clint had to swallow the emotion clogging his throat. "Are we talking about me, Dad?" he asked gently.

"Not entirely." Pete scrubbed a hand down his face. "I guess my little health scare got me thinking about my life and that I won't be here forever." He shrugged. "And Christmas has always been a tough time for me."

"Because Mom loved the holidays so much?"

"Yeah, and with both of you gone, well . . ."

"Dad, why didn't you ever tell me any of this?"

"Son, if we sat here all day, I wouldn't be able to get through the list of things I should have said and things I didn't do. Pride always got in my damned way. But when my ticker started giving me trouble, well, let's just say it was an eye opener." His father cleared his throat in a rare show of emotion. Clint always viewed his father as a big, tough, robust man, but right now he looked older, sadder, and, well, just tired.

"I shouldn't have stayed away so long," Clint said, surprised when his voice shook.

"I admit that I was surprised when you decided to live in California. Was it . . . was it because of the divorce?"

Clint toyed with the towel and swallowed hard. He finally inhaled a deep breath and then blew it out. "No, Dad. It was because of guilt. I left you and Mom during a dark time. The tavern was struggling. You two were always fighting. But I was always the glue that seemed to hold you two together, and when I left, it all fell apart."

"Son, you had to take the scholarship. It was your chance at an education and a baseball career."

"Yeah, I know." Clint laughed harshly and then leaned forward with both palms on the bar. "And I *failed*. Didn't get drafted. I wasn't good enough. For a long time I was too ashamed to come home a failure, knowing that if I had stayed, you and Mom might have made it." He didn't have the heart to mention Ava.

His father looked at him for a long moment, and something happened that Clint has never seen before. . . . His father was crying. He brushed at tears leaking out of the corners of his eyes, and his big, strong shoulders shook. "Ahhh, Clint. Damn."

"Here." Not knowing what else to do, Clint handed his father a few cocktail napkins and watched him blot the tears.

"Trust me. I know all about stubborn pride and the damage it can do. Look, I know you and Ava were young when you broke up and she might harbor some hurt feelings, but, Clint, if there's something between you two after all these years apart, imagine what could develop when you're together."

"I pretty much told her that, but—"

"No buts, Clint. And while we're at it, let me tell you something else. I'm proud of you. You worked your everloving tail off to make it to the major leagues."

"But I didn't make it."

"That's not the important part."

Clint lifted his shoulders and let out a sigh. "Thanks, Dad. For a long time I felt as if not making it was a failure, and it kept me from coming home as often as I should. But my journey was really a stepping-stone to coaching. I actually get more satisfaction out of teaching than I got out of playing. I'm looking forward to working for Noah Falcon."

"You'll be an asset to the coaching staff. But sit down. There's more I want to talk to you about. You might want to grab a beer."

"Okay." Clint felt his heart thud at the grave sound of his father's voice. He considered refusing the beer but then decided that he might need it. "You want something?"

"Yeah, I want a bourbon and Coke, but I'll settle for a Diet Sprite. Can't even have the Coke because of the caffeine."

"You're doing great," Clint said while he poured the drinks. "You've lost weight and already lowered your cholesterol. Give yourself some credit."

"Whatever . . ." His father waved a dismissive hand but then grinned. "But to be honest, I really do feel better."

"Seems like honesty is the word of the day," Clint said carefully. After sliding the soft drink to his father, he came around and sat down on a stool. They had about an hour before people started pouring in after the Christmas open house walk, but the staff would be arriving soon, and he wanted privacy. "Shoot," Clint said much more calmly than he felt.

"You know how your mother and I met, right?"

Clint took a swig from his mug and then nodded. "She was singing at a honky-tonk in Nashville. You convinced her to come to Cricket Creek to sing here at the tavern."

"Your mother is a talented woman, Clint. I kept her from pursuing her dream of being a singer-songwriter."

Clint frowned. "But you got married, had me. I thought she wanted to live here and raise a family."

"That's what I wanted." He tapped a fingertip to his chest. "When I'd catch her writing songs, I'd give her something to do at the tavern. When you came along, I made her feel guilty for doing anything other than raising you." He sighed. "I told myself I was doing the right thing. I reminded her that she was a wife and a mother. I called her songwriting a pipe dream that she needed to give up."

"Aw, Dad . . ."

"I know. I know. But once words are spoken, you can't take them back. But, Clint, in truth, I was afraid that if she became successful, she'd leave me. And it was my damned selfish pride rearing its ugly head. When things got tough around here, Maria wanted to write some songs, try to get published and bring in some money, but dumb-ass me argued with her. I told her she was needed here and not piddling around with her music."

254 *LuAnn McLane*

"Wow."

"Yeah." He laughed harshly. "Is it any wonder that she left me? I should have offered to sell the tavern and move to Nashville. I knew it was what she wanted but would never ask. I didn't want to give this place up. It had been in the Sully family for sixty years."

"Dad, that's understandable."

"Really? This is a building. She is"—Pete swallowed hard—"was my wife." He shook his head. "And karma sure came back to bite my ass, didn't it? Maria makes lots of money doing what she loves. She's won awards, Clint. I robbed her of that for many years. Stubborn, selfish pride sure is a cold-ass bedmate." A muscle jumped in his father's jaw. "All I had to do was support her dream and things would have been so damned different." He looked into the glass of Sprite and shook his head slowly. "You know that Keith Urban song, 'Stupid Boy'?"

"Um . . . yeah."

"That could have been written about me. I fenced her in until she realized that she could leave. And then she was gone."

"Did you ever tell Mom any of this?"

"Hell no."

"Maybe you should." Clint hesitated and then added, "You know she never bad-mouths you. She always just said that you two didn't see eye to eye."

"Well, she always did have class. One of the many things I loved about her."

"You still love her?"

"Yes, and I miss her every day."

"She might like to hear that."

"Ahh, Clint, your mother has a nice life. I don't want to do anything more to screw it up. I've done enough harm already." He pointed at Clint. "But if you still have feelings for Ava, then you should take this shot. If it doesn't work out, then so be it. But don't live with regret. Take it from an expert; it sucks. I'm telling ya, woo her."

Clint tilted his head and grinned. "Woo her, huh? You mean like standing beneath her bedroom window and singing?"

"Hell yeah, if that's what it takes!" Pete laughed and then clamped a hand on Clint's shoulder. "But you might start with something simple like chocolate."

"I'll keep that in mind," Clint said, relieved to see the twinkle back in his father's eyes.

"So, are you going to head on over there?"

"No. I think I need to give Ava time to adjust to the fact that I'm back. In the meantime, I'll put a game plan together."

"Smart thinking." Pete tapped his temple.

"And, Dad, thanks for talking to me man-to-man."

"It helped. And you know what?"

"What?" Clint asked and then drained the last of his beer.

"I might have played jolly old Santa every year, but this is the first time in a long while I'm really looking forward to having a merry Christmas. It's good to have you home."

7

It's Beginning to Look a Lot like Christmas

Ava helped Ronnie clean up the sparkles and glitter left over from several hours of ornament making with a roomful of rambunctious children. Their Saturday-afternoon Christmas Crafts for Kids workshop gave local parents a few hours to do some shopping around town, knowing their children were supervised and getting the chance to be creative. With only two weeks left before the big day, time was running out. Plus, the kids loved creating presents for their parents and friends.

"Did anyone actually get any glitter on the ornaments?" Ronnie grumbled as she dumped a dustpan full of it into the trash.

Ava laughed. "Good question. Hey, I can finish up here. Why don't you head on out. I know you've got something better to do on a Saturday evening. You just

might want to change from your elf costume first—
although you do look cute in it."

"It's not a costume. I am an elf." She pointed to her
pointed ears. "These are real. I bake cookies in a tree,
too."

Ava laughed. "I believe you."

"Hey, I'm going over to Sully's tonight with a bunch
of girlfriends. It's Christmas Carol Karaoke Night. It's
always a riot. Why don't you come with us?"

"Thanks, but I thought I might head over to make
cookies with my mom."

Ronnie stomped her elf boot, causing the bell on the
toe to jingle. "Ava, it's *Saturday* night. You need to let
your hair down and have some fun. Call up some
friends."

"Most of my friends are married with kids."

"Well, they need to get out too."

"I don't want to run into Clint," Ava admitted. In all
honesty, she was disappointed that all she'd seen of him
the past two weeks was when she spotted him stopping
by at Grammar's Bakery. Pete had actually been dropping by the shop dressed as Santa.

Ronnie hugged the broomstick to her chest. "I think
you do want to run in to him."

"I do not!"

Ronnie arched one eyebrow. "The man sent you flowers, bourbon balls from Rebecca Ruth, and a cinnamon
cake from Grammar's. I think he's sending a pretty clear
message. You need to call him! And the next thing on the
agenda is a kiss. Then you'll know if there's still something there."

Ava caught her bottom lip between her teeth and felt
a blush steal into her cheeks.

"What?" Ronnie dropped the broom and didn't even

flinch when it clattered to the floor. "You *kissed*! You've kept this juicy little tidbit to yourself! How was it? Amazing?"

Ava nodded glumly.

"Well, why don't you go after him? I bet today you get an Edible Arrangement or something. What does the man need to do? I don't get it."

"Ronnie, it's obvious that there's still something there, but I don't want to get hurt all over again."

Ronnie shrugged. "Well, if you ask me, I'd much rather get hurt than never know."

"I'm not asking you. Look, my wise little elf, I should never have told you about the kiss. It just sort of slipped out."

Ronnie put her arms akimbo. "Let me guess—because you can't stop thinking about the kiss? About him?"

Ava felt heat creep into her cheeks once more.

"Thought so."

Ava started walking around tossing trash into a big plastic bag. "It takes more than flowers and candy. Why doesn't he show up?"

"Maybe he wants you to think about him, you know, and miss him."

"I've missed him for fifteen years!" Ava said and then clamped a hand over her mouth.

"Ava," Ronnie said gently. "You didn't just tell me anything I hadn't already figured out. Give this a shot. What is the worst thing that could happen?"

"Like I said, I'll get my heart handed to me on a silver platter."

"No. I'm telling you, that's not the worst thing. Having a shot at happiness and not taking it? You're made of stronger stuff than that. Besides, Cricket Creek is a small town. Do you seriously think you can avoid him forever?"

Ava groaned.

"What do you have to lose?"

"Um, my heart, my self-esteem, my pride, my store."

"Your store?"

"I threw that in for good measure."

Ronnie rolled her eyes. "Okay look, why don't you come out with me tonight to Sully's Tavern? Christmas Carol Karaoke Night really is a blast, and if Clint totally ignores you or it goes way wrong, then I'll shut my pie-hole once and for all."

"You promise?"

"Elf's honor." Ronnie made a show of crossing her heart. "So you're coming?"

Ava inhaled a deep breath and then gave her a level look.

"I'll take that as a yes." Ronnie picked up the broom and handed it to Ava. "I'll come by and swoop you up at eight. Oh, and wear something sexy!!" She waved her hand over her head as she hurried toward the door.

After Ronnie breezed out the door, Ava stood there in the middle of the room holding on to the broom for support. "Now, how in the world did I just let that happen?"

Ava tidied up the shop, pretty much going through the motions, but her thoughts were hitting all over the map like a pinball in an arcade machine. Excitement, fear, and anger were pinging around in her head until she couldn't think straight. Ronnie, of course, was right in so many ways, but she was looking at the world through the eyes of a twenty-two-year-old. At that tender age, Prince Charming and the fairy-tale wedding were still somewhere on the horizon and on a Pinterest board. There was . . . *hope* of finding true love and living happily ever after . . . romantic notions that Ava had all but given up on. But were she and Clint still single for a reason? Did he deserve a second chance? Ava closed her eyes and sighed. Hope was being tossed to her like a life preserver in her sea of doubt.

Should she grab it?

Yes! The word rang out in her head like a giant gong. "Well, why not?" she said softly, but her voice sounded loud and clear in the empty shop. "Why the *hell* not." She picked up a smiling stuffed monkey that had fallen to the floor and hugged it to her chest, reminding herself that this wasn't about failing but about trying. This wasn't about getting hurt but finding out and, yes, about grabbing on to and clinging to . . . hope.

She pushed the monkey back and said to it, "Now, for that all-important question! What in the world am I going to wear?"

Ava laughed as she locked the front door and then took the stairs up to her loft two at a time, startling Rosie, who was perched on the sofa, looking out the window. Forgetting to scold Rosie for sitting on the back of the sofa, she said, "I'm going out tonight!"

Of course, all Rosie knew was the word "out" and bolted for the back door.

"Okay . . . okay!" Ava laughed and opened the door, letting the cold, crisp breeze cool her cheeks and chase away the rest of her doubt. This time of year meant long hours at the shop, but instead of feeling dead on her feet, she suddenly felt energized and ready to go!

8

This Christmas . . .

Clint popped the top off of a Kentucky Ale and slid it across the bar to Noah Falcon. The tavern was filling up fast, and there was a festive feel in the air that had everybody abuzz with conversation and laughter. Evidently, Christmas Carol Karaoke Night was a popular annual event in Cricket Creek. There were even prizes to be awarded.

"Hey, let's set up a time to get together and talk," Noah said.

Clint leaned closer to the baseball legend and nodded. "I'd like that. I'm living over at the high-rise across from the stadium."

"Good deal," Noah said. "Ty McKenna is home watching his kid tonight, but I'll introduce him to you next week."

"Thanks, I'm looking forward to it," Clint said. Noah Falcon was a hometown hero in more ways than one. First, for being a major-league baseball superstar and then for being a soap-opera heartthrob, but mostly for building the baseball stadium that brought prosperity back to Cricket Creek. Clint had once dreamed of following in Noah's footsteps, well, except for the soap opera part, but he was really looking forward to this opportunity. The Cricket Creek Cougars were a step below the minor leagues and competed in an independent professional baseball league designed to give players a chance to play the game and get noticed by scouts for the big leagues. Many of them either had gotten cut at the higher level or, like Clint, never got the shot to prove themselves at the higher level.

Clint slid a couple of beers over to another customer and then turned to his father, who was mixing a martini. "It's getting packed in here. When does the karaoke begin?"

"As soon as Mia Patrick steps up to the microphone and gets things under way."

"Isn't she also the public relations director for the Cougars?"

"Yeah, and married to Cameron Patrick, a Cougar player who got drafted into the minors and is doing quite well, I might add. She's cute as a button but a tough little cookie when it comes to business. Got me to buy a big ol' sign advertising Sully's out in center field. Oh, here she comes now."

Clint looked over to see a cute blonde hurrying to the microphone. She was wearing a sparkling silver dress and high heels that looked impossible to walk in, much less hurry in. "Good evening, everybody, and welcome to the third annual Cricket Creek Christmas Carol Karaoke party!" Beer bottles and glasses were raised, and a loud collective cheer went through the crowd.

"I just want to remind everybody that there is a big

box for canned goods right here behind me." She gestured overhead with her thumb. "We want to stock up the food bank for the holidays. And if you didn't already know, and I'm sure you do because I don't shut up about it, Heels for Meals—my charity with my friends Olivia, Jess, Madison, Sunny, Violet, Bella, Nicolina, and Myra—is going strong over at Violet's Vintage Clothing or you can access us online. Ladies, we've got a nice collection of donated designer shoes for sale just in time for the holiday season! All of the proceeds will go directly to local families in need of some extra help during Christmas and throughout the entire year.

"That said, here are tonight's karaoke rules. If you want to come up here and sing a song, it will cost you five dollars, the money going to Pete Sully's charity, Toys for Tots and Teens. Noah Falcon, Ty McKenna, and my dad, Mitch Monroe, have gotten together to donate lots of prizes including hats, T-shirts, and the grand prize of season tickets to the Cricket Creek Cougars baseball games. We've also got dinner at Wine and Diner, jewelry from Designs by Diamante, toys from A Touch of Whimsy, just to name a few. So dig into your wallets and whet your whistle. Oh, and if you have a little bit too much fun, if you know what I mean, there is Santa's sleigh . . . well, Santa's minivan, out front ready to shuttle people home.

"And let's not forget about the five bucks for a mistletoe kiss. If you're under the mistletoe and you hear three dings from the tip bell over at the bar, you have to stand there and wait for your kiss from the person who put up the five bucks . . . unless you want out of it—that will cost you ten." She waited for the whistles and applause to die down. "Let's get this party started!"

Clint joined the crowd and applauded. He leaned close to his father and said, "Wow, I'm impressed."

Pete nodded. "Our little town bands together and does big things."

"I agree," Clint said. He would have added more, but when he glanced over to the front entrance and saw Ava enter with Ronnie, the rest of what he was going to say evaporated in his brain. They paused at the coat check his dad had set up to accommodate the crowd, and when Ava slipped off her long leather jacket, Clint caught himself staring. She wore a tan skirt that hit above the knee and a shimmery gold button-down sweater that exposed the smooth column of her neck and just a hint of cleavage. Her hair was piled up in a loose bun with just a few loose tendrils caressing her face. Her jewelry was minimal, and she wore dark brown leather boots with chunky heels that added to her height. The look was timeless, classy, and yet Clint didn't think he'd ever seen a woman look so damned sexy.

"When you pick your jaw back up off the floor, I could use two Bud Lights," Pete requested.

Clint nodded absently to his father, not hearing a word he'd said because in that moment, Ava looked over at him. When their eyes met she didn't look away, but held his gaze. A slow smile spread across her face, making Clint's heart thud. Something had changed.

"Oh, for Pete's sake—and I do mean me," Clint's father grumbled and nudged him out of the way so he could grab the beers. But then Pete must have spotted Ava looking at Clint. He grinned. "Well, I'll be . . ."

"We're packed. Where's she going to sit?" Clint asked, worried that Ava might leave before he had his chance. But then a group of girls sitting at a round table over in the corner waved to her and Ronnie.

"Go on over and say hi. I'll hold down the fort here at the bar," Pete offered.

Clint shook his head. "I'll wait until they get settled before I head over there," he said. In truth, he needed time to gather his wits about him and figure out something clever to say.

"Okay. Let me know when you want to get your mistletoe kiss. It's over there . . ."

Clint looked over his shoulder to where his dad was pointing. "Seriously? At the hallway to the bathrooms? You can't avoid going under it."

Pete chuckled as he handed another beer to Noah Falcon. "I know. At some point you have to put yourself at risk, right, Noah?"

Noah laughed. "You got that right."

Clint shook his head and looked over at Noah Falcon. "It's for a good cause. I'm guessing it becomes pretty popular later in the evening. But I'd sure hate to get turned down with the ten-buck rule."

"Well, unless you're married," Noah said with a laugh. "Olivia is over there sitting with Myra, Jessica, and Madison. She'd be pissed if another woman tried to kiss me, so I've got a slew of tens in my pocket." He patted his jeans.

"Who came up with this mistletoe craziness?" Clint wanted to know.

"Mia did last year," Pete replied. "She's a money-making machine, especially when it's for a good cause."

A moment later, Clint was laughing until his sides hurt when Ava, Ronnie, and her group of friends stood up and got the karaoke started with "Grandma Got Run Over by a Reindeer." Ava was doing more laughing than singing, but Ronnie held her own, bringing the house down with the funny ending to the song.

Noah chuckled and pointed to the next group heading up to the microphone. "Ty is home with his son, Ben, so Jessica could come out tonight. In case you didn't recognize them, that's her daughter, Madison, and of course their aunt Myra, who used to run the diner until Jess took over."

"Jessica doesn't look too happy about singing," Clint observed while he watched Myra and Madison all but drag Jessica up to the stage.

Noah laughed and raised his phone to film the whole thing. "Ty is going to be so sorry that he missed this."

The trio did a very bad version of "I Saw Mommy Kissing Santa Claus," but still got a very big round of applause.

"Hmmm . . ." Pete got out his clipboard and made a note. "Could win the worst performance," he said with a chuckle.

When Olivia stood and started singing a beautiful rendition of "Blue Christmas," Clint observed Noah beaming with pride. During his baseball heyday, Noah Falcon had been known to be quite the playboy, but he sure looked at his wife with adoring eyes. With that in mind, Clint looked over at Ava's table in time to see her with her chin cupped in her palm, listening intently to the song. He thought about his dad's recent admission and knew it to be true. Christmas is blue when you can't spend it with the people you love the most. The first year after the divorce, Clint couldn't bring himself to come home to a broken family and had stayed in his dorm and eaten a frozen turkey dinner, wishing all the while for his mom's mashed potatoes and gravy. From that moment on, Christmas represented more sadness than joy. This Christmas, he hoped things would be different. His father nudged him and handed him a martini glass.

"Take this over to her, Clint. I'll get Mia over here to

help me behind the bar. She gets a big kick out of ringing the tip bell."

Clint took the delicate glass from his father's big hand. "Okay, but if you need me . . ."

"Go! You've been working your tail off all week. Have some fun tonight."

When Clint hesitated, Noah said, "Hey, if you need some extra help behind the bar, I'll step in for you."

"Thanks, Noah," Clint said.

"If you're wondering if I'm buttering you up, I am. I played college ball with Jake Barnet and he has really good things to say about you. I really want you on my staff." Noah winked. "Now, go get that sweet little toy store owner you've been staring at since she walked in."

"I think I will." He put the drink down for a second and reached in his pocket for his wallet. "Dad, here's five bucks. Ring the bell when you catch Ava beneath the mistletoe." Clint picked the glass back up, took a deep breath, and wished he had a drink of his own for a little liquid courage. He'd approached plenty of women over the years, and no one had ever made him feel nervous jitters the way he was feeling now. But they were good jitters, the kind he always felt with the bases loaded, two out at the bottom of the ninth inning. He was halfway over to the table when he saw Ava get up from her chair. His heart pounded when he saw that she was headed in the direction of the ladies' room.

Oh boy . . .

The mistletoe kiss was supposed to happen later, after Ava had a few drinks and he'd—what was the word? Oh yeah, wooed her. Clint looked over at his dad at the bar and gave him a "don't do it" look, but it must have been misinterpreted and he was given a thumbs-up. He saw his dad reach for the bell, almost in slow motion. If Clint didn't show up for the kiss, Ava would stand there feeling stood up. Clint looked down at the cosmopolitan and then drained it in four gulps. A moment later, the bell rang three times, bringing a cheer from the crowd.

9

It Must Have Been the Mistletoe

When Ava heard the bell ding, she looked up and, yep, there it was, *the mistletoe.* With a silly smile pasted on her face, Ava came to a halt even though she really wanted to bolt. Ava hoped that she had a ten-dollar bill tucked in her purse in case she wanted to pass, even though she probably wouldn't hurt someone's feelings by refusing the kiss.

Then she saw Clint heading in her direction, and her pulse started beating like the wings of a hummingbird. All eyes were on her, so she knew she had to make this funny rather than intimate, but the thought of being in Clint's arms made her feel warm all over and she had the sudden urge to rip off her sweater. She really needed to stop wearing sweaters.

"Are you going to take him or leave him?" someone shouted, and although Ava tilted her head and tapped her cheek as if considering the question, the ten-buck turndown never even entered her mind. Suddenly Clint was standing in front of her, and she had to remember to keep her cool . . . well, at least act like she was keeping her cool. Because she wasn't. So when he leaned over to give her a kiss, she artfully dodged his mouth, bringing laughter from the crowd. He tried again without success, finally grabbing her. With the crowd cheering him on, Clint dipped Ava over his arm and planted a big smacking kiss on her lips. And even though he'd kept it playful too, her lips tingled, leaving her longing for so much more. Whistles and applause had Ava laughing and feeling a little bit light-headed after the dip backward—or maybe it was the kiss.

Luckily, a moment later Mia started singing a slightly off-key but cute version of "Santa Baby," diverting the attention of the crowd away from their theatrical display. But when Ava would have gone back to her seat, Clint pulled her down the hallway where the offices were located. She followed, feeling a surge of excitement.

"What was that kiss all about?" Ava asked after they stopped.

"For a good cause."

"Oh, the charity?" she asked, slightly disappointed.

"No . . . for me. I wanted to send a message to the rest of the guys in the bar."

"And what would that message be?"

"That you're with me," he said in a low, sexy tone that slid over her like smooth Southern Comfort.

"You tasted like a cosmopolitan," Ava commented with a slow grin.

"Sorry. Dad made it for you, but I just downed it."

Ava raised her eyebrows. "You just tossed back a cosmo?"

Clint grinned. "Yeah. I always thought it was a girly drink, but it packs quite a punch." He took a step closer and her heart thudded.

"It's pink, but it's still a martini."

"Yeah, pretty but potent," he agreed, and his gaze dropped to her mouth. Ava realized that feelings she'd been fighting had been buried deep within her heart and had resurfaced stronger than ever. The cocky young athlete had returned to her a man who had been humbled by life but was better for the experience.

"Hey, wait. You owe me one now," she pointed out, wanting to see where this night was going.

"And you owe me a *real* kiss. I paid five bucks for it," Clint said. Before Ava could protest—not that she was going to put up a fight—he pushed her up against the wall and gave her a slow, sexy, bone-melting kiss that was more intoxicating than the glass of wine she had consumed. When he finally pulled away, he looked into her eyes. "What's changed, Ava?"

"Nothing ... even though I was fighting it tooth and nail," she said. She watched him frown, but then he gave her a slow smile as if understanding. "That's just it. My feelings for you *haven't* changed even after all of these years apart."

Clint ran a fingertip down her cheek. "You already know I feel the same way."

"I do," Ava answered softly. "Of course, we're adults now and have to get to know each other all over again, but that foundation of caring is still there, and I think it's something we can try and build upon."

"Are you telling me you're willing to take the risk after all?"

"Blame it on the mistletoe," Ava answered with a grin, but then she angled her head to the side. "Actually, a little Christmas elf told me that there are worse things than getting burned."

"And what would that be?" Clint asked softly.

"Having a shot at happiness and not taking it." Ava swallowed hard. "Never knowing what might have been . . ."

"Christmas elves are never wrong," Clint said in such a serious tone that Ava giggled.

"Ah, so you're a believer?"

"I'm head of the elves, remember?" he replied with a lopsided grin. "But yes. I'm a true believer in new beginnings and second chances." He leaned in and kissed her softly. "Now, what do you say we blow this Popsicle stand?"

"Don't you have to bartend?"

"Noah and Mia are helping Dad. The rest of the floor is covered. Besides, I could use a bite to eat. You?"

"Yes, I could eat, but most of the restaurants on Main Street are closed."

"Well, I'd offer to cook for you at my condo, but—"

"Let me guess. There's mustard, pickles, and beer in your fridge."

Clint chuckled. "Pretty much, but I stand behind the fact that I'm good chef. I'm just not stocked up right now. Guys only buy what they need at the moment."

"Well, let's head back to my place. We can throw together something. Besides, I need to look after Rosie."

"Sounds like a good plan to me. Is your car here?"

Ava shook her head. "No. Ronnie picked me up."

"Perfect, I'll drive you."

"I should let them know I'm leaving."

Clint shrugged. "You could send a text message instead of getting back into that crazy crowd."

"Point taken," Ava said. "And I already have my purse

with me." Besides, she didn't want to be anywhere else but by his side, or even better yet, in his arms.

After getting their coats, they headed outside into the crisp cool air. Ava felt a warm rush of happiness when Clint took her hand. It has been such a long time since someone had held her hand, a simple gesture that meant so much. He led her over to his car, and any remaining fear completely fell away, leaving excitement that was coupled with a sense of peace. The feeling was a heady experience. It might be cold and dark outside, but on the inside Ava was walking on sunshine.

When they reached the BMW, instead of opening the door, Clint drew her close and kissed her once more. His lips felt warm against her chilled skin, and she felt a tingle all the way to her toes. When Clint came up for air, he brushed her hair back and moved his mouth to her neck. "What are you doing?" Ava asked with a breathless giggle.

Clint lifted his head and gave her a slow smile. "Trying to make up for lost time," he replied, but his eyes turned serious. "I'm so sorry, Ava. I—"

"No." Ava put a gentle fingertip to his lips. "We don't need to go there, Clint. Listen. We were young, trying to find our way in this big old world. I didn't walk in your shoes, nor did you walk in mine. The past is, well, the past. Let's not dredge it up once more, but instead concentrate on the future."

Clint's brows drew together. "While I like the way you think, I would also like to explain why I stayed away so long. Don't you think you deserve answers?"

"No, because I'm done asking questions. We don't need to open old wounds. We're starting fresh. Let's leave it at that." Ava eased up on tiptoe and gave him a light kiss. "Okay?"

"Okay," Clint answered gruffly. "And I know there's no way to make up for lost time, but I'll tell you this. From this point forward, I want to make every moment count."

Ava gave him a trembling smile. "Deal."

"Let's seal it with another kiss." He dipped his head and kissed her softly, gently but with a slow, simmering heat that held promise of the passion to come.

A sudden gust of wind had them both laughing. "Guess we should get out of the cold," Clint said, but in truth, Ava hadn't noticed anything but being in his arms. It was still sort of surreal to her that he was back in Cricket Creek. After another quick kiss, Clint finally opened the passenger door for Ava. "I cannot stop kissing you."

"I like that!" Ava blushed with pleasure. It has been so long since she'd felt the butterflies-in-her-stomach reaction to a man, and it felt warm and wonderful. She climbed inside and rubbed her hands together. When Clint slid behind the wheel, she said, "This is a pretty sweet ride you have here, Clint."

Clint patted the dashboard and grinned. "Bought it off of a friend. Coaching paid the bills, but I made pretty good extra income doing some personal training for high school kids."

Ava nodded. There was so much she wanted to know. "Will you be coaching here in Cricket Creek?"

Clint pulled out of the parking lot. "I've been talking with Noah Falcon about joining the staff of the Cougars. I'm going to meet up with him this week. I might do some scouting too. I really enjoy discovering new talent, especially if it's at a smaller school that might get overlooked."

"You sound as if you have a real passion for coaching."

"I do. I wanted the head coaching job at SCU, but that job is locked up for a while."

Ava felt a stab of disappointment. "Oh, so you would have stayed in California if you had gotten the offer?"

"Well . . ." When they paused at a red light, Clint looked her way. "I have a confession to make."

Ava's heart started to thud. "Go on . . ."

Clint reached over and took her hand. "I felt such a connection to you while riding in the parade that it helped solidify my decision to move back."

"Seriously?"

Clint nodded slowly. "Yep . . ." He raised her hand to his lips and kissed her fingers. "And I'm glad I did."

Ava felt a rush of pleasure both from his admission and his warm lips on her cold fingers. "Me too," she said softly.

A horn honking behind them let Clint know that the light had turned green. He laughed, and she joined him. When they caught the next red light, Clint groaned. "Are we going to catch every doggone red light?"

"I hope not," Ava said, understanding his hurry. They couldn't get to her apartment soon enough. They had so much to find out about each other. "There's a concrete apron behind the shop where you can park."

"This feels kind of surreal, doesn't it?" Clint asked after he killed the engine.

"Yes, but in a good way." The low rumble of his laugh was so endearing that even though Ava wanted to be up in the apartment, she couldn't help but lean over the console and hope for a kiss. Clint didn't disappoint. He all but pulled her across the barrier and gave her a deep, long, lingering exploration of her mouth that stole her breath.

While Ava was still in a kiss coma, Clint got out of the

vehicle and came over to her side to open her door. Ava slid into his arms and they kissed again, oblivious to the cold, the breeze, the rest of the world ... until Rosie barked, bringing them somewhat back to reality.

Ava laughed. "Rosie must be standing by the kitchen door."

"Let's get up there and let her out." Clint took her hand and started walking.

Ava laughed as she tried to keep up. "Hey, your legs are longer than mine!" she protested, but the real problem was that her knees wobbled from the excitement and anticipation of what was to come.

"No problem." Clint came to an abrupt halt, pivoted, and scooped Ava up into his arms.

"What are you doing?" Ava asked breathlessly.

"In case you haven't noticed, I'm in a big hurry. I'm carrying you."

"Up the stairs?" Ava squeaked.

"I'm stronger than I look."

"Well, I'm heavier than I used to be," Ava warned him, but to her delight Clint carried her with apparent ease.

"Hush. You don't feel one bit heavy," Clint assured her. When they reached the small deck, Rosie started barking in earnest. "Someone else is in a hurry," Clint commented as he put Ava down.

Ava chuckled while she dug in her purse for her keys. "She's actually pretty good, especially for a puppy. The only thing she does is chew my shoes, and then she hangs her head in shame."

"You always did love animals," Clint commented. He laughed when Rosie practically jumped up into Ava's arms.

After petting the eager puppy, Ava let Rosie outside.

Clint helped her shrug out of her coat, and then she held out her arms for his leather jacket. "Can I get you something to drink before I round up something to eat?"

"No, thanks."

"I thought you were hungry."

"That was an excuse to get you to myself," Clint admitted. "We've got a lot of catching up to do." He dipped his head and gave her a lingering kiss. This was going to be the best Christmas he'd had in a long time.

10

A Christmas Love Song

Clint sat down on the sofa and then smiled when he heard Ava coaxing Rosie back inside with the promise of a doggie biscuit. She was still the same sweet-natured but down-to-earth girl that he had fallen in love with back in high school. Clint's grin remained when he recalled that she also had some sass when she got riled up, especially if it was something she was passionate about or if someone was getting bullied. Ava had been his best friend and his first love, and he was coming to realize that no one else ever really had the power to take her place. But after his parents' divorce, his heart had become guarded, and it felt so damned great to let that insecurity fly out the window and allow his true feelings to take center stage. Ava's little elf was right. Taking a risk was better than never knowing what might have been. "There you are," he said when she walked into the room.

"I needed to text Ronnie and let her know I'd left for

the evening." She set two glasses of sweet tea on the coffee table. "I also needed to get Rosie settled into her bed for the night or she would want to play forever." She grinned. "And I cheated and changed into jeans and a sweatshirt. I hope you don't mind," she added as she sat down next to him, tucking her feet under her legs just like she used to do.

"Ava, you look great in anything. And you need to be comfortable because we have a lot to talk about. For starters, why did you decide on a toy store?"

She immediately warmed to the subject. "It's no secret that family farms have struggled for a long time, and my parents' was no exception. For Christmas we'd always get handmade gifts instead of the latest electronic gadgets. Of course, I always wished for the latest toy being pushed on television, not realizing what treasures the wooden toys and handmade dolls were. When I asked for the Barbie dollhouse, my father built a handmade masterpiece that put the plastic version to shame. When the Christmas season is over, I'll put it back in its rightful place of honor in the front window." Her eyes misted over. "I've had countless offers to buy it, but I'll never part with it."

Clint reached over and took her hand.

"And I've tried to keep my prices low. I hate to think of a child without a present underneath the tree, you know? I've always admired your dad for heading up the toy drive each year."

Clint nodded. "My dad is a good guy. When I found out his health was on the line, I knew I needed to come home. I'm just sorry it took so long."

"Why did it?" she asked softly.

Clint took a swallow of the tea and then said, "I was so hell-bent on making the big leagues. Ava, I felt such guilt leaving them ... you. And when things didn't pan out for me, pride kept me away." He shrugged. "And in truth, for a long time I was angry with them for splitting up." He scrubbed a hand down his face. "Dad still loves her. He told me." He gave Ava a long look. "And he doesn't want me to make the same mistake." He leaned over and kissed her. "All I want for Christmas is a second chance."

Ava smiled. "Well, since you have an inside track with Santa, I think you might get your wish."

"I sure hope so," he admitted.

"And thank you for all of the gifts." She dropped her gaze. "I should have called you, but ..."

"Hey, don't worry about that. I was following Dad's suggestion to get your attention. I'm just glad it worked."

"Do you think your dad might ever try to patch things up with your mom?" she asked hesitantly.

Clint raised his eyebrows. "Well, I don't know, but I can tell you this much. Mom was really upset when I let her know about Dad's health issues. She's been asking about him every time we talk. I understand that there are people who, no matter how much they love each other, just can't be together, but if there's a chance, I sure hope they take it. Not for my sake, but for their own. Now tell me about your family. How are they doing?"

Ava smiled as she spoke of her family, especially her nieces and nephews, making him wonder if she wanted children. He didn't go that far, though, and ask. They finally decided to order pizza and ended up talking well into the night about everything from movies to baseball. ... It didn't matter because all Clint wanted to do was be with her. They ended up cuddling on the couch while watching *Christmas Vacation*, laughing at Clark Griswold competing with his neighbor.

When Ava fell asleep, it felt so right having her in his arms. He kissed her head and held her close, longing to make love to her but not wanting to rush before completely regaining her trust. Ah, but this was a start . . . a very good start. Christmas just kept getting merrier.

11

Toyland

"Ronnie, would you just look at these handmade doll clothes?" Ava held up a pink knitted sweater with a matching hat and booties.

Ronnie turned from stacking toy soldiers in a row. "Cute! Those will sell out this weekend. Did your mom make them?"

"A few, but the rest came from the sewing club down at Whisper's Edge Retirement Community. Clint went with me last night to pick them up."

"Ava, you're having a hard time keeping toys on the shelf. With less than a week before Christmas, we just might sell out of everything! But speaking of Clint, I'm guessing the rosy in your cheeks isn't just from the successful sales. Don't even try to deny it."

"I won't." Ava lit a sugar-cookie-scented candle and grinned over at Ronnie. "With those pointed elf boots and crazy twirling hat, you look as if you should be living in Whoville."

Ronnie rocked back on her heels, showing off the curled-upward tips of her boots. "Are the red-and-green-striped tights over-the-top?"

"Yes, but it's totally you."

"You mean that as compliment, right?"

"Of course!"

"Just checking." Ronnie looked down at the painted face of the toy soldier. "The details on these are incredible. It makes me think that they march all around the shop at night when the lights go out." Ronnie did a stiff-legged impression.

"You have a vivid imagination, my friend."

"I know. It's a curse, I tell ya. Have you picked out a present for Clint yet?"

"Gourmet pots and pans."

"What?" Ronnie paused from her new task of placing plush teddy bears on a round display table.

Ava shrugged. "The man enjoys cooking. He'll love them."

"He cooks too? You are one lucky chick."

"I know," Ava admitted. They might have been separated for fifteen years, but the loss of time somehow made reuniting even sweeter. All week, every night after work, Ava walked upstairs to a long kiss followed by a hot meal, and although Clint had to leave to help out at the tavern, he returned to spend the evenings with her. The fast-paced routine they had fallen into was exhausting but in a good way. Ava had never felt happier or more satisfied . . . in more ways than one. The thought made her blush.

"There it is again, the rosy cheeks." Ronnie grinned.

"Oh stop!" Ava said with a laugh. This Christmas she'd have Clint with her at her parents' celebration. While she loved their family gatherings, Ava always felt like she was floating in a sea of her brothers' wives and children, belonging and yet a little bit lost. But this year things were going to be different. Ava made a mental note to remember to invite Pete.

"I'm so happy for you. It's like being in the middle of our own personal Hallmark Christmas movie. All we need is a soundtrack. And, you know, a boyfriend for me, the sidekick and scene stealer."

"I can fix that," Ava said, and turned on the piped-in Christmas music.

"A boyfriend?"

"The soundtrack."

"Perfect!" Ronnie did a funny little elf dance to "Toyland" and then hurried across the shop to give Ava a hug. "We are kinda like babes in Toyland," she said with a giggle.

"Well, then, babe, as for the boyfriend"—Ava put her hands on Ronnie's shoulders—"when are you going to make a play for Braden?"

"I told you, Braden has a girlfriend, Ava. I won't be a home wrecker."

"That would only be if he were married."

"Still . . ." Ronnie turned and busied herself pouring silver candy kisses into a big red bowl sitting next to the cash register.

"When I was over at the bakery ordering more cookies, I overheard that he broke up with Stacy." Ava wiggled her eyebrows.

"Really?" Ronnie perked up at the news but then shrugged. "I mean, that's cool but whatever."

"Well, now, I have to wonder why Braden has come in here pretty often. He doesn't have any kids to shop for."

"To see you! You're neighbors and you used to babysit for him."

"To see me, right. That's why he brought you a cookie from the bakery last week."

"Because it was shaped like an elf and he thought it was funny."

"And he knows you like Grammar's cookies."

"Who doesn't?"

"Hmm ... and here he comes walking across the street now."

"What?" Ronnie squeaked.

"Hey, you're starting to sound like an elf," Ava teased, but Ronnie's attention was fixed on the young man heading their way. Reaching up, Ronnie touched her funny hat, licked her lips, and smoothed her puffy little skirt. Ava put a hand to her chest, remembering that breathless, fluttering feeling when Clint walked into a room. She pressed her lips together, thinking that young love was so fresh and exhilarating. But it could also be fleeting and uncertain. What Ava had with Clint was built on young love but was now deeper, stronger, and more powerful. Ava smiled softly.

And, yes, better.

Just as Ava had thought, Braden gave her a brief wave and then walked over to where Ronnie pretended that straightening the bows on the bears was extremely important.

"Oh hi, Braden!" Ronnie did a commendable job acting surprised. "What brings you in here?"

"Aw, just out shoppin' and I thought you might give me an idea of what to get my mom," Braden said in that slow cowboy way.

"Oh ..." Ronnie nodded. "But this is a toy store," she reminded him with a grin.

"I know." Braden tipped his cowboy hat back a notch. "But I was wondering if you might take part of your lunch hour to help me out? I'm heading over to the feed store, but I'll take you to Wine and Diner if you can help me find the perfect gift for my mom."

Oh, how in the world could Ronnie refuse Braden's oh so cute request? Ava had to smile.

Ronnie glanced over at Ava. "Oh, I don't know; we've been so busy."

Braden didn't miss a beat. "Ava? Can you spare Ronnie for a little while this afternoon?"

"Sure." Ava nodded. "Ronnie, I'll text you if we get swamped."

"Thanks," Braden said and turned back to Ronnie. "I'll drop on by around noon." And then, with a tip of his hat, he quickly went on his way.

"Well, now . . ." Ava said, but Ronnie had a deer-in-headlights look.

"I can't go walking around town dressed like this!"

"I told you that you didn't have to wear the costume every day."

"The kids love it, but that's here in the store. I can't go to lunch dressed like this."

"It's never stopped you before."

"And I wasn't with Braden!"

"Besides, it's kind of Hallmark movie–ish, don't you think?"

Ronnie laughed. "I think we're rubbing off on each other."

"And I like it! It was about time I let my hair down and lived my life. Now get back to work, my little sidekick. We're about to get busy."

The rest of the weekend passed in a holiday-colored blur. By Monday afternoon, the lack of inventory coupled with the threat of snow had Ava sending Ronnie home and closing A Touch of Whimsy early. Her decision to close also gave Ronnie the opportunity to go out to the Greenfield farm for a bonfire and ice skating party. Ava remembered how she'd loved the bonfires down at the Sullys' cabin by the river—sometimes shared with friends, but often just the two of them creating memories of their own.

"I know. I'm home early," Ava said to her delighted puppy. "Gives me time to wrap presents before Clint gets home," she said. She put her hands to her cheeks. "Home," she whispered and then smiled. She and Clint hadn't spent a day apart since the night of the mistletoe. While Clint rented the condo over by the stadium, she almost felt as if her loft had become his home. Their relationship had gone from zero to eighty in nothing flat, but everything about it felt right.

After changing into comfy sweatpants and a hoodie, Ava poured a glass of sweet tea and hauled out her Christmas gifts to wrap. She gave Rosie a pig's ear to keep her busy and then turned on her favorite Amy Grant Christmas CD. Hopefully, she'd have the presents wrapped and beneath the tree by the time Clint walked through the door. Wrapping was usually a task that Ava rather dreaded, but she found herself humming along with Amy Grant and happily adding little decorative touches to the gifts. When she got to the big box filled with the copper-bottomed cookware, Ava laughed, bringing a curious doggie look from Rosie.

"I know. I'm acting silly. I guess that's what being in love is all about. I just can't stop smiling."

When it got to be a little bit late, Ava began to wonder why Clint wasn't home. But she shrugged it off. He'd mentioned planning something special, and maybe he was like most guys and doing some last-minute Christmas shopping. Perhaps Sully's was simply too busy to allow him to take his dinner break. "I think I'll just take a hot bath," Ava said, getting an alarmed bark from Rosie. "Not a bath for you," Ava assured her dog. "I just need to soak these tired bones. By the time I'm done, Clint should be here."

12

Blue Christmas

Clint whistled his way down the hallway, heading for his father's office. The tavern was a bit dead, due to the threat of a snowstorm that the weatherman was still trying to track. In Kentucky, just a few inches of snow were enough to send loaves of bread and gallons of milk flying off the shelves, but they were saying this one could dump a foot of snow on them if the conditions were right.

Clint was anxious to get over to Ava's. Instead of visions of sugarplums, he'd had visions of Ava dancing in his head all day long. Clint closed his eyes and paused before he reached the office door. He'd taken the day to go Christmas shopping, and when he entered Designs by Diamante, the jewelry store over on Wedding Row, all he had intended to purchase was a necklace or maybe earrings. But instead he'd bought a ring.

At Clint's request, Nicolina, the talented jewelry designer and owner of the shop, started showing him necklaces, but his gaze kept traveling over to ring display.

With a soft laugh, Nicolina steered him over to the ring case, and a diamond droplets ring seemed to be calling his name. Framed in matte gold, the teardrop diamonds circled the finger. Earthy and elegant, the unique ring reminded Clint of Ava. The teardrops were a testimony that he would want to see only happy tears, and Clint realized it was the perfect gift.

Although they were going to her parents' house on Christmas Day, Clint wanted to give the ring to Ava tomorrow on Christmas Eve. He was going to finally say what he had been longing to say for the past couple of weeks. He loved her. He wanted this Christmas to go from being a second chance to a new beginning and he wanted the setting to be perfect. After thinking about it for a few moments, he smiled suddenly, knowing that his dad's cabin down by the river would be just right. They used to sneak there when they were teenagers, and the cabin was where Clint had told Ava he loved her for the first time.

"Perfect!" Clint said with a smile. "Who the hell knew I was such a romantic?" He had his work cut out for him since he knew he would need to air the cabin out and stock it with supplies for a special dinner. First he needed to stop by the tavern and let his father know his plans. But as he walked down the hallway toward his father's office, he overheard him on the phone.

And it stopped him cold.

"Maria, I didn't tell you about my heart condition because we're divorced." Pause. "I know we share a son together. But you gave up the right to know about me when you left. Don't give me that," he growled. Then he paused again. "No, I don't want your help! Clint is here."

Clint inhaled sharply and stepped back, leaning against the wall. When he was a kid, hearing his parents argue used to make him break out in a cold sweat, but this time all he did was shake his head. "Well, it may not have been your intention, but you are upsetting me, Maria." After a pause Clint heard, "Really? I know it's the holidays. Bury the hatchet? Look, if you're worried that I'm going to kick the bucket, you can stop. Clint has me eating rabbit food and exercising. I'm healthy as a horse."

Clint knew he shouldn't eavesdrop, but he couldn't help himself.

"Well, he shouldn't have told you. No, I don't need your help. Okay . . . okay, I will. Bye."

Clint stepped into the office and folded his arms over his chest. "Seriously? Mom wanted to come here and you just blew her off?"

"Only because you had to run your mouth and tell her about my damned heart."

Clint looked up at the ceiling and then back at his father. "She asks about you, Dad. She always does, and she's been asking nonstop since she found out you were having some health issues."

"She . . . she does?"

"Yeah. Look. I know how you feel. Putting your heart out there feels like you're up to bat, it's the bottom of the ninth, two outs, full count bases loaded, and you're down by one. What did you always tell me?"

"Swing with no fear."

"Exactly. That's what I'm trying to do, and I hope you'll do yourself a favor and do the same thing. Taking a risk is better than never knowing."

"Did I say that too?"

Clint grinned. "No, it was a wise little elf. And speaking of Christmas, I have some shopping left to do. Do you need me to bartend tonight?"

"No. Get your shopping done. I'll be fine."

Clint was about to tell him that he was heading out to the cabin, but the phone rang and his father started talking to a vendor. Instead, Clint grabbed the keys to the cabin from the hook on the wall and headed out the door. He'd call his dad later. Right now he had some work to do.

13

We Need a Little Christmas

"No, Ronnie, for the last time, I haven't heard from Clint," Ava said from where she shelved the last of the toys that they still had on hand. "He hasn't returned any of my calls or text messages yesterday or today."

"Have you talked to Pete?"

"No," Ava answered flatly. "If there were some kind of emergency or something, Pete would have called me. I think . . ." She swallowed hard. "I think that this thing between us has just moved way too fast for him and he's having second thoughts."

Ronnie stomped her elf boot so hard that the curled toe wiggled up and down. "Ava! It's Christmas Eve. You and Clint need to be together."

"Apparently he doesn't think so," Ava said, trying her best to keep her voice steady. "Look, he left me once before without looking back, and I guess he's doing it again. But listen, sweetie, you should go home."

"It's only noon. We'll have some last-minute shoppers."

"I can handle it," Ava gently assured her. "Look, I'm going to be okay. You can go."

"Oh, Ava, I just don't get it." Ronnie frowned and looked as if she were going to burst into tears. Ava knew the feeling but forced herself to keep a stiff upper lip.

"What can I say?" Ava shrugged. "Life is weird."

"This just *sucks*." A tear slid down Ronnie's cheek, nearly Ava's undoing. "This is not a Hallmark movie ending," Ronnie protested in a sad tone. "I mean, look, we're having a white Christmas and everything."

"Another reason you should go. The roads are terrible and getting worse."

"Ava, I have a four-wheel-drive truck. I'll be fine."

Ava walked over and put her arm around Ronnie's shoulders. "Hey, I'm going over to my parents' farm later on. After a glass of my dad's spiked eggnog, I'll be fine. Please, Ronnie. Head on out and enjoy the holiday. I don't want to think you'll be sad on Christmas Day. As a matter of fact, I'm going to close up in a little while."

Ronnie sniffed but nodded. "All right, but text me later, okay?"

"I will," Ava promised and gave Ronnie's shoulders a firm squeeze. "Now shoo!"

After Ronnie reluctantly left, it was difficult to keep her chin up any longer and Ava's lips trembled. Not wanting a customer see her dissolve into a puddle of tears, Ava was about to walk over and lock the door when a woman entered. After swallowing hard, Ava managed a wan smile. Wait . . . she looked familiar.

"Hello, Ava. I know it's been a while, but I'm Maria Sully."

"Clint's mom?" Ava asked and then felt silly. "Of course you are. May I help you?"

"As a matter of fact, yes." Her rich brown hair was cut in a flattering layered bob framing her face. Shiny cowboy boots peeked out beneath her jeans, and she wore an expensive-looking leather coat with a jewel-toned scarf artfully tied around her neck. Maria had to be somewhere around sixty, but you would never guess it.

"What can I do for you, Mrs. Sully?"

"I'm looking for Clint. I haven't heard from him since yesterday, and it's not like him not to return my calls."

Ava felt a flash of alarm. "Did you talk to Pete?"

She nodded. "Yes, and he said Clint had asked for the night off last night to shop, and he assumed he was with you. So he's not?"

Ava shook her head. "I've been trying to contact him too." She put a hand to her chest. "Have you been over to his condo?"

"He's not there."

"Oh . . ." Ava frowned.

"I have to ask, do you know why he might have left?"

"If you're asking if we had a fight or something, the answer is no. Quite frankly, I'm totally hurt and confused. I have to wonder if Clint was feeling overwhelmed about the seriousness of our relationship. But if he was leaving, surely he would tell you or Pete."

Maria shook her head. "Something isn't right. I'm worried sick, Ava. I'm going to head over to the tavern and see if Pete knows anything. In the meantime, if you hear from him, let me know." She dug inside her purse and pulled out a card. "My number is on here."

"Do the same for me, please. I'm going to close up the shop."

"Will do."

Ava followed Maria over to the front door and locked up. The snow was falling down once more, but Ava noticed that Maria was driving a sturdy-looking SUV. Even so, if this kept up, the roads would soon become impassable.

Ava went upstairs to her apartment to let Rosie outside. Her emotions hovered somewhere between worry and confusion. She'd thought that Christmas was going to be filled with joy, and nothing about Clint's behavior made any sense. Cell phone reception around Cricket Creek was good, so not answering his phone didn't make any sense either. She watched Rosie frolic in the deepening snow, smiling absently when her little legs suddenly got stuck. . . .

Stuck!

Ava's eyes widened, and she suddenly pictured Clint's sports car. "He must be snowed in somewhere," she whispered. But where? Ava racked her brain, going through the possibilities but coming up blank.

And then it hit her, and she snapped her fingers. The cabin! "It has to be it." Cell phone reception in the wooded area down by the river could be spotty, especially where the cabin was located. She smiled, knowing why Clint would go there. He'd mentioned wanting to do something special, and the little hideaway in the woods would be the perfect setting.

Ava picked up her cell phone and called Pete.

"Ava!" His voice boomed into the phone. "Have you heard from Clint?"

"No, but, Pete, I think he might be at your cabin down by the river." Joy shoved away the last of her doubt. She laughed. "In fact, I'd bet the farm."

"Really? Let me check and see if the keys are there. Nope. Gone! Ava, he must be snowed in with that little car of his. Girl, get ready. Maria and I will pick you up in my four-wheel drive and deliver you to his doorstep like Santa on his sleigh."

14

All I Want for Christmas Is You

Clint tried calling Ava for the millionth time but once again without any luck. He hadn't given any thought to poor cell phone reception. Make that no cell phone reception. He also shouldn't have trusted the weather report. "Ha! Yeah, this is a dusting up to an inch?" he grumbled. His attempt to drive down the road had been a slip-sliding, fishtailing mess.

He'd been so busy decorating and getting ready yesterday that he hadn't realized the snow was coming down until it was too late. There was already a good eight or so inches and it was still falling, with fat accumulating flakes. He was stuck. Snowed in. Clint raised his arms skyward. "And it's Christmas Eve!" he shouted. He shoved his fingers through his hair, wondering what Ava must be thinking, and groaned. "This is not good."

He wouldn't mind being stuck in the winter wonderland if only Ava were with him. Because of his state of mind, he couldn't even enjoy the beauty of the pristine snow covering the ground and clinging to the evergreens. With another groan, he turned away from the window, sank down onto the sofa, and stared into the fire crackling in the stone fireplace. His father had actually done some much-needed improvements to the cabin over the years, and it looked good. The floors had been refinished and the kitchen remodeled. It would have been the perfect little romantic setting. He'd even put up a small Christmas tree in the corner, but the twinkling lights did nothing to improve his gloomy mood.

"This just sucks."

In desperation, he wondered how long it would take him to hike to where he'd get cell phone reception. He already walked around every nook and cranny of the cabin, holding the phone up over his head. He'd done the same thing outside, even attempted to climb a tree.

Clint was getting hungry, but the thought of eating the amazing dinner he had planned for Ava all by himself took away his appetite, so he sat there and sulked. After a little while, he started to doze off, but he was awakened by the sound of an engine. Hoping he hadn't been dreaming, he stood up and hurried over to the window. In the waning light, he saw a slate gray Ford F250 approaching the cabin. Through the falling flakes, he saw that a big red bow decorated the grill.

With a whoop of joy, Clint threw open the front door just as his father emerged from the driver's side wearing a festive Santa hat. His mother? Wow, it really was his mother sliding from the passenger side, laughing as they approached the front door.

"Mom! When did you get into town? Dad! How did you find me?" He hugged his mother, who had tears glittering in her eyes.

"I had a little help," Pete said. "Oh right, and we come

bearing gifts." He raised his hand over his head and gave a signal. The back door to the extended cab opened and out stepped Ava, holding Rosie, who was sporting a festive green bow around her neck.

"Merry Christmas, son," he said and gestured toward Ava.

Ava hurried forward, slipping and sliding a little bit but laughing all the way.

"I hope you like your gift because it's nonrefundable," Pete said, getting a poke in the ribs from Maria.

"Better than my all-time favorite," Clint replied, "which was a remote-control car when I was ten years old."

Ava raised her palms upward. "And I don't require batteries."

"So what do you run on?"

"Love," she said simply.

Clint laughed and pulled her into his arms. "That's good because I have an endless supply."

THE
CHRISTMAS GIFT

Alexis Morgan

1

Bridey boxed up a pair of cupcakes slathered with pink icing and glittery sprinkles for Gage Logan, the chief of police in Snowberry Creek. She smiled to herself at the mental image of the big tough lawman sharing the treat with his nine-year-old daughter, Sydney.

As she set the box on the counter, the relief in Gage's expression was impossible to miss. "Thanks for saving a cupcake for me, Bridey. I promised Syd I'd bring her one if she kept her room picked up for a week without having to be nagged. If I'd forgotten—" Gage shuddered. "Well, let's just say it wouldn't have been pretty."

Bridey smiled as she took the money he held out. "The good news is that I stuck in an extra so you two can celebrate together."

The man's face lit up with a wicked grin. "Not to mention the added bonus: Syd can't nag at me for eating sweets if she's doing it, too. It's a win-win situation." Gage picked up the small box with great care. "Thanks again, Bridey. You're definitely a lifesaver."

"Anytime, Gage."

As he walked away, a movement in the far corner of

the shop drew Bridey's attention. One glance sent her pulse into overdrive, and she felt her cheeks flush. This made Seth Kyser's third visit this week, and it was only Wednesday. Seth had already staked out his usual table, marking his territory with his coat on the back of the chair and the newspaper open to the crossword puzzle.

He'd been coming into her coffee shop, Something's Brewing, for more than a month now, almost as long as he'd lived in the area. From what she'd heard, he'd moved into the old Sedgewick place on the outskirts of town. No one seemed to know much about the man, only that Seth paid his bills in cash and on time. Otherwise, he pretty much kept to himself.

Except when he came in here.

She glanced at the clock and then at her assistant as Seth finally started toward the counter to place his order. "Fiona, why don't you take your break before the on-rushing hordes from the high school head this way."

Her assistant immediately started for the back. "Boy, where has the time gone? I can't believe we're less than twenty minutes until the afternoon influx of kids."

Bridey laughed. Fiona had it right. While she was grateful for the steady business from the high school students, things got pretty hectic once the teenagers came pouring through the door. For the moment, though, there was just the one customer in the shop. She took a calming breath, determined to maintain the facade that Seth was just like any other customer who came through the door even if he wasn't.

From the first day he'd walked into her shop, her reaction to him had been far from ordinary. She'd yet to figure out exactly why. Certainly, Seth was a far cry from the kind of men she'd known in her previous career as the pastry chef in a high-end restaurant in California. For one thing, her ex-husband's taste in clothes had run to hand-tailored and expensive, not the flannel shirts and faded jeans that apparently composed Seth's entire wardrobe. And yet she found the casual attire soothing.

Today's shirt, a mix of deep forest green and blue, brought out Seth's green eyes. His sandy blond hair looked a bit damp, as if he'd been out walking in the rain. She tried to keep her appreciative glance quick, but she couldn't help admiring his lean, athletic build.

She had only one question for herself: When had plaid become so darn attractive?

Bridey realized she was staring. Kicking her smile up half a notch, she got down to business. "Mr. Kyser, what can I offer you today?"

He was on the quiet side, rarely saying more than the absolute minimum to place his order. Shifting from one foot to the other, he gave her a shy smile. "Call me Seth. A tall drip with extra sugar and cream and a refill. Two pastries. Your choice."

After pouring his first cup of coffee, she pulled out the two treats she'd set aside earlier on the off chance he came in again today. "Here's your usual blueberry muffin. The other one is a new recipe I've been working on for Christmas. It's a gingerbread cupcake with cream cheese icing. I've been playing around with the spices a bit and thought maybe you could let me know what you think."

He nodded as he pulled out his wallet. "Glad to. They smell wonderful."

When she rang up the total, he frowned. "It's usually more than that, Ms. Roke."

She shook her head as she counted out his change. "Please, it's Bridey, and the gingerbread is on the house.

I never charge my test subjects. I ask only that you be honest with your evaluation."

"Will do." His eyes twinkled. "Never been anybody's lab rat before."

Her cheeks flushed hot. "Hey! I never called you that. Besides, my pastries are far too good to feed to rodents."

He winked at her and retreated to his table, leaving her staring at his back. And if she took a few seconds to admire those broad shoulders, well, that was her own business.

Luckily, she'd managed to tear her eyes away before her assistant returned. The bell over the door chimed as the first bunch of teenagers entered the shop in a bright burst of noise and high energy. She and Fiona braced themselves and got to work. The rush was on.

Seth sipped his dark roast and savored the chance to watch Bridey Roke in action as she greeted each customer with a smile and friendly banter. He couldn't help but notice that she had singled him out to sample the new flavor of cupcake.

He ate the blueberry muffin first, preferring to hold off on the gingerbread until his second cup of coffee. Right now the line was too long, which gave him the perfect excuse to linger awhile longer here in Something's Brewing.

He hadn't meant to come in today, but he'd been too restless to stay home. A walk along Snowberry Creek had helped his mood, but somehow he'd ended up standing across the street from the coffee shop.

How the heck was he supposed to resist the potent combination of fresh coffee, delicious pastries, and Bridey Roke's bright gray eyes and pretty smile? As if sensing his gaze, she glanced in his direction. When she spotted the cupcake, she frowned. Oops. Not wanting her to think he didn't want to try it, he picked up his coffee cup and headed toward the counter for his refill.

There were only two people ahead of him, so it didn't take long for her to get to him. He held out his cup.

"I was saving the cupcake for my second round, not because I didn't want to eat it."

That was the most he'd said to her at one time. Thank goodness he hadn't stumbled over a single word. He'd learned to be grateful for such small miracles. His stuttering no longer ruled his life as much as it had in the past. Yet that didn't mean it didn't rear its ugly head once in a while, especially around attractive women.

And Bridey Roke was definitely that.

She filled his cup, automatically adding the extra cream and sugar he liked. "I'm glad to hear it. I was afraid that I had put you in an awkward position by asking you to do a test run for me."

"Not at all. I'm honored."

Since he'd already paid for the second cup with his original order, he'd run out of excuses to remain at the counter. After returning to his seat, he peeled off the wrapper and removed the plastic Santa decoration that was stuck in the top before tasting a piece of the cupcake without the icing. He kept his eyes focused on what he was doing because he suspected Bridey would be watching his every move.

He smiled as the complex flavor of cinnamon, ginger, and cloves hit his taste buds. Delicious, although the cloves threatened to overwhelm the other flavors just a bit. The added sweetness of the cream cheese icing complemented the other flavors perfectly.

When he was done, he gathered up his empty cup and wrappers and carried them over to the trash. As he slung the strap of his backpack over one shoulder, he wondered how honest he should be with his evaluation. Deciding Bridey would prefer honesty to platitudes, he paused by the counter. "Thank you for the holiday treat. The icing was just right. The gingerbread was moist and rich, but the cloves came across a little strong. I've always liked nutmeg better, so that might just be me."

His critique seemed to please her. "Thank you, Seth! I almost used nutmeg. I'll try it in the next batch. I want to start serving them as soon as I perfect the recipe. There's just something about the smell of gingerbread that puts everybody in the holiday spirit. In fact, that's what got me inspired to dig out all the Christmas decorations this morning and set the radio to a holiday music station. That's as far I've gotten, though, because it's been pretty busy today, not that I'm complaining. Busy is good."

As she spoke, she pointed toward the large wreath leaning against the wall behind the counter. Next to it was a box full of other Christmas decorations. Seth surprised himself as much as Bridey when he asked, "Do you want some help putting that stuff up?"

Bridey glanced at the pile of garland and the wreath. "I couldn't ask you to do that."

He was surprised by how much he wanted to help her decorate. "I've got some time on my hands. Besides, after eating those pastries, the exercise will do me good."

"Yeah, I get that," Bridey said, laughing. "If you're sure, I'd appreciate your help hanging the wreath. There's already a hook at the top of the window frame, but I can't quite reach it even if I stand on a chair."

"Sure thing." Seth tossed his pack on the nearest table as Bridey carried the wreath to the front of the shop. He climbed up on a chair and held the wreath up to the window. "Is this about right?"

Bridey cocked her head to one side and studied the wreath. "Perfect."

After he slipped the wire over the hook, he asked, "Does that garland go up h-here, too?"

This time Bridey didn't even hesitate. Between the two of them, they made quick work of the rest of the decorations while Fiona handled the few customers who came in. After Seth trimmed the window with the green garland that had Christmas lights running through it, Bridey had him replace the normal bell over the door with jingle bells while she set small vases filled with poinsettias and ivy on each of the tables. Seth liked that the two women felt comfortable enough in his company to sing along with the radio as they worked.

Finally, he hung a sprig of mistletoe over the pastry counter, providing a whole new layer to the temptations to be found in Something's Brewing. All told, it took less than an hour to transform the shop. Bridey was clearly pleased with the results, especially when she plugged in the lights around the window. "There, that definitely adds a bright touch of Christmas to the place. Thanks again, Seth. All of this would have taken me hours to do by myself."

"You're welcome. It does look n-nice."

Finally out of excuses to linger, he picked up his pack. "I'd better get going."

"Wait. Let me fix you a hot chocolate to go."

When it was ready, Bridey followed him toward the door. "And thanks for the feedback on the gingerbread cupcakes. I hope to try another batch on Friday morning."

Feeling more daring, he winked at her again. "S-save one for me. You know, for comparison's sake."

Bridey nodded. "I'll do that."

"I'll be here." Seth nodded at Bridey's assistant and started for the door. Friday was only two days away, but already the time in between stretched out unbearably. Even so, he had something to look forward to for the first time in months: cupcakes and another excuse to see Bridey.

2

On Friday morning, Seth wandered into his new studio. As he circled the room, he paused to examine a large piece of oak and then a smaller slab of walnut. There was no comfort to be found in tracing the grain lines in either piece, and their continued silence only depressed him. Always before, no matter what was happening with the rest of his life, the hidden beauty in the wood had spoken to him.

He'd been struggling for far longer than he cared to admit. The constant pressure to produce sculptures that were bigger, better, and ever more spectacular had worn him down and left little time in his life for anything other than work. As the joy in his art faded, he tried to find happiness in other places. Between his stutter and the demands of his work, he'd never had much luck with women, but he'd had high hopes for his last relationship. Unfortunately, he'd found out just how wrong he'd been about that when his girlfriend walked out after publicly announcing she was tired of playing second fiddle to a pile of lumber. That had been more than a year ago, and he hadn't tried dating since. Her abrupt departure had marked the beginning of this long dry period.

Dwelling on past failures was getting him nowhere. Determined to keep trying, he tested the heft of his favorite chisel and mallet as he studied the thick slab of solid cherry he'd picked out of his supply at random on yesterday's trip through the room. After studying the swirls of colors in the wood, he closed his eyes and put his mind to work. Utter silence. Not even a hint of what images might lurk beneath the smooth surface of the wood.

"S-son of a bitch!"

He tossed the chisel and mallet aside and stalked away. When he reached the door of his shop, he stopped. Guilt drove him back to the table to put his tools where they belonged. At least his carelessness hadn't damaged the chisel blade. Small comfort.

"Sorry, guys."

Seth patted the mallet as if it were a puppy before walking away. The gesture left him smiling. His family already thought he was crazy for abandoning his home in an upscale neighborhood in Seattle. If they found out he'd taken to talking to his tools, there was no telling what they'd do. His mother had already enlisted the help of his older brother and younger sister to assist in her determined efforts to get him to return to the fold.

Well, that wasn't happening. Even if Seth wasn't working right now, he liked everything about this place. A few weeks ago, he'd been taking a much-needed respite from the grueling pace he'd been keeping up in the city and found pleasure in the simple beauty of this rural setting. He'd spent hours cruising up and down the twisting roads that wound through the Cascade foothills when he'd spotted the "For Sale" sign posted in front of the ramshackle log house. He'd been searching for inspiration but found a new home instead.

Preferring to remain under the radar, Seth had returned to Seattle and instructed his lawyers to purchase the house in the name of his corporation. That allowed him to draw a sharp line between his new lifestyle and his prior one in the high-end art scene. It meant hiding who and what he was from his neighbors as he tried to rediscover his artistic inspiration in the small town. Although he hated the need for the deception, at this point he would try anything for the sake of his sanity.

Despite not being able to work, he enjoyed puttering around the house and took pride in how well the bookshelves he'd built in the living room had turned out. He might not be getting any serious work done, but he was learning how to relax again. It had been years since he'd taken the time to sit by a fire and read.

And speaking of taking time for the simple pleasures in life, he'd really enjoyed helping Bridey with her Christmas decorations. In past years, he hadn't bothered with any of that, but maybe this year he would. In fact, more than once he'd caught himself whistling one of the Christmas songs that Bridey and Fiona had sung while the three of them decorated the shop. That was definitely out of character for him, so maybe there was something special in the air here in Snowberry Creek that helped spread the holiday spirit. The idea had him smiling and looking forward to finding out what changes the season would bring next.

Having made his daily token effort to work, Seth snagged his backpack on his way to the front door. It was time to head into town. He needed to pick up his mail at the post office and buy some groceries if he wanted to eat dinner later. In between those two particular chores, he had one more stop to make, the real reason behind the whole expedition.

Today was the day Bridey had promised him another gingerbread cupcake to try. The thought had his mouth watering. However, even if she'd already run out of the cupcakes, he'd happily settle for whatever was left. After all, it was the chance to spend a few minutes with the attractive and friendly woman who had become the highlight of his week lately.

Twenty minutes later, he had to circle the block twice before finally finding a parking spot near Bridey's shop big enough for his twenty-year-old panel van. Back in Seattle, he'd used it only for hauling the various woods that were the medium for his art and for delivering his bigger pieces to the gallery that handled his work. The barn behind the house, which had been converted into a garage, housed a perfectly good sedan and a much flashier convertible. Neither one fit his current lifestyle.

Once he maneuvered the van in next to the curb, he hustled down the sidewalk toward Bridey's shop. He'd timed his arrival for that quiet moment between lunchtime and the late-afternoon rush. However, when he walked inside, he found himself at the tail end of a line that wound its way almost to the door. Looking around, he realized it must have been a half day for the high school.

His regular spot was already occupied by some boys sporting letterman jackets. Worse yet, there wasn't an empty table in the entire place. Disappointed, Seth resigned himself to getting his order to go. Would the cupcakes taste as good if he had to eat them at home? Yeah, but that didn't mean he'd enjoy them nearly as much.

As the line slowly snaked forward, a table opened up near the counter. With a maneuver that rivaled his best days on the soccer field, Seth tossed his backpack on the table and his jacket on the chair, successfully heading off a pair of teenage girls who had been zeroing in on the same spot. After identical disappointed sighs, they veered off to rejoin some friends in circling around the edge of the shop in case another table became available.

He fought the urge to do a victory dance on his way back to the counter to place his order.

Bridey nodded in the direction of the table he'd just staked out. "Nice move there, Seth. I thought for sure those girls would get there ahead of you."

Totally unrepentant, he grinned. "They're younger. I'm sneakier."

She laughed and set out a pair of cupcakes with his coffee. "And to the victor go the spoils."

"Thank you. The new recipe?"

Bridey nodded. "Two different versions. Let me know what you think."

"Will do."

Seth retreated to his table and peeled off the first wrapper, which was decorated with small candy canes. It was tempting to read something into her having his two cupcakes set aside seemingly for him, but that was no doubt wishful thinking on his part. She probably had a whole squad of regulars lined up to try out her newest creations.

One bite and he was sold. He closed his eyes and savored the moist cake, which had just the right amount of nutmeg. That flavor always brought back childhood memories of time spent in his maternal grandmother's kitchen. She used to make him plum tarts seasoned with nutmeg. Nona was also the only one who had never made him feel as if he failed to measure up just because he stuttered.

But all that was water under the bridge. It was amazing how people could overlook his hated impediment once his artwork started selling for five figures. He slammed the door shut on those memories. They wouldn't do anything to fix his current uninspired dry spell and would only diminish his enjoyment of his visit to Something's Brewing. Ignoring the constant buzz of the teenagers around him, he took his time finishing the two cupcakes as he picked up his pen and started working on the crossword puzzle.

Bridey wiped down the counter and scanned the shop to see what else needed to be done. The crowd had finally thinned out enough so that she could catch a breather. Her eyes swept across the room once more, this time coming back to where Seth sat working on a crossword puzzle. She liked that he did it in ink, a sign of confidence that seemed at odds with his rather shy demeanor. The newcomer to town was definitely a puzzle himself.

Before she made it to his table to see what he thought of her new recipe, the door to the shop opened. She smiled and waved at Callie Redding, a friend from high school and one of her best customers. She dropped by often to buy treats for her fiancé.

"Hey, Callie! Are you here to feed Nick's sweet tooth or your own?"

"Mine for now, but I'll need to take something home for Nick and Austin. They're up in Seattle for the afternoon, checking out a couple of building supply places that specialize in the stuff needed to restore old homes."

As Callie studied the few remaining pastries, Bridey felt compelled to apologize. "Sorry, but it's pretty slim pickings right now. The high school was on a half day, and I've been too busy to restock. A batch of coffee cakes just came out of the oven, but they need to cool before I can take them out of the pans."

Callie actually looked pleased by the situation. "Not

a problem. I can wait. Meanwhile, I'll take that last muffin and a tall hot chocolate. Do you have time to grab a cup of something and join me? It's been a while since we've had a chance to chat."

Bridey swallowed her disappointment at the missed chance to talk to Seth. Maybe he'd be engrossed in reading the newspaper until after Callie left. Not likely, but a girl could always hope.

She fixed two hot chocolates and carried them over to Callie's table. After sitting, she broached a subject that had been on her mind for a while.

"There's something I've been meaning to ask you, Callie. I know Nick has his hands full working on Spence's place, but I was wondering if he could take a look at my kitchen and give me some ideas about what could be done to make it more user-friendly. The place was set up for a sandwich shop, not a bakery like mine. It would involve tearing out the old cabinets and replacing them with new shelves."

Callie sipped her drink and set it back down. "Of course I can ask him. At least he can recommend someone to do the work for you."

Bridey nodded. "That would be good. I'd just want a rough idea of what the renovation would cost. I can't afford to spend a lot right now, so the work will have to be done in several stages."

The two of them moved on to other topics, chatting until some other customers came in. While Callie finished her hot chocolate, Bridey packed up several generous pieces of the coffee cake for her.

As Callie walked out the door, the scrape of a chair announced that Seth was up and moving. Darn it, anyway. But instead of heading straight for the door as he usually did, Seth sidled up to the counter.

She brightened her smile. "Hi! I meant to stop by to get the verdict on the cupcakes."

"The one with the red sprinkles and white icing had the perfect amount of nutmeg. Liked it best. Both were wonderful, though."

"Great. That's what I thought, too."

He glanced toward the group of women seated at the front table and frowned. Was there something wrong? He shifted his gaze back to her.

"Listen, Bridey. I didn't mean to listen in on your conversation with your friend. About the shelves, that is."

Where was he going with this? "As small as the shop is, it would be hard not to have heard at least part of what we were saying."

He nodded, but drew in a deep breath, as if bracing himself to say something more, something she might not like. "Feel free to say no, Bridey, but if you can tell me what you want, I can build the shelves for you. I have a lot experience working with wood, and I'm really good with my hands."

3

Okay, maybe he could've phrased that last part differently. There were all kinds of things he wanted to do when it came to Bridey Roke. Not one of them had anything to do with shelving. While waiting for her to make up her mind, he stared at the far wall and tried to act as if a refusal wouldn't matter. From the way she was biting her lower lip, she was either seriously considering his offer or trying to think of a gentle way to say no.

"Did you hear me also say that I couldn't afford to pay much for the work?"

Okay, so it wasn't him giving her second thoughts. "Not a problem. Pay for materials. That's enough."

She was already shaking her head. "I couldn't let you do that, Seth. That wouldn't be fair to you."

Her eyes zeroed in on the hole in the knee of his jeans, and he bet she hadn't missed the frayed collar and cuffs on his shirt. She'd never believe he didn't need the money, but these days he dressed for comfort, not to impress. Although for Bridey, he might make an exception.

"Minimum wage and materials, then. I'm between assignments, not unemployed. Doing this will help fill the time until I go back to work after the first of the year."

Hopefully this long dry spell would have played itself out by then. He had promised to deliver some new pieces to the gallery by late spring. One way or another, he needed to rediscover the joy in his art that he had lost.

Bridey didn't look convinced, but finally she nodded. "Let me show you what I'm talking about. You may not be interested after you see what a mess it is back there."

"Let me get a couple of things from my truck, and then you can show me."

He took off for the door before she could change her mind. Outside, he gave in to the big grin he'd been fighting to hold back. Things were looking up. This development meant more time in Bridey's company and something more constructive to do than moping around his shop waiting for a new project idea to hit.

Shelving might be a far cry from his usual work, but at least he'd be creating something from wood again. And had he mentioned spending more time with Bridey?

Late Saturday afternoon, Seth walked into the coffee shop clutching the plans he'd drawn up for Bridey's kitchen. After staying up most of the night to finish them, he hoped he'd come close to what Bridey had envisioned. If she approved the designs, he planned to tear out the old cabinets immediately and start rebuilding on Monday. Because Bridey couldn't afford to shut down the coffee shop for the number of days it would take him to do all the work at once, he'd have to work on one section at a time. He didn't mind, since that would stretch out the time he got to spend in her company in the cozy, inviting bakery.

Bridey finished packing up an order for another customer before turning her attention to him. "Seth, are you sure you don't have something better to do with your Saturday evening than ripping out my old cabinets?"

"I promise. I brought the plans for you to look at."

He flexed his grip on his toolbox. It had been a long time since he'd been this nervous about presenting a client with a hand-drawn sketch of a project.

Bridey studied the cardboard tube he'd held up. "Fiona, can you handle the counter alone for a little while? I have some business to discuss with Mr. Kyser."

Turning back to Seth, she smiled. "Let me fix you a coffee and grab you a snack. Then we can go over the details."

He waited out of the way of the other customers while Bridey fixed his drink and then followed her into the small office in the back of the shop. After motioning him to have a seat in the chair wedged into the corner, she sat down at her minuscule desk.

When they were both settled, he traded her the cardboard tube with the plans for the coffee and muffin she'd brought in for him. "I can make changes if things aren't exactly what you want."

She was already unrolling the stack of papers. He'd drawn a separate sketch for each of the different areas that she wanted to have done. Her eyes flared wide as she studied the top page.

"Wow, Seth! Are you an architect or draftsman? I was expecting a rough sketch on notebook paper, not something so professional looking."

"Not an architect. Had some training, though, and I have a lot of experience working with wood."

As she pored over each page in turn, her expression was difficult to interpret, but that didn't keep him from taking advantage of the chance to study her. Today she wore her dark brown hair in a messy knot high up on the back of her head, held there with what looked like a pair of chopsticks. His hands itched to tug them out and watch the dark strands tumble free. Then he'd—

The squeak of Bridey's chair when she leaned back to look at him cut off that line of thought.

"I've got to say, Seth, these are amazing. You have quite the eye for detail, and there's not an inch of wasted space in the designs. Seriously, it's as if you read my mind. I have only one concern. Are you sure you can do this for the money we discussed?"

"Yes, no problem. The materials aren't expensive, and I own all the tools needed to do the work. I'll get started now, if you like what you see."

"I definitely like what I see."

A sudden influx of heat in her gray eyes seemed to accompany her words, along with a slight flush to her skin. A rush of desire hit him, but he was never very good at flirting, although it hadn't really bothered him before now.

He settled for giving her his best smile. With Bridey, he was content to take it slow and see where things between them led. "I'll get started, then."

Bridey followed Seth into the narrow confines of the storage room. He immediately peeled off his flannel shirt, probably because it was already warm in the small room. Ordinarily, she would have said there was plenty of space in there for two people, but right now it seemed pretty darned crowded. Seth had his back to her as he studied the old cabinets he was going to tear out. He could handle that part by himself, but she wanted to help move her supplies so she'd know where everything ended up.

At the moment, though, she was having trouble concentrating on anything but the way the thermal shirt clung to Seth's body, showing off an impressive set of lean muscles as he easily picked up the first fifty-pound bag of flour and carried it out of the room. On the way by, he gave her an odd look.

Snap out of it! You're too old to be caught gawking at a nice set of shoulders!

Yeah, she argued with her inner self, *but you've got to admit those are some damn fine shoulders.*

She grabbed a big bag of sugar and carried it out herself, hoping Seth would think the bright pink flush in her cheeks was due to exertion, not embarrassment. At least he didn't say anything, but then, he always was quiet. Although it didn't mean he didn't communicate a lot with a simple look. Right now there was a suspicious twinkle in his dark green eyes, but there wasn't much she could do other than soldier on.

While he carried out the last few supplies, she arranged things so that she'd still be able to work in the kitchen despite the temporary chaos. While she gathered up the recipes she'd need in the morning, she checked to see what else needed to be done. Once again her wayward eyes found something better to look at as Seth strapped on a tool belt that rode low over his lean hips.

When he bent down to pick up his hammer, the papers she'd been clutching fluttered to the floor, scattering everywhere. Sheesh, what in the world was wrong with her? She knelt to pick them up, hoping Seth hadn't noticed. Unfortunately, one had fallen between two counters just out of her reach. A pair of her longest tongs would do the trick, but before she could grab them, Seth was there reaching for the paper.

His callused fingers brushed across hers when he handed her the recipe. "Here you go."

She cleared her throat. "Thank you."

"You're welcome."

"Um, I'll be in my office, you know, that is if you want me, um, for anything at all."

"Nice to know."

As he spoke, the fine lines around his eyes crinkled just enough to let her know that he found something amusing in what she'd just said. She replayed her words in her mind on her way to her office. Good grief. Had she really said "for anything at all"? On one level, the words were perfectly innocent. but if he suspected that she found him attractive—and she did—then he could have interpreted her statement as a come-on.

Figuring she'd only dig herself a deeper hole by trying to clarify what she'd actually meant, she retreated to her office. But as she closed the door, she was pretty sure she heard a deep chuckle coming from inside the storeroom.

Seth tossed the last of the debris into the Dumpster out behind the shop. Once he finished sweeping the floor in the storeroom, he'd be out of excuses to hang around any longer. Besides, he didn't want to risk making Bridey uncomfortable by lurking around now that the shop was closed.

She'd been pretty skittish right before she'd taken refuge in her office, not that he blamed her. Other than talking to him a few times when he came in for coffee, she didn't know anything about him. A woman had every reason to be concerned about being alone with a virtual stranger.

"Wow, you've made amazing progress, Seth!"

He jumped, sending his swept pile of dirt flying in all directions. How had she managed to sneak up on him like that? He started cleaning it up again. "Yeah, the demolition is done. Monday, I'll start putting stuff back in."

Bridey frowned. "About that. How early would you be able to start? I'm worried about all the noise bothering my customers. I probably should've thought of that sooner."

"How early are you here?"

"I come in at four thirty, but the shop doesn't open until seven. I close at six in the evening."

"I'll come early Monday and leave when the shop opens, if that's okay. You sure put in a long day, though."

"That's the price I pay for being my own boss. I only recently hired Fiona. Once she's fully trained, she'll take over closing for me at least a couple of days a week."

He understood the strain of being the only one on the payroll all too well. "Good. You don't want to burn out."

Bridey shot him an odd look as if he'd revealed something important. "True. And with that in mind, it's time for both of us to get out of here. We've both put in enough hours on a Saturday night."

Once Seth finished sweeping, he packed up his tools. Bridey was waiting for him by the door. "Thank you again for doing this, Seth, and for working around my schedule."

"Glad to do it." He smiled. "I'm new to Snowberry Creek, but there's a lot I like about the town. It's warm and friendly, especially your shop."

His remark clearly pleased her. "I'm glad you feel that way. I wanted to create a place where people felt welcome to linger over a cup of coffee and their favorite pastry."

"Well, you've definitely succeeded."

They walked out into the brisk air together. Seth had parked close by, so they came to a parting of ways all too soon.

"See you on Monday, Seth."

As she walked away, he put his toolbox into the back of his van and tossed his tool belt in beside it. He slammed the door and gave in to the temptation to watch Bridey a little longer. A flashing light down the street caught his eye and gave him what might be an excellent idea.

Hoping he wasn't making a major mistake, he loped after Bridey. She heard him coming and stopped, her expression curious but not worried.

"Did you forget something in the shop?"

He shook his head and pointed across the street. "My fridge is pretty empty, so I thought I'd grab dinner across the street. I hate to eat alone."

Okay, that was a lie. He'd rather eat alone than spend time trying to carry on conversation with most people. Bridey was an exception to that rule.

She looked across at the Creek Café. "You know, that sounds good to me, too. I think tonight's special is Frannie's pot roast, which beats the heck out of leftover soup."

He did a mental victory dance but kept his response a simple. "Good."

As they cut across the street to the Creek Café, Bridey looped her hand through Seth's arm. The small contact carried quite a wallop, sending a jolt of hungry awareness rattling around inside his chest. If she were aware of the effect her touch had on him, she gave no sign of it.

Inside the café, she let go, but he didn't blame her. These people were her friends and customers. Seeing the two of them together could cause rumors to fly across town, especially if they acted like a couple instead of two friends grabbing a quick meal together.

Luck was with them. The busboy was just clearing a booth in the back corner. "There's a spot."

Bridey followed in his wake as he wound his way through the crowded diner. As he did, it occurred to him that a booth might not have been the best choice. Should he sit across from her? Yeah, he probably should. What he really wanted to do was slide in right next to her, but he didn't want to crowd her.

Damn, why was this stuff never easy for him?

They'd almost reached their destination when someone called Bridey's name. Seth would have preferred to ignore the summons, but Bridey caught his hand in hers and tugged him over toward another booth. He recognized the woman from the other day in the coffee shop. Bridey performed the necessary introductions.

"Seth, this is my friend Callie Redding and her fiancé, Nick Jenkins, most recently of the U.S. Army." She paused to smile at the couple before adding, "And this is my friend Seth Kyser. Looks like we're not the only ones who decided to let Frannie do the cooking tonight."

Seth nodded at Callie and shook Nick's hand. "Nice to meet both of you."

The other man turned his attention to Bridey. "Callie mentioned you wanted me to stop by your shop. Something about shelving you need done. Would Monday work?"

Bridey grimaced. "Sorry, Nick. I should have called Callie before now. Seth offered to build them for me."

Nick looked relieved. "No need to apologize. I'm glad you found someone so quickly."

On the other hand, Callie's eyebrows shot up in surprise. "Why don't the two of you join us, and you can tell us all about what you have in mind, Seth. For Bridey's shop, that is."

Although clearly that wasn't what she meant at all. The last thing Seth wanted was to be grilled by one of

Bridey's friends on their first not-quite-a-date. Thankfully, Bridey headed her friend off at the pass.

"We don't want to intrude. Besides, Seth and I will be talking business, which I'm sure you'd find boring."

That might have been true for Nick, but it was apparent that Bridey's refusal only heightened her friend's curiosity. "If you're sure. Maybe I'll give you a call tomorrow so we can catch up on things."

"Sounds good. See you two later."

Bridey held his hand firmly as they walked over to the booth they'd been aiming for. She took the seat that faced away from her friends while he took the opposite side.

Should he be concerned that Bridey had refused her friend's invitation? As much as he'd like to think it was because she wanted to have him to herself, it was more likely that she wanted to maintain the image that this was strictly a business meeting.

She answered his unspoken question. "Callie is one of my best friends and I really like Nick, but it's been a long day. I don't have the energy to hold up my end of a four-way conversation."

Her eyes slid to the side briefly before once again looking directly at him. "I'd rather spend the time with just you. I hope that's okay."

It was well beyond just okay. "I'm not a big one for talking."

She smiled at his comment, looking a bit shy. "I've noticed, but I like that about you. It's soothing. Most people don't appreciate the value of silence."

"I like being with you, too."

"That's good, Seth, considering how much you'll be doing around my shop for the foreseeable future."

Before he could figure out what to say to that, she

turned her attention to the menu, studying it as if she'd never seen it before. He gave up and scanned his as well.

When the waitress arrived to take their orders, Bridey handed back the menu. "I'll have the pot roast and iced tea with my dinner. Seth, have you decided?"

"The same."

As the waitress walked away, he had a small bout of cold feet. What if Bridey chose this moment to grill him about his past? He didn't want to lie to her, but he wasn't yet ready to fill her in on all the details about his long dry spell. It was easy to see that she was working herself up to asking him something. He braced himself and waited.

"So, tell me, Seth. Why nutmeg instead of cloves?"

He laughed. "B-because my grandmother was famous in our family for her plum tarts. No one else could duplicate her secret recipe, although they tried. All I know for sure was that she preferred nutmeg to cinnamon, and something gave her tarts a little extra bite."

Somehow he thought Bridey would understand his grandmother's stance. He was right.

"I get that. I used to be the pastry chef in an upscale restaurant down in California. Other places were always trying to rip off my recipes."

She looked pretty fierce there for a second, but then her expression softened, saddened. "There was a time I thought about publishing my own cookbook. That way people would at least pay for the privilege of using my creations."

"You should still do that."

"That's sweet of you to say." She sighed and toyed with her silverware. "I was never a big enough name, so most likely no one would care enough to buy the book."

He would bet his last dollar that she was parroting someone else's opinion on the subject. And that someone had meant so much to her that his words carried enough weight to destroy her dream. Feeling daring all of a sudden, Seth reached over to take her hand in his. He brushed his thumb back and forth across her knuckles. "He was wrong, you know."

Bridey looked puzzled. "Who was wrong, Seth?"

"Whoever told you not to try. Failure hurts, but it won't kill you. Not trying at all is what sucks your soul dry. Don't underestimate yourself, Bridey. You have a real gift for what you do."

Although she didn't say so directly, her soft smile proved his comment pleased her. Bridey stared down at their hands for several seconds before looking up. "You're a nice man, Seth Kyser."

He laughed again. "G-glad you think so."

Unsure what more to say, he turned the conversation in another direction. "So what other goodies do you plan to add to the menu for the holiday season?"

Bridey gave him a wide-eyed look. "Why, Mr. Kyser, are you volunteering to be a test subject again?"

He leaned back, doing his best to look innocent. "Anytime, but right now I'm just being curious."

Bridey frowned a little. "I do want to change things up a bit, but it's hard to come up with a lot of different ideas without making things too complicated. Although now that I have Fiona to help, things should be easier. I'll be adding a couple of seasonal drinks. Eggnog and a pumpkin spice drink, for starters, and a new spice tea, as well. I've already started baking gingerbread cookies and some cream cheese spritz cookies you might like. I've also gotten quite a few orders from people for boxes of my cookies to give as gifts. I started offering those last year, and people seem to really like them."

Seth made a mental note to order a few boxes for his

agent and some other people he did business with. "I can see why. They get to enjoy Christmas cookies while you do all the work."

She laughed. "There is that, but really I don't mind. I love this time of year. Everybody seems friendlier, and all the decorations make the world a prettier place. As far as I'm concerned, you can never have too many lights or candles. I inherited my mother's snowman collection. I really don't have room in my apartment for all of them, but I don't care. I put them out anyway. Unpacking them is like seeing a bunch of friends I haven't seen in a while, and they remind me of her. How about you? Do you have any favorite traditions?"

He shook his head. "I haven't even put up a tree in ages. However, I have to admit helping you put up the decorations in the shop might have inspired me to make more of an effort this year."

Then their dinners arrived, and the conversation became more intermittent. But even when the silence stretched out as they ate, just sitting across from Bridey made the time special.

4

The shelves in the storeroom were nearly done. Bridey wouldn't miss the noise and the clutter, but she would miss Seth. Until she came up with another project for him to tackle, their morning time together, which she'd come to look forward to each day, was about to come to an end. Granted, moments after letting him in every morning, she'd been up to her elbows in flour and sugar, getting the morning's baking done while he drilled and hammered and sawed away in the storeroom. And yet . . . simply knowing he was around made her happy.

He was definitely a hard worker. To get him to take even a short break, she had to resort to bribery, usually her next attempt at the perfect gingerbread cupcake. With Christmas getting closer by the day, she had only a short time to refine her recipe.

Today, however, she had planned a special surprise for him, an almond kringle, another of the specialty desserts she wanted to serve during the holidays. It was a traditional Scandinavian coffee cake, one she'd never before tried to make. Once Seth became engrossed in his own work, Bridey cranked up her favorite Christmas music, collected all the ingredients, and got busy. Ensuring the crust would be flaky and light was a three-day process, which involved adding another layer of butter each day and then chilling the dough overnight. Now all she had to do was roll it out and add the filling. After the crust was the right size, she spooned a mixture of almond paste and butter along one half of the dough and folded it over to seal in the filling. The last step was to brush the top with butter and then sprinkle it with sliced almonds. While the kringle baked, she finished decorating a batch of sugar cookies that were cut into Santa and snowman shapes as she sang along with the music.

An hour later, the kringle had cooled enough to eat. What would her favorite test subject think of it? She waited until Seth finished what he was working on before knocking on the doorframe to get his attention. "Ready for a break?"

"Always."

He removed his safety glasses and set them aside before following her out into the kitchen. They'd taken to sharing a cup of coffee and a snack about this same time every morning. Something else she would miss when he was done.

After he settled himself at his usual spot at the counter, she set a small plate down in front of him. She'd covered it with a napkin to hide the surprise.

"What's this?"

"My first attempt at making an almond kringle. I researched online for some traditional recipes to use. I don't expect to have hit perfection, so please think of this as my opening salvo."

Seth looked positively reverent as he studied the small slice of coffee cake. "It looks wonderful, but I have one question for you. How did you know it was one of my favorites?"

"Oh, I didn't. I just wanted you to be the first to try it."

She blushed and gripped the edge of the counter with her shaky hands to hide how much this meant to her. If she could put her own individual stamp on the recipe, it might be the first step in a new project for her: that cookbook she'd always wanted to do. Doing a whole section on holiday desserts seemed to be the perfect place to start. For now, though, she wasn't ready to share that idea with anyone, not even Seth.

Seth took a bite and then a second. Eyeing the rest of the kringle on the counter, he said, "Damn, that's good, Bridey. I hereby volunteer to eat that whole thing by myself!"

His honesty soothed her nerves enough that she could release her death grip on the counter. "Great! That gives me a starting point."

To her surprise, Seth set his fork down and stood up. He took a slow step toward her, getting close enough that her entire field of vision was filled with the red and black plaid of his flannel shirt. His big hand rose up to gently lift her chin until she met his gaze.

"Thank you for trusting me with your creations, Bridey."

While he spoke, his gaze zeroed in on her mouth. Thanks to the demands of running her own business, not to mention a definite skittishness when it came to men since her divorce, her dating skills were a bit rusty. Even so, she was sure that Seth was about to kiss her.

God, she hoped so.

Maybe he needed to be sure she wanted him just as much. She leaned in to his palm, letting him know she liked his touch. Then she grabbed a fistful of flannel and tugged him closer.

Seth was a man of few words, but his actions spoke volumes. He pulled her into a full-body press as his mouth settled over hers with a definite take-no-prisoners attitude. The brush of his lips sent the temperature in the kitchen soaring. His kiss tasted of almonds and dark roast coffee. Bridey could've feasted on that flavor for an eternity. There was a slight tug as Seth pulled the chopsticks from her hair, setting it free to tumble down to her shoulders.

He smiled against her lips. "I've been wanting to do that for days."

As his fingers slid through her hair, she felt his touch right down to her core. His other arm tightened around her waist as he lifted her up onto the counter, bringing her to his eye level. He put a hand on each of her knees and spread them apart to make room for himself there.

Oh yeah, she liked that. She trailed her fingers down his cheek, finding the hint of stubble arousing. "Kiss me again, Seth."

"Gladly."

This time, she parted her lips at first touch, welcoming the invasion of his tongue. He took his time and did a thorough job of kissing her. For the moment, he made no move to take it any further, letting her set the pace. When she tugged his shirt up to stroke her hands along the warm skin of his back, he murmured his approval.

Finally, he drew back just enough to rest his forehead against hers. "I can't believe I'm saying this, but unless you want to delay opening the shop today, we need to stop."

His words took a second to sink in, but then he turned his wrist so she could see his watch.

Good grief. She was due to open the door in less than ten minutes! "Oh gosh. I completely lost track of time, and it's all your fault!"

Seth settled his hands on her waist and lifted her down off the counter. His smile was a tad wicked. "You know, I think there's a compliment for me in there somewhere."

She liked this teasing side of Seth's personality even if their heated encounter left her blushing. Thank goodness one of them had the presence of mind to keep things from getting completely out of hand. She noticed Seth seemed to be waiting for some kind of response. Rising up on her toes, she pressed a quick kiss to his cheek.

"Yeah, there was a compliment in there somewhere, but now I've got to get ready to open."

He stepped back. "I'll go put the chairs down for you."

"That would be a big help."

After he disappeared into the front of the shop, she checked to make sure her clothes were all in order. When she started to twist her hair back up in a knot, she could only find one of her chopsticks. Fine. A pencil would have to do.

With Seth's help, everything was ready just as the first burst of customers came through the door. They were regulars, so she could fill their orders without having to think about it too much. Good thing, too, because her encounter with Seth had left her a bit frazzled.

She was eager to be alone with him again, and that had her feeling off balance.

When there was a break in the foot traffic, she ducked into the kitchen to take care of a few last-minute shop details. Seth was just heading out the back with his toolbox. He stopped when he heard her coming.

She joined him at the door. "Good, I was hoping to catch you."

He looked concerned. "Everything all right?"

"Everything's fine. I was wondering if you'd like to

have dinner with me tonight. We can go to the diner again if you'd like or maybe try someplace else."

His smile was all the answer she needed. "I'd like. I'll be back when the shop closes."

The jingle bells over the front door rang, dragging her back to reality. "Gotta go. See you tonight."

Seth drove straight home, planning on crawling back into bed for a few hours. As much as he loved working in Bridey's shop, four a.m. wakeups were excruciating, especially when he was used to staying up late and then sleeping in. However, for Bridey's company, he'd change his ways without complaint.

After unlocking the front door, Seth headed for the kitchen, thinking a second breakfast before that nap sounded really good. He had just cracked three eggs into a bowl when there was a knock on the front door. He wasn't expecting any deliveries, and his family never dropped by without calling first. In fact, they usually insisted that he come to them.

He took the pan off the heat and headed for the front door.

There was a strange pickup truck parked in the driveway and a tall man prowling back and forth on the front porch. When he turned around, Seth recognized Nick from the diner the other night.

He opened the front door. "Hey, Nick, what brings you out here?"

"Sorry to show up unannounced, but I just missed you at Bridey's. There's something I wanted to discuss with you."

What could that be? "I just made a fresh pot of coffee and was fixing myself some breakfast. Care to join me?"

"I've already eaten, but coffee sounds good."

Seth led the way into his kitchen and filled a big mug for his guest. "Have a seat, Nick. I'll finish up, and then we can talk."

Nick made himself comfortable while Seth scrambled the eggs. When he finally joined Nick at the table, the other man took a deep breath as if bracing himself to spit out something unpalatable. Seth buttered his toast and waited him out.

"Okay, here's the thing. Evidently the town has a tra- dition of decorating all of the buildings along the main drag for Christmas. The mayor wants to up the ante this year and really pull out all the stops in the hopes of at- tracting more tourists to town."

With a sly grin, he added, "Well, actually, I think she's more interested in attracting their wallets."

Seth still wasn't sure what this had to do with him. He concentrated on eating his breakfast while he waited for the other man to get to his point.

Nick paused to sip his coffee. "The town council is looking for volunteers to help put up the lights and dec- orations. It can get done in one day if enough people pitch in to help."

He shrugged his shoulders and shook his head. "Cal- lie's mother immediately volunteered my services, so I'm already on the hook to do some of the heavy lifting. Since Bridey has been raving about the great job you're doing for her, I thought maybe you'd be willing to help out, too. We didn't have your phone number, so I tried to catch up with you at Bridey's place this morning."

Seth pointed out the obvious. "Bridey could have given you my number and saved you a trip out here."

Something about Nick's expression had Seth thinking Nick was hiding something. "Okay, so I'm guessing she did give you my number. Why didn't you call?"

The man didn't even pretend to be embarrassed by his deliberate ambush. "Because, my friend, it's harder to say no in person than it is over the phone."

They weren't actually friends, not yet anyway, but Seth already liked him. "Sneaky, Nick. Did they teach that in the army?"

The man looked smug. "I prefer to think they only polished my already impressive skill set. So, what do you think? Are you busy next Saturday?"

No, he wasn't. The only question was whether he was ready to get more involved with his new neighbors. He'd left Seattle for some much-needed privacy. On the other hand, if he was going to make Snowberry Creek his home, maybe he should pitch in. He also suspected that Bridey would approve if he decided to help. That was the clincher.

"Yeah, I can do that. What time and where?"

"We'll all meet up in the parking lot at the Community Church at eight o'clock sharp on Saturday morning. For what it's worth, the local churches are going to provide breakfast and lunch for everyone."

This was getting better and better. Seth's mother would die to find out her artist son would be doing common labor and getting paid in potluck fare. He couldn't wait to tell her.

"Yeah, I'll show up on Saturday."

"That's great, Seth. I'd apologize for putting you on the spot, but from what I've heard about the mayor's plans, I suspect we're going need every helping hand we can find."

"Could be fun."

Clearly Nick had a different opinion on the subject, but he didn't say so. He finished his coffee and carried the mug over to the counter. As he started for the door, he stopped to stare at the bookshelves and cabinets Seth had built along the wall surrounding the natural stone fireplace.

"Nice work. Did all that come with the house?"

"No, I put them in."

Nick moved in for a closer look. "This is quality work, Seth. Have you been building cabinets for long?"

No, he'd done it only to keep busy. Rather than lie about it, he simply said, "I like working with wood."

"Bridey mentioned you had work lined up after the new year starts. If you ever have room in your schedule for some small jobs, let me know. I'm remodeling that big old Victorian my buddy Spence left to Callie, and I could sure use someone with your skills. I'm okay with routine carpentry, but you've sure got an artist's eye for bringing out the best in the wood."

Of course he had no clue that he was touching on such a sore subject—but there was no use in burdening Nick with his problems. The man meant well. There was no way for him to know that Seth was struggling right now.

"I'll keep that in mind."

Nick started toward the door again. "Well, thanks again, Seth. Maybe we'll run into you and Bridey at the diner again one of these nights."

"Could be."

After seeing Nick out, Seth headed for his workshop, all thoughts of taking a nap gone for now. The reminder he'd be seeing Bridey again in a few hours left him reenergized.

After flipping on the overhead lights, he headed straight for his worktable, meaning to sketch out a few more details on another shelving unit he wanted to suggest to Bridey for her office. The huge, rectangular slab of cherry was right where he'd left it the other day. Determined to ignore it, Seth spread out his plans on the other side of the table and got ready to work.

Except he couldn't. Instead, he found himself staring across at the wood. Odd that one strip of color was almost the exact shade of Bridey's gingerbread cupcakes. There was even a lighter streak that could be the icing. He rounded the corner of the table to stand squarely in front of the thick board, his pulse racing as it hadn't in months. Maybe ever.

One by one, images superimposed themselves on the smooth surface of the wood in his mind's eye. Rather than risk losing them, he ripped a sheet of white butcher paper off the roll hanging on the wall and laid it out beside the board, holding the corners down with whatever he could grab: a stapler, a hammer, his coffee cup, and a Slinky.

Taking a deep breath, he started sketching out all the elements that would make up the carving. When it was finished, he stepped back and studied the drawing. Perfect. Not only that, but the carved sign for Something's Brewing would make a great Christmas gift for Bridey. Maybe being around her bustling productivity at the bakery had given his own creativity a boost. Whatever the source of his inspiration, he couldn't wait to make that all-important first cut into the wood.

5

Bridey dialed Seth's number again. Still no answer. If something had happened to prevent him from being able to join her for dinner, surely he would've called. Seth wasn't the kind to blow off a friend like this. She'd give him another ten minutes and then give up.

After those ten slowly stretched into fifteen, she started to let herself out the front door of the shop when she spotted a group of Christmas carolers making their way down the street toward her shop. She closed her eyes to appreciate their sweet harmony. When they reached the front of her shop, they were just finishing the final chorus of "Joy to the World," one of her favorite Christmas songs. Back when her parents were still alive, her mother would hum that song while she wrapped gifts and baked cookies.

Deciding the singers deserved a reward for sharing the gift of their music, she said, "Can you wait here a minute?"

When they nodded, she ducked back into the shop to bring out a tray of cream cheese spritz cookies decorated to look like miniature wreaths. The carolers made quick

344

work of the goodies, clearly pleased with the treats she'd offered them. When they were finished eating, they rewarded her by launching into a cheerful chorus of "We Wish You a Merry Christmas." As they sang, a strange car swerved to the curb right in front of where Bridey stood, startling her. As soon as the driver stepped out of the car, she relaxed.

Seth smiled at the carolers and started right for Bridey. He stood quietly at her side during the rest of the performance. As they launched into the next song, he pulled several bills out of his wallet and stuffed them into their donation can. Bridey didn't know how much he gave them, but there was no mistaking the pleased surprise on the face of the man who was holding the can.

When he and the other singers finally moved on down the street, Seth said, "Sorry to have kept you waiting. Got caught up in something and lost track of time. I'll understand if you're angry."

She offered him a reassuring smile. "No. It's all right. I was more worried than angry. I was afraid something had happened."

"I am s-sorry."

He started to raise his arm as if to hold her hand but then let it drop back down to his side. Maybe he thought she wouldn't welcome the gesture right now, and she didn't know how to tell him she would without embarrassing herself. Did he feel as awkward as she did about where they were in their relationship? Did they even have one?

Rather than stand there and dither, she pointed toward the Creek Café. "Shall we head down to Frannie's place?"

Seth stared at the neon sign down the way. "I was kind of hoping you'd like to go somewhere else tonight." He hesitated before adding, "We're likely to run into some-one we know at the diner again. Although, if that's what you'd prefer, that would be fine."

Where was he going with this? "What would you pre-fer, Seth?"

This time he did reach out to brush the back of his fingers along her cheek. "To have you all to myself."

The night was chilly, but his touch was delightfully warm. It made her want to snuggle close to soak up his heat. Did she really want to spend the evening at a crowded restaurant? No, she wanted Seth all to herself.

"So what are our options? I have to work tomorrow, so I can't be out late."

Seth stared down at her for several seconds. "We could pick up a pizza and go to my place."

She liked his way of thinking. "To tell you the truth, I've been around enough people today. A pizza and just the two of us sounds like the perfect combination."

He was already reaching for his cell. At the same time, he opened the passenger door of the car for her. "They make a wicked veggie pizza at that place down the street."

"Perfect!" As she slid in to the front seat, she gave him a wink. "But make sure they hold the onions and go light on the garlic."

"Yes, ma'am."

Half an hour later, Seth pulled into his driveway and stopped. Ordinarily, he would have parked in the barn, but all too soon he'd have to get the car back out to take Bridey home. He wished like hell that she would spend the night in his bed, but he suspected it was too soon to suggest it.

"I like your place, Seth. Log homes might be rustic, but they always look cozy to me."

He tried to see it through her eyes. "I was hooked the second I saw it. Like I'd finally come home."

The only other time he'd had that same blow-to-the-gut feeling was the first time he'd seen Bridey, but he kept that fact to himself. "We'd better get moving before the pizza gets cold."

Inside, he sent her to the living room while he grabbed plates and silverware from the kitchen. When he came back, Bridey was standing at the front window staring out into the night. She looked cold to him, so after setting the plates down on the coffee table, he put a pair of logs in the fireplace along with a few pieces of kindling and wadded-up newspaper. When he had it all arranged to his satisfaction, he struck a match and held it to the edge of the newspaper. He fanned the fire until it was well established and burning brightly.

Bridey joined him to watch the flames. "I envy your real fireplace. I have one of those little gas ones in my apartment, but it's just not the same."

He slipped his arm around her shoulders and held her close. It was hard to tell if the surge of warmth he felt was coming from the fire or the woman at his side.

Pizza sounded good, but at the moment he was far more interested in the delectable woman standing next to him.

He gave in to temptation and kissed her. She didn't resist, but neither did she give herself over to the moment like she had earlier in the day. He took it down a couple of notches, still holding her but trying to give her some space.

At least Bridey didn't pretend to not understand what he wanted from her. "Seth, I've been thinking about things since this morning, and I wanted to talk to you about it. Please don't get me wrong. I love spending time with you, but it's been a while since I've been involved with anyone. Can we take it slow and see where the evening takes us?"

As much as he wanted this woman in his bed, he valued her companionship and needed to make sure she was comfortable before things headed in that direction. Plus, his disappointment was diluted with relief because she wasn't rejecting him completely. "No pressure, Bridey. We can eat pizza, watch television, talk, whatever makes you happy."

Her smile brightened and she pressed a soft kiss to his cheek. "So let's check out this veggie special you were raving about."

They ended up on his couch making fast work of the pizza. As it turned out, he was hungrier for more than just Bridey. They washed it down with a couple of local microbrews and then settled back to watch the fire.

"Music or television?"

Bridey set her empty plate on the coffee table and then snuggled in closer to Seth on the oversized couch. "Music. Something soft and easy."

He used the remote to turn on a soft-rock station and knocked the volume down until it provided a soothing background noise. He was glad Bridey didn't mind his long silences. Right now he was content just simply sitting with her.

Two, maybe three, songs played without either of them speaking a single word. The peace wasn't going to last long, though. There was a new tension in Bridey. Maybe she wanted to go home but was reluctant to say so.

"What's wrong, Bridey?"

She gave him a startled look. "Nothing's wrong at all. I was just wondering if maybe I slowed things down too much. You seem pretty content just sitting here to-gether."

"What have you got in mind? Because I can tell you right now, I'm definitely up for anything."

She glanced down as if to verify the truth of that statement. When she realized what she'd done, she groaned and buried her face against his shoulder.

Cute. Rather than leaving her to wallow in embarrassment, he lifted her up onto his lap. Granted, now she could probably feel the effect she was having on him, but he couldn't wait another minute to kiss her.

For the second time that day, he let her hair down so he could play with it. Her arms snaked around his neck and held on for dear life as their kiss rivaled the intensity of the roaring fire. Bridey broke away long enough to shift positions to straddle his thighs, bringing the heat of her core directly against his erection. Groaning with pleasure, he filled his hands with the soft curves of her ass.

Bridey made one of those sexy little noises and rocked against him, fanning the flames of his desire for her. He wanted to carry her to the bedroom, strip them both naked, and take this to its logical conclusion.

Unfortunately, he'd come equipped with a conscience. Bridey had made it clear that she wanted to take things slow, not to mention she had an early start in the morning. Cursing himself for a fool, he caught her wandering hands in his before the last vestiges of his control shattered completely.

"Bridey, we need to stop. Now." He brushed her dark hair back from her face and traced the curve of her lips, which were swollen from his kisses. "Although once again, I can't believe I'm actually saying that."

She blinked at him, her eyes briefly unfocused, but

then she nodded and sat back, giving them both some badly needed space. Her smile was rueful as she drew a ragged breath. "So much for going slow. Sorry about that."

The moment could have been awkward, especially when it felt as if he'd lost all ability to speak, but it wasn't that way at all. Bridey leaned in closer to kiss him again before scrambling off his lap to perch on the edge of the coffee table in front of the couch. It took every bit of restraint he could muster to stop himself from yanking her right back into his arms.

She pushed her hair back behind her ears and tugged her clothes into place. He refrained from saying out loud that he liked when she looked a bit rumpled.

"Should I take you home?" He'd forced himself to make the offer, although the last thing he wanted was for her to leave.

"Yes, I suppose so." Once again, she tried to straighten her clothes, maybe using them as a shield between them. "Not that I want to leave, especially in the middle of . . . this. Us. You know."

Yeah, he did.

Bridey paused as if she'd lost her train of thought, her cheeks flushed a little rosy. "It's just that my alarm goes off so darn early."

Unfolding himself from the couch, he said, "I'll get my keys."

She caught up with him before he'd made it halfway to the kitchen counter, where he'd tossed his keys and wallet. "I meant what I said, Seth. I don't want to leave at all, but if I stay, we both know what's going to happen."

Where was she going with this? "I didn't assume anything, Bridey, when we came here. And remember, I know exactly how early your day starts."

"I know you didn't assume anything, Seth. You're not that kind of guy." Bridey put her hand on his chest right over his heart. "But I'd rather it be when we have more than an hour, two tops, together. Slow and easy would be so much better than rushed. Okay?"

Oh man, that was a helluva image! "It's definitely okay, but we'd better go while I still remember what good intentions are."

She laughed as they headed out into the night. For her sake, he was glad that she lived fairly close because it was getting pretty late. She refused to let him walk her to the door, choosing to kiss him one last time in the front seat of his car before heading into her first-floor apartment by herself. Seth waited until she was safely in the door and the lights came on. She pulled aside the curtains in the front window and waved at him one last time. Out of excuses to linger, he drove away.

And because she'd said "when" they took that next step, not "if," he smiled all the way back home.

6

Bridey stacked the last two dozen gingerbread cupcakes on the tray. They smelled heavenly, if she did say so herself. They were her donation to the potluck luncheon for everyone who was pitching in to decorate the town for the holidays, and Seth was going to deliver them to the church. She shouldered the heavy tray just as he came through the back door after taking the first load out to his van.

"Here, let me help you with that."

She surrendered her burden under protest. "I carry trays like that all the time."

He offered her one of his bad-boy grins. "But then you'd miss the chance to watch me showing off my muscles."

When he held out his arm at a right angle to flex said muscles, she fanned her face and pretended to swoon. "Why, Mr. Kyser, how shall I ever express my gratitude for all your manly help this morning?"

His easy smile morphed into something more seductive. "I have some thoughts on that I'd love to share with you."

She'd love that, too. "Did I happen to mention that I'm closing the shop on Monday? I have some business in Seattle to attend to that morning. I thought I'd sleep in, then drive up to meet with my attorney and maybe do some Christmas shopping afterward."

Seth had been almost to the door. He spun back in her direction, nearly dropping the tray in the process. Only quick reflexes and a bit of luck kept all of her hard work from hitting the floor in a flurry of crumbs. With exaggerated care, he set the tray on the nearest counter and closed the distance between them in two steps.

"Did you say you could sleep in?"

Smart man. He knew exactly what she was saying. They'd had dinner together almost every evening, mostly carryout from one of the local restaurants. Separating at the end of the night was getting increasingly harder.

"Yep, that's exactly what I said."

To her surprise, he looked a bit hesitant. "Would you like some company?"

"I was hoping you might want to come along. My appointment shouldn't take more than an hour, so we'd have the rest of the afternoon to do what we please."

The smile was back in full force. Seth swept in to kiss her hard and fast. When they came up for air, he asked, "What do you think about driving up Sunday after closing time to spend the night someplace nice?" After another kiss that curled her toes, he added, "Someplace with room service."

"Hey, Seth, didn't you say there was one more tray to load? Whoops. Sorry."

Neither of them had heard the door open again. Nick was already making a hasty retreat. "Look, no rush. I will, uh, I'll be out here. No rush. I'm gone. Never mind me. You two just carry on."

As the door slammed closed again, he was muttering, "Carry on? I can't believe I just said that."

Bridey rested her forehead against Seth's chest, which shook with laughter. Okay, that was too funny. "That sounds lovely, Seth. I'll pack a bag and be ready to go at five thirty."

Then she gave him a soft shove. "You'd better get going. We both have work to do."

"Fine, I'll go." Seth tugged her back into his arms for another kiss. "But I'm telling you, tomorrow night can't get here fast enough."

Then he grabbed the tray and disappeared out the back door. As she watched him leave, she smiled.

The past few holiday seasons had been lonely ones, but with Seth in her life, this one promised to be extra special in so many ways.

Six hours later, Seth plunked his lunch on the table and collapsed onto one of the metal folding chairs in the church basement. They'd been hard at work since early that morning, but unfortunately, they'd finished decorating only one side of the street.

It didn't help that he was so distracted. The thought of having Bridey all to himself for the better part of twenty-four hours had him wanting to run down the street whooping and hollering. The last thing he wanted to do was climb another ladder.

Nick joined him. He looked as tired as Seth felt. "I can't believe we still have that much left to do."

Seth didn't bother to answer. Instead, he poked at the food on his plate with a fork. It looked kind of like beef stew but with a mashed potato topping. Nick evidently had no reservations about the food, judging by the way he was packing it away. He happened to glance up and caught Seth watching him.

He grinned and picked up another forkful of food. "Soldiers never pass up the chance for a hot meal. Oddly enough, no one has ever figured out how to schedule combat around mealtimes."

He took another bite. "Besides, I like shepherd's pie."

Seth couldn't fault the man's logic. He took a bite of the casserole and was pleasantly surprised. The two of them finished off their meal in short order, but neither one was in a particular hurry to get back to work.

Nick topped off his coffee. "Don't tell Callie, but for all my bitching about having to do this today, I'm actually enjoying myself. Snowberry Creek is a little smaller than the town I grew up in, but we had days like this where everyone pitched in to help on a project."

Seth had nothing to compare it to. "I grew up in the city, so we didn't have that connection with our neighbors. Here in Snowberry Creek, everyone has been really friendly, but not in your face about it, if that makes sense."

The other man laughed. "Except when someone shows up on your front porch uninvited to ask how you feel about hanging Christmas lights."

"Yeah, except for that."

He noticed that the rest of the crew they'd been working with were already making their way to the door. "Looks like it's time to get back to work."

Nick grumbled, "Yeah, those lights won't hang themselves."

They carried their trays over to the cleanup squad and headed back to the business district. When they got there, Seth realized the next storefront due to be decorated was Something's Brewing. Deciding it wouldn't hurt for Bridey to see him at work, he picked up the pace.

"Come on, Nick. Hustle your ass. I want to stake out the coffee shop before anyone else does. You got me into this, so the least you can do is help me impress Bridey."

The former soldier dutifully kicked it into high gear. "Considering what I walked in on this morning, I don't think you need any help impressing the woman. However, I will do my best to make you look good."

Before they'd even gotten their ladders set up, Bridey came outside with tall cups of her latest concoction, peppermint mocha hot chocolate, along with a couple of pastries for each of them. Nick lit up like one of the strings of lights they'd been hanging.

"Woman, you keep feeding us like this, Seth and I are going to have to buy bigger jeans."

Seth noticed that didn't keep Nick from accepting her offering. "Don't worry. We'll work it off. Plenty left to do."

She stood close to him as the three of them checked the progress being made. "Think it will all get finished today?"

He nodded. "The lights are the slow part. The people filling the planters are almost done. Once they finish, some of them will pitch in, too."

"That's good." Bridey gave him a hesitant look and dropped her voice. "I hope you don't mind postponing leaving for Seattle for an extra hour tomorrow night. The mayor wants everyone to show up when she throws the switch on the lights at six o'clock."

He hated any delay, but he understood that she was part of the business community here in town and needed to show her support. "That will be fine as long as we can leave right after the lights come on."

"Sounds good to me." She gave him a quick hug, the promise in her eyes hot enough to drive away the damp chill in the air.

Seth fought the urge to blow off working so he could drag her off to someplace more private. Unfortunately, Nick had already started up the ladder. "Hey, Seth, can you hand me the first string?"

"Sure thing." But before doling out the lights, Seth leaned down close to Bridey's ear to whisper, "Sunday evening can't get here fast enough."

She whispered back, "I feel that way, too." Then she kissed his cheek and added, "By the way, I'm packing something black and lacy that only you will get to see."

He groaned and closed his eyes. "If that was meant to help me get through the day, it won't. How am I supposed to get any work done with my imagination running wild?"

She sashayed toward the door. "Not my problem, big guy. Deal with it."

He stared after her, plotting his revenge. Unfortunately, he had other obligations right now.

"Seth? The lights? I know they're not as interesting as whatever Bridey just told you, but I'd really like to get done sometime this century."

He definitely needed to get his head back in the game if they were ever going to finish stringing the lights. It took all of Seth's strength to drag his attention back to the job at hand. "Sorry, Nick. I'll get them."

As he opened the next box of lights, he glanced at his watch. Twenty-seven hours and counting. He wasn't sure he'd survive.

While he waited to hand Nick the next string of lights, Seth studied the picture of a certain jolly old elf that Bridey had just hung in her shop window. It had been years since Seth had put together a wish list, but maybe it wouldn't hurt to drop a hint or two.

Hey, Santa. I know just what I want for Christmas. I promise to be good.

Although come to think of it, his idea of good and Santa's thoughts on the subject might not be at all the same. Laughing, he opened another box of lights and started doling them out to Nick.

7

Bridey shut off the lights and posted the sign in the window that indicated the shop would open at noon on Monday. She'd planned to close for the day, but Fiona had offered to cover for her. It would be her first time handling the shop by herself, but Bridey wasn't worried about how she'd do.

Seth was on his way, setting off a flurry of butterflies inside her chest. It wasn't that she was having second thoughts, but this was a big step for the two of them. A huge step. Was he as nervous as she was? She hoped so.

Although she'd gone out with a few men since her divorce, this was first time she'd met someone she wanted to get involved with beyond a few casual dates. Seth made her feel appreciated, something she'd been missing in her life since long before her marriage had ended.

She peeked outside where everything glistened with new snowfall. The deep green boughs on the fir trees were already tipped with a heavy layer of white. An artist couldn't have painted a prettier picture. Across the street, a young father was pulling two small children on a plastic toboggan. The kids were having a fine time as they held out their mittens and tried to catch snowflakes as they fell.

It was nice that nature had cooperated with the mayor's plans by dropping five inches of new snow on the ground since noon. As pretty as it was, it was a relief that it wasn't sticking to the roads.

She wanted nothing to interfere with their plans for the night. A glance at the small suitcase sitting by the door had her smiling. Ever since she'd told Seth about the black lace, he'd been pestering her with questions, wanting details, but she'd held strong. A woman was entitled to her secrets. He'd see the negligee soon enough, and a little mystery only added to the anticipation.

Someone knocked at the rear entrance of the shop. She hurried through to the kitchen and unlocked the door. "Sorry, I was watching for you out front."

Seth stomped his feet to knock off the snow before coming inside. "All the close parking was taken. I left the car on the next street over and walked."

He studied her attire. "I'm glad you're dressed warm. It's cold out there."

His cheeks were rosy and his stocking cap was dusted with melting snowflakes. "Do you need something to warm you up?"

She'd been thinking about a tall coffee, but Seth obviously had a different idea. He swept her up in his arms for a big hug and a long kiss.

When he released her, she asked, "Did that help?"

His smile was a tad wicked. "I can honestly say that it fanned the flames. Are you sure we need to hang around for the light show?"

"Yes, but we can leave as soon as the mayor flips the switch." She checked the time. "The ceremony starts in twenty minutes. Allowing for the mayor giving a short speech and a ten-minute walk back to your car, I'm thinking we'll be on the road to Seattle in forty-five minutes tops."

Seth's smile faded as he followed her back out into the shop to retrieve her suitcase. "A speech? Seriously?"

Bridey shrugged. "She's a politician. Mayor McKay won't simply turn on the lights and walk away. She's also been asked to remind folks donations are still needed for the fund-raiser to refurbish the playground at the elementary school next spring. I thought I'd donate a gift certificate for a cake for a birthday party."

Seth frowned. "What's wrong with the playground?"

Bridey zipped her parka and turned out the lights. "The equipment is old and doesn't meet current safety standards."

He took the bag from her. "Sounds like a good cause. Can anyone donate?"

"I think they'd appreciate anything you could do to help out. With the city's budget so tight, there's just not any money left over for extras."

She shivered as they stepped outside. "You're right about it being chilly. Maybe that will encourage the mayor to keep it short."

Seth wrapped his arm around her shoulders as they walked. "We can only hope."

Outside, they hurried down to where the crowd was gathering near the bandstand in the park. As they crossed the street, a snowball came flying from out of nowhere to hit Seth in the middle of his chest. It didn't take long for him to spot Nick and Callie approaching from the other direction. The former soldier already had another snowball ready to launch. Not to be outdone,

Seth gathered up a double handful of the stuff and prepared to return fire. Bridey tried to stay out of it, but Callie wasn't having any of that. She lobbed a snowball at Seth and then a second one at Bridey. Seth defended his woman's honor, but she did her own fair share of fighting back.

As both couples continued their attack, other grownups and a bunch of children chose sides and joined in the impromptu battle with a lot of good-spirited namecalling and jeering when someone missed their target. Seth whooped and hollered along with the rest of the crowd, having a great time ducking and weaving to avoid incoming fire from the other side. When he saw one heading straight at Bridey, he jumped in front of her to take the blow himself.

She threw her arms around him for a quick hug. "My hero!"

"Damn straight!"

Then he gave her a quick kiss and rejoined the battle. The flurry of snowballs slowed down only when someone over by the bandstand started ringing jingle bells to get everyone's attention, signaling it was time for the lighting ceremony. The snowball fight broke up, and everyone made their way down to gather in a circle around the steps of the bandstand. Callie and Nick fell into step with Seth and Bridey. The four of them found a spot where they could see the podium that had been set up. There was a group of people already gathered in the bandstand.

Nick nodded in their direction. "I see the town council is out in full force."

The mayor must be a believer in promptness because she stepped up to the podium right at six o'clock. The crowd fell silent as she started to speak. "I want to thank everyone for coming tonight, especially those who pitched in to make this night possible. . . ."

Seth only pretended to listen to what she was saying. Right now all he could think about was how good it felt to have Bridey tucked into his side. Anyone who saw them standing together would know they were a couple. It had been a long time since he'd had this sense of belonging not just to someone, but also somewhere.

He'd always been a homebody, finding it easier to keep to his own company than constantly worry about his stuttering. But right now, in this place, he was part of something larger, and he liked how it felt. All those hours he'd put in stringing lights gave him part ownership in tonight's event. It was more than having Bridey in his life, but she certainly played a large role in anchoring him here in Snowberry Creek.

Meanwhile, the mayor had moved on to talking about the auction, which would be held on December 23. Maybe he could donate a sculpture or two to the cause. His artwork was sold under his legal name of Geoffrey Kyser rather than Seth. He could always have his agent handle the donation to distance himself from the process.

Eventually, though, he needed to tell Bridey what he did for a living, but he wasn't ready for that. Far too often in the past people had treated him differently once they found out who he was. It would devastate him if that happened when she learned he was a famous artist, and not just Seth, the guy who built her shelves. His last girlfriend had walked away because of what she saw as his obsession with his art, and what he'd felt for her paled in comparison to how much Bridey meant to him.

Once he finished her Christmas present, he'd use it to explain the artist was the same down-to-earth man she knew, the one who wore jeans and flannel. Geoffrey was the persona who filled out the professional uniform of well-tailored suits.

"Is everything okay, Seth? You look worried."

Bridey's question dragged him back into the moment. He smiled down at her. "I'm fine, and it sounds like she's about done talking."

The crowd grew silent when Mayor McKay held up a switch box. Then she called out, "Start the countdown!"

Everyone chanted the numbers, their voices growing louder as they approached zero. When the last number rang out, the mayor threw the switch, and the night was transformed into a winter wonderland. The trees in the park had been festooned with white lights, and the bandstand had been decked out in the traditional red, green, and blue. Behind them, the drifting snowflakes softened the bright lights along Main Street into a gentle glow.

He wanted to capture the moment somehow. A photograph would work, and he could certainly snap one with his cell phone like so many of the others in the crowd were doing. That would record the details but not the spirit of the moment, with its richness and warmth despite the cold nip in the air.

"This was worth waiting for."

Seth could only nod, although he was thinking of something other than the twinkling lights and the crisp beauty of the snow. And from the heat in the depths of Bridey's eyes, he wasn't the only one.

"Should we head straight back to my car or take the scenic route and admire more of the lights along the way?"

She stared down the street briefly and then rose up on her toes to kiss him. "Let's go light up the night ourselves."

He wished like hell that he had a gift for fancy talk,

but his relationship with the spoken word was adversarial at best. He settled for simply kissing her again in the hope she knew what he was trying to say.

And maybe she did because, as she took his hand and set off down the street toward the car, her sweet smile added to the wonder of the night.

8

After checking in at the front desk of the hotel, Seth made arrangements for their luggage to be taken up to the room while the two of them headed into the small bar located in one corner of the lobby. When they were seated, he ordered a champagne cocktail for each of them. When their server returned with the flutes, Seth said, "I thought a celebration was in order."

She sipped the champagne, finding the bubbly drink refreshing. "And what are we celebrating?"

Seth gave her a solemn look. "Our noble victory over Nick and Callie in the great snowball war."

Bridey suspected it was more likely Seth had picked up on her nervousness and was trying to take things slow and easy. She appreciated his thoughtfulness and went along with his ploy. "You actually think we won? As I recall, Nick got you twice before you even had a chance to throw one back."

"Yeah, but I hit him straight in the face, definitely a lethal blow." Then he grinned. "Besides, they're not here to argue the point, are they?"

She liked this fun-loving side of Seth. Holding up her

glass, she clinked it against his. "Then to the victor go the spoils!"

His eyes flared wide, his smile turning a bit predatory. "I like the way that sounds. . . ."

She studied him over the rim of her drink. "I thought you would."

Half an hour later, they left the bar and stepped into the elevator. The doors closed with a soft *whoosh*, and they were whisked upward to the top floor of the hotel in a matter of seconds.

Bridey wasn't sure what she'd been expecting when she'd let Seth make all the arrangements. Certainly nothing quite as fancy as this place—not that she was complaining. Well, not exactly anyway. It was hard not to worry about the cost, but Seth clearly wasn't concerned about it.

Should she say something? No. He wouldn't appreciate her concern about the state of his finances, even if it did remind her that there was a lot about this man she didn't know. He never spoke much about his past or his family background. All she knew about his job was his assertion he had work lined up starting after the first of the year. He hadn't been very specific about what the job entailed, but she figured it must be along the same lines as what he'd done for her. Maybe that realization should've left her questioning the wisdom of her decision to spend the night with him, but she hadn't been exactly forthcoming about her past herself.

When they reached their room, Seth swiped the key card to unlock the door. He reached inside to turn on the lights and then stood back so she could enter first.

"Wow!"

Bridey wasn't sure if she was talking about the spacious room or the panoramic view. She wandered closer to the window and stared down at the brightly lit city below. Just like Snowberry Creek, Seattle was decked out in her best holiday finery. Even though Seth was normally the one of few words, right now all she could do was repeat herself. "Wow!"

Seth joined her at the window, where she could see his reflection in the glass. From his pleased expression, it seemed the single word had been praise enough. He stood close enough for her to feel his warmth but without crowding her. Maybe she wasn't the only one who was intimidated about taking this next step in their relationship.

For a short time, she was content to hold Seth's hand as they enjoyed the view below them in total silence. The peaceful moment didn't last, though. She could feel her own tension rising and suspected that Seth knew it. The last thing she wanted was for him to think she regretted being there.

"Would you like to go out to dinner?" He paused to study their reflections in the window. "Or maybe you'd prefer to go back home?"

She seemed to be stuck on one-word answers. "No."

He looked a bit puzzled as he faced her directly this time. "No, you don't want to go out to dinner? Or no, you don't want to go back home?"

"Let me try that again." She drew a deep breath, hoping it would help calm her. "No, I don't want to go out to dinner; nor do I want to go back home. Everything I want tonight is already right here with me."

To prove her point, she placed her hands on Seth's chest, one right over his heart. She left it there, taking comfort from the strong, steady beat of his pulse. He covered her hand with his, adding another layer of warmth.

"Something made you skittish."

The truth would be better than any lie she could come up with on short notice. She glanced around at the lush room that surrounded them. "I wasn't expecting anything quite so grand. It took me by surprise."

"And you worry about the money."

At least he looked more amused than insulted when she nodded. "Well, maybe a little."

"The manager is a family friend. He gave me a special rate in return for some work I did for him a while back."

Nothing in his behavior made her think he was lying, but she also sensed there was something more he wasn't telling her. Not that it really mattered. She wouldn't embarrass either of them any further by prying into his personal business. Besides, she had other, more important things on her mind right now.

Seth brushed his fingertips across her hair. She'd worn it up tonight just for him since he'd mentioned how much he liked setting it free. She savored the simple contact, knowing it was only a precursor to what the night would bring.

"Let's order some room service. Maybe a variety of snacks to whet our appetites." He put a small emphasis on the last statement, making it clear which appetites he was talking about. Then he added, "And perhaps some wine?"

"That sounds good. Perfect, in fact."

After they made their selections, the two of them chatted about nothing in particular as they waited for their food and drink to arrive. When the knock at the door finally came, Bridey took advantage of the interruption to take her bag and slip into the bathroom while Seth let the waiter in with the cart.

It didn't take her long to exchange her clothes for the

black lace confection she'd teased Seth about earlier. The satin and lace skimmed down her hips to stop halfway down her thighs, and the neckline plunged down to hug the top curves of her breasts. Oh yeah. Seth was going to love it. After checking her hair, she touched up her lipstick and then spritzed on a small splash of her best perfume.

Maybe it took her longer than she thought because Seth knocked softly on the door. "Would you like a glass of wine?"

"I'll be right out."

Taking yet another deep, calming breath, she opened the door and stepped out into the room. Seth had been in the process of pouring them each a glass of wine. The instant he saw her, he froze, causing him to overfill his wineglass. He cursed and set the bottle aside.

"Sorry if I startled you." Even though his reaction pleased her deeply.

He stared at her, his eyes slowly drifting downward and then back up to her face. His mouth widened into a hungry smile. "You look amazing!"

He'd packed a lot of approval into that assessment. Pleased, she held out her hand. "About that wine?"

Seth scooped up both glasses and headed straight for her. "I didn't know if you preferred white or red, but this is one of my favorite local vintages."

She sipped the wine, savoring the rich taste. "It's delicious."

He set his own glass aside. "Can I fix you a plate of food?"

She studied the array of cheeses, fruits, and pastries. Good. Nothing that couldn't sit for a while.

Placing her glass next to Seth's, she once again rested the palms of her hands against his chest and then slowly reached higher to encircle his neck. Rising to kiss him, she countered his offer with one of her own. "Why don't you take me to bed instead?"

Kissing Bridey tasted like a rare vintage that went straight to Seth's head. The pounding of his pulse drowned out all awareness of their surroundings except for the lush feel of the woman in his arms. He wanted to take her hard and fast. Bridey deserved better: a seduction, not a claiming. But as he drew in her alluring scent, he wasn't sure if he had enough control to pace himself. The sweet press of her breasts against his chest only added fuel to the fire.

Even the delicate satin and lace that offered all those enticing glimpses of her pale skin underneath was too much of a barrier between them. Bridey must have been having some of the same thoughts because her hand wandered south to trace the bulge beneath the fly of his slacks. Her eyes dropped to half-mast and her kiss-swollen lips tipped up at the corners. "Take your shirt off."

Who was he to argue? His fingers fumbled a bit with the buttons, but he quickly shed the first layer of his clothing. His white T-shirt went sailing right after it. He kicked off his shoes and then reached for the buckle on his belt, groaning when Bridey stopped him.

"Slow down." She softened the command with a smile. "Just a little. Let's enjoy this."

He'd do his best, but did she have any idea the effect she was having on him? She went willingly into his embrace, murmuring her approval when he settled his hands on the enticing curves of her bottom and lifted her up enough to press his erection directly against the juncture of her thighs.

"Bridey, my control is about shot. Black lace and your beauty is a potent combination."

She dug her nails into his shoulders just enough to sting. "I'm yours, Seth. Make love to me."

He kissed her deeply again before leading her over to the king-sized bed. There he knelt down to grasp her gown by the hem and slowly tug it upward, taking his time to admire each new inch of her skin that was revealed, turning the process into one long caress.

Bridey raised her arms so he could strip the gown the rest of the way off. After tossing it aside, he turned his attention to releasing the clip that held back her hair, setting it free. He loved the soft tumble of dark silk framing her face and brushing against her shoulders. He'd dreamed of threading his fingers through it as he took her. This time, when he reached for his zipper, Bridey didn't stop him, her eyes following his every move. When he'd stripped away the last of his own clothing, there was nothing left between them except for that last scrap of lace. Now that they'd reached the moment, time had seemed to slow down.

He touched her mouth with a fingertip and then dragged it down to follow the elegant curve of her jawline, her throat, to pause at the pulse point at the base of her neck. From there he traced the top curves of her breasts and then down past them to test the small indentation of her belly button.

Her breath caught in her throat as he continued to follow a path down her body. He closed his eyes as the pad of his finger brushed against the damp heat at her core.

She moaned as he tested and teased, moving his fingertips in slow circles over the thin layer of lace. Abruptly, she retreated a step to perch on the edge of the bed.

There, she supported herself on her elbows and arched her back, drawing his attention to her breasts.

Before following her down onto the bed, he reached for one of the foil packets he'd scattered on the bedside table. Once he'd taken care of that chore, he stretched out next to Bridey. Where to begin? He started with a kiss, taking his time and doing a damn thorough job of memorizing her taste. While their tongues tangled, he tested the weight of her breasts with the palm of his hand, kneading each of them in turn until her nipples pebbled up hard.

Continuing to nip at her breasts with his lips and teeth, he eased his hand inside her panties. As soon as he touched her, Bridey gasped and tried to pull him over her.

"Take these off for me, honey."

Bridey froze briefly but then did as he asked. Minx that she was, she took her time and made sure he watched every move she made. When she dropped the panties onto the floor, she pushed him over onto his back and straddled his hips. His eyes about rolled up in his head when she rocked against him.

He let her have her fun but reclaimed her breasts with his palms. She covered his hands with hers, making it clear that she wanted more, harder, faster. He'd reached his breaking point and used his superior strength to flip them both over until he had her anchored beneath him.

"Bridey?"

She nodded, knowing what he was asking, and shifted her legs to welcome him into the cradle of her body. She grasped his shaft with a gentle touch and guided him right to where they both needed him to be. In a series of quick thrusts, he buried himself deep within her slick heat.

When she gasped, he froze. "D-did I hurt you?"

She ran her hands up and down his back as if comforting him. "No, just give me a second."

He'd give her forever if that's what it took. When at last Bridey let out a long breath, she smiled up at him. "Like I said, it's been a while."

Before he moved inside her again, he teased her with soft kisses on her forehead and cheeks before settling his lips firmly over hers. It didn't take long before she drew her legs up to wrap around his hips and dug her fingertips into his shoulders. It was all the encouragement he needed.

This time, when he flexed his hips hard, her response was pure pleasure. Within seconds, she was urging him on, reinforcing her demands by lifting her hips up to meet his thrusts. That snapped his tenuous hold over the driving need to claim this woman as his own.

Rising over her, he held himself up with his arms fully extended to give his hips room to move freely. The building pressure became his sole focus. From the expression on Bridey's face, it wouldn't take much to send her flying, too.

Seconds later, she shouted his name and threw her head back on the pillow, her eyes squeezed tight as she rode out her release, which pushed him right over the edge with her. The rest of the world narrowed down to the connection between the two of them.

After riding out the last shudders, Seth rolled to the side and took Bridey with him, tucked in at his side. Once his brain started working again, he'd do his damnedest to find some way to tell her how much this meant to him. Until that happened, he held her close and hoped she already knew.

9

Morning came painfully early, with the first rays of sunlight pouring through the windows. Bridey studied her companion, tilting her head up to watch Seth sleep. His strong jaw had darkened with his morning stubble. She couldn't resist running her fingers across it, enjoying the bristly feel.

Seth toyed with her hair in response. "Good morning."

She hadn't really meant to wake him, but then again, she wasn't sorry that she had. His eyes opened just the smallest bit, but already he was smiling. Considering how happy she'd been to wake next to him, it was comforting to know he felt the same way.

"What time is your appointment this morning?"

His voice was gravelly and deeper than usual. She liked it. "Not until eleven."

He glanced past her to the clock on the bedside table. "Four hours. Plenty of time."

"For what?"

He took her hand and guided it down beneath the covers. "I bet you can guess."

Oh yeah, she loved the way this man thought, but she had a few ideas of her own. Laying her finger across his lips, she whispered, "I was thinking a hot bath would be a great way to start the day. Did you see the size of that tub? It's definitely big enough for"—she reached down to stroke the length of his shaft—"both of us."

Seth nipped at her finger, catching it with his teeth and then gently sucking on the tip. The small tug fired a jolt of pure desire straight through her. His green eyes glittered with greedy heat. "How about we start here and end up there?"

And that's what they did.

Three hours later, Seth walked hand in hand with Bridey as they window-shopped along the streets in downtown Seattle, pausing to admire the shop windows in all of their holiday finery. He mentally compared them with those he'd helped put up back in Snowberry Creek. On the whole, he thought the small town came out on top in that contest.

Bridey was clearly entranced by everything she saw, her clear gray eyes sparkling with happiness. He hoped part of that stemmed from the night they'd shared.

Their immediate plan was to grab breakfast at one of the local restaurants. Afterward, while Bridey met with her attorney, Seth would hang out at a nearby bookshop. She'd find him there when she was done, so they could do some Christmas shopping together.

He couldn't remember the last time he'd actually looked forward to buying Christmas presents. The past couple of years, he'd done most of his shopping online, but he couldn't wait to hit the stores with Bridey. Maybe he could find a sweater for his mother and some handmade jewelry for his sister. His brother was always harder to buy for, but the bookstore would be worth a shot.

Bridey tugged on his arm. "Seth, I asked how about that place on the corner?"

He blinked and realized they'd reached the end of the block. "Sorry. I was shopping in my head."

Okay, that didn't even make sense to him. He tried again. "Yes, that place is fine. And sorry. I was thinking about what I should buy for my family."

She frowned a little as he held the door to the restaurant open for her. "Funny, but that's the first time you've mentioned them. Do they live nearby?"

He nodded. "Yes. I guess we haven't talked much about our lives outside of Snowberry Creek."

Seth didn't want to go into detail and was relieved when she didn't press. Instead, when he didn't continue, she took his hand and gave it a quick squeeze. "I vote today is only for the two of us, not responsibilities. Well, other than my meeting. Agreed?"

The time was coming soon when he'd tell her everything but not today. The last thing he wanted to do was ruin the carefree spirit of their time together. "Agreed! Now, we should probably hurry if we want to eat before your appointment."

Bridey headed for a small table in the back corner of the restaurant. He let himself be towed along in her wake, only too glad to postpone talking about his past. He just hoped keeping his secrets didn't come back to bite him.

Even after lingering over a late dinner, Seth wasn't ready for their time together to come to an end. Walking out of the restaurant, he caught sight of one of the horse-drawn carriages that gave tours of the city. It was just turning the corner about a block away. On impulse, he grabbed Bridey's hand and took off running down the street.

"Come on!"

They were both a bit breathless by the time they caught up with the carriage. After paying the driver, Seth helped Bridey up into the seat and then climbed in after her. After settling in with his arm around her shoulders, he said, "I know you have to be up early in the morning, but I'm not quite ready for our evening to end."

"Let me worry about tomorrow." Bridey snuggled in closer to his side. "Besides, this is the perfect way to get into the holiday spirit!"

She was right. Even the coach was draped with garlands of greenery and red bows, and the horse's harness had strings of bells that chimed softly as it moved. As they passed by the iron pergola located in Pioneer Square, Bridey waved at the Santa, who was ringing his bell and greeting passersby. "I've always thought the pergola is beautiful, especially this time of year, when it's all decked out for the holidays."

"B-beautiful is right."

Not that he was talking about the decorations or even looking at them at the moment. Instead, he was captivated by the woman sitting next to him. He caught her chin with his fingertips and gently tipped her face up so that he could kiss her. Bridey smiled against his lips and then tilted her head back farther for him to deepen the kiss. It was a perfect moment, one he knew he'd cherish forever.

It was ten o'clock by the time they were back in Snowberry Creek. Seth tried to hide his disappointment when

Bridey asked him to drop her off at her apartment. It was probably for the best, though. Despite the energetic night and morning they'd spent, he doubted he'd be content to simply sleep in the same bed with her.

He took the long way around so they could see the Christmas lights in town one more time on the way to her place. Bridey stared out the window with evident delight. "I'm glad the mayor decided to do this. It's really lovely even though the snow is already gone."

She turned to smile at him. "I can't remember the last time I really looked forward to the holidays. Where I worked in California, we did a big catering business on the side. From Thanksgiving through New Year's was a busy time for us. It made it hard to relax and enjoy something as simple as Christmas lights."

He pulled into her parking lot and found a spot near her building. She was already out of the car when he came around to her side. He hesitated before popping the lid of the trunk because he wanted to hold her one last time before they returned to their familiar routines.

He gathered her close and nuzzled the side of her neck, drawing in her scent and appreciating the chance to feel her pressed against his body. "The past twenty-four hours were perfect."

The dim glow of a nearby streetlamp showcased her pleased smile. "It was wonderful, Seth."

"We'll do it again." He pressed a kiss to her temple. "Soon."

"Agreed, but now I should let you get home."

He got her suitcase and bags from the car and carried them for her. Bridey kissed him one last time before unlocking her door.

While he waited, he said, "I'll stop by the shop tomorrow to measure the shelves for your office."

He hadn't phrased it as a question, but Bridey responded as if he had. "Okay, but only if it isn't taking you away from something else you should be doing."

"It won't." When it looked as if she was going to protest, he added, "I promise.

That much was true. He was too buzzed to go to bed anytime soon. He planned to go home and work on her sign most of the night. Then he'd crash for a few hours before showing up at the shop. "I'll be there after the lunch rush. Save me a couple of muffins."

He gave her one more kiss and walked away.

It had been one heck of a morning. Bridey had been away from the shop for only one day, but it felt like a lot longer. Her rhythm had been off since she'd unlocked the door at four thirty. It had been years—*years*—since she'd burned even one pan of muffins, but she'd managed to ruin three. That's what she got for daydreaming about a certain man.

After she finished coping with that disaster, she'd knocked over a cup of coffee, sending it splashing down the front of her last clean apron. At least it had hit her and not a customer.

The only bright spot had been when Fiona announced that everything had gone smoothly on Monday. So starting the next week, she'd take over closing the shop three days during the week and alternate working weekends with Bridey. Ever since opening the shop two years ago, Bridey had done everything by herself.

What would she do with all that free time?

No sooner had she posed the question when one possible answer came strolling in the back door of the shop, his toolbox in hand and a smile on his face hotter than the huge ovens in her kitchen. He set the toolbox down on the counter and headed straight for her. He stopped just out of reach with a puzzled look on his face.

"What?"

His eyebrows rode down low over his eyes as he stared at her. "Not sure about that smile."

She laughed. "Fiona is going to start closing the shop for me three days a week and will work alternating weekends."

"You'd mentioned that was the plan."

He held his ground, so she closed the distance between them. "I was wondering what I could do with all that free time and in you walked. Seemed like the Fates were answering the question for me."

His callused hand cupped the side of her face with such gentleness. "I like that answer."

"So do I." She wrapped her arms around his waist and laid her head against his chest. "I've never had time off during the Christmas holidays. It's a gift I didn't expect to receive, but it's one I will be glad to share with the right person."

"And what would you like to do with all that time?"

The longer she stayed in his arms, the harder it was for her to remember that this was her place of business. "Let's start with dinner tomorrow night and go from there."

"My place and I'll do the cooking." He punctuated his suggestion with the kind of kiss that should have set off the smoke alarms.

"I'll be there. Should I bring my overnight bag?"

"Yes." His seductive glance packed a lot of meaning into that one word as he backed away and reached for his toolbox. Then, with a mock frown, he made shooing motions at her. "Now, you have customers, and I have work to do."

He was right, but that didn't mean she wouldn't rather watch him measuring shelving instead of pouring another cup of coffee. With more than a little regret, she headed out front to help Fiona with the rush of teenagers coming through the door.

10

Seth paced the length of his workshop and back. How many times had he circled the room? Time was moving both too slowly and too fast. The minutes ticked away one by one, each pushing him closer to the moment of truth. Somehow he kept finding excuses not to tell her about his artwork, even though he knew she wouldn't react well to learning that he had kept such a big secret from her.

The past three weeks had been the happiest of Seth's life. He and Bridey had spent nearly every night together. They'd celebrated her first official Saturday off by buying a carload full of Christmas ornaments and then picking out the perfect tree at a nearby Christmas tree farm. It had taken them three hours and two bottles of wine to decorate his house. The end results had been breathtaking, especially the part where they'd made love on the floor beneath the twinkling lights on the tree.

Considering how few hours of sleep he'd been getting, he should have been running on empty, but he wasn't. In fact, he couldn't remember a time when he felt more energetic.

Just yesterday, he'd finished another set of shelves for Bridey, but all of his real work had taken place right here in his shop. The sign he intended to give her for Christmas had taken him until the wee hours of that morning to complete. It was some of his best work in years, although he suspected his agent wouldn't see it that way. Nor would he understand why Seth wanted to invest so much creative energy in a sign for a small-town coffee shop.

He wouldn't see the love that Seth had carved into it right along with the image of Bridey smiling down at the riot of cupcakes and muffins that had been hidden in the swirling grain of the wood. He'd also finished two smaller pieces for the auction to improve the playground at the local elementary school.

Both sculptures had been delivered to the mayor's office in time for pictures to be included in the last-minute advertising in the area. The accompanying documentation had included the certificates of authenticity and a promise that the prominent Northwest artist Geoffrey Kyser would attend the auction in person. He'd also had his agent let it be known in the local art community that the pieces would be part of the auction. Hopefully, that would bring out a few more people.

Now the auction would begin soon, and he was battling major doubts about the wisdom of having gotten involved at all. It would have been far simpler to maintain a low profile if he'd made an anonymous cash donation instead.

However, now that he'd decided to make Snowberry Creek his permanent home, he couldn't continue hiding who he really was from his friends and neighbors, much less Bridey. The bigger issue was how to explain to her why he'd felt compelled to hide at all. He should've known that the longer he delayed telling her, the harder it was going to be. If she took it wrong, if she walked away from him—

She meant too much to him for him to even consider the possibility that Bridey might not be able to accept his reasons for not being completely forthcoming with her. Surely she'd see that she knew who he was in all the ways that mattered—the man who was head over heels in love with her. He hadn't shared that last part with her yet, either. It didn't seem fair to confess the depth of his feelings for her until she knew everything about him.

The clock chimed the hour. He had intended to present her with the sign first and explain everything before going to the auction together. Unfortunately, she'd called him an hour ago to say she was closing early and would meet him there.

So much for well-laid plans. All he could do was punt and hope he could get her alone long enough to explain everything before the event really got started. Plan B also included waiting until she left for the auction to let himself in the back door of the shop. Bridey had given him a key so that he could finish up the shelves yesterday, and he'd conveniently forgotten to give it back to her.

He'd take the gift-wrapped sign to her shop and then head straight for the auction. Crossing his fingers that he wasn't about to destroy the one good thing in his life, he gathered up everything he needed and headed out into the night.

Bridey hated lying to Seth, but she was still finishing up his Christmas present. They'd agreed to exchange gifts on the night of the auction because the next two days promised to be busy. On Christmas Eve, they were going to a party at Callie's house after the evening service at church. Seth had also made plans for the two of them on Christmas Day, but he was being all mysterious about those. She'd be less worried about it if he wasn't so obviously feeling a bit twitchy about whatever he had in mind.

For now, the plum tarts were due to come out of the oven. She'd finally figured out the last secret ingredient needed to re-create his grandmother's recipe as he'd described it to her—ground ginger. It gave the plum filling just a bit of a bite without overpowering the nutmeg Seth loved so much. When the timer buzzed, she took the pan from the oven.

The spicy smell filled the air, making her smile. Seth was going to love them. He took such pleasure in the simple things in life, one of the many things that drew her to him. He understood that there was more to living than maintaining an image, things like friendship and trust and even love.

She had no doubt that was exactly what she felt for Seth. There was still a lot she didn't know about him, but that was okay. She'd hadn't been in much of a hurry to drag the sad details of her own past out into the light of day; she could hardly fault Seth for feeling the same way.

After setting the tarts out of sight in the storeroom to cool, she ducked into the small restroom in the back of the shop to fix her makeup and check her clothes for stray smears of flour. The sweater and slacks were dressier than her usual attire, but not too fancy. It had been hard to decide what to wear to a small-town event being held in the high school gym.

She was about to pick up her purse and keys when she heard a knocking coming from the front of the shop. Who could that be? She was sure she'd posted the "Closed" sign and turned off all the lights.

As soon as she recognized the man standing outside the door, she wished she'd already made her escape out the back. She still could, but unfortunately Russell had already seen her. Her ex-husband was nothing if not determined and might very well follow her to the high school. The man wouldn't think twice of making a scene to get his way.

He'd never do such a thing on his home turf, where image was everything, especially around his family. It had been only when he got her behind closed doors that he'd unleash his never-ending criticism of everything she did. It had taken every scrap of courage she had to walk away from their marriage. If she'd stayed, there would have been nothing left at all of the woman she wanted to be.

Here in Snowberry Creek, Russell wouldn't care if he humiliated her in front of everyone she knew. Worse yet, no doubt Seth would rush to her defense, and she could only imagine how that would turn out. Seth never talked about his slight stammer, but she'd noticed it got worse when he was in a crowd. The thought of him confronting Russell at the auction had her marching toward the door.

She turned on the lights in the shop and unlocked the door. Russell strolled in as if he owned the place. He probably thought he did, since she bought it with part of their divorce settlement. He looked around with just the barest hint of a sneer. "What a delightful little shop you have here, Bridey. Quaint, but definitely a step down for you."

She wanted to smack him. Bracing herself for the worst, she asked, "What do you want, Russell? I have plans for this evening."

She took pride in how calm she sounded. For a brief second, he let his mask slip, showing his anger, but he had himself back under control in an instant.

"I'm here, Bridey, because it's time for you to come home."

At first she couldn't make sense of what he'd said because it was that last thing she would have expected to hear from him. Russell had been only too glad to see her disappear from his life. He'd made that much abundantly clear.

"I don't know what kind of game you're playing here, Russell, but I am home. Snowberry Creek is where my life is now."

The sneer was back, which didn't help his cause one bit. On the contrary, it made it that much easier to see through his thin facade of charm. He was still the bastard who'd all but destroyed her with his lies and cheating ways. His hand-tailored suit and expensive Italian shoes did nothing for her, not anymore. No. She'd developed a definite preference for well-worn flannel and faded denim.

Russell sidled closer, making it clear that he wasn't going to leave until he got his way. She stood her ground and waited to see what argument he'd try next.

"I know you have reason to be unhappy with me, Bridey, but you were never the type to hold a grudge. Come home with me, and I'll do everything I can to make up for my past mistakes. We both know how much you loved working at my family's restaurant. We could be happy again."

Seriously? She scoffed at him. "You cannot believe I'd still fall for that bunch of hooey." Tired of the whole discussion, she sighed. "Listen, I've said no, so just leave. I have somewhere else to be, and I don't want to be late."

She should have known he wouldn't take rejection well. "Dammit, Bridey. You can't make me believe that you actually prefer life in a place like this after what the two of us had."

Her own temper surged to the forefront. "I thought we had something special once, Russell, but I'm not the one who threw it away. You did that, and I doubt you've changed."

"But—"

She cut him off before he could launch another bunch of lame excuses. "But nothing, Russell. We both know you don't want me back, and I sure as heck don't want you. I have someone else in my life, someone who'd never lie to me the way you have. So quit wasting my time and tell me why you're really here."

Instead of answering her, her ex-husband laughed. "Can't you come up with a better excuse than some fictional boyfriend? I hired a private investigator to check up on you. It didn't take him long to report back that you spent all of your time here at the shop. Hell, outside of your customers, the only man he ever saw hanging around was some low-rent handyman."

Bridey wasn't about to drag Seth into this mess. "I cannot believe you'd stoop so low. We haven't spoken in close to two years, and all of a sudden you're here begging me to come back. Why?"

Finally, he got to the truth of the matter. "Fine. I'm here because my grandmother's health is failing. She thinks the two of us are only separated, and I never told her any different. She's still very old-fashioned, especially on the subject of divorce."

Bridey had always liked the fierce old lady. "I'm sorry to hear she's not doing well, but I won't help you lie to her."

"It wouldn't be lying, Bridey. Not if you'd give me a second chance to make things work between us." He looked around the shop again. "I'd even pay you for your time. She doesn't have long left. It would make her so happy to think we'd reconciled."

Sensing that his arguments weren't working, he kept going. "You would have free rein at the restaurant, too. I'll admit that the place took a bit of a hit when you left and took your recipes with you."

Yeah, that last part made sense. His family's high-end restaurant was the one thing that had always been important to Russell. "What happens if she learns the truth? And she will, because I'm not coming back."

Experience had taught her that the madder Russell was, the slower he spoke. Right now, the words left his mouth as if he was having to force them out one at a time. "My grandmother still holds the majority interest in all our family restaurants. She has made it perfectly clear that if I don't get my life in order, she'll relinquish control to my cousin Tony from back East. I won't let that happen. He'll destroy the place."

Maybe so, but Bridey had no interest in his family's power plays. It was time to end this discussion. "I'm sorry, but you'll have to settle for telling her the truth. I won't pretend to be your wife, not when you quit being my husband in any real sense long before our divorce was finalized. Now, for the last time, leave."

But when Russell took a step, it was toward her with his hands clenched in fists.

11

That was odd. When Seth arrived at Something's Brewing, the back door was unlocked and the lights were on. If Bridey was inside, maybe he'd have a chance to explain things before they reached the auction after all.

He stowed the sign inside the kitchen and made a second trip outside in the pouring rain to fetch the small, tabletop Christmas tree he'd bought that held one more special surprise for Bridey. After that, he grabbed his garment bag so he could finish changing for the auction. Back inside, he looked around and spotted Bridey's purse and keys sitting on the counter.

Okay, so she had to be around somewhere. He quickly arranged the tree, straightened the few ornaments, and then plugged in the lights. After leaning the sign against the counter below the tree, he had everything ready to show Bridey. He started to call out her name when he heard voices coming from out in the shop. He didn't recognize the guy's voice, but the level of tension in Bridey's was all too clear. Who the hell was he?

The next words out of the jerk's mouth clarified the situation. Bridey's ex-husband was out there telling her he wanted her back. Seth held his breath and ignored the pain in his chest as he waited to hear her answer. It didn't take long. Good. She wasn't buying that line of bullshit the guy was selling.

Even so, Seth wouldn't tolerate him disrespecting Bridey. Not when he could do something about that. He ducked back into Bridey's office to change. He already had on his dress shirt, pants, and shoes. All he needed to do was slip on his black bow tie and the jacket to his tux. When he was ready, he let himself out the back door and drove his convertible around to park in the front of the shop. Drawing a deep breath, he headed for the front door and hoped Bridey would forgive him for springing this on her with no warning.

He walked in just as her ex clenched his hands into fists and took a step toward Bridey. At the sound of the door opening, the other guy froze and looked back to see who was joining the party.

Seth bypassed him and headed straight for Bridey.

Bridey was so focused on her ex-husband's growing agitation that it took her a few seconds to recognize the well-dressed man who had just walked into her shop. When she finally did, all she could do was whisper in confusion, "Seth?"

He nodded as he deliberately walked between her and Russell to reach her side. Still ignoring her ex, Seth brushed a quick kiss on her cheek. "Sorry to keep you waiting, darling. It took me longer to get here than I expected."

Russell fell back a step as his gaze bounced between her and Seth a couple of times. "Who the hell is this guy?"

Good question. At the moment, Bridey wasn't sure herself. Seth's answer left her even more confused.

"I'm Seth Kyser, although I'm better known in the art world as Geoffrey Seth Kyser. Bridey and I are attending a community event where they're auctioning off two of my sculptures to raise money for a local cause."

He made no offer to shake hands but instead tipped his head to one side as he studied Russell. The haughty expression was one she'd never seen on his face before. "And you would be?"

Russell countered the question with one of his own. "You're Geoffrey Kyser? The sculptor?"

The name hadn't clicked with Bridey until Russell said it. She stared at Seth, trying to bring this new image into focus alongside what she knew of him after spending so much time together these past several weeks. There were several artists in the Northwest whose names were nationally known, and Geoffrey Kyser was one of them. None of this made any sense. Why on earth would an artist of his caliber work for minimum wage building shelves for her?

The two men were too busy posturing to pay any attention to her at the moment. Seth remained at her side, but it felt more like he was staking out his territory.

She hated it.

Seth continued talking to Russell. "Yes, I am, but you have me at a disadvantage."

Russell held out his hand. "I'm her husband, Russell Roke."

Seth ignored the gesture, and his smile turned predatory. He slid his arm around Bridey's waist, holding her tight enough that she couldn't escape without a struggle. "Don't you mean ex-husband? She's told me all about you."

No, in fact, she hadn't, but Bridey didn't argue the point. When Seth glanced down at her, his green eyes softened into something like concern. It was the first time since he'd walked in the door that he looked like the man she knew. "Isn't Russell the one who works at some little place in California?"

Russell clearly didn't appreciate the implied insult. "It's a five-star restaurant, and I'm not an employee. My family owns the place. Now, if you'll excuse us, my wife and I have some unfinished business."

It was well past time for her to speak up for herself. "There's nothing left for us to discuss. You heard me. I have my own life here in Snowberry Creek, and you're not part of it. Tell your grandmother whatever you want to, but leave me out of it."

He made one last attempt to turn on his charm. "You don't mean that, Bridey. I know you're upset about how things were between us, but you have to admit that it was as much your fault as it was mine."

Okay, enough was enough. "I don't know how you came to that amazing conclusion. You were the one who couldn't keep his pants zipped."

For the first time, Russell's betrayal no longer had the power to hurt her. She pointed toward the door. "It's over between us. Now, leave. I have somewhere I need to be."

Instead of heading for the door, Russell charged toward her. "You bitch! Damned if I'll let you ruin it all for me!"

Before he'd gotten two steps, Seth spun Russell around and shoved him back in the other direction, right out the door into the pouring rain. "You've got one minute to drive away before I call the cops. The chief of police is one of Bridey's best customers, so that pretty much guarantees you'll end up in jail for threatening her."

Then Seth turned the latch to make sure Russell couldn't get back in. For the longest time, he stood staring out into the night, his shoulders slumped as if the effort had exhausted him. She was still trying to assimilate everything that had just happened when Seth finally turned around.

"I w-was g-going to tell you."

She didn't want to hear it. Not now. He should have guessed how she felt about liars, and yet he continued to pretend he was . . . what? A carpenter? A handyman? As an excuse to get closer to her? But why, when he was an artist whose work was displayed in world-class museums?

Unable to get her head around the whole shift in her perception of him, she latched on to the only thing that she could. "I'm late for the auction. Where did I leave my keys?"

"On the counter in back." Seth started for the kitchen. "I'll get them for you and lock the back door. My convertible is parked out on the street, so we can go out the front."

"What convertible?" He drove a sedan and that old van. Had anything about him been real?

He disappeared into the kitchen without answering, so she looked out the window to see for herself. Sure enough, a sleek convertible was right outside. She didn't recognize the model, but she knew an expensive vehicle when she saw one. Another bit of proof that he was exactly who he'd claimed to be.

The jerk! The confrontation with Russell and the betrayal by Seth combined to leave her furious beyond words. No way she was going to get into that car with Seth—Geoffrey—whoever the hell he was. She'd walk first.

Bridey was out the door and halfway down the block before Seth caught up with her. He planted himself in front of her, sliding from side to side when she tried to get past him.

"I'm walking there."

He gently caught her hand in his. "N-no, you're not. I know you're m-mad, Bridey. Maybe you have a right to be, but it's raining. Let me drive you."

She stared at his hand until he released her.

"P-please, Bridey. Let me do that much."

"Fine."

He helped her into the passenger seat and then hustled around to the other side as if he were afraid she'd try to escape. The engine roared to life with a heavy rumble of power. As he pulled away from the curb, she stared out the passenger window. The Christmas lights outlining every roof line and window they passed were a blur, but she couldn't tell if that was due to the raindrops on the glass or the tears running down her cheeks.

Seth forced himself to drive to the high school when what he really wanted to do was head straight back to Something's Brewing and get things settled between them. What he wouldn't give to find a way to turn back the clock, to hit rewind, anything that would let him go back to the moment when everything went off track.

He had never wanted to hurt Bridey, but that's exactly what he'd done. He'd gone rushing in, hoping to play hero. Instead, he'd joined her ex-husband in the ranks of liars in her life.

The rain was coming down harder than ever, so he pulled up in front of the covered entrance to the high school. "I'll let you out here so you don't get d-drenched. I'll park and be right back."

She silently climbed out of his car and walked away. Okay, so chances were she wouldn't be waiting for him. Fine. He'd track her down. Making things right with her was too important for him to give up easily.

Sure enough, there was no sign of her anywhere when he walked into the building. A few seconds later, he spotted her down the hall. On the surface, Bridey looked calm, but he knew better. Kicking it into high gear, he caught up with her before she joined the throng of people heading into the gym. Taking her arm ever so gently, he tugged her over toward a nearby corner.

"Bridey, please let me explain."

She gave his hand a pointed stare until he let it drop back down to his side, but then her expression softened just enough to give him some glimmer of hope. "This is hardly the place for lengthy discussions."

No way was he going to let her walk away. Not until he had his say. Either she'd accept his explanation or she wouldn't; all he could do was share his truth. "Please, Bridey. I n-never meant to hurt you. I moved here when my art dried up. When I volunteered to build your shelves, I hadn't worked in months. You've got to believe me when I tell you that it's because of you that I've been so happy living here and being just plain old Seth."

He swept his hand up and down in front of his tailored jacket. "This isn't me. Not really."

She was already shaking her head, but before she launched her next refusal, someone called his name—his real name.

"Geoffrey Kyser, there you are! I'm so pleased you made it. I wanted to thank you personally on behalf of Snowberry Creek for your generous donation to our auction."

Seth shoved his pain deep down inside and pulled his

public persona around him like a cloak before facing the mayor and her entourage. "Mayor McKay, I'm sorry I couldn't get here sooner."

"Not a problem. If you don't mind, the press would like to take pictures and do a short interview before the auction gets started."

She paused to look at Bridey and then back at Seth. "Ms. Roke, I hope you don't mind if I borrow Mr. Kyser for a few minutes."

Bridey's smile was so damned sad. "No, Mayor, not at all. I know how much it means to everyone to have an artist of his caliber here tonight. Besides, I'm supposed to be helping in the kitchen."

The mayor waved the reporters forward, and just that quickly, the two of them were surrounded by flashing cameras and a staccato rush of questions. Seth hoped his answers were at least marginally coherent because watching Bridey walking away, leaving everything between them unresolved, just about killed him.

12

Two hours later, Bridey let herself back into the shop. She should've gone home, but she wasn't up to it. Not yet. The thought of facing her empty bed, where she and Seth had spent so many happy hours, made her physically ill.

At the auction, she'd made a token effort to help, but she hadn't been able to stand watching everyone fawning over Seth. Then there were all the questions from her well-meaning friends. How long had she known Seth was famous? And why hadn't she told anybody?

Finally, claiming a bad headache, she'd made her excuses and left, catching a ride with the police chief and his daughter. Inside, she left the lights off in the front of the shop and headed for the back. When she stepped into the kitchen, only part of her tension drained away because everywhere she looked, there was something to remind her of Seth: the shelves he'd built, the stool where he normally sat when they shared a cup of coffee, the decorations they'd hung together, and the special plum tarts she'd made for him for Christmas.

The man had definitely left his mark not only on her

heart, but in her sanctuary as well. She'd just have to ignore all of those things, because baking was the only thing that brought her any kind of peace. Right now, it seemed unlikely she'd feel like attending the Christmas Eve party at Callie's house tomorrow night, especially without Seth. Unfortunately, she had promised to bring the dessert, so she'd make a double batch of Nick's favorite brownies and call it good.

Maybe if she worked long enough, late enough, she'd be able to fall asleep without dreaming about Seth and what might have been. She could only be grateful that she hadn't actually told him that she loved him.

It wasn't until she went to preheat the oven that she noticed the small Christmas tree on the back counter along with a large Christmas package all tied up with a huge red bow sitting on the floor beneath it. Off to the side, a couple of hangers and a garment bag had been tossed on the back counter. Where had all of that come from? There was only one logical answer—Seth.

She'd been wondering how he happened to arrive at exactly the right moment to help her deal with Russell. He must have come in the back door and overheard their conversation. Great, he'd heard her ex refer to him as a low-rent handyman. And white knight that he was, Seth had still rushed to Bridey's defense.

That might not excuse him for not telling her who he was, but she was pretty sure she owed him an apology. She wandered closer to the package. Lying right next to the package was a small envelope with her name on it. She opened it and pulled out a small gift card, which read *To Bridey, with all my love. Merry Christmas—Seth.*

Although she tried not to read too much into that bit about his love, it was clear the package was for her. What could it be? There was a tear along the top edge of the paper. It wouldn't hurt to peek, but she couldn't see much. The hole wasn't big enough to reveal anything except it was made from wood.

Her hands reached out of their own accord to untie the ribbon and then gave the torn paper a tug to extend the rip a little farther. Now she could make out a couple of letters—an S and then an O. Was that next letter an M?

Ignoring the inner voice that chastised her to leave it alone, she gave in to temptation and grabbed the paper with both hands and let it rip. When she'd stripped the rest of the wrapping out of the way, her heart about stopped.

It was a hand-carved sign for her shop.

It was signed by the artist: Geoffrey Seth Kyser.

It was stunning.

Seth had carved a picture of her holding a basket that was overflowing with muffins and cupcakes. Both she and the pastries looked almost real, as if someone could pluck one of her creations right out of the basket. She took three steps back to get a better perspective on the amazing piece of artwork.

Did Seth really see her as that beautiful?

"Yes, I do."

She hadn't realized that she'd asked the question out loud, nor had she heard him come in.

Turning to face him, she blinked back her tears and managed a bit of a smile. "Seth, it's amazing. Simply amazing."

"G-glad you think so."

He hovered near the door with his hands in his pockets as if unsure of his welcome. With his tie loosened and his jacket draped over his arm, he looked more like the Seth she knew—and loved.

"Meant to surprise you with it before we went to the

auction and explain everything, but you called to say you'd meet me there. Then I was going to hang it and then find you before things got started. Couldn't do that because Russell was here hassling you."

Seth wandered closer and tossed his jacket aside. He paused in front of the carving and reached out to trace one of the letters. "I m-moved here to get away from the stress of my family and all the d-demands on my time. Not to mention, my stuttering can make speaking in p-public excruciating."

His expressive eyes looked so sad. "What I said earlier about not w-working in months was true. It wasn't until I realized how m-much I loved living here . . . and especially how much I loved you, that it all came back to me. It's been hell, but for the first time in months, the wood is speaking to me again. I'd stared at this blank piece of cherry for weeks when all of sudden I saw your gingerbread cupcakes and your pretty face hidden there in the wood. I not only finished this for you, but the two pieces for the auction."

He paused to glance back at her with a look of wonder on his handsome face. "And now there's this huge chunk of walnut in my shop that's clamoring for my attention."

Her heart ached for him even as her breath caught in her throat. She knew what it was like to lose the joy of creation. Living with Russell had done the same thing to her. It wasn't until she came home to Snowberry Creek that she'd found it again. Did he realize what he'd let slip? That he loved her? The last of her anger and confusion drained away. He'd shared his truth with her; it was time she did the same.

She closed the small distance between them and held out her hand. "Hi, I'm Bridey Roke. It's nice to meet you, Geoffrey Seth Kyser."

His smile turned up to full wattage as he shook her hand. "Please call me Seth. Geoffrey is who I pretend to be when I have to wear a tux and impress someone. Much to my mother's dismay, I spend most of my time in flannel shirts and faded jeans."

She grinned back at him. "Me, I love a man in a flannel shirt, at least if that man is you."

Seth's eyes widened. "You love me?"

She nodded. "Very much."

With a whoop, he picked her up and twirled her around. "That's the best Christmas present anyone has ever given me."

He followed that up with a deep kiss that curled her toes and left both of them gasping for breath. When he finally set her back down, she pointed toward his favorite stool. "And with that in mind, why don't you have a seat? Since we'd planned to exchange gifts tonight, I have something for you, too."

He settled himself in his usual spot while she set out two plates, forks, and napkins. Seth followed her every move as if he were afraid she'd disappear if he didn't keep an eye on her. When she carried the tray of tarts out of the storeroom, his eyes lit up. "Plum tarts?"

She set one in front of each of them. "Merry Christmas, Seth. I think I have figured out your grandmother's recipe."

He took one bite and then a second. "That's it! The perfect blend of sweet and tart with just a bit of a bite! You couldn't have thought of a more perfect gift for me."

She watched as he devoured the rest of his tart and reached for a second. Before he started on that one, he asked, "What was the secret ingredient?"

"A touch of ground ginger." She paused to take a deep breath. "And this recipe and the one for my gingerbread cupcakes will be the first ones in my own cook-book."

Seth stopped midmotion to stare at her. Then he set his fork aside and stood up to tug her back into his arms. "I'm so proud of you."

He kissed her again, holding her with such care, as if she were the most precious thing in the world to him. "I love you so much, Bridey. You complete me."

"Oh, Seth—"

Seth put his finger across Bridey's lips to keep her from speaking. When he was sure she'd remain quiet, he lifted her up on the counter. As she watched, he walked over to the tabletop tree and pulled a small box from inside its branches. "This was the other present I wanted to give you for Christmas, Bridey."

He opened the box to reveal a ring with a square-cut emerald flanked by two small diamonds. "Bridey Roke, will you do me the honor of marrying me, even knowing that the famous artist and I are a package deal?"

Her eyes filled with tears as she reached out to hold his face with both hands. Her touch banished the last bit of the evening's uncertainty. "Yes, I'll marry you, Geoffrey Seth Kyser."

Seth slipped the ring on Bridey's finger. "We need to celebrate, but not here. How about we drive out to my place, light a fire, and see where the night takes us?"

Bridey held out her hand to admire her ring. "I love the way you think, and I love you. Let's go!"

Seth immediately lifted her down off the counter. "Good, because I've already got a bottle of champagne chilling."

"Perfect!"

As they walked outside, all the twinkling lights up and

down Main Street took on a whole new beauty. This was the most special Christmas in his life, but there was one more thing he had to tell Bridey.

When they were in his car, his smile faltered a bit. "You should know that I've already told my mother I'd be bringing my fiancée with me to the family gathering on Christmas Day. She can't wait to meet you."

Bridey swallowed hard. "Are you sure?"

"You'll be the best Christmas present I've ever given her." When he looked at the woman who held his heart, he couldn't help but grin. "But just in case, we should save some of the tarts for her. She loves them, too."

About the Author

Alexis Morgan is the author of the Snowberry Creek series. She and her husband make their home in the beautiful Pacific Northwest. Alexis shares her office with two parakeets, who rock out to her favorite music and keep her company while she's writing. A lifelong avid reader, Alexis loves spending her days creating worlds filled with sexy warriors and the strong women who love them. She has been nominated for numerous industry awards, including the RITA from the Romance Writers of America, the top award in the romance genre.

CONNECT ONLINE

www.alexismorgan.com
facebook.com/amorganauthor
twitter.com/alexis_morgan

ENJOY MORE BOOKS BY THESE AUTHORS!

ALSO BY JOANN ROSS

The Homecoming
One Summer
On Lavender Lane
Moonshell Beach
Sea Glass Winter
Castaway Cove

ALSO BY SUSAN DONOVAN

Sea of Love

ALSO BY LUANN MCLANE

Playing for Keeps
Catch of a Lifetime
Pitch Perfect

ALSO BY ALEXIS MORGAN

A Time for Home

LOVE

ROMANCE
NOVELS?